# Earning It

## A NOVEL

## E.F. Dodd

Sugar Beaver
BOOKS

My mother told me to be a lady. And for her,
that meant be your own person, be independent.
—HONORABLE RUTH BADER GINSBURG


For all the ladies out there, and their moms, including my own.
Love you, Mama. Thanks not just for being you
but for making me into me.

*The* second Saturday in May dawned bright and beautiful—the perfect day for an outdoor wedding. From a guest room window, Rae looked out at the crisp blue sky, dotted with fluffy white clouds. The waxy green leaves of the magnolias lining the drive to Jackson's house swayed lazily in the breeze, stirring the mild humidity. Their satiny blossoms gleamed with an almost translucent sheen, as though even they had dressed for the occasion.

"But, Rae," Giselle whined, her voice sounding tinny in Rae's ear, "how can this be happening?"

Rae closed her eyes and asked the all-knowing female office manager in the sky for patience . . . and to get her off the phone before Kez walked in. "Giselle," Rae said, "nothing has happened. My office is in contact with the photographer *and* the magazine who hired him. Those pictures won't see the light of day. Not today, not tomorrow, not ever. Trust me."

"I do trust you," Giselle wailed, and Rae pulled the phone from her ear to preserve her hearing. "It's just that everyone has been so hateful since the separation and now . . ." A pitiful yet carefully delicate sniffle came over the line. "These pictures could make it so much worse!"

*No*, Rae thought, *what made things worse was you sleeping with an NFL star three weeks after his wife gave birth to twins. And, oh yeah, he's also the brother of your not-quite-ex-husband.* Impulse control was not Giselle's strong suit.

"Calm down, Giselle," Rae said, rubbing her forehead to ease the tension there. She did *not* have time for a headache. Nor did she have the time to dedicate to Giselle's bullshit. The NFL player with questionable morals was her client, and Giselle was a problem for him, which made her Rae's problem too. The woman was like a stubborn UTI no amount of cranberry juice would flush away. Rae was going to throttle whoever gave Giselle her cell number. But that would have to wait.

"I promise you," Rae said, keeping her voice steady and even. "Those pictures aren't going public, and this won't impact the divorce settlement. I've already spoken with everyone involved, and they all agree this needs to be kept quiet."

"Even Avery?" Giselle asked, and Rae didn't miss the hint of excitement in her voice. Avery was the wife of the NFL player and Giselle's soon-to-be ex-sister-in-law. Rae liked Avery, even if she questioned her taste in life partners. Client or not, sleeping with your brother's almost-ex-wife while your own wife was breastfeeding two brand-new babies was a complete dick move. But without those types of douchey decisions coupled with her innate talent to diffuse them, Rae's PR business wouldn't be as successful as it was.

"Yes, Giselle, even Avery," Rae said, careful to keep her voice modulated and even. "She's on board with the plan. Just sit tight for the next few weeks until this blows over." Rae paused for effect then said, "Which means you do not call Avery's husband, understand?"

Giselle sniffled again, and even over the phone, Rae knew it was an act. The witch was reveling in the havoc she'd caused, just as she had done dozens of times before her marriage finally imploded. Rae's temples began a slow, methodical throb, and she stifled a groan while she waited on the inevitable pushback from the other end of the line.

As though on cue, Giselle asked, "But what if—"

Rae's voice was sharp when she interrupted, "No what-ifs, Giselle. I mean it. If I hear you called him, or bothered Avery in any way, this story will get a whole new spin with you at the center. Do you understand me?" It was a risky move, because it wouldn't paint her client in the best light, but Rae believed it was worth the gamble.

Giselle's waterworks dried up in an instant. "Are you threatening me?" Her normally breathy voice had a shrill edge to it.

"Giselle," Rae said, her voice deadly quiet in the face of impending hysterics, "I do not make threats. I make things happen. You do not want to learn the things I can make happen to you. Are we clear?"

There was a pause, during which Rae imagined Giselle weighing the cold hard cash she'd lose if she ignored Rae's warning against the sadistic glee she'd get from dragging Avery even further into her drama. Her greed was what Rae was banking on. There was another sniff, followed by Giselle's agreement. "We're clear," she said.

There wasn't a hint of Marilyn Monroe in her voice now. Rae had never been fooled by Giselle's act. She might play the blonde bubblehead, but Giselle was no dummy. Manipulative, vindictive, and spiteful? Sure, but not stupid. She was getting a good deal in the divorce and knew Rae had the power to yank it, and more, away if she stepped out of line. Whatever cheap, temporary thrill she might have gotten from calling Avery to rub salt in a wound wasn't worth the resulting fallout.

"Very good," Rae said and hung up. Thanks to her efforts, Thanksgiving at the running back's mansion might be awkward this year, but at least this latest snafu wouldn't impact his impending contract negotiations or lose him any endorsements. It wouldn't make the news, either, and for that, Rae had more than earned her fee.

She closed her eyes and took a few cleansing breaths to rid herself of the toxicity generated by the call. Her friends could kid her all they wanted about her aversion to talking about feelings, but there was no denying how much messier things became once feelings were involved. Willing the tension winding up in her skull to relax, Rae focused on the importance of the day. Her best friend was getting married, and she didn't want any leftover vitriol to intrude. In with the happy, out with the angry. Not your typical woo-woo mantra, but it worked. The tight bands that had formed around her head began to loosen, and the throbbing at her temples subsided.

When she opened her eyes, Rae looked back out the window of the guest room where she and the rest of Kez's bridesmaids had gathered that morning. She watched the mad scramble of florists, caterers, and others hustling to create the wonderland Rae knew Jackson had promised Kez. A large white tent for the reception was being erected to the right of the pool. On the other side of the backyard, neat rows of wooden chairs with golden cushions faced an arbor made of tiger lilies and daylilies interwoven with yellow irises. The vibrant colors of the flowers drew everyone's attention to where the two lovers would exchange vows.

*No pale colors for Kez,* Rae thought. There was nothing pastel about her friend, which was reflected in the bright jewel tones she'd selected for her wedding. The bridesmaids' dresses hung in a neat line on a rod in the corner, their deep-wine shade burnished by the sunlight flooding into the room. The color not only matched Kez's floral selection but complemented each of her bridesmaids, from Rae's olive-toned skin and dark hair to V's peaches-and-cream complexion and blonde tresses. All of them would be beautiful today, but none more so than Kez.

After everything Kez went through with her ex, Miller, Rae wondered whether Kez would ever open up to someone else. Then, in Kez's harebrained scheme to attend Miller's high school reunion, she'd met Jackson, and that was it. After a few bumps, the two of them came together in a whirlwind love affair that culminated in Jackson proposing last December. He'd used his nana's engagement ring but had the wedding band custom-made. It was a simple platinum band engraved in a continuous circle of the words "I love you."

Rae viewed Jackson's appearance in Kez's life as more welcome than crocuses breaking through the snow after a long, gloomy winter. He made Kez glow, lighting her up from the inside with a happiness that radiated around her. It was the look of a woman in love. Of course, it helped that Jackson reflected that same look tenfold. The man was head over heels in love with her friend. Rae couldn't be happier for them.

A flute of champagne appeared in front of her. The pale pink nails on the hand holding the drink told her it belonged to V.

"You're slipping," V said. Taking the thin-stemmed glass, Rae arched an eyebrow in question. With a quick glance at her wrist, as though a watch rested there, V replied, "It's after ten in the morning, and you don't have a drink in your hand."

Rae laughed and sipped, enjoying the dance of the bubbles on their way down her throat. "Guess I'm a little distracted." She gave her friend a once-over, taking in her freshly scrubbed face and loose blonde curls. "Plus," Rae said, "aren't you supposed to berate me for drinking *before* noon? Encouraging my breakfast time intake of alcohol seems to go against your status as one of the rising behavioral health specialists in our state."

To counter Rae's point, V drank from her own glass. "I'm a *pediatric* mental health specialist," she corrected. "Last I checked, you were over the age of eighteen and able to make your own, if somewhat dubious, life choices."

Rae laughed and touched her glass to V's. "Thanks for the vote of confidence, Doc."

"Anytime, Spin Doctor," V said. They watched the frenzy below for a minute, then V smiled. "If you'd told me a year ago that we'd be at Kez's wedding today, I'd have called you crazy."

Behind them, the door opened, and Kez walked in with her mother. The rest of the women swarmed around her, but Rae and V stayed at the window. In her loose lounge pants and matching top, she looked gorgeous with a cascade of red hair over her shoulders and a face free of makeup. They caught each other's eyes as Kez hugged a younger woman before coming over to give V a quick hug. Then V moved away to speak with Kez's mom and sister, Hudson.

Watching people scurry around like ants building a palace for their queen, Kez toyed with the diamond teardrop at her throat. "It's hard to believe this is all for me," she said, her eyes soft and voice wistful.

Rae grinned. "Is it really?"

Kez gave her a playful poke in the shoulder. "You calling me a diva?"

"If the tiara fits," Rae replied with a shrug.

As Kez laughed, Rae took stock of her friend. Even though she knew Jackson and Kez were solid, given Kez's history with commitment issues, Rae had worried that once the wedding day was here, Kez would need a flask hidden in her bouquet to get down the aisle. Looking at her now, though, she emanated a serene calm.

"You ready?" Rae asked.

Kez's eyes sparkled and her lips tilted up. "I know it sounds ridiculously cliché, but I feel like my whole life has been leading up to today."

Rae pretended to gag. "You sap."

The light in Kez's eyes didn't dim. "You asked," she said and dropped an arm around Rae's shoulders. Given their height difference, Kez could easily tuck Rae under her arm. With a squeeze, she said, "Thanks for being here today."

Pulling back in surprise, Rae asked, "Where else would I be?"

While any celebration with an open bar was normally an automatic RSVP for Rae, weddings were *not* her thing. The ceremony portion specifically. She'd never understood the appeal in standing in front of dozens (or hundreds) of people, more of whom were acquaintances than close friends, just to tell the person who already knew it that you wanted to spend your life with them and no one else. It seemed redundant and unnecessary, but those were not sentiments to share with the bride a few scant hours before she was set to do exactly that.

Kez's hazel eyes were warm with gratitude and a hint of teasing. "I know hearts, flowers, and lovey-dovey stuff aren't really for you."

Rae's arm snaked around Kez's waist, returning her hug. "It's a sacrifice I wouldn't make for just anyone."

"I know, and I appreciate it."

Used to defusing emotional scenes instead of encouraging them, Rae dropped her arm. With a slight lift of her shoulders, she said, "You're not just anyone."

Before Kez could respond, Rae looked at the gaggle of women in the small room. "Couldn't find more people to be in your wedding?"

Kez blushed, a little embarrassed at the big to-do. "I know, I know."

A few hours later, Rae's long hair was twisted into an elegant up-do, complete with carefully placed clear stones that winked like stars against her dark mane. The makeup artist used bold shadows and liner to enhance Rae's green eyes and give them a feline tilt. As she looked at her reflection in the handheld mirror, she smiled. There was no question. She looked stunning.

"You like it?" the aesthetician asked.

"You've outdone yourself," Rae responded. The young woman beamed and accepted the tip Rae took from the pocket of her robe. Rising so the next bridesmaid could take her place, she moved to stand behind Kez. Two girls worked on her makeup while a third tackled her hair. The bridal party had taken over the master bedroom and the two downstairs guest rooms. Female voices echoed through the first floor, mingling with the music playing on the sound system.

"You look gorgeous!" Kez exclaimed, meeting her eyes in the mirror.

"I know." Rae smirked.

With a subtle shake of her head, so as not to dislodge any bobby pins, Kez said, "No one could ever count modesty as one of your flaws."

Noticing Kez's empty champagne glass, Rae asked, "Need a refill?"

"I'd love one, but I don't think we have any left in here. Would you mind checking in the kitchen?"

Rae wound her way back through the room, dodging pairs of heels, makeup bags, and other assorted female accoutrements. It was a proverbial minefield of estrogen in there. Her bare feet padded silently over the hardwood floors, down the hall, and into the kitchen. While rummaging in the back of the refrigerator, she recognized Jackson's deep baritone coming from the front of the house. Once she unearthed the champagne, Rae snagged it and shut the door. She jumped a foot when she realized Jackson was on the other side.

"Jesus Christ," she said with a gasp. "You sneaky bastard!"

His lips quirked into an affable grin. "It's hardly sneaking if I'm in *my* house, Rae." Blue eyes went to the bottle in her hand. "For you or my bride?" he asked.

"I could be cruel and tell you she needs some liquid courage to get down the aisle," Rae teased. "But the two of you are so disgustingly in love, you'd know I was lying."

The tanned skin around his eyes crinkled as he laughed, his full lips splitting into a wide smile beneath his beard. "One day, Rae, you'll know what it is to be this in love."

Carefully, she tamed her features so he wouldn't see the pain he'd unwittingly caused. She gave his beard a playful yank. "Looks like you traded in the mountain man look for that of a distinguished gentleman today."

Jackson stroked the closely trimmed dark hair on his chin. "I have to look like a man who deserves her."

Even as cynical as she was, Rae was touched by the sweet sentiment. She squeezed his forearm and gave him a warm smile. "If any man does, it's you."

And he did. Jackson James Jenkins, or "Triple" as his friends sometimes called him, was a true rarity. Jackson had been undaunted by Kez's somewhat misguided attempt at closure with her ex *and* her initial resistance to their obvious attraction for each other. His resolve was founded in a genuine but not overblown belief in what he could offer her. He'd accepted her hesitancy and scaled the barriers she'd put up to protect her heart, knowing he had to prove he was worth the risk. In the end, the start of something new with Jackson helped Kez get the closure she wanted.

He gently grasped her elbow. "That means a lot to me, Rae."

She smiled and turned to go but froze in her tracks when she heard *that* voice. The sound of it triggered reactions throughout her entire body, from the tiny hairs at the nape of her neck going spiky, to her breath seizing in her lungs while her heart tried to escape from her ribcage, and ending with her feet rooting to the floor. Her blood whooshed in her ears while her mind struggled to convince the rest of her she was imagining things. It wasn't him. It couldn't be him.

But when he entered the kitchen, adjusting the cuffs of his shirt, she saw that he was indeed there. Tall with broad shoulders tapering to a trim waist, his dark hair was shorter now, and he sported a faint scruff on his chiseled jawline. But when he smiled at Jackson, his deep brown eyes lightened to the familiar cinnamon mocha she'd lost herself in so many times.

"Your dad's looking for you. He said you need to—" When he noticed Rae, he stopped talking. Molten-chocolate eyes traveled over her body, and she felt every inch of the journey but resisted the urge to gather the lapels of her robe. It was like he was cataloguing every part of her to review later. The champagne hit the counter with a loud clunk, and she held onto the ledge of it to keep herself upright, her feet still practically welded to the floor.

Oblivious to their silent interaction, Jackson said, "Hey, man, sorry. I'll be right there." Then, with an apologetic laugh, he added, "I'm forgetting my manners. Rae, this is Donovan McLeod. Van, this is—"

"Regan Murphy," Van said, his voice threaded with husky disbelief, as though equally stunned by her presence in Jackson's kitchen.

Jackson blinked. "Uh, yeah." Looking between them, he finally noticed Rae's death grip on the countertop. "You two . . . know each other?"

Rae didn't respond, her brain still taking a hiatus from making her body function, but Van had no such qualms. Never taking his eyes off her, he said, "Last time I saw Regan, I was wearing nothing but a towel, so yeah, I guess you could say we know each other." The bravado in his voice didn't quite reach his eyes though. The beseeching look in them and the tension radiating from the stiff line of his shoulders were both at odds with his playboy comment.

The hint that he wasn't as flippant as he sounded about their chance reunion only made things worse. The floor swayed under her feet, or maybe she was swaying. Either way, having Donovan McLeod standing less than five feet away was seriously screwing with more than just her equilibrium. She tried to form words in response to the bomb he'd dropped on Jackson, but her short-circuited brain kept her silent.

Jackson's eyes widened when he looked at Van. "What did you say?"

Without breaking eye contact with her, Van replied, "I said we know each other."

Rae watched the irritated bulge of Jackson's jaw. "That's not the part I'm talking about."

Van looked away from her, and Rae sucked in a breath, her body slowly rebooting.

"Oh, you mean the part about the towel?" he asked with an air of nonchalance but couldn't fully mask the catch in his voice on the word "towel."

"Uh, yeah, *that*," Jackson said, arms crossed and blue eyes boring into Van.

Rae's heart thudded like a cartoon animal's as she debated whether to flee. Normally, she'd never consider running from a man. Except for the night she'd run out on Van, that is. But right then, with the face of her past standing just across the counter, sprinting out of there like her hair was on fire had a certain appeal.

With a guarded look, Van said, "That wasn't exactly true." His dark eyes flicked back to her, and again she felt the tingling caress of them on her skin. It heated her from the inside as he looked her over, eyes lingering at the top of her robe. His throat bobbed with a rough swallow. "I put the towel on after she left."

His words and the corresponding memory hit Rae like a defibrillator. "Oh no. No, no, no, no," she said, straightening her spine and pointing at Van. "Don't even think about it," she warned.

"Did I say something wrong, Regan?" Van's voice was laced with a challenge, as though daring her to correct him.

Her skin prickled at the sound of her full name on his lips, but she ignored it. Waggling her pointed finger at him, she said, "You don't get to say anything at all to me, *Donovan*." The tic beneath his eye let him know he hadn't missed the emphasis on his full name.

Jackson gave his collar an anxious tug as Van and Rae smoldered at each other across the island, her with anger and him with . . . well, Rae didn't want to linger too long on what was behind the heat in Van's gaze. Jackson said, "I'm not sure what is going on between the two of you, and I don't want to sound like a total douche, but I'm getting married to the woman of my dreams in a few hours. Can we postpone any bloodshed until tomorrow?"

Rae jerked her eyes away from Van and over to Jackson. *Damn*, she thought, *no time for a mini meltdown today.* Her hands smoothed down the panels of her robe. Van's eyes followed the movement, and the weight of his gaze was palpable, pressing over her in a way she *did not* want to think about.

With a forced smile at Jackson, she grabbed the champagne. "Nothing to worry about, Jax. Today is about you and Kez and"— she glared at Van—"*no one* is going to spoil it for you." With what she hoped was a reassuring nod, she swept out of the kitchen, giving Van a wide berth and ignoring the *zing!* sensation of his eyes on her backside.

"Regan!"

She heard him call out but didn't slow down. It wasn't the full sprint she'd envisioned earlier but more of a subdued trot down the gallery hallway. She prayed silently that Jackson wouldn't let him follow her.

Near the end of the hall, she ducked inside the half bath and locked the door. Setting the bottle of champagne on the floor, she grabbed the sides of the vanity. In the mirror above it, her reflection stared back at her with wild eyes and flushed cheeks. She gulped in air, holding it in her lungs for a count of four then releasing it on a slow exhale. Closing the toilet lid, Rae sank down onto it, dropping her head between her knees and trying not to hyperventilate. But for the elegant updo, she would've been pulling her hair out. In—one, two; out—one, two.

"How is it even possible they're friends?" she muttered between deep breaths. Rae wracked her brain for any recollection of Kez mentioning Donovan. But that was nonsense, because if she had, there would've been no need to even think about it. If Kez had said *anything* about Donovan McLeod, the curves of the letters spelling out his name would've been seared in her mind like a brand. There'd been no mention of him—she was sure of it.

A knock at the door startled her, and she banged her elbow on the toilet tank. "Rae, you in there?" V called through the solid oak.

As she rubbed her elbow, Rae swore in her head. "Yeah, just a second!" she said. She flushed the toilet for cover and washed her hands, letting cold water rush over the pulse points at her wrists. Turning her gaze to the mirror, she put on the controlled mask she used when dealing with unruly clients, recalcitrant ex-girlfriends, and irate agents. Once she was sure her expression wouldn't betray the gamut of roiling emotions within, Rae opened the door with a practiced grin.

V's pretty face creased into a worried frown. "You okay?"

"Yeah, I'm good," Rae said, brandishing the champagne. "Just had to make a quick pit stop."

V remained skeptical, so Rae delved into her PR agent bag of tricks and plucked out the tried-and-true tactic of distraction. She tucked a loose curl behind V's ear. "What's with the sour face? You look like you're going to a funeral, not a wedding."

"I couldn't find you," V said, the lines between her brows deepening.

"Here I am!" Rae responded a little too brightly, holding out her arms in a wide arc. *Focus on the movement, not the face,* she telegraphed silently.

"Why are you being weird?" V asked.

Fooling a roomful of reporters was one thing. Pulling one over on one of her best friends was much more complicated.

"What's weird about me getting more booze and then using the bathroom? That sounds pretty normal to me," Rae said, mentally crossing her fingers that V would drop it.

V's brow remained furrowed, so Rae poked her between the eyes. "The ladies Kez hired are good, but I don't think even *they* do instant Botox."

V slapped her hand away. "Quit it!" She gave Rae one more long look. "You sure everything's okay?"

"Of course it is," Rae said, her smile going brittle. "Why wouldn't it be?"

After a moment's hesitation, V shrugged, and Rae let her smile dim before her face cracked open. V said, "I'm probably keyed up because I want today to be perfect for Kez. No drama, you know?"

Rae flashed back to the dramatically chiseled features currently in the kitchen, looking *way* too good in a tux. The rumble of male voices carried down the hall, and Rae put a hand on V's shoulder. Keeping her touch light, even though she wanted to shove her, Rae nudged V back toward the bedroom. "Well, by all means, let's bring her some refreshments! Can't have her getting parched on the big day, can we?"

Together, the two of them opened the double doors to the master suite. Jackson's house, soon to be his and Kez's house, dated from the 1850s. He'd lovingly restored every inch of the place over the years and added modern conveniences. One was widening the doorway to the master bedroom and putting in barn doors that rolled apart on a huge metal bar.

Kez turned in her seat at the sound of the doors opening. "There you are!" she cried. "I thought you'd gotten lost."

Rae forced herself to smile. "No such luck, I'm afraid. I'll have to suffer through this lovefest with everyone else."

"Oh, please," Kez said. "You know the reception will be worth the fifteen minutes of romantic stuff you have to stand witness for. Plus, I heard there were lots of hot single guys here," she said with an exaggerated jiggle of her brows.

Rae almost lost her grip on the champagne.

Kez chortled. "See! I knew you were excited about new prospects!"

*More like terrified of old flames*, Rae thought to herself. Today would be a long day.

Van's eyes locked on the swish of Regan's hips as she hurried away from him. Coming around the corner and seeing her had sent shockwaves rolling through him. Her being in nothing but that silk robe nearly brought him to his knees. Now, watching her walk away was more than he could stand. He made a move to go after her, but Jackson's hand on his arm stopped him cold.

"You want to tell me what the hell that was all about?" Jackson asked, curiosity mixing with concern in his tone.

Reeling from the first glimpse of Regan in five years, Van pounded a frustrated fist on the countertop. "Why didn't you tell me Regan Murphy was one of Kez's friends?"

One brow crept up and Jackson said, "Probably because I don't think of Rae as Regan Murphy. Even if I did, how would I know that would mean anything to you?" He leaned a hip on the counter, making it clear he wasn't going anywhere until Van provided some sort of explanation.

Van flattened his hand against the hard, cool surface and tried to calm down. Anger at Jackson was misplaced, especially on his wedding day. He was right—there was no way he could have known about Van's history with Regan, because Van hadn't told him.

He'd met Jackson in Charleston, well after he and Regan broke up. At the time, Jackson was overseeing the installation of several intricate reclaimed wood pieces in the lobby of one of the upscale hotels in town. Van was there to speak at a conference then offer a training course to the hotel's security. Both jobs took longer than expected, but the upside of it was that they'd gotten to know each other and become close friends. So close, in fact, that Jackson had asked Van to be his best man.

Images he'd banished from his thoughts played like a highlight reel in his mind. *Regan.* She was here, in the flesh, and as beautiful as the day she'd walked out on him.

Jackson shoved his shoulder. "Dude, seriously. What is going on?"

Jolted from his memories, Van straightened his tie and checked his watch. "Your dad sent me to bring you back to the smokehouse. The photographer is ready for the groomsmen photos."

Jackson had converted the old smokehouse into a man cave of sorts, complete with a wet bar and humidor. The wedding photographer had foamed at the mouth about the chance to get "manly" pictures, whatever the hell that meant.

"You really expect me to just let this go?" Jackson asked, gesturing to where Regan had disappeared.

Van scrubbed a hand over his jaw. "Yeah, I do. At least until a time that isn't your wedding day and a place with an endless supply of tequila."

Jackson was never one to hide his emotions, nor did he ever really try. They played out across his face, telegraphing his thoughts. It was why he was a shitty poker player but a great friend. When he shook his head with a small smile, Van knew he was off the hook.

"Fine," Jackson said. "But that time and place will come soon."

Van gave a quick nod, relieved at the reprieve. They left the kitchen and crossed the foyer, stepping into the bright sunshine on the front porch. Shading his eyes, Van saw Jackson's father waving at them from across the lawn. "We've been spotted," he said. Their shoes clicked across the stone pavers lining the walkway to the smokehouse. The rest of the groomsmen roamed around the building while a petite brunette strung with pounds of camera equipment darted among them. Jackson's dad pointed in their direction and said something to her.

"Finally!" she chastised. "I can't exactly take groomsmen photos without the groom!"

"Sorry, Mitzi," Jackson said, giving her his trusty twinkling grin.

She clucked in reproach but smiled back. "We'll have time for apologies later. I've got to get shots of you all before I start on the girls. If I could get you to move inside, we'll get this show on the road!"

*Like* any well-adjusted person, Rae took her heartbreak over Donovan, or Van, as Jackson had called him, along with all the memories of the life they'd started to build together, and threw it all in a proverbial box. She slammed the lid, slapped a lock on it, shoved it into the deepest recesses of her mind, and vowed not to think about him, them, or any of it ever again. When he waltzed out of her past and into Jackson's kitchen, that carefully hidden box started to rattle. The feelings inside it raged against the confines placed on them, threatening to burst forth and consume her.

She could practically hear the lock cracking open as she stared across the lawn at the groomsmen. Tucked away in Jackson's laundry room, she had a perfect view of the wedding photographer corralling them into various groups and poses. Among the guys, Van stood out in bold relief, his familiar frame drawing Rae's eyes like a magnet. He was tall but not the tallest in the group or the most classically good-looking. Some would call his features too angular, sharpened further by the close-cropped haircut. The naturally firm set of his lips gave him a somewhat dour countenance. And even when he did smile, most would say the half-curve was more mocking than pleasant, like he was in on some private joke at their expense. But to Rae, he remained the best-looking man she'd ever seen. She didn't think he'd changed at all in the past five years. If anything, he looked better.

"What are you doing in here?" V asked from behind her.

Rae let out a little shriek, jumping back from the window. "Holy shit! You scared me!" She placed a hand on her chest. "Don't sneak up on me! What are you doing in here?"

"I was hardly sneaking. You weren't paying attention." V plucked out a few towels from the closet behind Rae. "Kez asked me to grab some spare towels." She glanced out the window and grinned. "Oh, I see what you're doing," she said. "Picking out tonight's lucky guy?" she asked with a sly wink.

*If only it were that simple*, Rae thought. She tried to laugh off V's question. "You got me," she said with false enthusiasm. Rae stepped closer to V, subtly herding her from the room. But V held her ground.

"Who is that?" V asked, pointing out the window.

Rae didn't look. She didn't need to. There was only one groomsman V didn't know. Rae's palms started to sweat. "Who?"

Confusion passed over V's face, changing to disbelief. "You mean you didn't notice the broodingly sexy guy next to Jackson? I find that hard to believe."

This was not good. Not good at all. Rae couldn't let V catch the scent of her past with Van. There wasn't room on the day's schedule to deal with it. If Rae had her way, they'd never deal with it. With practiced nonchalance, she said, "I noticed, but I haven't decided yet."

That was not a lie. She *had* noticed Van and her mind was staggering under the weight of too many memories for her to make any decisions. Like whether to find the closest flat surface and ravage him—or the closest kitchen knife and stab him to death. Desperate to hide her rising panic, Rae seized on the one topic she knew was a surefire distraction.

"I also noticed that Dave looks damn good in a tux," she said. Dave was one of Jackson's oldest friends and yet another fortunate result of their brief trip up north. V met him when they'd gone to see Jackson perform at a local bar. Dave was the bartender, and V had fallen hard for him, much to her pretentious parents' dismay. It was a little outside the box for a doctor to date a bartender, but the two of them were smitten. They'd made long distance work, and there were rumblings about Dave moving to North Carolina.

V beamed and went back to the window to stare at her boyfriend. "He does, doesn't he?" Satisfied that V's attention was on how good Dave would look *out* of his tuxedo, Rae breathed a little easier.

She started to walk out of the room, but V lingered, her fingers touching the windowsill as she chewed her lower lip. "I have it on good authority he'll be at the wedding, Doc," Rae said. "You don't have to keep watching him." V blushed and followed her out.

Rae looped her left arm through V's right as they strolled toward the sounds of female laughter. "I don't think I'll ever get over this house," she said.

V tilted her head back to look at the rough-hewn beams above them. "I know. It's freaking huge." When Kez had met Jackson last fall, she learned he was a former CPA who now ran what he called a "restoration business." In his words, he essentially restored anything from old cars to antique drink machines. His "little business" was a thriving enterprise with customers all over the United States. Customers who paid big bucks to have Jackson rehab their neglected antiques or design something wholly unique for them. Jackson was, to put it mildly, loaded. Not that Kez cared about that. She would've loved him as much if he were poor as a church mouse. Plus, her law practice offered her a more than comfortable living.

The hall they walked down ran the length of the first floor. At one end was the laundry room they'd just left, along with a couple of guest rooms. The master suite was at the other. Not exactly how Rae would've laid it out, given the amount of clothes she had. Traipsing up and down that hallway to change out loads of laundry was not her idea of a good time. She'd asked Kez about it. Her response had been a hearty laugh. *"If that's the only thing I have to worry about in this marriage, I think we'll be fine,"* she'd said.

Rae and V passed the formal dining room on the right. Through a wide opening, the great room arched upward on their left. Wood rot had allowed Jackson leverage with the historical commission to knock out the walls that had separated the space into smaller rooms, and now the living area flowed into the updated kitchen and breakfast nook. Wide, sliding glass doors spanned the opposite wall, giving a view directly to the pool out back. An enormous stone fireplace occupied the center of the wall between the living room and the master suite. Jackson had salvaged most of the original hardwoods on the first floor. He'd done a beautiful job not only restoring the house but updating it into a home that was functional in the modern era—laundry room placement aside. Rae knew it couldn't have been a simple task to drag an antebellum mansion into the twenty-first century.

A shudder ran down Rae's spine as she peeked into the kitchen, half expecting Van to materialize in front of her. "Chilly?" V asked.

"Hmm?" Rae responded, her mind still on Van.

V pulled Rae to a stop before they reached the master bedroom, peering closely at her face. "What's going on with you?"

*Crap!* Rae thought. "I, uh, guess I'm still getting my head around the fact that Kez is getting married today."

"You sure that's all it is?" V's training in behavioral health made her a living, breathing lie detector sometimes. She could sniff out a half-truth almost as quickly as Kez could suss it out on cross-examination. But Rae was the mistress of spin, so she did what she did best—deflect and dodge without truly giving an answer.

Rae squeezed V's hand. "Yep, just thinking about one of my best friends walking the plank."

V chuckled. "Somehow, I don't think you should use that line in your wedding toast."

"You may be right," Rae agreed with a grin. "I'll have to dig deep to find some lines about true and everlasting love and all that happy horseshit."

"You're such a poet." Sarcasm dripped off V's words. "You have already written the toast, right?"

"Wouldn't you like to know?"

⚜

"Okay, Jackson, now let's get one with you and Franklin," Mitzi called from behind her camera.

Jackson's three-year-old nephew, Franklin, was a blue-eyed, blond-headed little imp who Van could tell would grow up into quite the lady-killer. For now, he was still shy and hung onto his dad's pants leg. He peered out from behind the man, refusing to cooperate.

"What's the matter, bud? You don't want to have a picture with your old, ugly uncle?" Jackson asked. He hooked his thumbs in the side of his mouth, drawing it down into a grotesque frown while closing one eye and rolling the other.

Franklin giggled and buried his face in his dad's thigh.

"Aw, c'mon, buddy," Jackson pleaded with him, this time with a normal face. "If you do, I promise I'll let you drive the tractor later."

At that, Franklin's eyes lit up, and he dashed over to Jackson. With a laugh, he scooped his nephew into his arms, and they posed for a few photos. Seeing Jackson with the young boy made Van wonder whether he and Kez planned to have kids. Hell, he wondered whether *he'd* ever have kids. Thoughts of a little girl with bright-green eyes and dark hair popped into his head. *Shit*, he thought. *That imaginary little girl looked a lot like the gorgeous woman I ran into in the kitchen.*

He tried to clear his head with a shake. It was no more effective than spraying sugar water to ward off mosquitos. Thoughts of Regan dominated his brain. It was as though seeing her had jarred loose every memory he had—memories he'd worked hard to keep buried. Like the way her hair smelled like coconuts and, after they'd spent the night together, so did his pillow. Or the taste of her skin after her shower. Van stifled a groan and adjusted his trousers. If he didn't stop that train of thought, his dick was going to be like Where's Waldo in Jackson's wedding pictures.

"Hey, man, you joining us or what?" Jackson's voice brought him back to the present. While Van was walking down memory lane, the rest of the groomsmen had lined up for a group photo. Even Franklin was in place. The photographer looked impatiently at the open space next to Jackson.

"Sorry!" He jogged over and stood in the spot she indicated. "Sorry, man," he said under his breath.

"Don't worry about it," Jackson said through his smile.

Mitzi moved them through various posed and "candid" photos. After a few minutes she said, "Okay, fellas, I need a few of just the groom and his best man." All the guys except for Jackson and Van dispersed. "Don't go far," Mitzi said. "We still have a few more group shots."

Hearing Jackson mutter under his breath, Van asked, "Not ready for all your close-ups?"

Jackson gave a weak half laugh. "For as much as we're paying for these photos, I guess I should be glad she's taking so many. But really, how many shots of me 'talking' or 'laughing' with my friends do there need to be?"

"It's not like you have a good side, bro, so she'll need to sift through thousands to find one she can use," Van teased.

"Not all of us are Abercrombie models," Jackson retorted.

"You're dating yourself, old man. Abercrombie is no longer what it was when we were in school."

"Neither are you." Jackson laughed.

Van made a show of straightening his tie. "The ladies would beg to differ."

"I know of at least one lady in that house"—Jackson jerked his chin toward his home—"who agrees with me."

The hook was baited and dangling in front of him, but Van refused to bite. "Nice try, Jackson." The two friends stared at each other then heard the camera click and whir.

"These are going to be some of the best shots!" Mitzi said, scanning through the images.

"Good grief," murmured Jackson. In a louder voice, he said, "Mitzi, I think the best shots are going to be of my bride. Isn't it time you start their pictures?"

"Smooth, real smooth," Van whispered.

"Let's just hope she agrees," Jackson whispered back.

"That's so sweet," Mitzi said with a sappy smile. She checked her watch. "You're probably right. I can get shots of the girls while they're getting ready so I capture the complete process. I'll send the wedding planner over to you boys to talk about what happens next."

"Isn't you getting married the next thing that happens?" Van asked.

"If only it were that easy," answered Jackson.

They watched Mitzi pick her way across the grass and meet up with a taller brunette in a lavender suit. The two women exchanged a few words, and Mitzi gestured in Jackson's direction. The taller woman made her way over to them, her mouth set and eyes stern.

❦

"You keep disappearing!" Kez giggled when Rae and V came into the bedroom. The giggle was the first sign maybe Kez had had too much champagne. She wasn't a giggler . . . unless there was champagne involved. It was like the fizz of the drink infected her laugh or something. She was still in her satin robe that had "Bride" embroidered on the back. Her makeup and hair—an intricate updo consisting of braids, twists, and carefully placed curls—were finished, and she looked flawless.

"I found her spying on the groomsmen from the laundry room," V reported.

Kez sipped more champagne. "Really?" she asked. "The groomsmen and not the bartenders?" Her eyes widened. "Wait, wait, wait! I know exactly which one she was looking at!"

Even though she knew Kez couldn't know about her and Van, Rae's blood still ran cold. Kez's fingers fanned out as she fluttered a hand in the air, grasping at the memory. Just how much champagne had she had?

"It's the dark and sort of moody one, isn't it? You know, the one with the cheekbones and the artful stubble!" Kez said, drawing a hand down her own cheek in emphasis.

Frustrated at Rae's lack of response, Kez snapped her fingers. "You know the one I mean!" The glass in her other hand tilted dangerously toward the floor.

V stepped in and took it from her. "Maybe you should slow down on the champagne a bit, Kez."

"I might be *just* this side of tipsy," Kez admitted.

"I think you've crossed to the other side," V corrected.

"Not the point." Kez drummed her fingers on the table in front of her. "What is his name?"

"Whose name?" V asked.

"The guy Rae was looking at! It's right on the tip of my tongue. Devon? No. Donald? Definitely not. God, what is his name?" Kez's brows knit together with the effort she was making. With a final slap to the tabletop, she said, "Donovan! That's it!"

"Oh, him," said V. "He's the one who missed the rehearsal, right?"

Kez nodded. "Yep, that's him. He had some work thing, so he didn't fly in until late last night. I'd never even met him until this morning. Between all our schedules, we couldn't ever get together."

"How do he and Jackson know each other?" Rae asked cautiously.

"They met when Jackson was working on a project down in Charleston. That's where Donovan—well, actually, he goes by Van—lives. They bonded over bourbon, and the rest is history."

"Well, you're right about one thing," V said. "His cheekbones are killer. A little on the glum side but still cute."

"Cute isn't the word I'd use," Rae muttered.

V's brows raised, her interest piqued. "And how would you describe him?"

Rae flushed but quickly answered. "Puppies are cute—even *some* babies are cute. A man that looks like him isn't 'cute.' The only words for a man like that are steamy, sexy, or extremely fuckable."

Kez sucked in a breath and fanned herself. "Damn, Rae. It's a good thing I'm guaranteed to get laid tonight."

Everyone in the room laughed, and Rae was glad for the diversion.

3

The door to the bedroom opened, and Mitzi stuck her head in. "Hey, ladies!" she said. "Y'all ready for some photos?"

Kez waved her into the room. "Mitzi! Come join the party!"

Mitzi and all her equipment came into the room. Her dark hair sat on top of her head in a messy bun. Various cameras hung around her neck, each with a different-colored strap. Her black tank top and jeans made her blend into the background while she captured everyone around her.

"Don't you all look gorgeous!" she said. She took off one camera and placed it on the bureau. The other she used to focus on Kez and clicked off a few shots.

"Make sure you get my good side," Kez said, cupping her hands around her face and hamming it up.

From behind the lens, Mitzi said, "Rae?"

"Yep?" Rae responded.

"Ms. Williams wanted you to come outside for a few minutes," Mitzi said.

"What did I do to get sent to the wedding warden?" Rae asked.

"Careful," V warned in a hushed tone. "She has eyes everywhere."

Kez shuddered. "I know she was highly recommended, but I also think she would've helped hunt down the Von Trapp family."

"So what does she need me for?" Rae asked Mitzi.

"Something about needing to go over things with you and the guy who missed rehearsal."

Rae gulped. "With whom exactly?"

Mitzi pulled a list from her pocket and ran her finger down it. "The best man, Donovan McLeod."

The room tilted a bit. Rae grabbed a champagne flute and took a drink. "He's the best man?" she asked Kez.

She nodded in response. "Yeah, didn't I tell you that?"

"No, you didn't." Rae chugged the rest of the champagne. This was not good.

"Well, looks like you get to spend a little one-on-one time with Mr. McLeod," Kez said, cocking her head and batting her lashes at Rae. The rest of the girls in the room oohed like they were all still in fourth grade.

"What's next?" Rae asked, clutching the empty flute and wishing she had a whole bottle. "Sitting in a tree K-I-S-S-I-N-G?"

"If you're lucky," Kez answered, giving her a little shimmy.

Mitzi laughed with the rest of them then said, "Rae, if I were you, I'd get a move on. Ms. Williams doesn't like to be kept waiting." The idea of an unhappy Ms. Williams killed the laughter in the room.

With no choice but to obey, Rae changed out of her robe into yoga pants and a button-up shirt to avoid messing up her hair. She left her friends behind with all the joy of a condemned woman headed to her fate. Time with Van was not tops on her list for today or any other day in the future.

The girls had called him broody, but that wasn't it. The man was just intense. *Very* intense in all aspects. She willed away a shiver and gave herself a mental pep talk that Van was nothing more than a problem to solve. Her job revolved around her ability to do that, so it was no problem. He was just a man. Albeit a man who'd smashed her heart into a thousand pieces, almost ruined her career, and humiliated her all in one fell swoop. But she'd emerged from the wreckage of her old life stronger than ever, and she'd be damned if she'd let him think he'd broken her.

"Uh-oh," said Van, watching the lady in lavender stalk toward them. "Who's that?"

"Lilah Williams, the wedding planner." Jackson grimaced.

"She looks . . . formidable?"

"That's one word for it," said Jackson.

"What would you call her?"

After a momentary pause, Jackson said, "Terrifying."

Van laughed at the idea of his friend fearing the well-dressed, willowy woman, but his humor was short-lived.

"Jackson!" The wedding planner's voice cracked like a whip, and Van managed not to jump . . . barely.

"Yes, ma'am, Ms. Williams?" Jackson answered dutifully.

She clapped her hands together like a teacher settling an unruly preschool class. "We need to go over the groomsmen's duties." Her steel-gray eyes settled on Van. "Is this the best man?"

Before Jackson could answer her, Van stepped forward and offered his hand and his best smile. "Yes, ma'am. Donovan McLeod at your service."

The woman's handshake crushed his bones. "No, Mr. McLeod. If you were at *my* service, you wouldn't have missed the rehearsal last night."

Van flushed under his collar, flexing his fingers to restore feeling in them. "My apologies. I was delayed by—"

Her hand sliced through the air, cutting off his response. "Why you were delayed isn't relevant. It only matters that you were not present, so you missed the run-through. As you probably figured out, you're paired with the maid of honor. Have you met her?"

He shuffled his feet like a kid who'd forgotten his homework. "Um, no, ma'am, I haven't—"

She cut him off again. "You will escort Ms. Regan Murphy. As you two are the most important parts of this ceremony other than the bride and groom, rehearsal is essential to make sure you are familiar with your responsibilities. Since you missed it, the three of us are going to spend time together now. I've asked Mitzi to have Ms. Murphy join us."

Van stood shell-shocked. "Did you say I'd be escorting Regan Murphy?"

Ms. Williams sniffed and tugged at the hem of her suit jacket. "I certainly didn't stutter, Mr. McLeod. Yes, you, as best man, will be with the maid of honor, Ms. Murphy."

Van heard Jackson snicker behind him. "I'm with Regan?" he asked him.

"A state of affairs I think you're familiar with," Jackson said.

Van swiveled back to Ms. Williams. "And Regan is coming out here?"

She released a long-suffering sigh and closed her eyes, seeking patience or deliverance from Van's stupidity. To Jackson, she asked, "Is your friend . . . slow?" Her voice oozed annoyance.

Jackson barked out a laugh. "Not normally, Ms. Williams."

Ms. Williams leveled her icy stare at Van and spoke slowly. "Yes, Mr. McLeod. Ms. Murphy will join us momentarily."

Her glance over his shoulder made him turn around. Regan was making her way down the stone steps at the front of Jackson's home. When she reached the bottom, her gaze swept over him like the barrel of an artillery tank, coolly calculating the distance necessary to launch a decimating barrage into enemy territory.

"She looks like she could spit nails," Jackson said quietly as the three of them watched Regan approach.

Van responded with a noncommittal sound, preoccupied with being able to see her again. Toned legs in tight pants made quick strides and, within moments, she stood across from him. Green eyes landed on him briefly then skittered away to Ms. Williams.

"You wanted to see me?" she asked the wedding planner.

Ms. Williams brushed nonexistent dirt from her skirt. "Yes, Ms. Murphy. Since Mr. McLeod didn't join us last night"—she gave Van a reproachful look—"we need to go over the duties of the maid of honor and best man."

"Duties?" Regan asked, still refusing to look at him.

Ms. Williams dipped her head in a quick nod. "Yes. Each of you will hold the rings for the couple. Ms. Murphy, you'll have the groom's ring, and Mr. McLeod, you'll have the bride's ring."

"Right, I have his with my stuff back in the house," Regan said, hiking a thumb over her shoulder in the direction from which she'd come. "I hope you like etched rose gold and diamond baguettes," she said to Jackson.

"My wife wouldn't do that to me," he responded confidently.

"She's not your wife yet," Regan said with amusement in her eyes.

"Rae," Jackson said in a warning tone.

"God, you're so easy to get riled." She laughed. "I promise it's platinum, like you agreed on. Even *I* wouldn't try to sneak in a fake one on your wedding day. Too bad I didn't think of that at the rehearsal though."

Even Ms. Williams managed a semblance of a smile at Regan's antics. "Very good, Ms. Murphy. Now, you'll be the last bridesmaid before Ms. Walsh comes down the aisle. I understand she has kept her music for her entrance a secret from everyone but you?"

Regan grinned. "Yes, ma'am, that's correct."

"I trust everything is set up to have it play once you've reached your place at the altar across from Mr. McLeod."

Van's heart tripped as the words "at the altar" reverberated through his brain. He'd dreamed of being with her at an altar, except they'd be the ones exchanging vows. They'd talked about it being on a beach, just them and a few close friends. Regan had wanted simple, with as little pomp and circumstance as possible. She'd be barefoot, and he wouldn't wear a tie. It would've been perfect.

Regan's smile withered when she looked at him. "Yes," she said in a clipped tone. "I'll have everything ready."

"Good, good. Once the recessional starts, you two will precede the new Mr. and Mrs. Jenkins down the aisle. I prefer my bridesmaids loop their left arm through the groomsmen's right and rest their hand right below the man's elbow. Since we didn't have the chance to see how that worked last night, let's do that now, shall we?"

Ms. Williams's long fingers rippled in the air like sea anemones courting a clown fish, encouraging Regan and Van to couple up. Regan gave no outward sign she'd willingly touch him, so he took her left hand. She frowned and pulled away.

"A problem, Ms. Murphy?" Ms. Williams asked, a critical downturn to her mouth.

Regan drew in a deep breath, and Van prayed for a positive outcome. On an exhale, she said, "No, ma'am. No problem." She fisted her hand, and he felt the sting of her knuckles against his ribs as her arm passed through his. He grunted at the contact but refused to flinch. Their arms linked awkwardly, since she was still trying to stand as far away from him as possible.

Ms. Williams arched a thin brow. "Maybe with a little more finesse during the ceremony, dear."

Regan tried to pull her hand away, but Van covered it with his. There was no way in hell he would give up the opportunity to touch her. She looked over at him, sparks flying from her green eyes. "What are you doing?" she asked through clenched teeth.

He stroked her hand. "We have to make sure everything looks perfect, right? I want to make sure we do this like Ms. Williams wants. Should we try it again? Only this time, maybe don't punch me."

Regan grumbled under her breath but slowly withdrew her hand from his arm. With refined grace, she eased toward him and gently slid her arm back through the crook of his. Her small hand rested lightly below the bend of his elbow. He tightened his arm against his side, forcing her nearer. The side of her body aligned with his. He felt her quick inhale and placed his hand over hers, savoring the feel of her next to him. His whole body reacted to her proximity, starved by her absence and craving more of her.

"Much better, Ms. Murphy!" Ms. Williams praised. "You will walk together down the aisle and then separate at the last row of seating. Let me see you take a few strides together." She directed them to walk in front of her. "And Ms. Murphy?"

"Yes, ma'am?" Regan answered.

"Try to let Mr. McLeod lead you," she instructed.

Van stifled a chuckle. "Shall we?" he asked Regan.

"Lead on, asshole," she responded in a voice low enough only he could hear her.

"You always had a way with words," he said as he walked in the direction Ms. Williams pointed.

"So did you," said Regan. "Only your way was to twist them into lies."

He winced as her barb hit its mark. "Regan, please," he said.

"Stop, just stop. I'm going to walk down this fucking aisle with you because it's my best friend's wedding. We're going to smile and pose for a million pictures. We're going to fake our way through the reception and then never see each other again. As I recall, keeping people from seeing the truth is something at which you excel. One could almost say your *job* depends on it." Her voice shook behind her smile.

Before he could respond, Ms. Williams called out, "Excellent, you two. It seems I may have misjudged you, Mr. McLeod. You are not the simpleton I thought you were."

"Er, thank you?" Van said.

"Ms. Murphy, thank you for joining us. You're free to go," said Ms. Williams, as if she were letting Regan off with a warning.

Regan dropped his arm like it was on fire and started for the house without a backward glance. He missed the press of her body against his, but that longing didn't keep him from enjoying the view of her ass as she hustled away. Yoga pants were a goddamn miracle.

Jackson came up beside him. "This thing between you and Rae won't be a problem today, will it?" he asked.

Van tore his eyes from Regan's backside and looked at his friend. "No, it won't be. I wouldn't do that to you on your wedding day. Despite what she"—he jerked his chin toward Regan's retreating form—"thinks, I'm not that big of an asshat."

Jackson's eyes were troubled as he looked toward the house. "Tell me you didn't totally fuck her over, man. She and Kez are closer than sisters, and I don't want to start married life with my wife hating one of my best friends."

Van rubbed a hand over his hair and sighed. "She definitely thinks I did."

Jackson groaned, and Van hurried to finish. "If I could have five minutes alone with her, I can show her she's wrong. I swear I didn't do what she thinks I did."

Jackson clasped Van's shoulder. "Two hundred and fifty people are coming to this wedding. That doesn't include the caterers, musicians, DJ, or any of the other staff we hired. I don't think any of us are going to have five seconds, much less five minutes alone with anyone."

Van's shoulders sagged in defeat. Jackson slapped him on the back. Reaching into the breast pocket of his suit coat, Jackson pulled out a long, slender box. "Tell you what," he said. "I was going to have Rae deliver this to Kez."

Hope sprouted in Van's chest, and he reached for the box. Jackson held it out of his reach and smiled, but his eyes remained serious. "This might get you five minutes with Rae, or it might not. Although somehow, I don't think a five-minute explanation is going to erase whatever happened between you." He handed Van the box. "Good luck, man."

Van clasped Jackson's free hand and pulled him in for a bro hug. "Thanks, brother."

# 4

Once out of earshot of Ms. Williams, Rae mumbled curse words all the way back to the house. Stomping up the stairs, she brushed at her arm to scrub off the feeling of having it pressed into Van's side. He looked positively divine in a tuxedo, and she remembered all too well what he had going underneath it. She shivered at the thought.

With another deep, cleansing breath, she opened the front door. When she reached the bedroom, she found Mitzi still taking pictures. Kez had stopped drinking and was posing with the ladies of her family—her mom, sister Hudson, and Hudson's daughter, who'd serve as the flower girl. A crown of flowers perched on the child's head, and her red curls bounced as she laughed. Her dress was a mini version of the brides-maids' dresses, with cap sleeves and an ivory sash at the waist.

Kez glanced at Rae. "Looks like you survived," she said.

"Barely," Rae answered as she closed the door behind her. V handed her a glass of champagne, which she accepted gladly.

"The caterers brought in a light lunch for us," V said. The buffet table set up across the room overflowed with salads, sandwiches, and finger foods.

"If that's a light lunch, I can't imagine what's being served for dinner tonight," Rae said.

"I know, right?" V said.

Rae walked over and fixed herself a plate. Breakfast felt like hours ago, and she was suddenly starved. As she piled bites of charcuterie on her plate, V came up beside her.

"How'd things go with Van?"

Rae bobbled her plate. "What?"

Her friend looked at her questioningly. "Um, with Van? The reason Ms. Williams summoned you?" V put a hand on Rae's arm. "What is going on with you today? You're as jumpy as a stray cat in a room full of rocking chairs. Are you sure you're okay?"

Rae sighed and took her plate to a corner of the room, signaling V to follow her. With a quick peek to confirm Kez was still preoccupied with her family, Rae said, "I need to come clean about something."

V's eyes widened, and she set down her plate. "Okay . . ."

"Donovan and I," she started. "Well, we, um . . ." Rae paused and put her plate next to V's. She twisted her hands together and looked out the window.

"What is it, Rae?" V asked, reaching out to her friend.

"You know how you and Kez always want to delve into the dark secrets of my past love life?"

V's nose crinkled in confusion. "Yeah?"

"Well, you only have to walk outside and join the groomsmen to do that now," she said.

"Wait, what?" V asked.

"Donovan McLeod is my past love life," said Rae.

V's blue eyes rounded. "He's what?" she squealed.

V's high-pitched squeak made Kez turn in their direction. "Shhhh!" Rae implored her, but it was too late. Kez had excused herself from her mother and was headed their way with questions shining in her hazel eyes.

"What's with the heavy discussions on my wedding day, you two? It's supposed to be a party, haven't you heard?" Kez asked.

"Are you going to tell her, or am I?" asked V.

"Tell me what?" asked Kez.

V stared at Rae, who tried not to fidget under her reproachful gaze. "Fine," she huffed. "Today isn't the day for this discussion, but I don't see any way around it. You're finally getting the answer to your questions about my love life."

"What are you talking about, Rae?" Kez asked.

"You always say I should talk to you girls about 'the guy,' as you call him." Rae's fingers hooked into air quotes. "Well, 'the guy' showed up here this morning."

"What? Who?" Kez fired questions at her and looked around as though whomever they were talking about was in the room.

"Donovan," said Rae.

"Donovan?" Kez repeated.

"Donovan," Rae confirmed.

Kez sank down into a chair. "So you're saying my fiancé's best friend, the best man in my wedding, is the guy who dicked you over all those years ago?"

Rae swigged champagne. "In a nutshell, yep."

Kez grabbed the glass from her and chugged. "Well, fuck," she said.

"My thoughts exactly," said Rae, poking glumly at a prosciutto roll.

Kez jumped from bride to lawyer in two seconds flat. "Well, obviously, you and V will switch places in the wedding. He can't walk you down the aisle! That would be too weird. And you have roughly"—she looked at the clock on her bedside table—"an hour before we have to be dressed and ready for the last pictures, so you'd better start talking."

"Uh, what?" Rae asked.

"I need the story so I can evaluate whether Donovan even gets to stay at the wedding," Kez said, hands on her hips.

"Okay, let's all take a breath here," said V, always the voice of reason. "This is big news we need to process before we make any decisions."

Kez opened her mouth to argue, but Rae jumped in. "V's right, Kez. It's three hours before you say 'I do.' It's too late to change anything with the wedding, including who's escorting whom down the aisle. I can handle Donovan. It'll be fine."

Kez looked at her friend for a long moment then said, "Well, you'd know better than I would whether you can or can't, since I have no idea what the hell happened between the two of you. But again, you've got an hour to tell me." She turned to the rest of the wedding party. "Ladies, if I could get your attention for a few minutes?"

The balance of the women in the room faced them. Kez smiled. "Thank you. I hate to ask, but since I'm the bride, I guess I can ask anything today." Laughter rippled through the room. "I need a few minutes with these two, so if you all could take your lunch into the living room, that would be great. I'd say we could go out there, but I don't want to risk Jackson seeing me before the ceremony."

"Of course, Kez," said Hudson.

"Don't dally too long, Kesler," her mother cautioned, nervously toying with the string of pearls around her neck.

"I won't, Mama, I promise. Just need a moment with my girls," said Kez. Placated, her mother smiled and herded the bridesmaids toward the door. Hudson opened it, only to find Van on the other side with his hand raised to knock.

⬯

Van covered his surprise at the opening door with a practiced smile. "Ladies," he said.

The woman at the door looked back to Kez, silently asking permission to let him in. She, Regan, and a girl he thought was named V clustered in a far corner of the room. Kez narrowed her eyes on him and smiled. Only it wasn't really a smile, more like a wolf baring her teeth.

*Uh-oh,* he thought.

"It's okay, Hudson. You can let him in," Kez said.

The women and the photographer filed past him until the only women left in the room regarded him with thinly veiled hostility. He toyed with the box in his hands as he stalled in the doorway.

"By all means, Donovan," Kez said in a syrupy voice, "do come in."

He stepped forward and held out the jewelry box. "Jackson asked me to deliver this to you, Kez," he said.

Her eyes softened at the mention of Jackson's name, and her smile became genuine. The look on her face was one of pure love. Envy ran through Van's veins, followed quickly by regret. Regan had looked at him like that when they were together, and if things hadn't gotten so screwed up, it could've been her preparing to walk down the aisle to his side.

Kez reached for the box and traced a hand over it before setting it on the table next to her. "Is that all you needed, Donovan?" she asked, and he understood how one of her witnesses must feel at trial. Those hazel eyes lasered onto him and searched for answers.

He resisted the urge to loosen his collar or shuffle his feet. He was a grown man, for God's sake, not a kid who'd gotten called into the principal's office. Van met her searching look and didn't cower. "Actually, Kez," he said, "I was hoping to speak with Regan for a few minutes."

Kez moved in front of her friend like a guard dog. "I don't think that's the best idea," she said. V moved to flank her, letting him know she agreed.

He readied himself to plead his case, but from behind Kez, Regan said, "Calm down, Counselor." She shouldered between her friends.

"Rae," said Kez, still glaring at Van, "you don't have to—"

Regan interrupted, "I don't have to do a lot of things, Kez. But as your maid of honor, I do have to make sure your wedding day goes off without a hitch. And"—she sneered at Van—"if that means giving five minutes to this cockroach, I can do that."

Okay, so having her think he was a cockroach was a problem, but at least she'd agreed to talk to him. Van counted that as a win. He nodded at the porch door. "Regan, could we maybe . . ."

She brushed past him and jerked open the door, signaling him to go in front of her. He walked toward her, but Kez's voice stopped him.

"Donovan?" she asked.

He turned back. She had the jewelry box in her hands and questions in her eyes. "Did Jackson know about . . ." She gestured between him and Regan.

He shook his head. "No, he didn't." Relief washed over her face, and she nodded.

Van resumed his path to the door. For a second, he worried Regan would shut it behind him and throw the lock. But she followed him outside and closed the door behind her. She stood a few feet away with her arms crossed. He considered reaching for her but knew it would be a mistake. Instead, he clasped his hands behind his back and rocked on his heels.

"You're wasting your five minutes," she said when he didn't immediately begin talking.

"You're even more beautiful than the last time I saw you," he said.

Her eyes flashed. "Fuck you, Donovan." Her lip curled in disgust. "Or should I say *Agent* McLeod?"

"You left without letting me explain," he said.

"What was there to explain?" she spat. "Our entire relationship was a lie. I didn't even know your real name!" The anger in her voice was raw and jagged.

"Regan, please," he said, hands outstretched. "Just give me the chance to talk to you."

Her laugh was bitter. "You think you can explain a year of lies in the next three minutes? Give me an explanation for blowing up my life with no warning at all? Taking everything I'd worked my entire life for up to that point and lighting it on fire? That's a tall order even for someone as gifted in bullshit as you."

His hands clenched and fell to his sides. "I was doing my job, Regan." Hurt blazed quickly in her eyes, disappearing in an instant. Too late, he realized how those words sounded to her. "Wait, that's not—"

She held up a hand. "Save it, Agent McLeod. You've answered the one question I had all along—whether anything we had was real or I was a means to an end. I guess I know the answer now."

Throwing caution to the wind, he reached for her, taking her hands in his. "Regan, please, that's not what I meant at all. You were never just part of the job."

She jerked away from him. "So you didn't use me to get access to Hasselhoff?" she asked.

"Regan," he said, stepping toward her.

She backed up a step with a harsh laugh. "You can't even deny it, can you?"

God, he was screwing this up. What might be his only chance was slipping through his fingers. "Please," he begged. "Give me a chance to explain everything to you."

"You had a chance," she said. The ice in her voice reached all the way to his bones. "You had so many chances. When you took me to bed and let me call you a name that wasn't your own. Every promise, every touch, every kiss were all chances to tell me. None more so than each time you told me you loved me." Her voice broke on the last words.

"Regan," he breathed, gutted by the pain in her voice. He wanted to go to her, take her in his arms, and hold her. But he stayed where he was, fisting his hands to keep from reaching for her.

Regan cleared her throat, and her face emptied of emotion. It was her public face, unflappable and cold—and it hurt to have her use it on him. Like he was just another PR problem she had to defuse. "This was a mistake." She turned and went back into the house.

"Dammit!" His shout startled the caterers setting up in the tent below the porch. Furious with his failure, he stomped down the back stairs. Jackson was right. He'd been foolish to think he could explain everything in a few minutes. Now that he'd laid eyes on her again, desperation clawed at him like an animal. He had to make her understand that what they'd had was real, that what he'd felt for her was *real* and not part of his assignment.

5

As soon as the door shut behind Rae, Kez and V rushed over, their faces twin expressions of concern. "What happened?" asked V, touching Rae's shoulder.

"Same shit, different day," Rae answered, pushing past her two friends. If she could put distance between them, it would be easier to avoid rehashing the scene from the porch. She didn't want the stain of Van and her to taint Kez's wedding day. She should've guessed the two of them wouldn't let her off that easily.

"That's not an overly informative answer," said Kez, stepping in front of Rae. "Why don't you start at the beginning?"

Rae tried again to put them off. "We don't have time to get into it. You're getting married in just a couple hours. *That* needs to be the focus of today, not my bullshit with my ex."

Kez rolled her eyes into an imperious look. She patted her updo with an air of confidence. "You know they can't start without me, right? We've got as much time as we need, Rae. Your delay will only make people wait longer to see how good I look in my dress."

With a snort of laughter, Rae knew when to give in. She sank down onto the foot of the king-size bed. Kez's request seemed simple enough, but it still hurt to think about how her relationship with Donovan had started. Tucking her feet underneath her, Rae said, "I'll try to give you the highlights."

*It was a Monday morning like any other in Charleston, South Carolina. August had come in with a vengeance, layering the wet heat of humidity over the Low Country like a damp blanket. Rae wrapped her hair into a twist and secured it with a clip at the back of her neck, fanning herself with her hand. All it did was move the hot air around. Caviar and Bananas, the little sandwich shop she'd come to for lunch, had AC; however, the continuous stream of people coming in and out meant it was working overtime just to make the small space bearable, much less cool.*

*Why she'd chosen to walk over in this heat escaped her at that moment. After a single block, her shirt had wilted and clung to her body. She plucked the fabric from her skin, willing the AC to infuse into her clothing for the walk back.*

*"Caprese sandwich with a side of sauteed brussels for Rae," the clerk called out.*

*Rae moved toward the counter and reached for it, but a large male hand took it before she could. "Hey!" she said in protest.*

*The hand's owner turned, and Rae forgot about the heat. Standing in front of her was the sexiest man she'd ever seen. He was tall but not towering—which was important given her diminutive stature—with broad shoulders and sharply defined cheekbones. His light-brown hair needed a trim, but it was his eyes that hooked her. They were dark brown and framed by gorgeous lashes. It wasn't fair for a man to have eyes that pretty.*

*Dressed in scruffy chinos and a worn T-shirt with faded lettering, he wasn't a typical Charleston dandy. Even in ninety-five-degree heat with one hundred percent humidity, those guys wore their blazers and bow ties. In* his casual to the point of frayed outfit, he didn't fit the preppy mold, which made him all that more attractive to Rae. She'd been fending off the local fops since she'd moved there six months ago. This guy was a far cry from those preening peacocks.

"Did you need something?" he asked. His voice was deep and smooth, and Rae's ovaries took notice.

She gave herself a mental slap. "Yeah, you took my sandwich."

He looked at her quizzically. "No, I didn't."

"Yes, you did."

He took a step toward her. "No, I didn't. It's a sandwich for Ray." He pointed to his chest. "I'm Ray."

She pointed to the paper wrapper, through which the balsamic had started to bleed. "No, it's a sandwich for R-A-E." Her finger pointed back to her. "That's me."

He blinked then looked at the sandwich. "Well, hell," he said. "My bad." He handed her the sandwich. "Sorry about that . . . Rae, was it?"

Rae took the proffered paper-wrapped parcel. "Yeah, well, actually, it's Regan." Why had she told him that? No one called her Regan. Not since kindergarten when she was teased and called Ronald Reagan by some little bastard at recess. Even at five, she'd been capable of making executive decisions. She came home that day and informed her parents her name was now "Rae" and that was that.

He smiled, showcasing perfectly white teeth and a dimple in his left cheek. "Well, that will certainly make things easier."

"What things?" she asked, concentrating more on the sandwich than the man who'd held it. She needed to get back to the office—with her lunch.

He tucked his hands in his pockets, his grin stretching wide enough to activate his other dimple. "We can't very well call out the same name in bed. That would be awkward."

*Rae's eyes rounded, but she kept her cool. "Excuse me?" she asked, doing her best to look down her nose at him. Which was difficult, given their height difference. But she thought she'd managed it pretty well.*

*With a laugh, he closed the distance between them, giving her a whiff of his oaky cologne. "Kidding, I'm kidding!" he said, smile still in place. "But we need to sort through the name issue. I'll have to call you Regan since you'll be calling me Ray. How's that?" he asked. "Ray Edwards. Nice to meet you." He stuck out a hand.*

*Rae looked at it then took it with her sandwich-free one. "Regan Murphy."*

*"Nice to meet you, Regan."*

"Wait, wait, wait," said Kez, tilting her head in consternation. "I thought you were going to tell us how you met Donovan."

"That is how I met Donovan," Rae said.

"What?" asked V, equally flummoxed.

"When I met Donovan, he introduced himself as Ray Edwards," Rae explained.

"Why on earth would he do that?" asked Kez.

"Because when he met me, he was working undercover for the FBI investigating Benson Hasselhoff," Rae said.

Recognition lit Kez's eyes. "Isn't he that guy who got indicted on federal drug charges like"—she paused and looked at Rae—"five years ago?"

"That's the one," Rae replied. "He was also my boss," she added. Looked like all the dirty laundry was getting aired out today.

"Your boss?" V cried.

"My boss," Rae confirmed.

Kez sat down next to Rae. "How did we not know that before today?"

Rae downplayed her friends' shock with a simple shrug. "Probably because I didn't tell you. But that's not the actual point of this anecdote."

"Sorry, sorry, but we are going to come back to that," said Kez, rolling her hand in a continue motion. "Why did he give you a fake name?"

"Because that 'chance' meeting at the market wasn't chance at all. Donovan set the whole thing up to meet me."

"But why?" asked Kez.

"To use me."

"Use you?" V asked. "For what?"

"To bring down my boss," Rae said.

Kez and V rocked backward, each looking stricken and appalled. "Oh my God!" said Kez.

"One of the same thoughts that went through my head," said Rae with a sad smile. The memories still cut her, but she hid the residual pain to avoid any big spectacle. No matter what Kez said, Ms. Williams made the schedule, and heads would roll if anything interfered with it.

Kez put an arm over her shoulders. "How long did you date?"

"Long enough to live together."

"Holy crap," said V in amazement.

"Oh yeah, everything was hearts and flowers and unicorn farts until I found out the whole thing was a lie. He was undercover, and since I was semi-high up the food chain, I guess I made a good mark." She looked quickly at her friends, struck by the need to reassure them that she had nothing to do with any of her boss's misdeeds. "I had no clue what Hasselhoff was doing. I just handled PR for the hotels."

The truth of the statement didn't dull the slap of humiliation that had become somewhat of a constant in Rae's life. She no longer thought about it every day, but it lurked there just beneath the surface. Its favorite time to come out of the shadows was at three or four in the morning when her anxiety was already peaking over something else. *That* was prime time for her past to pop up and remind her that the man she'd loved, the one guy she'd wanted as a permanent fixture in her life, had lied to her on a consistent basis since they met. As had the man who'd shaped her early career. How could she pride herself on building a career based on her ability to sort through the lies, ferret out the truth, and hold people accountable when she'd been hoodwinked herself? Even years later, it made her break out into a cold sweat.

Kez squeezed her shoulders. "Of course you didn't know, honey. That thought never even occurred to us." V nodded in solidarity, and Rae was buoyed by her two friends' unwavering confidence in her character.

"How did you find out who Van really was?" asked V.

Rae laughed, the sound hollow. "It was a total fluke thing."

*"Ray," she called as she opened the door to their condo. He didn't answer, and she moved from the foyer into the living room. "Ray?" she called again, and again there was no response. Slipping out of her heels, she padded down the hall to the bedroom and pushed open the door. The shower was running in the master bathroom. That'd been why he hadn't answered her.*

*Well, she thought, I'll pop in there and surprise him. She unbuttoned her blouse and hung it in the closet. Unzipping her skirt, she slipped it off and crossed the room to put it in the dry-cleaning bag. Passing by the small desk, she noticed Ray's briefcase hanging halfway off the corner. She went to move it back farther onto the desk so it wouldn't fall, except she nudged it too far to the side, and it did just that. Its contents spilled onto the floor on contact. Crap!*

*Hurriedly, she started scooping up papers, not reading them until one caught her eye. She recognized names that she knew were on the guest list for a party her boss was hosting next week. Several names were circled. Why would Ray have this? She glanced furtively at the bathroom door then gathered the other papers. In for a penny, in for a pound, she figured.*

*Rae rifled through the stack of papers and broke into a cold sweat when she found a memo marked "Confidential" and addressed to "Agent Donovan*

McLeod." Who was that, and why did Ray have it? Her stomach alternated between clenching and roiling, and her hands shook a little when she set the paper aside and went back to the briefcase.

A zippered pocket on the underside of the lid bulged slightly. With another quick glance at the bathroom, her hands trembling, she opened it and reached inside. Her fingers closed around a square leather object. When she pulled it out, it looked like some type of wallet. Opening it, she saw it was a badge. Federal Bureau of Investigation. A chill ran through her as she looked at the identification above the gold badge. It was for Agent Donovan McLeod. Only the picture was of Ray.

She heard the water turn off and scrambled to her feet, dropping the badge on the bed. She couldn't process what she'd just found. Her mind refused to wrap around the enormity of her discovery. That not only was Ray not Ray, he was some kind of federal agent. For more than a year, she'd shared her bed . . . her life with a stranger. But why? Why had he done this to her? What did he want from her? Was she in trouble for something? She could think of nothing about her that would interest the FBI.

"Regan, honey, is that you?" Ray—Donovan—called from the bathroom.

Rae didn't answer. She couldn't breathe. Her lungs felt like they'd filled with sand and the room closed in around her. She needed to get out of there. Her heart pounded in her chest as she raced to the bureau and blindly took out clothes. Juggling them in her arms, she managed to stoop down, grab her sneakers, and run out of the bedroom.

"Regan?" he called again.

She was almost at the door when she heard him discover the opened briefcase. "Shit!" he said. He emerged from the bedroom stark naked. Her hand was on the door. "Regan, wait, please!"

She turned to look at him. "Who are you?" she asked.

He stopped short. "Regan, I—"

"Who. Are. You?" she asked, enunciating every word.

*He didn't answer for a minute then said, "You saw the badge. You know who I am."*

*Tears flooded her eyes. "I thought I did," she whispered and jerked the door open, fleeing into the hall.*

Kez gave a low whistle, and V took Rae's hand. "That's crazy!" V said. "And you haven't seen him since then?"

Rae shook her head. "Nope, other than the news coverage when they arrested my boss about a week later."

"That's so awful," said Kez, her eyes downcast.

What had been awful was her entire friend group in Charleston questioning whether she'd been involved in the shadier aspect of her boss's dealings. That was bad enough but easily handled by the FBI's lack of interest in her once Hasselhoff had been arrested. If she'd been involved, obviously, she'd have been caught in the same net that trapped him. The real kicker, though, was that she'd introduced Donovan to all of them as "Ray Edwards," security specialist. Hell, she'd met *his* friends. Probably FBI plants who knew all along she was getting played and got a good chuckle out of it.

The sheer, overwhelming shame she felt at being so stupidly naive and trusting had almost been her undoing back then. But the humiliation that pushed her out of Charleston also brought her to Charlotte and, if she were honest, into friendships that were much more solid. Because after a smattering of calls to "check in" during the immediate aftermath of Hasselhoff's arrest, when Rae's unfettered access to cool clubs and fancy parties ceased to exist, so did most of her friendships.

Kez and V cared about Rae, rather than what list she could get them on or celebrities she had access to. They were true friends who didn't think for a second she could've been involved in anything Hasselhoff was doing. The two of them had found the crack in the defenses she'd fortified like Fort Knox after Charleston and ensconced themselves in her life—for better or worse—messy emotional entanglements included.

She tried to lighten the mood, taking Kez's hand. "It was horrifically shitty, but hey, it's what made me move up here and meet you two, so there's a silver lining."

The three of them were silent as Kez and V digested Rae's story. Never one to dwell—because if she did, her brain might implode—Rae hopped off the bed. "C'mon, ladies," she said, grabbing a bottle of champagne and three glasses. "Kez is getting married in about"—she checked the clock—"two and a half hours, so let's drink up and celebrate."

Kez and V didn't look ready to let the subject drop.

"Hey," Rae said, "no long faces today. This is a wedding, not a wake."

It took a little coaxing, but they joined her, and each took a glass.

Rae raised hers. "I can't give my toast yet, but I'll give you a little preview." She turned to Kez. "Kez, when I moved to Charlotte and met you, I was at a low point in my life. It was your friendship that helped pull me out of the darkness and into the light. And I'm so happy that I'm here today to see you get your very own happy ending. Cheers, babe!" She clinked her glass to Kez's and then V's.

"Dammit, Rae," Kez said as she fanned her face to dry the tears forming in her eyes. "If that's the preview, there will be no pictures after your toast, because I'll be blubbering like a baby."

V dabbed at her own eyes. "Who knew Little Miss Feelings Are Toxic had anything like that buried inside?"

"Save the diagnoses for later, Doc," Rae quipped and gave V a side hug. "You know, for when I've come to grips with the fact that I walked down the aisle with my ex. And trust me, I have *plenty* of feelings right now. They're vacillating between elation for Kez and pure, unadulterated loathing for Donovan."

Kez's mother poked her head in the door, a worried frown creasing her brow. "I'm not pushing, Kesler, I promise, but Mitzi says you girls need to get dressed for the next set of pictures."

Kez motioned her inside. "It's fine, Mama. Thanks. Everyone can come back in. I just needed a last-minute huddle with my girls."

Hudson appeared at her mother's shoulder and glanced around the room. "What'd y'all do with Mr. Tall, Dark, and Handsome?"

Kez looked at Rae. "The jury is still out on what we're going to do with Mr. McLeod."

Van's face when he stormed into the smokehouse must have been a dead giveaway that things hadn't gone the way he'd hoped. Jackson tapped his hand of five-card stud on the table and waited. The other guys seated around the table watched while Van paced back and forth like a caged lion. Jackson leaned back in his chair and reached for the cigar smoldering in the ashtray next to him. He took a few puffs and regarded Van through the smoke. When it was obvious Van would not volunteer what happened, Jackson asked, "Went that well, did it?"

Van halted his pacing and looked at Jackson. "About as well as it did for Custer at Little Bighorn."

"I don't see any bullet holes," Jackson said, "so you're ahead of the game there."

"I fucked up, man," Van said and slumped in defeat.

Jackson called to another groomsman across the room. "Jordan!"

A dark-haired guy with a neatly trimmed beard and multiple piercings in his ear looked up. "What's up?" he asked.

Jackson stacked his cards and put them on the table. "I need you to finish this hand for me." Leaving his spot at the poker table, he walked over to the liquor cabinet. Opening the door, he pressed a recessed panel in the bottom and revealed a small, refrigerated compartment. From it, he pulled a frost-covered bottle of tequila. He grabbed two glasses then closed the cabinet.

"Let's go, McLeod," he said and walked out the back door. Van followed him to a small flagstone patio that held two Adirondack chairs and a table. Jackson set the glasses on the table, cracked open the tequila, and poured generously into each glass. He handed one to Van. "You'll have to do without the lime, but with tequila this good, that shouldn't be a problem."

Van accepted the drink. "I'm a shitty best man."

Jackson sipped his own drink, carefully adjusted his slacks, and eased into one of the chairs. "What makes you say that?"

"Bringing all this shit to your door the day of your wedding."

Jackson crossed an ankle over one knee. "You didn't know Rae was going to be here, Van."

"Yeah, but I should have waited to talk to her until after the wedding. Hell, I probably shouldn't have tried to talk to her at all."

"Sit down, Van. Try talking to me," Jackson said, his tone casual.

Van sat. Blue smoke passed in front of them as Jackson took an occasional drag on his cigar but remained quiet. Van often used the technique of waiting out a suspect. A prolonged silence often resulted in people filling it. Usually because their guilt squeezed the words out of them like pus from an infected wound. Turned out, he was no different.

"She thinks I used her, man."

"Did you?" Jackson asked, puffing serenely on his cigar.

"No!"

Cocking a brow, Jackson continued. "Then what makes her think that?"

Van dropped his head into his hands and groaned. Jackson nudged his drink toward him. Sitting back in the chair, Van picked it up and drank. The cold liquor ran down his throat with a freezing burn. Van closed his eyes. "You remember the Hasselhoff case I told you about?"

"That was some big drug thing, right?"

"Yeah, Hasselhoff was using his hotels and clubs to run drugs, from Miami to DC. His operation was headquartered in Charleston. Easy in, easy out through that port, plus I-26 linking right with I-77. The premier hotel was the Carson, on the corner of King and Wentworth."

"Okay," said Jackson, letting Van set the pace of his story.

"He'd hired a new head of PR. She was young, just out of grad school, a rising star. Benson snapped her up to bring a unique shine to the crown jewel of his hotel collection."

"The Carson," Jackson confirmed.

"Yeah," Van said.

"Just a hunch," said Jackson, "but did this young rising star have long dark hair, big green eyes, and a wicked sense of humor?"

"She certainly did." Van sighed. "You should've heard the team clamoring for the undercover assignment."

Jackson grinned. "I bet. You were the lucky winner?"

Van took another drink. "I was the right age, had the right look, so yeah, they picked me."

"And through her, you'd reach him," said Jackson.

"That was the plan," Van said, remembering how he'd naively thought it wouldn't be a problem for him to use Regan to help make the case. Easy in, easy out once Hasselhoff was in cuffs. That all changed the moment he met her.

"Did the plan change?"

"No, the plan didn't change," Van said. "But the circumstances certainly did." Meeting Regan Murphy in the flesh had thrown him for a loop. She'd been so vibrant, so alive, so . . . *her*. He'd been smitten almost instantly.

Between puffs on his cigar, Jackson asked, "How long were you under?"

"I'd been assigned to the case for two years but was undercover as Ray Edwards just over a year."

Jackson gave a low whistle. "Long time. How long before you fell in love with Rae?"

Van's answering laugh was rueful. "You mean before I fell in love or before I was ready to admit it?"

Jackson chuckled knowingly. "Whichever one you can pinpoint."

He leaned back in the chair, staring without seeing the rolling fields in front of them. "I probably started falling the day I met her but didn't realize it until about six months in."

"So what happened, Van?"

"We'd moved in together, or rather, I'd moved into her place."

"Let me guess, her place was in the Carson," Jackson said.

Van nodded. "It was."

"Perfect setup for your case."

"That was how the bureau saw it."

"How did *you* see it?" Jackson asked, rolling his cigar between his fingers.

Van's heart was heavy. "There wasn't a day I didn't want to tell her the truth. Tell her my real name. Say 'fuck it all' and run away with her to Bali."

"But you didn't," Jackson said.

"No," Van said. "I didn't. I picked the case over her, and I've hated myself for it ever since."

"Sounds like maybe Rae has too."

"There's no question she has, Jackson." Van sat forward, his hands dangling between his knees. The weight of Regan's disgust toward him rested on his shoulders like a dismal cloak, threatening to crush him.

"No, I guess not," Jackson said. Blue smoke floated in the breeze. "The question is, what are you going to do to change that?"

6

*Mitzi* buzzed in and out of the room, her camera snapping at every turn. She photographed the bridesmaids getting dressed and took a few pretend makeup shots. The sound of the shutter clicking in the background was constant as the ladies completed their finishing touches. Then it was time to get Kez into her dress.

Back in February, Kez had spirited Rae and V down to Atlanta to go dress shopping with her. As with most everything else, Kez had a specific idea of what she wanted. They'd made appointments all over town, but their first stop was Winnie Couture. From the sparkling chandeliers to the crushed velvet upholstery, the place oozed southern elegance. They'd sipped champagne and plundered the racks, each choosing multiple dresses for Kez to try on. While Rae and V settled into cozy wing chairs, Kez slipped behind the thick blush-colored curtains of the dressing room.

When she emerged in the first dress, Rae knew they weren't going anywhere else. She and V instantly put down their bubbly and shrieked their approval. Kez looked like a goddess.

The sleeveless gown was bright-white satin with a low neckline. It draped over Kez's long frame as though made just for her. The skirt was straight, with a high slit, designed so the silky fabric flowed around her legs when she walked. The front was relatively plain, but the back was made of fine netting, sewn with long ropes of Swarovski crystals. The look replicated that of the back-drape necklace she'd worn the weekend she and Jackson had met. It was, in a word, perfect.

As Rae and V unzipped the garment bag holding the dream dress, the smooth satin spilled out, and all the girls in the room oohed and aahed in unison.

Kez beamed. "It's gorgeous, right? I know that makes me sound like such an asshole, but I can't help it," she said.

"Kesler, language!" her mother scolded but couldn't hide a smile.

Rae laughed. "Today, of all days, it's acceptable for you to sound like an asshole." She glanced at Kez's mom. "Sorry, Mrs. W."

Kez dropped her robe and stood there in nothing but the tiniest pair of nude lace panties. She covered her breasts with her hands and practically vibrated with excitement as Rae brought the dress over to her. With one hand on V's shoulder to steady herself and Rae holding the dress open, Kez stepped into the skirt. The three of them shimmied the dress over her hips, and Kez slid her arms through the straps of the bodice. Rae pulled the hidden zipper up the back and fastened the tiny hook at the nape of Kez's neck.

V stepped away and grabbed the familiar khaki shoebox with elegant white script. That was the other thing they'd found—the most fabulous shoes on the freaking planet. They were skyscraper-high Louboutin heels in red crepe, covered in crystal spikes. The kinky contrast with Kez's dress was divine. Kez slipped her feet into the shoes and stood before the floor-length mirror.

"Holy shit," she breathed, her eyes wide. She brushed a hand down the front of her dress. "I'm getting married." With tears in her eyes, she clasped her mother's hand.

"You look gorgeous, baby," her mom said with tears in her own eyes.

"Don't forget the finishing touch," V said. In her hand was the slender box Van had delivered earlier.

"Sounds like you already know what's in there," said Kez.

"Rae and I may have given suggestions, but we don't know what he finally chose," V said.

Kez opened one end of the box and withdrew the signature blue box wrapped with a white bow. Gingerly, she untied the bow and opened the box to reveal a black velvet jewelry box. Pulling it out, she cracked it open and gasped. Diamonds winked out from the dark satin. Three strands of diamonds, to be exact.

"Christ on a bicycle," said Rae, captivated by the twinkling lines of stones.

"Well," said V, "they aren't going to wear themselves." She took the box from Kez's quaking hands and eased the necklace free. Gently, she pushed on Kez's shoulders to make her stoop so V could get the necklace over her updo and around her neck. Once the clasp was fastened, V stepped back, and Kez faced the room. A few sniffles could be heard as they drank her in.

"You look amazing, Kez," said Rae.

"There's a note," said V, holding up a small envelope.

Kez waved it away. "I can't read that now! I'm barely containing the waterworks as it is. If I read that, we'll have to delay the ceremony an hour so I can fix my face."

V laughed. "Fine, I'll tuck it over here." She placed the note beside the bed. She walked back to join Rae and Kez. The three of them joined hands, forming a tight circle.

"Be honest," said Kez. "Neither of you thought I'd be the first one down the aisle."

"First or last doesn't matter," said V. "You are the most beautiful bride I've ever seen. I'm so happy for you, Kez."

Kez started to get misty-eyed but fought through it. "Thanks, V."

"I'm glad you got over yourself enough to see what you'd be throwing away if you didn't give Jackson a chance," said Rae.

Kez rolled her now-dry eyes. "Gee, thanks, Rae."

She squeezed Kez's hand. "Seriously, though, I'm so glad things turned out this way for you two."

"Me too," said Kez. "But, Rae, about Donovan—"

"Don't worry about him," Rae interrupted. "He and I can civilly coexist for the length of the ceremony and the reception. I won't let him ruin your wedding, Kez."

"But I—" Kez tried again.

"Seriously, Kez, don't worry about it," said Rae with finality.

Kez's niece, Edie, interrupted any further discussion. She popped between Kez and Rae. "So pretty," she said and clapped her pudgy little hands together. Everyone laughed, and Kez kissed the top of her head.

Ms. Williams stuck her head in the door. "Why, Ms. Walsh, don't you look stunning!"

Kez smoothed her skirt. "Thank you, Ms. Williams."

The wedding planner took inventory to confirm everyone was dressed and presentable. "We have about ten minutes before we start. If you ladies will line up, we'll move into the great room for your flowers. Ms. Walsh, you stay out of sight until it's time for your trip down the aisle. Everyone ready?"

A chorus of *yes, ma'ams* met her question, and they all fell in line behind her. Rae stood back and let others pass in front of her. As maid of honor, she would be last in the bridesmaid line. Ms. Williams's assistant handed them their bouquets as they came through the doorway into the great room. When she took her flowers, Rae looked back at Kez.

"You all good?" she asked.

Kez's smile was pure joy. "So good," she answered.

Van took his place next to Jackson in front of the arbor made of vibrantly colored flowers. He couldn't name half of the blooms but had to admit it made for a stunning backdrop. Van was amazed at the number of people seated in rows. He leaned toward Jackson. "Did anyone turn down their invitation to this thing?"

Jackson stifled a laugh. "Doesn't look that way, does it?"

Van heard the first chords of "Can't Help Falling in Love" playing. Instead of Elvis, a woman sang in a soft, sexy contralto. He looked at Jackson, who shrugged.

"Kez wanted our wedding to be different," he said.

The back doors of Jackson's house opened, and the bridesmaids began their journey toward them. Van's heart sped up as women filed out of the house. Finally, Regan appeared in the doorway, and everything else faded away. She was a vision. The cut of her dress was simple, but it highlighted her delectable figure. As she started down the stairs, shapely legs peeked from the slit in the front. Sunlight winked off the jewels in her hair, making her look otherworldly.

Van watched her eyes roam the audience as she walked, and she gave a special wave to Jackson's nana seated in the front row. He wondered how they knew each other. Reaching the altar, she cupped Jackson's elbow. "Don't worry, she's right behind me," Regan said in a stage whisper. Van laughed along with everyone else. As the song ended, she took her place across from Van.

Jackson's gaze was riveted to the now-closed back doors. He seemed seconds away from saying screw it all and going to get Kez, rather than waiting for her to come down the aisle. A guitar riff sounded, catching Van off guard. When he recognized the song, he couldn't help but smile. Jackson's soon-to-be wife was pretty badass. Guests looked around, puzzled, but rose when the doors slid back open. The woman of the hour appeared in all her radiant glory. A spiked red heel landed on the last step right as Tom Petty sang, "Here Comes My Girl." Jackson tipped his head back and laughed, obviously loving Kez's choice of processional music. His bride beamed at him from her father's arm on her way down the aisle.

"Hurry up, baby!" Jackson called, risking the wrath of Ms. Williams.

Van thought Kez might sprint the rest of the way, but she restrained herself. When she reached them, Jackson leaned down to kiss her, but the officiant stopped him.

"Woah there, buddy," she said. "We haven't quite gotten to that part yet." It seemed laughter would be the running theme of this ceremony. Properly chastised, Jackson stepped back. Kez handed her bouquet to Regan and took Jackson's hands in hers.

The tall woman between them smiled at the crowd. Her long black hair hung in a solid sheet over her shoulders, and she wore a vibrant red pantsuit with four-inch black patent heels. Using the word "different" to describe this wedding was like calling Bernie Sanders slightly liberal. Given the setting, Van hadn't been expecting a traditional ceremony, but this was beyond anything he'd imagined.

"Friends, family, and everyone in between," the dark-haired woman began, "we've gathered together this afternoon to witness the union of Kesler Walsh and Jackson Jenkins. They've included all of you in this day because you each hold a special place in their hearts. They wanted all of you to bear witness as they pledge themselves to one another and forsake all others."

She paused and smiled. "That being said, the bride has given me strict instructions to keep this as short as possible to allow more time for the reception." Chuckles arose from those seated behind them. "With that in mind, it should come as no surprise that a woman who walks down the aisle to Tom Petty has written her own vows and asked her groom to do the same." Kez grinned, her eyes dancing. "Ms. Walsh, the floor is yours," said the officiant with a sly grin.

Kez took a deep breath and looked at Jackson. "Jax," she said in a strong, clear voice. "When I met you, my life was in turmoil, and I was struggling to find solid ground. The last thing I expected was to be standing in front of an altar with you eight months later. And yet, here we are." She laughed. "We're here because you became my solid ground. You pulled me from the cold, dark waves of uncertainty that threatened to drag me under and guided me to a haven of love and understanding. You give me solace in times of sadness, hope in times of fear, and laughter in times of joy." Her voice wavered, but her eyes never left Jackson's face.

"So," she paused to sniffle, "for all you've already given me, I give you these vows. I vow to be your shelter in every storm and your light in the darkness. I vow that you'll never find yourself alone, because I'll always be there. Whether it's to celebrate, to mourn, to laugh, or to cry, I'll be there for all of it. I'll be your lover, your friend, your confidante, and your protector. I'll be everything I can for you, because you're already everything to me. I love you, Jax."

*Holy shit,* thought Van. Jackson was one lucky bastard. He looked over at Regan and saw her fighting back tears. She met his eyes, and for a second, he saw the longing he felt reflected back at him in her gaze. As quickly as it had appeared, it vanished, and she returned her attention to Kez and Jackson. A small glimmer of optimism bloomed in Van's chest. Maybe his cause wasn't as lost as he'd thought.

Jackson's voice shook with emotion when he said, "I knew I should've gone first." Kez laughed. He looked at the woman in the red suit. "You sure I can't kiss her and move on to the man and wife part?"

Red Suit grinned. "You've got to get to the man and wife part *before* you kiss her. Priorities and all, you know?"

Jackson lifted Kez's hand and kissed her knuckles. "Kez, the first night I saw you, my black-and-white world became Technicolor." He waved one hand toward the flowers arching above them. "From that day to today, the colors have only gotten brighter. Having you in my life makes its timbre richer, its texture a little thicker, and the chords that much sweeter." He stopped and smiled down at Kez as she blinked back tears.

"Kesler Walsh, soon-to-be Jenkins, I promise to be the one who makes you laugh and hardly ever makes you cry. I promise to always make time for you, even if it's just a quick text to say I love you. I promise there will never be a day that goes by without you on my mind and in my heart. I promise to love, honor, and cherish you as long as we both shall live. And finally, I promise to try to understand why you need so many shoes and give you half my closet to put them in."

"Only half?" Kez asked with a watery laugh.

Laughing along with everyone else, the officiant stepped back up to the couple. She said, "I will now ask the best man and maid of honor to please provide the rings." Van reached into his pocket and pulled out a small band. He saw Regan pull a larger one from her thumb. Together, they dropped them into Red Suit's outstretched hand.

She looked at Kez and Jackson. "These rings in my hand represent the vows and promises you've exchanged today before all these people. When they slide onto your fingers, they represent the commitment those words inspire. It is my hope, and the hope of those gathered here today, that the continuous circle of the rings will remind you every day that marriage is not a destination but a journey. One that has no beginning and no end, just a moment-to-moment opportunity to love and be loved, until death do you part."

She handed Kez's ring to Jackson. "As you place this ring on Kez's finger, please repeat after me: I give you this ring as a symbol of my devotion to you as my wife and of my decision to bind my heart to yours."

Jackson repeated the words softly as he slid the slim platinum band onto Kez's ring finger.

Handing Jackson's ring to Kez, the officiant said, "As you place this ring on Jackson's finger, please repeat after me: I give you this ring as a symbol of my devotion to you as my husband and of my decision to bind my heart with yours."

Slowly, Kez slid the larger band onto Jackson's finger as she, too, repeated the words.

With a brilliant smile, Red Suit addressed the couple. "Kesler and Jackson, in the presence of your family and friends today, you vowed to love and commit to one another for all eternity. With those words and an exchange of rings, you have formalized that commitment and sealed the bond between you. Therefore, it is my pleasure to pronounce you husband and wife." She tapped Jackson's shoulder. "*Now*, you may kiss the bride!"

Jackson pulled Kez into his arms and gave her a kiss so hot it seared the air. When he lifted his head, Kez was still holding onto the lapels of his tux.

"Ladies and gentlemen, it is my pleasure to present, for the first time, Mr. and Mrs. Jackson Jenkins!" The crowd cheered as Kez and Jackson turned to face everyone, both grinning from ear to ear. "Best Day of My Life" by American Authors played as they came down the aisle.

Van held an elbow out to Regan, and she tucked her hand into it. He leaned down and whispered into her ear, "That was different."

She looked over at him. "Did you expect it wouldn't be?"

"I guess I was expecting a 'love, honor, cherish' with a bit of Jesus thrown in there."

"Well, then you definitely don't know Kez," Regan said.

"No, I guess I don't," he said as they reached the end of the aisle. She dropped her arm from his, and he instantly missed her. For an awkward moment, they stood there. Before he could say anything, V appeared, giddy and rosy with happiness, and stole Regan away.

Van felt a hand on his arm and saw Red Suit standing next to him. She smiled and extended a hand to him. "I'm Evelyn Sands," she said in a sultry voice. "We didn't get to meet last night."

He shook her hand. "Donovan McLeod, nice to meet you. That was an . . . interesting service."

She laughed. "Yes, can't say I've ever had one quite like it." Evelyn nodded after Regan. "Is Rae your girlfriend?"

Van jerked in response to her question. "What? No, she's not my girlfriend. She's . . ." He didn't know how to finish that sentence.

Evelyn gave him a knowing look, her dark brows drawing into a pensive frown. "I see," she said.

With a puzzled smile, he asked, "You see what?"

She patted his shoulder. "I see you need to get yourself together if you want a chance—first, second, or otherwise—with her. Good to meet you." Evelyn walked off, leaving Van staring slack-jawed after her.

Ms. Williams clapped her hands in staccato succession. "All right, all right, I need the wedding party to line up, please. We have to make your grand entrance to the reception!"

They'd finished the last round of pictures, and Rae was starving. The photos took so long, she missed the happy hour food. *Dammit!* She'd been lusting after those cheesesteak egg rolls and the fried risotto balls. Her stomach grumbled in protest.

"All I can offer is a mint, I'm afraid," Van said at her elbow.

She hadn't noticed his approach and jumped at his sudden appearance, emitting a tiny gasp of surprise. "What are you doing?" she asked.

He nodded at Ms. Williams directing the traffic of the wedding party a few steps away. "What I'm told," he answered. "We have to get in line for our introduction at the reception."

Rae groaned.

"I'll try not to take that personally," said Van.

"You should," she shot back. Saying nothing, he offered her his elbow. Reluctantly, she placed her hand in the crook and let him guide her back to their position in line.

"So what's our plan here?" Van asked.

"What are you talking about?" Rae responded, her mind still on the egg rolls. She angled her body as far away from his as she could without being obvious. They resembled two tangled paper clips connected solely by a right angle but unable to escape each other.

"Our entrance," Van said, dimpling down at her. "What's the plan? A slow, measured stroll then break into a dance routine?"

"Why on earth would we do that?" Rae risked looking up at him and instantly regretted it. His dark-brown eyes were warm and bright with laughter, sucking her in. Hurriedly, she turned to face forward again.

"Just something to spice up our entrance a bit," he said, seemingly oblivious to her reaction.

She dropped his arm, needing to make something crystal clear. "We are not on a date, McLeod."

"I didn't say we were, Regan." His voice was even and unbothered, which only irritated her further. He'd been that way when they were together too. Always even keeled in the eye of her storm of emotions. Back then, it kept their arguments from being too intense or too hurtful. His calm demeanor forced her to dial back her seething anger, or frustration, or any other countless emotions fired off by her hair trigger. Today, it had the opposite effect.

She scowled at him, looking between rather than into his eyes. "Let's get something straight. I may have to stand next to you and smile pretty for the camera. I may have to let you escort me into the reception. But it's all smoke and mirrors. None of it means I have any feelings toward you—other than loathing and intense hatred."

"Duly noted," he said with that same infuriating calm. "But aren't those the same thing?"

Rae's bottled emotions boiled over, and she lashed out at him. "I don't know why it should surprise me that you can stand there and act like nothing is wrong. You did just that for over a year back in Charleston."

"Enough, Regan," he said, his cool facade cracking a bit. "If you won't let me explain what happened, then you don't get to keep throwing it in my face."

"That's where you're wrong," she said, the angry words scorching her throat. "As the one you completely humiliated, I have every right to throw that and more in your face whenever I want."

His lips flattened, and he said nothing. Those stupidly dreamy eyes turned dark and melancholy. When the couples in front of them moved forward, he reached for her hand and drew it through his arm. They moved in stony silence, seething behind picture-perfect smiles. Being next to him, touching him, was unnerving and brought up memories she'd worked hard to bury—including the night she'd left Charleston.

She'd fled the condo that day with nothing but an armful of clothes and her car keys, sneaking back in the next day to get the rest of her things. Except her cell phone, having seen enough true crime stories to know that if "Ray" was really in the FBI, he could use it to find her. Paying cash, she'd checked into a hotel in Mt. Pleasant for a few days.

A week later, she watched along with the rest of the world as her life imploded. Reporters salivated over the coverage of Van and his cronies arresting her boss on federal drug charges. News of his hotel empire being a front to traffic narcotics along the East Coast erupted on every station. According to CNN, the FBI tracked him for years but could never get close. At least not until a "long-running undercover operation" provided the break they needed. She felt like a first-class idiot. Not only had her boss duped her but so had the man who took him down—Special Agent Donovan McLeod.

After the collapse of Benson Hasselhoff's drug enterprise, Rae had worked her ass off to resurrect her career. Turns out, folks in

PR didn't care if you'd worked for a drug dealer, provided you still had connections and the ability or tenacity to get things done. She tapped every contact she had, and it paid off. A former bigwig guest whose son Rae rescued from scandal helped her land a position with McLaren and Associates in Charlotte. Within a few years, she'd solved enough crises to become the youngest partner at the firm. Pretty soon, it became obvious she was on track to run the place. Rae had risen above the ashes of her old life and was doing fine. Better than fine. Her life was going great. At least it had been until a few hours ago, when Donovan McLeod ambled back into it with his melted-chocolate eyes and pleading expression.

Van cursed himself for the millionth time as he saw the hurt Regan tried to hide under her anger. If he'd come clean to her the night he'd planned to, none of this would've happened. Well, he hoped it wouldn't have happened. She still would've been angry and upset, but at least *he* would've been the one to tell her.

"Regan, I—"

"Ladies and gentlemen, may I present Ms. Regan Murphy and Mr. Donovan McLeod, the maid of honor and best man!" The DJ sang out their introduction, and it was their turn to enter the tent.

"Smile, asshole," Regan gritted out from behind her own pearly whites.

Doing as she asked, he plastered on a grin and walked into the tent. Edison bulbs swayed on long lines extending from the center outward. Crisp white linens and an extravagant floral centerpiece topped each table. A four-tiered cake decorated with exotic flowers sat in one corner, with bars in the other three. It was quite the scene.

Van decided to take advantage of the moment. "Time to make an entrance," he whispered into her ear.

"McLeod—" she said but couldn't finish her warning because he'd already twirled her away from him. Her skirt swirled around her legs, and he tugged on her fingertips to bring her back. Having no choice but to comply, she spun back to him. Her hand landed on his chest, and he cha-cha'd the two of them across the room.

"You are such a dick," she said with a snarl behind her smile.

"Smile for the cameras," he replied as he heard shutters clicking around them. He ended their impromptu performance with an extravagant dip, his arm bracing her lower back. A mere breath separated their faces as he looked down at her.

"I'll get you for that little stunt," she said with quiet fury, but her smile never slipped. With a flick of his wrist, he pulled her upright and flush against his chest.

"I look forward to it," he said. He kept her from charging away from him by placing her hand back in the crook of his elbow. Slowly, he led her to the receiving line, where she promptly jerked her hand from his arm.

Van took his place beside Regan as they waited for the newlyweds to be announced. Being near her put his senses on high alert, and he noticed everything about her from the smell of the perfume she'd always worn—a light scent, with a spicy undertone—to the way her olive skin glowed under the lights, a smattering of freckles barely visible on her high cheekbones. He physically hurt from the need to touch her but knew after the stunt he'd pulled, he'd draw back a bloody nub if he tried. Her anger was like a rabid beast standing between them, gnashing its teeth and flexing its claws in a warning to stay back.

"And now, for the first time as husband and wife, Mr. and Mrs. Jackson and Kesler Jenkins!" Jackson and Kez sauntered into the room, sporting cheek-cracking grins. Happiness emanated from the couple, and a sharp twist of envy wormed through Van's gut. He was happy for his friend, but standing this close to the woman he'd planned to marry—yet being as separate from her as if he were on another continent—cut deep.

"God, they look happy, don't they?" Regan said with an almost wistful tone in her voice.

"They do," Van replied.

She jerked, as if she hadn't meant to say anything aloud. With one last scowl in his direction, she turned on her heel and left him staring after her. Their duties as a "couple" complete, he had no way to keep her from leaving.

"What did you do to my honorary granddaughter?" Jackson's nana sidled up next to him. In her tailored lace gown and elegant updo, she was more Jane Fonda than Maggie Smith.

"What makes you think I did anything?" he asked, giving her a peck on the cheek. "And how do you know Regan?"

Nana patted his cheek affectionately. "I met her the same weekend I met Kez. I guess you could say we bonded over both being Old Fashioned girls." Nana chuckled, and Van wished he understood the inside joke. Nana went on. "As for your first question, I'm old, not blind," she said. "I know the look of a man who's screwed up. And you, my dear, have that look. So what did you do?"

"It's more a question of what I didn't do," he said, watching Regan weave through the clusters of tables.

Nana watched him watching Regan and smiled. "Well, is it too late to do it now?"

Without taking his eyes from Regan, he said, "I hope not." God, did he hope not. Seeing her again reopened a hole in his life he'd patched over with kindergarten paste and errant duct tape. Her presence destroyed the shoddy repair he'd put in place and spurred him on to fix it—and things with her—in a much more permanent manner.

Nana linked her arm with his, and they made their way to her assigned table. "Well, Van, for your sake, I hope you're right. And for her sake, I hope *I'm* right."

"Right about what?" he asked. He pulled out her chair.

She smiled up at him then hit him with a zinger. "That you're not the complete jackass she seems to think you are."

# 8

*After* the last guest took their seat, caterers deployed trays of champagne with military precision. At a nod from Ms. Williams, Rae moved to stand between Kez and Jackson. She tapped a fork against her glass to gain the attention of the room. Folks quieted down and turned her way.

"Thank you, ladies and gentlemen. For those of you who don't know me, I'm Regan Murphy. Kez has been my best friend for the better, and worse, parts of the last five years. You may wonder why the role of maid of honor fell to me when Kez is surrounded by so many wonderful women. However, it was a straightforward decision with no room for debate. I'm the bossiest and love the sound of my own voice, so who better to be the maid of honor?" Chuckles came from the audience.

Rae looked down at her friend. "Kez, you're one of the strongest women I know. You take on the burdens of your friends and family without complaint. You celebrate their successes before your own and comfort them during their times of grief. Never once have you put your needs ahead of anyone else's. You are the definition of selfless, and I treasure you as a friend." Kez's eyes shone with unshed tears, and Jackson wrapped his arm around her shoulders.

"I knew it would take a special man, or at least a *magnificent* pair of shoes, to get you to dedicate a day to yourself and walk down the aisle in front of four thousand of your closest friends." Rae gestured to the expansive crowd gathered under the tent, and Kez laughed out loud. To Jackson, Rae said, "You, Jackson, are that man, and, in case you're wondering, you *are* a more important part of this proceeding than the shoes." He laughed and gave her a thumbs-up.

She grinned back at him. "I can honestly say that I've never met a man like you. You are the man who unabashedly and unequivocally puts Kez first. She is your center, your heart, and anyone who sees the two of you together can see that." A collective *aww* went through the crowd, and Jackson kissed Kez's temple.

"But," Rae said, "even more important, you call her on her BS and don't let her bulldoze right over you." The awws turned to laughter as Kez fixed Rae with a teasingly threatening stare. "I say that's more important because it provides her the balance we all seek in life. To find that in another person is one of the rarest gifts, and I couldn't be happier for my best friend that she found it with you."

She held her glass aloft and faced her audience. "I ask you to raise your glasses with me as we toast Kez and Jackson. May your life together be long, your days be filled with sunshine, and your nights be spent wrapped in each other's arms. To Kez and Jackson!"

The guests cheered, and Rae took a drink. She leaned down and wrapped an arm around each of the bride and groom. "Congratulations, you two," she said.

Kez's grin trembled as she held back tears. "That was beautiful, Rae. Beautiful and perfectly you."

Rae laughed. "Well, I tried to work a line in there about hot, sweaty sex but didn't want your Aunt Haley to keel over with a heart attack."

Jackson grinned and put his arm around Rae's waist. "Thanks for that, Rae. And I'm not just talking about sparing Aunt Haley's heart."

She gripped his shoulder. "You're a good man, Jackson." Leaning down, she whispered in his ear, "But you'll do well to remember, there are places in this state—dark, cold places—that you can drop a body and not even Indiana Jones could find it." Her smile was flat and her eyes calculating. "And I know each and every one of them."

He paled a little underneath his tan. "You really are a little terrifying," he said.

Rae gave his shoulder a friendly pat. "Glad to see we understand each other."

Kez asked Rae, "What did you say to him?"

She gave Kez a placating smile. "Nothing for you to worry about."

"Rae!" Kez hissed and half rose from her chair.

Jackson's hand on her shoulder kept her semi-seated. "Calm down, Gorgeous," he said, rubbing his broad palm over her back. She looked from him to Rae, not happy about being kept in the dark. He kissed the tip of her nose. "As long as I keep you happy, neither of us has anything to worry about," he told her. Rae touched her glass to Jackson's and laughed.

The chime of flatware against crystal brought everyone's attention down to Van. He stood behind his chair but didn't move closer from his position at the opposite end of the table. Lifting a glass in the air, he cleared his throat.

"It's never hard to follow a beautiful woman," he said, looking directly at Rae. She focused on a point above his left shoulder to avoid the twin tractor beams of his eyes.

"I'll drink to that," called someone in the crowd.

Van grinned. "But after Regan's charming and heartfelt toast, it is today." The crowd laughed, and he went on. "I had a speech—or toast—prepared, but I don't think I'll use it. Instead, I'll speak straight from the heart." Rae felt her own heart speed up, anxious to hear what Van would say.

"Jackson, I can only echo Regan's words about Kez and say that they apply equally to you. You are often a man among boys and not just because of your height." Jackson laughed.

"You're a man who stands behind what he believes in, even if it's outside the popular view. You've never shied away from doing what was right or persuading others to do the same. You're a man of great conviction, and you needed a woman equally strong in her own right. Big shock, the woman who fits that bill is a lawyer."

The guests laughed along when Van chuckled. Even Rae couldn't help but crack a smile.

"Kez, I only heard about you a few months ago and just met you today, so I can't claim to know you. But I know that I've never seen my friend as happy as he is when he looks at you, or talks about you, or just breathes the same air as you. That tells me you're more than his wife, Kez. You're the sunrise in his mornings and the stars in his evenings. You're what lights his world." Van's gaze shifted to Rae, and this time she didn't avert her eyes. "As someone who had that once and stupidly let it slip away, I know how precious it is." He looked back at Jackson. "So today, I want to celebrate you finding it and encourage you to cherish it. To Kez and Jackson!"

Rae's hand shook as she toasted her friends. She finished the glass in one swallow and searched for another. Luckily, there was a never-ending stream of servers at the ready. She greedily accepted a glass and chugged it, willing the alcohol to chase away the feeling of Van's eyes on her during his toast. Little niggling strains of doubt wiggled into her psyche.

What if he wasn't the heartless bastard she'd painted him to be? She'd lit out of Charleston as fast as humanly possible after uncovering his deceit, offering him no chance to explain. For the next few years, she concentrated on working from the shadows as the PR magician behind the scenes. She'd sanitized the few personal details about herself online and used her initials with no picture on the firm website, making it as difficult as possible for her past to catch up with her. Or for the most devastating part of her past to find her. Of course, that's assuming Van had even looked for her. Given his background, she was pretty sure he could've found her if he'd tried. Which meant he hadn't cared enough to try. Right? Confusion clouded her thoughts because that didn't fit with what he'd just said. But then, he'd been very good at saying all the right things, so why would that have changed?

She risked a look down the table and stumbled into his stare. Quickly, Rae looked away before she got sucked into the unholy vortex that was Donovan McLeod. Again, all those emotions she'd shoved down years before strained to break free and wreak havoc. She'd resisted the urge to find out about him, pushing it away and out of her mind every time it reared up. She'd refused to wonder what had happened to him, whether he'd moved on and fallen in love with someone else. What his life was like without her. Giving in to his request to talk would be like opening Pandora's box. Releasing what was inside would knock her carefully crafted world right out of orbit. Internally, she shook her head. No, there was no way she was going to let him back into her good graces or her heart.

❧

*Van jogged down King Street through the late-September fog. The sound of his sneakers striking the pavement was the only noise that early in the* morning. Charleston, as a city, was a late riser. Folks didn't get much of a jump on the day but worked their way into it at a leisurely pace. The summer heat had relented at last, and he took advantage of the break to get a run in before work.

He lengthened his stride, eager to get back to Regan. When he'd risen at what she referred to as the godforsaken hour of five o'clock, she'd snuggled back down into the covers and sighed. Her long, dark hair spilled across her pillow, and when she kicked her bare leg out over the comforter, he almost dove back into bed with her. If he hurried, he could shower and slide under the covers before she got up. That thought had his feet quickening all on their own.

Swiping a key card at the entry of the Carson, he jogged across the ornate lobby to the bank of elevators. The same card gave him a direct ride to their penthouse condo. The doors opened silently, and he again carded his way into their home. The high-beamed ceilings framed an exquisite view of the city out the living room window, but he passed by it without looking. His attention was solely on reaching their bedroom and stealing a few minutes with Regan.

He shed his T-shirt as he walked through the bedroom door, toeing off his shoes when he reached the bed. Van knew he needed a shower, but the sight of her sprawled out in bed pulled him like a magnet. Regan never slept in anything more than a tiny pair of boy shorts. He knew today's were a startling shade of red. His mouth watered as he looked at her. Her pretty pink toenails stood out against her tan skin. Van let his eyes wander all the way up her exposed leg, smiling at her peaceful expression. It never ceased to amaze him, given she was such an unstoppable force when she was awake. Her lips pursed as she slept, and the tiniest snore sounded as she shifted in her sleep.

Van dropped his shorts and slipped between the sheets next to her. Heat emanated from her body and drew him in. With a hand on her cotton-clad hip, he gently rolled her into him. She stirred slightly and rested a hand against his chest. He kissed her forehead, and she gave him a sleepy smile. Her hand moved south.

"No shower this morning?" she asked, her fingers trailing down his stomach. The scent of mint on her breath made him grin. She'd hoped he would come back to bed and had brushed her teeth just in case.

Her unabashed enthusiasm for the physical side of their relationship thrilled him. After a year, he'd gotten used to the way she used her body to show him how she felt. He didn't need her to put it into words—he could feel it in each of her kisses or the way she'd stroke his shoulder as she passed by him. Each touch said "I love you" more loudly than words could.

He angled toward her and positioned her leg over his hip. "I didn't want to miss a chance to climb back in here with you."

Her eyes drifted open, and her hand dipped lower on his body until her fingers wrapped around him. She grinned. "Feels like that run was pretty invigorating." The gentle pressure of her fingers elicited a groan from his lips, and he flexed his hips, pushing into her hand. Regan's smile turned to one of feminine satisfaction, and her fingers tightened on a downward stroke.

"Into teasing this morning?" he asked, sliding a finger under the edge of her panties. She hummed low in her throat as he traced the curve of her ass. The hum changed to a growl when he moved down her thigh, rather than up.

"Now who's teasing?" she asked. He laughed and captured her lips in a long, slow kiss. His tongue delved into her mouth, tasting her. She moaned and arched against him, wrapping her leg tighter around his waist. He rolled on top of her without breaking the kiss. Threading his fingers through her hair, he tipped her head back. Taking full advantage of her upturned chin, he kissed down her throat.

Regan's knees pressed into his ribs, drawing him closer. "Ray," she whispered, her fingers in his hair, guiding him toward her breast.

Her use of his fake name made his heart twist. He planned to tell her who he really was. He'd even put together a file to go over when he broke the *news and had broached the topic with his unit leader. To say he had clearance to tell her was a stretch, but at least now doing so wouldn't be total career suicide. For the past four days, he'd wanted to tell her the truth, and each time he'd chickened out.* Tomorrow, *he thought.* Tomorrow, I'll tell her the whole truth. Then I'll make love to her and have her call out my name. *He only hoped he wasn't fooling himself into believing that when he did finally tell her the truth, she would understand. She'd see his pursuit of her boss was wholly separate from what he'd built with her. They'd be able to get past that and move on with their lives . . . together.*

*"Hey," Regan said softly, touching his face. "Where'd you go?"*

*As he looked into her deep-green eyes, he prayed he was right and she'd forgive his deception. Van kissed her. "I'm right here, baby. Right where I always want to be."*

As he watched Regan from his seat at the opposite end of the table, Van remembered that September morning. She was right. He could've told her then, or any of the other dozens of times they'd made love, or over coffee, at dinner, or any other time. In the beginning, he didn't know whether he could trust her. Meeting her had been an assignment. But a real relationship grew out of it. Within a matter of months, he knew Regan wouldn't have betrayed him. But he'd let the lie stretch on, because even if she wouldn't have blown his assignment, she might have ended things. The truth was, he'd been a coward, too afraid of losing her to come clean. Then his lies caught up to him when she'd unearthed the truth on her own.

Regret about the years he could've had with her cascaded over him. God knows there had been no one in his life since. Sure, he'd wasted his time with casual flings and errant one-night encounters, but there hadn't been a woman in his life since Regan had walked out of it. If he'd just told her, he could've been seated next to her instead of at the other end of the table. She still could've been his. Van loosened his collar and adjusted his tie, needing more air. It was like his past deceit was strangling him. He excused himself from those seated around him and left the table.

He walked to the bar against the far side of the tent. Given that dinner was being served, there was no line. "Whiskey, neat," he said to the bartender. As soon as the glass was in front of him, he snatched it up and tossed it back. "Another," he said.

The young man hesitated, so Van placed a fifty-dollar bill on the bar. *"Another,"* he said. The fifty disappeared, and the whiskey appeared in its place. Van reached for it, but a hand on his arm stopped him from drinking it.

"This is how you're going to fix things with Rae?" Jackson asked, keeping his voice quiet and expression neutral.

"There is no 'fixing things' with her," Van said, discretely wrenching his arm out of Jackson's grip.

"Not if you keep drinking straight whiskey," Jackson said as he leaned casually against the bar.

Van rubbed the back of his neck, feeling guilty for taking the groom away from his new bride. "Go back to your wife, man. I won't embarrass you or myself tonight." Jackson made no move to leave. Van forced a smile to his lips. "I'll take this drink and finish my dinner like a good little boy, okay?"

Jackson smiled, still not budging from his place at the bar. "In that case, I'll wait here while you do. Kez is surrounded by the elderly female contingent of her family, so I've got time to kill."

This time, Van's answering smile was sincere. "You haven't been married for three hours and you're already abandoning Kez in her hour of need?"

Jackson laughed. "She'll have plenty of chances to throw me to the wolves tonight, so I'm sure she'll get her payback."

Van finished his drink, and they made their way back to the table. He got through the rest of the meal but had no recollection of the food or any conversation around him. His body was present, but his mind was on Regan. Jackson was right. He needed to fix things with her. Whether or not it bought him a second chance, he had to get her to hear him out. When she'd disappeared from Charleston, he couldn't immediately drop everything to find her. Hasselhoff was in custody, but it was an active investigation of which he was a lead agent. Going AWOL to chase a girl wasn't an option. And then, once he could've . . . he didn't. Because he couldn't face her. He'd been a fool and a coward then, and he hated himself for it. But now, there was no case to come between them, and he couldn't hide from this opportunity to explain himself. He'd be a fool to waste the fortuitous opportunity tonight gave him at the bottom of a bottle of whiskey.

# 9

As the first strains of "I'll Be Your Lover, Too" by Van Morrison flowed from the speakers, Kez and Jackson drifted together for their first dance as man and wife. Rae stood on the perimeter of the dance floor with the rest of the wedding guests, watching Jackson enfold Kez into the circle of his arms. Their bodies came together to the soft beat of the music, and Rae smiled as she saw Kez link her hands behind Jackson's neck. Their twin expressions of happiness were positively blissful.

From behind her, Van said, "You always did like this song." His presence at her back made her body tingle, like the two of them were connected by hidden wires, buzzing with energy.

Ignoring her hyperawareness of him, Rae kept her eyes on the newly-weds. Her voice dripping with disdain, she said, "Old news, McLeod."

He laughed and his breath passed next to her ear. "Still such a fire-cracker," he said.

That made her face him, furious she couldn't haul off and smack the tar out of him. "Fuck. Off. Donovan," she said, clipping out every word but maintaining her smile. To the casual observer, they were just two guests having a pleasant conversation.

He didn't budge. "Now that I've found you, I'm not going to walk away, Regan."

They locked eyes in a standoff worthy of a spaghetti western, neither willing to back down. Rae's heart raced as she tried to maintain calm while also picturing her hands in a vice grip around his neck. Her fingers digging into the tanned skin above his collar, squeezing until the laughter left those stupidly gorgeous brown eyes of his. The rasp of his stubble against her fingers, his quick inhale of breath at her touch. The vision did nothing to slow her heart rate. "I'm not having this conversation here," she said.

"Fine," Van replied. "It's been five years," he said. "What's another few hours? But make no mistake—we are going to talk, Regan. Or, at least this time, I'm going to talk and you're going to listen without running off."

"Why would I care about anything you say, McLeod? You used me to advance your own career while blowing mine to smithereens! You humiliated me in front of everyone I knew. Even now, if it got back to my clients, who would hire a PR rep who not only couldn't sniff out an FBI sting but was the pawn who set it into motion? Everything about us could ruin me all over again. And what, you think I'm just going to line up for that? Say 'Thank you, may I have another?' Are you insane?" Her hands itched to make contact with his smug face, and she struggled to maintain her fraying control.

His eyes narrowed, and he glanced around, careful to make sure their conversation remained as private as it could. "If you'd stuck around instead of running, none of that would've happened. If you'd heard me out back then, Regan, I could've—"

She cut him off. "Nothing you could do then or can do now will make me listen to the bullshit that falls so freely from your lips." She whirled away from him, but his hand shot out and curled around her shoulder. Things were veering into dangerously obvious territory. A few of the other guests looked their way, and Rae saw the interest on their faces. There was no way to wriggle out of his grasp without drawing more attention.

"Tonight, you're going to hear me out," he said in a low tone. "I'm not letting you go again."

"Who says you have any choice in the matter?" she hissed, working her shoulder around in an attempt to dislodge his hand. The warmth of his fingers seeped into her skin, an intoxicating heat that spread through her body. Damn his stupid pheromones!

A smattering of applause signaled the end of the first dance. "All right, ladies and gentlemen," the DJ said, "I invite you to join the newly minted Mr. and Mrs. Jenkins on the dance floor. Here's a little John Mayer to help set the mood."

"Slow Dancing in a Burning Room" began to play.

With his hand still on her shoulder, Van guided her onto the dance floor. "Seems an appropriate song, don't you think?" he asked with a glint in his eye.

Rae could either knee him in the balls and run, giving the curious guests plenty of fodder for their gossip, or she could let the man she'd vowed never to see again hold her against his chest. There was only one real option. A PR maven having a meltdown at her best friend's wedding wasn't just bad for the friendship, it was bad for business too. Rae didn't make scenes. She cleaned them up for other people. She had to dance with the bastard. She knew it, and judging by the smirk on his face, so did Van.

He placed her hands on his shoulders, letting his fingers ghost down her arms. Her skin tightened in response to his light touch. Settling his hands at the base of her spine, Van pulled her in close enough she could feel the rise and fall of his chest as he breathed.

"You're a complete asshole. You know that, right?" she asked, keeping her eyes on a spot over his shoulder.

"I do," he said. Those two words shut down her ready stream of insults and made her look at him in surprise. His eyes were soft, and his lips curled into an apologetic smile. He looked contrite, which stymied her response.

"Well, at least we agree on one thing," she muttered.

His laugh was as warm as she remembered. "I think we can also agree that you look amazing in that dress."

*Don't fall for it again. You know it's just another one of his lines*, she cautioned herself. "Thank you," she said without returning the compliment. Even though he looked sinfully handsome in his suit.

They moved in a slow circle to the beat of the music. "I've missed you, Regan. I don't think you have any idea how much."

Tears pricked her eyes as she fought to maintain her composure. A fight she'd been ready for, but not this outpouring of emotion. She couldn't handle Van's incessant probing at her reopened wound.

"Not enough to try to find me." Her voice quavered "Yeah, I ran, but did you even bother to look?"

As soon as the words were out, she wanted to pull them back. Rewind the moment and say anything else. Anything that wouldn't reveal how badly it had hurt to know that if he'd wanted to, he could've found her. Could've long ago forced the conversation he claimed to want to have so badly. But he hadn't, and the ache of that knowledge had never gone away.

He looked down at her, his eyes somber and his mouth in a worried frown

"Regan, I—"

"Never mind," she said, almost frantic. Seeing him again, surrounded by all the love and happily ever after in the air, was pushing her close to the breaking point. She was barely holding it together. "I can't do this, Donovan. Not here, not tonight. I can't." A firm press of her fingers into his shoulders accompanied her plea, as though she could push her request into him and force him to stop talking.

"Okay, sweetheart, okay," he said and fell silent. The heat of his embrace seeped through the satin of her dress, his breath tickled her cheek, and she drew in his cologne with each inhale. In that moment, she was surrounded by her past with him, not the lies and deceit but the memories of nights spent a breath apart with limbs intertwined. As they danced, Rae didn't consider past heartbreak. For that brief period, she let the past in through the gentle pressure of his hands on her waist and found solace in the arms of her former lover.

All too quickly, the song ended, and the dance floor filled with people moving their bodies to the beat of the latest pop song. Rae dropped her arms and stepped away from Van. For a few seconds, they stared at each other. Rae didn't want to think about the emotions playing across his face, because they hid what he'd really done to her—used her as a stepping-stone for his own career while sabotaging hers. There had to have been a way for him to save her from the fallout back then, but he hadn't even tried. He was content to let her reputation be shredded and her life turned upside down while he sailed on with the Hasselhoff bust as a feather in his cap. Except, given the desolation reflected in his gaze, she wondered now if that were true. Had she been wrong about him? Was what they'd had been as real to him as it was to her? She spun on her heel and left the tent, seeking quiet away from the revelry inside. A few steps into the warm night air and she sucked in a deep breath, struggling to keep her composure.

"Rae?" a kind voice floated toward her. Without even looking, Rae knew Nana had followed her outside. For Rae, Nana was the number-one upside of Kez being with Jackson. Other than her best friend getting her happily ever after, of course. They'd met when Nana had essentially taken over Kez and Jackson's date night, inviting Rae along for the ride. All of them bonded over good bourbon and a home-cooked meal. Over the past few months, Rae had gotten to know Nana even better, their relationship fueled by their shared passion for potent cocktails and killer fashion. Even though Nana lived in upstate New York, they kept in touch with emails, texts, and FaceTime. Rae's parents passed away when she was still in college, and she'd never known her own grandparents. Nana's appearance in her life as a sort of surrogate had been an unexpected joy.

With her gaze still on the woods in the distance, Rae replied, "Hey, Nana. Just popped out for some air."

Nana's arm came around Rae's waist, and she gave her a tight, one-armed hug. "You know better than to bullshit a bullshitter," Nana said. "You came out here to get away from Donovan."

Rae put her arm around Nana's small shoulders. "Nothing gets by you, does it?" She took a second to admire the cut of Nana's gown. "You look fabulous, by the way."

"With age comes wisdom, or so they tell me," said Nana. "Which is why your attempt at flattery, as true as it may be, will not distract me. Want to talk about it?"

"I'd rather swallow a dozen rusty razor blades then gargle with hot rubbing alcohol," Rae said. "But I also don't want you to worry about me on your grandson's wedding day, so I'll sum it up. A long time ago, I thought he was the one. Turns out he wasn't the person I thought he was. As in, he pretended to be someone else the entire time we were together. Once I found out, I left. I haven't seen him since, then today he pops up as Jackson's best man. It's thrown me for a loop, but nothing a little whiskey and a lot of distance won't cure."

Nana shook her head. "Based on how you two looked when you stopped glaring daggers at him, that distance part is going to be harder to come by than you think. But," she said with a last hug, "the whiskey part is easy. I'll even help you get started."

Rae laughed and followed Nana back into the party.

Van left Regan alone after their dance, but the look on her face when he'd tried to talk to her lingered in his mind. She'd looked desperate to avoid talking about their past, as though delving into it would shatter her into a million tiny pieces. In his experience, seeing such raw emotion on her was rare. He wanted to push her, to plead his case, but she'd looked so uncharacteristically fragile that he'd kept his mouth shut and appreciated the chance to hold her close. Now, he settled for keeping track of her as she moved around the room. She talked with different guests and danced with her girlfriends. His palms burned from where they'd touched her earlier, and he longed to have the chance again. Leaning against the bar, he nursed his bourbon, heeding Jackson's advice from earlier that night.

He watched his best friend cut the giant cake with help from his wife. Kez dodged as Jackson pretended he was going to smash the first bite in her face. With a hand at her waist, he tucked her in close and gently fed her. She licked his finger, and even from his post at the bar, Van could see Jackson's reaction. They would need to find some privacy before the reception ended, he thought.

Sneaking away for a few stolen moments with Regan flashed into his head but faded quickly. She'd sooner leave the room with Ted Bundy. The image of Regan with any other man made Van finish his drink in one gulp. So much for pacing himself. He signaled for another.

The DJ's voice boomed. "If I could have all the single ladies join the bride on the dance floor, please. It's time for the bouquet toss!"

Young women crowded around Kez, and she took a small bouquet from Ms. Williams, who then shooed the women back several paces and placed Kez front and center. Initially, Van didn't see Regan, but on his second pass, he saw her hiding near the back. With her tiny frame, it was easy for her to lurk behind the taller girls clamoring for the bouquet. Kez looked over her shoulder, eyes calculating, and made a few practice swings.

The DJ counted down, "Three . . . two . . . one!" The bouquet sailed in a high arc, flying over outstretched arms and grasping hands, tumbling through the air until it collided with Regan's chest. Shock morphed to horror on her face as she reached up on instinct to catch the flowered projectile. Her cheeks paled and her lips moved, but only fractured syllables came out. Kez threw her hands up in a victory pose and rushed to hug her.

Laughing at Regan's appalled expression, the DJ said, "Looks like someone wasn't expecting the bride to have such an arm! All right ladies, it's the fellas' turn! Someone get the blushing bride a chair and bring out the groom!"

Kez released Regan, who'd recovered enough to stumble over to the side, and made her way to the chair set up in the center of the dance floor. It dawned on Van that if he caught the garter, he'd be able to dance with Regan again. Inspired by the thought, he hustled to the front of the group of single guys.

Jackson was already kneeling in front of Kez with a roguish twinkle in his eyes. She hid a laugh behind her hand and raised a red-heeled foot off the floor. Jackson cupped her heel in one hand and eased the other up her calf. Her dress wasn't one of those poufy things, so he couldn't disappear underneath it, but as his hand tracked higher on Kez's leg, her eyes glowed. *Oh yeah*, Van thought, *they're definitely sneaking away after this.*

Jackson's hand disappeared north of Kez's knee and reemerged a few seconds later, holding a tiny circle of blue lace. After easing it over her shoe, he leaned up and kissed his bride, then raised his hand, twirling the garter around his finger. The crowd cheered and laughed. Van took stock of the guys standing near him and recalculated his position. That lacy piece of elastic wasn't going far, so he needed to stay in front. Regan remained on the sidelines, holding the bouquet and looking slightly ill.

Once again, Ms. Williams positioned everyone to her exacting specifications, and the DJ gave them a countdown. Jackson let the garter fly, and it headed straight for Van. He raised his hand, ready to pluck it from the air. At the last second, someone snatched it away. "Yes!" he heard the guy say while winking at Regan. Playing along, she laughed and crooked her finger at the little punk.

"Lucky man!" called the DJ.

His opportunity to talk to Regan disappeared in front of Van's eyes as the guy walked over to her. He hadn't been in the wedding party, so he wasn't one of Jackson's close friends. Regan held out her hand to introduce herself, and the jackass kissed it instead of shaking it. Anger surged within him, and Van started toward them.

"A word to the wise, G-man," V said, seemingly materializing next to him.

Van jumped at the sound of her voice. "Jesus," he said.

"He's got bigger things on his plate than you, honey," V said. "Plus, if you march over there and toss her over your shoulder, even the Holy Trinity won't be able to save you from Rae's wrath."

He looked at Regan. She and the garter thief were laughing and posing for a picture.

The thought of doing that had crossed Van's mind. Right after the vision of decking the guy talking to her. Van felt like he could puke, but he heeded V's advice and stayed where he was.

V patted his shoulder. "Good choice," she said and walked away.

The DJ's voice boomed over the microphone. "All right, ladies and gentlemen, here comes the fun part! Ms. Murphy, if you would have a seat right there, please." He pointed to the chair Kez sat in a few minutes ago.

Now recovered from her initial shock, Regan embraced the moment for the spectacle it was and sauntered to the chair. She crossed one leg over the other, taking full advantage of the slit in her dress. Whistles and catcalls sounded around them, and she tipped her head back and laughed, the sound hitting Van squarely in the chest.

"And now, good sir," the DJ said to Garter Guy, "if you would assume the position."

The asshole rubbed his hands together. Van thought his head might explode from anger, or jealousy, or whatever else you wanted to call the volatile emotions running through him at that moment.

Once the asshat reached his mark in front of Regan, the DJ continued, "All right, you two, you know the drill. The higher you place that garter, the longer the two newlyweds will stay married." He looked at the guy. "I know it's a chore." Everyone laughed while Regan pouted, playing along. "But suffer through it for your friend Jackson."

The guy got down on one knee and took Regan's slender ankle in one hand. He looped the garter over her shoe and smiled at her. She grinned back and shifted in her seat. The garter began a slow slide up her leg. The higher it climbed, the slower time seemed to move. The interloper's hand paused at Regan's knee and lighthearted *boos* sounded around them.

Regan laughed again and said, "Let me see if I can help you out a bit." She lifted her leg up and put her foot on his shoulder. The boos changed to cheers when the garter slid over her knee and started up her thigh. When he stopped again, Regan put her hand over his. "What, you don't want them to be happy?" she asked. Still laughing, she looked out over the crowd, and her eyes landed on Van.

*10*

*The* laugh died on Rae's lips when she saw Van. Standing ramrod straight with his fists clenched so tightly she wondered if his bones hurt, Van was the quintessential scorned lover. He frowned so strongly it hollowed his cheeks. But his eyes alone were enough to telegraph his envy. If looks could kill, the poor guy at her feet would've keeled over dead, shredded by the scattershot of flaming jealousy arrows Van sent his way. The brush of lace on her mid-thigh tore her attention from Van.

"Um, I don't think I can go any higher," the guy said, his fingers resting on the garter. His smile turned a little naughty. "At least not in public."

Normally, a cute young guy with a hand on her thigh was exactly what she hoped to score at a wedding reception. But tonight, the urge to take things further wasn't there. The weight of Van's stare rested heavily around her like a force field scrambling all other signals to her sexual receptors. Irritating as it was, it didn't change her lack of interest in the guy.

"As tempting as that offer is," she said, "I think I'll pass."

He pulled his hand back, and she closed the slit in her dress. "Can't blame a guy for asking," he said with a grin.

"Well, folks," the DJ announced, "after that performance, I think Jackson and Kez have a shot at being together until they are old and gray! Give these two a hand for being such good sports!"

Rae kissed the guy's cheek, and they posed for a few more pictures. She looked for Van but didn't see him. Kez and Jackson appeared for another round of photos. Rae was pretty sure if they wanted a flipbook of every second of this wedding, they'd have one.

Once Rae's garter partner left, Kez said, "Thanks for making that sacrifice for our happiness." She grinned after the guy, and Rae wished she could summon even an ounce of heat for him. But there was nothing, not even the tiniest, lamest sparkler that had been left out in the rain. No need to let Kez see that though.

"Letting an attractive young guy slide his hand up my thigh? Yep, pure torture. But, that crap about the one who catches the bouquet being the next one down the aisle better be complete garbage," Rae said.

The bouquet toss and garter pitch both seemed outdated and designed solely to humiliate as many people as possible. She'd felt a little nauseated when she'd seen the flowers rolling blooms over stem straight for her. But when that garter had traveled toward Van . . . she'd strained to see if he could catch it—and if she were honest, been a little disappointed when he didn't.

Looping her arm through Rae's, Kez said, "Come join me and V for a drink." They moved to the bar, where V sat with Dave.

Jackson leaned against the bar and smiled at Kez. He signaled the bartender, and a tray of six glasses of bubbly appeared. Jackson passed glasses to V and Dave then handed one to Rae and one to Kez. He looked behind Rae and motioned to someone. Without turning, she knew it was Van. Rae could feel the shift in the air at his approach, like an antelope sensing a lion. Jackson handed him the fifth glass and took the last one for himself. When he dropped an arm over Kez's shoulders and gathered her into his side, it left Rae standing next to Van. Neither acknowledged the other, but she knew he was as aware of her presence as she was of his. She forced herself not to fidget.

"Well, guys," Jackson said, kissing Kez's temple. "We did it!" Rae laughed along with everyone else and clinked her glass with theirs. She took a sip and avoided looking at Van.

"We're so happy for both of you," said V.

"I'll second that," said Dave, his arm around V's waist.

"Next stop: paradise," said Rae. "And I, for one, cannot freaking wait to get on that plane! But I still think you're nuts doing a group vacation as your honeymoon."

Kez had broached the idea when they first started planning the wedding. She and Jackson had considered a destination wedding but knew Nana wouldn't jet off to the Caribbean. So Kez came up with the idea to bring some of the wedding party on the honeymoon. It would give Jackson guys to golf and gamble with, while she could bring her girls to sunbathe and spa. Not your typical weeklong sextravaganza with the "Do Not Disturb" sign hung up the entire time, but Rae wasn't about to turn down a tropical vacation. Work had been insane, and she was ready to unplug and drown in cold drinks and hot cabana boys.

"Oh, thank God," Kez said, putting a hand to her chest in relief. "I was so worried you'd change your mind and not come."

Rae laughed at the ridiculous idea anything could keep her from getting on that plane. "Girl, you know how crazy work has been for me lately. I'm tempted to leave now, before some other crisis pops up. Why on earth would you think I wasn't coming?"

A worried frown replaced Kez's smile. "Well . . ." She looked at Jackson, then back to Rae. "I wasn't sure whether you'd bail now since . . ."

"Since what?" Rae asked, now confused herself. "Why do you have that weird look on your face?"

"I think what Kez is struggling to say," Van said, "is that she worried you wouldn't come once you found out I was going."

A cold knot settled in Rae's stomach as her dreams of whiling away the next seven days under a brilliant sun, sipping frosty drinks and watching sailboats cut through crystal-clear water, crumbled. "*You're* coming?" she asked, finally looking at Van. Her head swam at the news. Then she cursed herself for being an idiot. He was the freaking best man. *Of course* Jackson would've invited him. How had she not thought of that until now? She should've paid more attention when Kez listed who was coming, but all she'd heard was "week in the tropics." The rest of the details she'd either glossed over or tuned out, figuring they didn't matter. That was coming back to bite her in the ass.

*This can't be happening,* she thought. A week in the Caribbean with Donovan McLeod? At one time, that would have been a dream come true. Except for one problem—she'd never wanted a dream vacation with Donovan McLeod. She wanted it with Raymond Edwards, a man who existed only on paper. Would there ever be a day when he didn't ruin things for her?

Van's lips curved downward, and his dark eyes clouded. "It's an easy problem to solve," he said. "I just won't go."

Rae glared at him, her fingers tightening on the champagne flute in her hand. "What did you say?"

He flinched at the venom in her tone but held his ground. "I said I won't go."

"Oh, so you're going to play the martyr?" she sneered at him.

"Regan," Van said. "My going will obviously ruin it for you and probably everyone else."

Rae's full fury from five years ago resurfaced with a vengeance. She grabbed Van's elbow. "If you all will excuse us for a minute," she said to the group. Before anyone could reply, she hiked up her skirt and dragged Van into a corner.

⊰❧⊱

"You do not get to make *me* into the asshole!" Regan whispered once they were alone, releasing his arm only to jab him in the chest.

"Ouch!" he said, rubbing his sternum. Manicures hurt. "What are you talking about?" he asked.

Truth be told, he was having a hard time concentrating on anything except a week with her on a white sand beach. Thoughts of her in a bikini, or possibly *less* than a bikini, kept playing through his mind. Sure, he'd offered not to go and, if he had to, he'd honor that offer. But he'd sell his soul to the highest bidder for this chance.

Seeing her that morning made all other thoughts, including any related to the Cayman trip, scatter from his mind. Jackson had been sparse on the details, saying Kez invited a few of her friends. Van was certain he would've remembered if Jackson had mentioned Regan, but then again, he hadn't put it together that Regan and Rae were the same person. Why would he? What were the chances?

Her fingernail poked his chest again, breaking into his thoughts. "You'll look all self-sacrificing by bowing out of this trip, while I'm the crazy ex. I don't think so, McLeod. You're going on this fucking trip."

*You're damn right I am, sweetheart,* he thought, inwardly rejoicing at her insistence. He knew he couldn't seem too eager. He had to play this right, so he tried to play it cool. "Regan, I don't think that's the best—"

"I could give two shits about what you think is 'best,' McLeod. You owe me." Her voice was flinty, little shards of anger chipping off and flying toward him. She planted her hands on her hips, which made champagne slosh from her flute onto the floor. He imagined she was mentally dismembering him and enjoying every slice and dice.

Her point, though, was one he couldn't deny. He owed her for what had happened. No, for what *he'd* done to her. But he never dreamed he'd make up for it with a tropical getaway. He'd envisioned something akin to waterboarding or the removal of his fingernails.

"So you're okay with going on vacation with me?" he asked, needing to hear her say it. He couldn't think of a better setting than a week on an island to convince Regan that what they'd had was real.

"I'm not going on vacation with you," she snapped. "I'm going on vacation with my two best friends and their husband and boyfriend. You just happen to be taking the same flight to the same resort for the same amount of time."

"Okay," he said.

Regan searched his face for deceit. "Okay?" she asked, eyes narrowed into wary slits. Her entire body radiated suspicion, from the rigid set of her shoulders to the squinted, gunslinger stare she gave him.

He aimed for nonchalance and gave a small shrug. "Okay," he said again. "You want me to go, I'll go."

Regan stepped forward, angling her head back to glare at him. If she'd had pistols, her hands would've been on the hilts of them. Their bodies were now within inches of each other. Eyes the color of jade blazed up at him. "Make no mistake," she said, her lips biting off the words. "*I* don't want you to go. Kez and Jackson want you to go. You and I will have as little to do with each other as possible."

All he had to do was lower his head and he could kiss her. Her full lips were plump and slightly parted. He felt her breath on his face, could smell the sweetness of the champagne she'd been drinking. *Now is not the time*, he told himself. She could turn tail and run or, more likely, gut him like a pig and leave him to bleed out. But in the Caymans, they'd be thrown together almost every day, whether she wanted to admit it or not. And she couldn't leave—or murder him—without also ruining Kez's honeymoon. Was it shitty to use his best friend's honeymoon to trap his ex-girlfriend into hearing him out and hopefully giving him another chance? Yes, it was. Was he still going to do it? Yes, he was.

Van took a conscious step back. "Whatever you want, Regan."

She scowled at him a moment longer and then screwed on a smile to disguise her real feelings. Regan extended her arm. "Then by all means," she said, "let's go give everyone the joyous news."

God help him if everything she'd just locked down inside ever ripped its way free. He was pretty sure it would destroy them both.

They rejoined their friends, all of whom looked more than a little worried. "So when do we leave?" Regan asked Kez.

Kez's eyes moved from Regan to Van, not sold by Regan's unnaturally wide grin. "Um, tomorrow morning?"

Regan laughed, the sound almost authentic. "You don't sound too sure of yourself, Kez. If I were in your shoes, I'd have the time I was leaving for my honeymoon down to the second."

Kez blinked. "Tomorrow morning. We're all on the eleven o'clock flight to Grand Cayman."

"Perfect," said Regan. She looked at V and Dave. "I hate to ask, because I know V will want to be there at the crack of dawn, but can I bum a ride to the airport?"

Dave laughed. "Sure," he said. "And I promise I won't let her get there any earlier than nine o'clock."

"You're a prince among men," said Regan. V rolled her eyes.

While Regan was busy talking to V and Kez, in a shade above a whisper, Jackson asked Van, "You sure you're okay with this, man?"

Van clasped his shoulder. "I'm more than okay with it." He looked at Regan. "You may have given me my second chance," he said.

"Make sure you don't fuck it—or my honeymoon—up," Jackson said with a grin.

Regan waved at someone, and Van turned to see who it was. His molars ground together when he saw Garter Guy. What did *he* want?

Regan said something to the bartender, who smiled and poured two shots. Scooping them up off the bar, Regan said, "Well, if you all will excuse me, I owe that young man a shot." She sashayed toward the douche and handed him a glass. They toasted then tossed the shots back. Regan rocked onto her tiptoes and whispered something into his ear. With an eager smile, he offered her his arm and led her onto the dance floor.

Van hadn't realized he was walking toward them until Jackson's hand landed on his bicep. "Let her go, Van," he said. Van flexed against his friend's hold, but Jackson didn't budge. "How is you making a scene not fucking things up?" he asked. "You'll have an entire week with her. Rather than start any farther in the hole than you already are, how about you take a beat to figure out how you'll use that week to get what you want?"

Van dragged a hand through his hair. "You're right, you're right," he said.

"I usually am," said Jackson.

Still looking at Regan, Van asked, "So you'd be okay if Kez were dancing with someone else?"

"Hell no," said Jackson. "I'd rip his arms off and beat him to death with them. But Kez doesn't hate me, so I'm ahead of the game. Unlike you."

Van groaned and slumped onto a stool. Kez excused herself from V and Dave to join them. She perched on the seat next to him, bumping him gently with her shoulder. "You know," she said, "I'm supposed to hate you.'"

He spared her a glance then tortured himself by keeping his eyes on Regan. If that guy's hand dipped any lower, he would not be responsible for what happened next. He dragged his attention back to Kez. "I sense a 'but' in there somewhere," he said.

She shrugged. "I always knew there was a man from her past. She was the one woman more emotionally closed off than I was. If I'd ask her about it, it was like someone flipped a switch. She'd shutter herself away and change the subject. Based on what she told me today, you're the one who did that to her."

Even without more detail, her description of what he'd done was painful to hear and made him feel even worse. Jackson was right. He was in a deep hole with a long way to climb. He figured winning Kez over was a good place to start. "I can't deny that I hurt her," he said. "But you have to believe me when I say I never meant to."

"That's where you're wrong, Van. I don't *have* to do anything." Kez brushed back an errant curl and gave him a small smile, and with it, a flicker of hope. "However," she went on, "I see the way you look at her. That's not something you can fake. So, while there's no doubt in my mind that you gave her a royal mind-fuck all those years ago, I'm not completely against the idea that maybe, just maybe, she should hear you out."

Van smiled and took her hand in his, giving it a grateful squeeze. "Thank you, Kez."

She patted the top of his hand, somewhat reassuringly. "I'm not saying I'll help you with anything, but I won't stand in your way." Kez hopped off the barstool and faced him. "But if you fuck her over in any way, shape, or form, I promise you they'll find Jimmy Hoffa before they find you." She gave his cheek a light swat and smiled. "Now, I'm going to dance with my husband."

*11*

*Rae* couldn't concentrate on whatever her dance partner was saying. She was sure it was fine, maybe even witty, but it didn't matter. The press of Van's eyes on her was too distracting. She didn't have to see him to know he was looking at her. She could feel it against her skin.

Her partner's—she thought his name was Brian but wasn't sure—hands dropped lower on her hips. He'd been thrilled when she reconsidered her earlier decision to brush him off. But now, she had second thoughts about her second thoughts. The itch to bat his hands away was strong, but she didn't. Not that he wasn't cute, because he was. Not because he wasn't a good dancer—he was. He was all the things she'd normally look for and encourage to come her way. Usually, their dance would've ended with some quality time in one of Jackson's guest rooms. But tonight, she couldn't get any of her trusty man-trap vibes to fire up. Every attempt she'd made fizzled, foiled once again by Van's stupid anti-sex laser beam vision. *Dammit!*

Determined to put Van and his pesky forcefield out of her mind, she wound her arms around Probably Brian's neck and pulled him closer. He came willingly. His lips brushed her cheek, and they continued dancing, bodies moving in sync with one another. Rae smelled his cologne, warm and masculine without being overbearing. She could tell there was a solid male form under his dress shirt and suit jacket. This guy was the epitome of perfect wedding hookup, yet her nether regions were more desolate wasteland than erogenous zone.

Rae groaned inwardly, steeling herself to the challenge of ignoring Van and focusing on Probably Brian. She could do this. Tonight wasn't different from any other time she'd picked up a guy over the last few years. It was a practice she'd almost perfected. This time would simply require extra effort. Surely, that was all it would take. "You know," she purred close to Probably Brian's ear, "we could keep dancing, or"—she ran a hand down his chest—"we could . . ."

Rae felt the curve of his cheek next to hers as he smiled. "We certainly could," he said, his hand skimming down her hip.

*You can do this,* Rae thought. *You need to do this.* The repeated mantra did nothing to generate any real interest in Probably Brian, but she soldiered on with the plan.

Linking her hand with his, she led him off the dance floor and away from the watchful brown eyes of the man who'd broken her heart. Outside, it was easier to breathe. Rae looked up at the stars and took a deep inhale of the jasmine-scented night air. Pea gravel crunched under their shoes as they walked along the path. Unfortunately, they didn't make it beyond the lights of the party before Van blocked the way to the house.

Rae watched the sleeve of his jacket tighten around his biceps when he crossed his arms and gave them a disapproving frown. "Regan," he said, and she hated the way she still loved how his voice rolled over every letter of her full name.

She clamped down on Probably Brian's hand, scarcely resisting the urge to stick her tongue out at Van. "What are you doing out here?"

"I saw you leave and wanted to make sure everything was all right." Van shot a pointed look at Probably Brian's hand in hers.

Rae bristled at his intrusion, sidling closer to her dance partner. "Everything is fine, McLeod. Go back to the party."

Van relaxed his posture a bit, tucking his hands in his pockets, but didn't move out of their way. "Brian, is it?" he asked. Van's question seemed conversational, but she heard the hard undercurrent. Most people wouldn't have picked up on the sharper edge to his tone, but she knew him so well it was easy to discern. At least . . . she *thought* she'd known him well.

She felt Brian's hand twist a little in hers. Van made him nervous, so he wasn't a complete idiot. "That's right," Brian said. Rae felt a small sense of vindication at the confirmation. "And you're Van, the best man."

Van's smile was small and fleeting. "That's right. Would you give Regan and me a minute?" he asked. Though posed as a question, it was more demand. The implied "fuck off" hung awkwardly in the air around them.

"Uh, I don't know," Brian said, looking between the two of them. Rae could read him as easily as a children's book. He'd left the party on what he'd seen as a surefire mission to get lucky with a bridesmaid. A confrontation with Van hadn't been on his radar. Now that it was, he weighed whether Rae was worth whatever Van was going to dish out.

She had to give him credit, though, for not turning tail immediately and abandoning her. While it was obvious he wanted to avoid any drama, he wasn't comfortable leaving her with Van. She'd sized him up correctly: Brian was a decent guy who didn't deserve to get roped into her drama. Van was her problem to deal with, not his. And she had to admit his departure would not be any significant loss. She'd started to wonder if she needed to do CPR on her libido, except for the fact it was ready and raring to go now that Van was there.

Rae patted Brian's chest. "Sorry, slugger," she said. "Tonight's not going to happen." Leaning in, she whispered to him, "But I have it on good authority Kez's second cousin Liz is easier than a nursery rhyme but a lot freakier. Good luck."

Brian's disappointment changed quickly to a reignited optimism for how his evening would end. He dropped a kiss on her cheek. "It was nice to meet you, Rae. Thanks for the dance."

Once he was out of earshot, Rae's hands fisted on her hips. Just because she was secretly glad Van interrupted her tryst with Brian didn't mean she wasn't going to give him a piece of her mind. He wasn't her keeper, nor was he her protector. He gave up the right to be either one a long time ago.

"Dammit, McLeod! Who the hell do you think you are?" Rae shoved him in the chest. He didn't budge but reached to steady her when she slipped in the small gravel. She slapped his hands away. "I'm fine!"

Once it was clear she wouldn't face-plant, he slid his hands back into his pockets. "Where were you going, Regan?" he asked. Shadows dappled his face but didn't lessen the intensity of his stare. Yep, he was mad all right. But so was she!

"Where do you think? And what business is it of yours, anyway?"

"Why?" he asked, ignoring her second question.

"Why not?" Rae crossed her arms.

Van stepped closer, frowning. "We leave for Grand Cayman in the morning."

"I wasn't planning on putting him in my carry-on," she said, rolling her eyes.

He took another step toward her, light from the tent letting her see more of his expression. There was misery there, resting quietly under the anger she'd seen earlier. "I can't stand the thought of you with someone else."

"I hate to break it to you, buddy, but there have been lots of some-one elses," she said. Watching the hurt surface past the anger and hang desolately across his features didn't provide the satisfaction she hoped it would. Instead, she regretted twisting the knife to make him hurt like she did.

But Van didn't limp off and nurse his wounds. Instead, he bent down so they were eye-level. "Does that soothe the pain I caused, Regan?" Van took her by the shoulders when she tried to turn away, holding her lightly but making her face him. "If it does," he continued, "then take your best shot. Take as many as you need for as long as you want. I'll be your own personal punching bag if it means that someday you'll let me explain what happened."

Rae stilled in his grasp, held captive more by his words than by the gentle grip of his hands. He sounded so earnest, so honest, that she almost succumbed to the practically gravitational pull she felt for him. Would it be so bad to hear him out? Maybe—

A loud shout, followed by laughter, came from the reception below them. Music drifted up the hill, showing the party was still in full swing. Rae stepped backward, and Van's hands fell from her shoulders.

Her skin prickled where he'd touched her, and she rubbed her arms. She couldn't say if it were to chase away the feeling or hold onto it.

"Cold?" Van asked and took off his coat.

"No, I'm fine," she said, even though she was anything but. She was, instead, a wheeling tumult of indecision and too many emotions. She was in no state to deal with Van. Her defenses were down and, if she weren't careful, she'd fall victim once again to his silver tongue. He'd have her talked into listening to him and out of her cocktail dress before she knew what hit her. As fun as the latter might be, she was not ready for the former. Not by a long shot.

He shrugged back into his jacket. "Then shall we head back?"

Her only answer was to walk away from him and reenter the tent. Rae headed to the bar without looking back, needing as much distance from Donovan McLeod as she could get.

The bartender gave her a practiced smile. "What can I get you?" he asked.

"Bourbon," she said, resting a hip on a bar stool. "And leave the bottle."

"Um, well, I don't think I can . . ." he stuttered.

"It's fine, Paul," said Jackson from beside her. "If Rae asks for the bottle, she gets the bottle."

"Thanks," she said, glancing over at him. He'd shed his suit jacket and rolled up the sleeves of his shirt. Intricate tattoos roped down his muscled forearms.

He eased onto a stool next to her and signaled for a glass. When it came, he filled hers first, then his. After giving hers a small clink, he sipped his drink. "Rough night?" he asked.

She tossed back a healthy swallow of her own drink. "You could say that," she answered then downed the rest in a second swallow.

Jackson put a finger against her wrist. "You know as well as I do, it tastes a lot better if you sip it."

"Takes longer to do the job that way," she said, refilling her glass. His reproachful look made her scoff, but she took a smaller sip.

Jackson twisted his glass on the bar, looking at it instead of her. "And what job is that, exactly?"

"Erase the last five years?" she asked with a sad laugh.

Jackson nodded and sipped his drink. "You know you can't erase them, but you can make up for them."

"When did you start writing riddles?" She took another small swallow of her drink, grudgingly admitting to herself that Jackson was right about sipping it.

He chuckled but didn't answer, just sat with her as she drank. Jackson was good at just being there. Not filling in a silence with a lot of forced nonsense that no one wanted to hear. She could tell he was worried about her, but he wasn't going to pry or give any unsolicited advice. And that she appreciated. But she also didn't want to monopolize the groom on his wedding night.

After a few minutes, she asked, "Where's your wife?"

Jackson let her change the subject and surveyed the crowd. "She was with Nana when I walked over here, so I assume they're still hanging out."

"She didn't want to come help play intervention?"

He touched his glass to hers. "Seems like I'm not doing the best job of that right now." Leaning back, he propped an elbow on the bar. "Why don't you stay here tonight, Rae?"

"Worried about me?"

"Not worried, but . . ." he hedged.

Rae laughed and swirled the liquor in her glass. It made her think of Van's eyes, and she pushed the glass away. "Whatever you want to call it, Jackson, worry or concern, don't waste your wedding night doing that. There are other things—and one special person—you should spend the night *doing.*" She wiggled her eyebrows at him. He grinned.

She gave him a playful shove. "Go find your wife. Take advantage of her in a dark corner or underneath one of the immense trees circling this place. Hell, take her to your cavernous bedroom and don't come out until morning." Rae held up three fingers in a semi-salute. "I'll behave myself. Scout's honor."

"Why do I think your only merit badge was in ball busting?" he asked.

"Cause you're a very smart man. And since you're so smart, you'll heed my advice and go get your bride." Jackson hesitated and Rae sighed, pushing the bottle away from her. "Better?"

"Much," he said and went in search of Kez. Once he'd gone, Rae grabbed the bottle and hopped off her stool. She wobbled a bit but regained her balance easily enough to know she was tipsy but not quite drunk. Weaving her way out of the reception, she vowed to fix that.

❧

Van hadn't followed Regan to the bar, and he'd felt marginally better when he saw Jackson sit next to her. He knew his friend was doing his level best to make sure she did nothing, or anyone, she'd regret the next day. He shoved away the memory of Brian's hands on her. God knew he had no claim on the woman anymore. But seeing her with anyone else tore him in two.

He looked back to where she'd been sitting with Jackson. Neither one of them were there. He scanned the crowded tent, fighting against the anxiety generated by her disappearance. Across the room, he saw Jackson lean down to kiss Kez, but he didn't see Regan anywhere. What if she'd circled back to find that Brian guy? With grim determination, he stalked around, looking for her. After an hour, he hadn't found her but saw Brian with a young blonde, maybe the aforementioned Liz.

Leaving the tent, he made one lap around the perimeter but still didn't find Regan. He walked toward the house, his dress shoes clipping smartly against the flagstone of the lower patio. When he reached the back stairs, he heard the soft, rhythmic clank of a chain. To his left, the porch swing barely moved in the far corner. Someone was sitting—or rather slumping—in it.

Quickly, he climbed the steps. It was darker on the porch, but between the moonlight and the lanterns lining the pathway below, he saw that the person on the swing was a woman. When the dim light reflected off the jeweled stones in her hair, he knew it was Regan. Her turning up a bottle served as confirmation.

"Regan?" he whispered, trying not to startle her.

She squinted in the darkness and then laughed. "Well, if it isn't the ghost of boyfriends past!" Judging by the slur in her words and the fact she didn't immediately tell him to fuck off, he was guessing she was well past tipsy.

Regan patted the swing beside her. "Have a seat, McLeod." Yep, that sealed it. She was drunk.

He approached cautiously, sure at any minute she'd bolt. Instead, she dropped her feet to the floor and slid over to allow more room for him. Careful to sit an appropriate distance from her, he eased down onto the swing. Regan kicked her foot and set the swing in motion while taking another slug out of the bottle. Van really hoped it hadn't been full when she started.

He motioned to the booze. "Mind if I have a swig?"

Wordlessly, she passed it to him. Van tilted it up and took a swallow. Thank God Jackson sprung for good bourbon. When Regan reached to take it back, he considered telling her she'd had enough. But staying next to her trumped any need to keep her from being hungover tomorrow. To his relief, she set the bottle beside her rather than taking another drink.

Cocking her head to the side, she looked at him. Then she closed both eyes for a second and opened only one. That bright-green eye traveled over his face in a continuous loop. A loud hiccup interrupted her one-eyed inventory of him. She put a hand over her mouth. "'Scuse me."

"No problem," he said. God, even three sheets to the wind, she was gorgeous.

She listed to the side, still staring at him out of one eye.

"You okay?" Van asked.

Regan flipped a hand in the air. "I'm fine," she slurred. "But if I open both eyes, there's two of you. And I can barely handle one." She huffed out an irritated breath. "You know, the gentlemanly thing to do would've been to let yourself go."

A laugh slipped out before he could stop it. "I'm sorry, what?"

She poked his shoulder. "*I said* the gentlemanly thing for you to do would've been to let yourself go. Delve into the donuts in the breakroom, lay off the gym, and stew in your alleged misery at losing me. But noooooooo," she drew out the word, punctuating it with a slash of her hand. "Not the world-famous Agent McLeod. His body is apparently still a fucking temple."

He could feel her desire as her eyes swept from the top of his head to the tips of his shiny dress shoes. Her pupils dilated, and she mumbled, "A fucking temple."

She shifted closer to him on the swing, her fingers resting lightly on his forearm. Her hip pressed against his, and she laid her head on his shoulder. Tilting her face, she nuzzled his neck, which sent lightning bolts skittering into his bloodstream. Heat pumped through him like a furnace when she wiggled even closer, pressing her thigh to his.

"Mmmm," she hummed. "You still smell good."

Regan's nose rubbed against his neck. When he felt the rasp of her tongue against his skin, Van had to grip the seat of the swing to keep from taking her into his arms. He wouldn't take advantage of her while she was drunk, but things hadn't gotten to the point of no return just yet.

"Still taste good too," she murmured. Hot kisses feathered down his neck as her breasts grazed his bicep. A groan escaped his lips. Her hand slid under his suit jacket and roamed over his chest. "So firm," she breathed. In an amazingly agile move for someone who'd tried to pickle themselves in a vat of bourbon, she kicked one leg out and settled on his lap.

Van's hands went to her waist while hers gripped his shoulders. They were a breath apart. The way her lips parted and her gaze softened, he knew she was going to kiss him. He also knew she was drunk and he should stop her. If he didn't, he was a world-class tool. He knew all of that, and yet he didn't move her off his lap, nor did he pull away from her. As she leaned toward him with hazy eyes, his hands slid down over her hips, took two handfuls of her luscious ass, and squeezed. She moaned and rocked into him, and there was no way she didn't feel how hard she made him.

Her tongue darted out to moisten her lips, and he tracked the movement. She noticed and smiled. He toed the floor and set the swing in motion. Her skirt rustled as the hem brushed the stone floor. Van reached up and cupped her face in his hand. Regan leaned into his palm. His thumb traced her cheekbone, and he guided her down.

Regan's mouth skimmed over his in a kiss so light he almost didn't think it was real. He curled a hand around her nape, pulling her closer. His tongue probed gently at the seam of her lips, seeking entrance. She opened them on a sigh, and he breathed it in as he deepened their kiss. He tasted the whiskey she'd been drinking as his tongue swept inside her mouth. Her lips were eager under his as she angled her head for better access to him. Her tongue teased his with a delicate rolling motion and he groaned. He felt the scrape of her teeth over his bottom lip when he finally pulled back.

"Regan," he whispered reverently.

"Shh," she said against his lips. "Don't say anything, please." Her voice trembled, and he felt a tear slide down her cheek.

Concerned, he pulled away to look at her. "Regan, what's wro—"

One small hand over his mouth stopped his question. She swiped at her cheeks with the other. "I can handle kissing you and, with a little more of that"—Regan pointed to the bottle beneath them on the swing—"I'd probably tumble right back into bed with you. But the one thing I'm not ready to do is talk to you."

The elation he'd felt at having her back in his arms evaporated. He didn't want some quick fuck she'd regret before the sun came up the next day. Van wanted so much more with her. He kissed the palm covering his lips, and she gave him a sad smile. More tears threatened to fall from her glittering green eyes. It shattered him. Gently, he lifted her off his lap and placed her snugly against him. Her head lolled against his shoulder, and he kissed her temple.

A soft push from his heel put the swing back into motion. Regan tried to grab the whiskey bottle and almost toppled over. Van grabbed her shoulder. "Easy there, beautiful. I don't think you need any more."

With a soft *thunk*, her head landed back on his shoulder, and she looked up at him from beneath her lashes. "You're not the boss of me," she said sleepily.

He bumped her chin lightly with the ridge of his knuckles. "Don't I know it."

She burrowed into his side. "You're so snuggly," she mumbled, her eyes drifting closed. Between the long day, the alcohol, and the slow rocking of the swing, she was close to passing out.

"Don't think that because I'm using you as a human pillow that I've stopped hating you."

"Of course not," Van replied, stroking her arm.

She yawned and inched impossibly closer to him. "'Cause I still totally do. Hate you, that is."

"I know, baby, I know."

After a few more indistinct mutterings, Regan's breath evened out, and Van felt her body go limp against him. "Regan," he said, keeping his voice low. She didn't stir. "Let's get you to bed, princess," Van said. He stood and lifted her carefully into his arms, looping one of her arms around his neck. She rested her head on his chest with a quiet exhale. After grabbing the heels she'd kicked off at some point, he crossed the patio and let them into the house. As he turned the knob, he was careful to keep a tight hold on her sleeping form.

Earlier in the day, Jackson had assigned him the downstairs guest room closest to the pool. He passed through the darkened kitchen and into the long hallway. The door to his right was closed but not shut. A nudge of his foot opened it, and he surveyed the chaos leftover from the parade of bridesmaids earlier in the day. Someone had shoved his duffle bag into a corner to make way for a rolling rack and collapsible table, which was covered in what had to be four thousand brands of makeup.

Cradling Regan against him with one arm, he swept the random articles of feminine crap off the bed and onto the floor. He lowered her down to the bed, and she rolled to her side. She bent one knee and Van watched as her dress parted to expose toned, tan legs. His hand ached to caress her skin, but he held back. Staring down at her, it occurred to him there was no way she could sleep in her dress. The satin would wind its way around her into a twisted mess. Van looked around them. Despite the explosion of femininity in the room, there was nothing in there that would work.

Van pulled his phone from his pocket and sent a text: *I need a pair of your wife's pajamas.*

# 12

*Rae's* head pounded. Overnight, her tongue had transformed into a huge cotton ball. The taste in her mouth could only be described as unholy and demonic. Her body ached in places she hadn't known existed the day before. The only comfortable thing was the solid source of warmth at her back that spread across her shoulders. When that solid warmth shifted on an exhale, Rae's eyes popped open. Looking down, she saw a tanned forearm draped across her stomach. What the hell had she gotten into last night? She remembered the wedding, the toasts, dancing with . . . Brad? Bobby? Brian! That was his name.

Had she gone to bed with him? Another look at the arm confirmed the owner was dark-haired, not blond. She was 85 percent sure Brian had been blond, so chances were good she wasn't with him. The only other guy she'd spent any time with was . . . *Oh shit.* She wouldn't have. She couldn't have. But all the evidence was that she had. She could turn her head and find out. One little peek over her shoulder at the man behind her. But . . . she wasn't ready to know just yet.

On her next downward glance, she paid more attention to her outfit. Whatever it was, it wasn't hers. The tank top was too long, as were the bottoms. Her best guess was that she was wearing a pair of Kez's pajamas. But who'd dressed her in these PJs? Based on her present company, she had a feeling she knew the answer.

"I can hear the wheels turning in that pretty head of yours," Van's deep voice rumbled behind her.

Instead of answering, she tried to twist away from him. Rather than let her go, he wrapped his arm tighter around her. "No running this time, Regan," he said.

Rae stiffened. "I have to pee, McLeod."

Van's stubble scraped her shoulder. "Just don't sneak out the window." He lifted his arm to release her. Slinging her feet over the side of the bed made her stomach roll in protest. Hot, putrid bile rose to the back of her throat, putting an even worse taste in her mouth. To quell the first wave of nausea, she put her elbows on her knees and held her aching head in her hands, breathing slowly. Fighting back the need to vomit, she stood up and faced Van.

He propped himself against the headboard and the sheet slid down. Even in her wretched state, she had to take stock of the specimen in front of her. Had the man done nothing but work out? His chest was broad and tan, with a light sprinkling of hair. When he adjusted the pillow, his abs flexed, and her stomach flipped for a totally different reason.

"See something you like, Regan?" Her eyes met his, and he grinned, folding his hands over his taut stomach with a smirk. The move emphasized the bulge of his biceps. Whirling around, she stalked to the bathroom, the sound of his laughter following her.

She slammed the door behind her and took a deep breath that almost came out in a shriek at her reflection. Someone might have changed her clothes, but they'd left her updo alone. It now resembled a nest constructed by a rat who'd drunk even more than she had. Knotted tendrils hung in her face, and the carefully placed curls were now clumps of hair held up by a few straggling bobby pins. The fancy jewels winked dejectedly from the disheveled mess. She looked . . . awful. No, awful would be insulted by the association with the bedraggled hot mess in the mirror. Not the look you wanted when waking up in the arms of an ex-lover. *Shit!*

After answering nature's call, Rae plucked out the drooping bobby pins and then, with some additional effort, removed the ones still wedged into her scalp. Her hair hung in straggly curls, but at least it no longer resembled strips of felt. Turning on the faucet, she splashed water on her face and wiped off the remnants of her makeup. Using her fingers, she combed out the worst of the knots from her hair. While she fought with a stubborn tangle, a knock sounded against the door.

"Regan," Van called through the wood barrier.

Ignoring him, she gave her hair a vicious yank, and the snarled strands loosened.

He knocked again. "Everything all right in there?" he asked.

She knew he wasn't leaving, and she was too hungover to slip out the window. There was no way she'd survive a tumble into the flower bed. With a resigned groan, she unlocked the door and threw it open. "What do you think?" she asked.

It was a miscalculation on her part, because she was eye to eye with Van's chest. Her gaze dipped lower and tripped over his boxer briefs. Very short, very snug boxer briefs. *Fuck me,* she thought. The man was delicious, with narrow hips, toned abs, and other hard-to-miss male attributes. The sight was better than all the ibuprofen and coffee in the world because it made her forget about the ache behind her eyes and the churning in her stomach. Other, much more pleasant sensations flowed through her system as she counted the ridges across his abdomen.

Over her head, he gripped the top of the doorframe, giving her an eyeful of tanned, sinewy muscle. He loomed over her, dragging his eyes down her body. "From my perspective, everything looks good." His gaze landed on her breasts. "Very good," he said, his voice husky with something more than sleep.

The air between them crackled with tension, sexual and otherwise. It made the hair on her arms stand up, as though even it wanted to get closer to Van.

*Get a grip,* Rae thought, surfacing from the pheromonal stupor generated by Van's semi-naked proximity. She glared up at him and crossed her arms. "You could at least put on some clothes," she said.

Van leaned down, invading her personal space. "Do I make you uncomfortable?" he asked.

"Your morning breath does," she said and shoved at his stomach.

He pulled back with a slight smile. "Well, someone was occupying the bathroom, so I couldn't brush my teeth."

She stepped aside. "Be my guest," she said, gesturing to the sink.

Van came into the bathroom, intentionally brushing against her as he passed. "Thanks," he said.

Rae shivered and moved into the bedroom, closing the bathroom door behind her. Her bridesmaid's dress lay crumpled in a heap by the bed. As best she could remember, she'd left her phone in the master bedroom. She wouldn't disturb the newlyweds on their first morning as a married couple. They hadn't even left for their honeymoon. A thought wiggled at the back of her brain, then it roared forward like a street bike boosted with nitrous. *HONEYMOON!* She was supposed to fly to the Caymans that morning with them, V, Dave, and . . . She glanced at the closed bathroom door. Van. *Shit, shit, and double shit,* she thought.

After rolling up the pajama bottoms so she didn't add falling on her face to the list of morning mortifications, Rae padded into the hallway. She heard voices coming from the kitchen. When she rounded the corner, she saw Jackson and Kez, or rather, she saw Kez's hands raking down Jackson's back. He had Kez pinned against the island, her head thrown back as he kissed the hollow of her neck.

Before he could get much farther, Rae cleared her throat. "Sorry to interrupt," she said.

Jackson paused but didn't lift his head. Kez looked at Rae over his shoulder and grinned. "Good morning, sunshine," she chirped.

Rae rolled her eyes. "Please tell me you started some coffee prior to dry humping."

Kez's hands grabbed Jackson's ass as she laughed. "Next to the stove," she said and kissed Jackson's chin. Ignoring their groping, Rae grabbed a mug from the cabinet and poured a cup of coffee. Adding a splash of milk and a little sugar, she sipped and savored the first hit. Thank God for caffeine. A few hundred more mugs of this and she'd feel almost human.

Kez extricated herself from Jackson and poured her own cup of coffee. "Fun night?" she asked, all wide-eyed innocence.

Rae's eyes narrowed to suspicious slits. "What do you know?"

Gold eyes danced over the rim of Kez's coffee cup. "What don't you remember?"

"Don't make me beg for details of my own downfall," Rae said. She pouted at Kez. "Have pity on someone whose head feels like it's stuck in a vice while bongos are being played inside it."

"It's seven o'clock on the morning after I got married, and I'm not currently being ravaged by my sexy new husband. I'm the one who deserves to be pitied," Kez said.

Jackson kissed her bare shoulder. "For the record, Counselor, it was your idea to get out of bed." His blue eyes shimmered. "I had a distinctly different plan."

"It's too early for this much sex in the air," said Rae. "Especially when I'm not getting any of it."

Kez's eyes twinkled. "You sure about that, Rae?"

Setting her cup down, Rae said, "It might have been five years ago, but I know that a little whiskey cannot erase sex with Donovan McLeod from my memory banks." At least, she hoped it hadn't.

"Glad to hear it," Van said from behind her. Rae swore to herself. She needed to put a bell on him so he'd stop sneaking up on her. He shuffled into the kitchen, wearing nothing but a low-slung pair of sweats. When he reached into the cabinet for a mug, the lines of muscle in his back tensed and bunched beneath his skin. After he fixed his coffee, he leaned against the counter and looked at Rae.

Jackson wrapped an arm around Kez's waist and pulled her in front of him, resting his chin on her shoulder. She kissed his cheek and then asked Van, "Those pants didn't come with a shirt?"

He brushed a hand down the lines of his stomach and smiled. "Just thought after marrying that old bastard, you'd appreciate a look at a set of abs."

"Oh, is someone else joining us?" Rae asked, making Jackson laugh and Van scowl.

She returned his scornful look and asked, "Will someone please tell me how I ended up in bed with this jackass?"

Van waited to see if Kez would offer an explanation, but she stayed quiet. Okay, it appeared he would be the one to do the explaining. He ran a hand through his hair, unsure of where to start. "Well, Regan, you . . . I . . . we . . ."

"Yes, those are the usual pronouns, McLeod," she said. "But they shed no light on how I ended up as the little spoon."

Jackson stepped in and answered, "Well, it started with a text from this asshole for a set of my wife's pajamas."

"What?" Regan asked with a laugh then grimaced and rubbed her temples. Van imagined if she could get an IV of coffee, she'd take it.

Releasing his wife, Jackson crossed to the counter and gave Van a good-natured shove out of the way. He grabbed a bottle of ibuprofen from the cabinet and passed it to Regan.

"May God bless you with endless orgasms," Regan said gratefully as she shook out several pills.

Jackson laughed and shook his head. "Anyway, my response to his request was less than . . . accepting. But once I understood he needed them because you'd essentially drunk an entire bottle of bourbon and passed out, I didn't kill him."

"Passed out?" Regan asked, looking at Van.

Van rubbed his neck and nodded. "You passed out in my bed."

Regan scrutinized Van, eyes boring into his skull to get answers. "The real question, McLeod, is how did I *get* into your bed?"

Anger at her insinuation lanced through Van. Sure, he might've accepted a little more from her than he should've. But he hadn't crossed any lines. She'd been the aggressor, not him. And he'd taken care, not advantage of her. His hands clenched on the counter behind him. "Well, I certainly didn't force you in there!"

Her hands tightened around her coffee mug. Van watched her struggle to piece together the scattered details from the night before. "The last thing I remember is sitting on that swing." She jabbed a finger toward the French doors leading to the back patio. "So, again, I ask, how did I get into *your bed*."

Van tried to rein in his response. He'd be just as snarky if he were in her shoes, so he needed to show a little compassion. Matching her anger wouldn't help anything. "Technically, you passed out on the swing. So I carried you into the bedroom."

Regan's brow wrinkled, and he knew she was searching through the alcohol fog for any clue about what he was saying. "You found me passed out on the swing?" she asked.

"No," he said, answering only the question she asked and volunteering no details.

"Okaaaay," she said. "If I don't get the question right, then I don't get the answer, huh? How about this—*when* did I pass out?"

This was a minefield that could obliterate the minimal progress he'd made. He had to tread carefully. "While we were . . . sitting on the swing," he hedged. He tried not to squirm under her stare.

"Sitting," she said, obviously skeptical. Well, he thought, they *had* been sitting. That she'd been sitting on his lap while she kissed him and he cupped her ass were mere details. Details he believed were wise to leave out.

"Yep," he said. "Sitting."

Before Regan could continue her inquisition, Kez said, "As much as I love this game, we have to be at the airport in two hours. And I'm guessing you don't want to spend the next week wearing my pajamas." She pointed at Regan. "You need to get home and get your suitcase. That I'm hoping is already packed."

Van would've been perfectly happy if Regan had spent the next week in nothing but the soft tank top and pants she'd worn to bed. Especially if she also spent the week braless, like he knew she was right then. He lifted his coffee to his lips as he watched Regan come to grips with the fact that she had less than two hours to get home, clean up, and get to the airport.

Most women would've panicked, but Regan handled crises for a living. She'd probably been packed for a week, with everything on the list he was sure she'd made tucked into place. He watched her mentally clicking through what still needed to get done before they left. Even hungover, she was efficient.

V and Dave walked into the kitchen, already dressed for the day. "Hey there, sleepyheads," V said. She took in Regan's disheveled state and Van's bare chest, furrowing her brow. "Okay, what did I miss?"

"Nothing," Regan said quickly. "I've got to get home and get my stuff."

V leaned into the hallway and produced a large rolling bag. "No, you don't," she said.

Regan's brows spiked. "Why do you have my suitcase?"

V assumed a very motherly posture, hands on her hips with a bemused smile. "C'mon, Rae. Like I didn't know you were going to sleep late this morning?"

Pointing to the clock on the stove, Regan said, "It's freaking seven-thirty in the morning. How is that late?"

Dave looped an arm around V's shoulders. "This one insisted we went to her place last night to finish packing. Then we had to get up at five o'clock to go by Rae's and grab her stuff too."

Van stifled a laugh as Regan fought against her gratitude for V's help. She tugged on her hair and twisted her lips to the side. "You understand that key I gave you was for emergencies, right?" There was no actual heat behind her question though.

V sniffed. "How is the fact that you have no clothes here when we're leaving for vacation *not* an emergency?"

Regan groaned but crossed over and gave V a hug. With a shake of her head, she said, "Please tell me you packed the black bikini I had laid out," she said.

Van's ears perked up, and he envisioned Regan in scraps of black held together by tiny strings.

V returned Regan's hug. "Duh," she said. "I threw in the white strappy one next to it too."

Van's imagination ran wild, conjuring a picture of straps crisscrossing over Regan's toned stomach and possibly running between the cheeks of her firm ass. He had to get control of himself. Otherwise, everyone would know how much he looked forward to her bikinis. He cleared his throat, and V glanced at him. Her bright-blue eyes homed in on him while her lips twitched impishly.

"You disappeared last night," she said. Her sapphire gaze shifted to Regan. "So did you."

V paused, awaiting an answer that Regan refused to give. Van would volunteer nothing. He heard Kez try to disguise a snicker with a cough. When it was apparent Regan would not break and confess, V turned to Van. She didn't speak, just leveled those baby blues at him in part question and part command. Van prayed for strength.

Undeterred by his silence, V slid onto a bar stool. When she continued to stare at him, Van regretted his decision to saunter out shirtless. He'd done it to goad Regan, but now, being the focus of her two best friends made him long for a shirt. Or possibly a bulletproof vest.

Dave slid a mug of coffee to V. She accepted it with a smile and lifted it to her lips. "Should be an interesting flight."

Van stepped away from the counter and said, "I'm gonna go grab a shower."

"And a shirt?" asked V. Their laughter followed him out of the kitchen.

# 13

*An* hour later, the women stood in the driveway watching the guys and the Uber driver wedge all the luggage in the car while still leaving room for the six of them. Their efforts to fill the car resembled a game of Tetris. After a shower and a second cup of coffee served with toast V made, Rae was rejuvenated. Her headache was gone, and she no longer worried about needing to use the little white bag in the seatback after takeoff.

Kez discretely pulled a twenty from her purse while admiring her husband's backside. "I'll bet you twenty bucks Jackson asks how many shoes I packed in the next thirty seconds."

"I'm not taking a sucker bet," said Rae. "I'm surprised he hasn't already asked why you need so much stuff, given his plan to keep you naked."

With a grin, Kez tucked away the twenty. "Half of the fun is unwrapping the present," she said.

V laughed. "Plus, he's got to know that at least one of those bags has nothing but either lingerie or itty-bitty swimsuits in it."

Kez slid her arms through each of her two friends' and sighed, "I'm so glad you are coming with us." She glanced sideways to Rae. "You're good with this, right?"

From behind her large sunglasses, Rae watched Van load luggage into the car, taking in the flex of taut muscles under his T-shirt as he shifted bags around. "I still think you're crazy for inviting us on your honeymoon, but who am I to judge? After all, I'm the one about to spend a week in the islands with my ex-boyfriend that I haven't seen in years." She shrugged. "What could go wrong?"

"You have separate rooms," Kez offered in half-hearted comfort.

Rae lowered her glasses and looked at Kez, being careful to keep her voice low. She doubted Van could hear them, given that he and Jackson were locked in a boisterous exchange about which bag to put where, but she wasn't taking any chances. "We were in bed together within hours of seeing each other again."

Bits and pieces of the night before came back to her, like watching a movie through a gauzy curtain with someone else choosing what scenes to play. She couldn't recall what happened on that swing but knew *something* had. Van had been a little too cagey while answering her questions. Plus, a hot guy combined with good booze usually added up to one thing. Except she'd had a little *too* much good booze to be an open and willing participant in anything. Van wouldn't do that to her though. She knew that without question. He was a lying snake, not a total piece of shit.

According to Kez, after getting Van's text, she and Jackson had come to the guest room and found Rae sleeping soundly in her bridesmaid's dress. Kez had supplied the pajamas *and* been the one to dress her. Rae was, according to Jackson, resistant to moving out of Van's room. She'd crawled back in bed, flipped them all off, and fallen back asleep. Van assured them he would take care of her, and they'd gone off to enjoy their wedding night.

"Well, last night was . . ." V labored to put her thoughts into words. "An aberration," she finished. "I mean, weird stuff was happening all over the place. Hell, Kez got freaking married!"

The sound of a door slamming brought their attention back to the SUV. The guys and their driver leaned against the hatch, looking pleased with themselves.

"Watch this," Kez said out of the side of her mouth. She held up a small carry-on. In a louder, fake sweet voice, she asked, "I guess this is a bad time to ask if anything else will fit?"

The men groaned in unison, and Jackson prowled up the drive. Beneath his beard, his mouth was a firm line of disapproval. Rae heard Kez swallow back her laughter at her new husband's overly stern appearance. When he reached them, Jackson said, "The only other things going in this car are the six of us. And that's if no one breathes the entire way to the airport."

Undeterred by his gruff growl, Kez rose onto her toes and whispered something in his ear. Jackson's head jerked back, eyes wide. "Are you serious?" he asked. She gave a sly nod. He snatched the bag from her hand. "Van can ride on the roof," he said and spun toward the car, taking the small bag with him.

Rae gave Kez a knowing look. "Sex toys or lingerie?"

"What makes you think it's not both?" Kez smirked and headed to the car.

"You're terrible," V called after her, but even Miss Prim and Proper had to laugh at Kez getting Jackson's goat so easily.

When they exited the car at the airport, it was reminiscent of the old gag of paper streamers popping out of a fake can of peanut brittle. Van was the shortest of the guys, and even he'd ridden with his knees at his chest. Rae wasn't sure how Jackson had contorted himself into the SUV. They exploded from the confines of the vehicle like circus clowns as soon as the driver pulled to the curb.

Jackson stood and stretched, his T-shirt riding up and giving everyone a glimpse of toned abs and a snippet of his tattoos. Kez, newlywed that she was, couldn't resist running a finger over that strip of skin. He caught her hand and kissed her fingertips. Rae watched their exchange, wondering for the thousandth time why they'd planned a group honeymoon. If it were her, she wouldn't spend any time clothed, much less with other people.

Turning away from the public groping, her eyes landed on Van. He was working the kinks out of his back. When he laced his fingers behind his head and leaned back, Rae noticed the tattoos on the underside of his biceps. *Those are new*, she thought. She'd been too distracted by her own mortification earlier to see them.

"Enjoying the view?" V whispered in her ear.

Rae yelped at her friend's sudden appearance next to her. "Jesus Christ, V! Are you trying to give me a heart attack?"

V's blue eyes danced merrily at Rae's over-the-top reaction. She nodded discretely at Van. "Seems like you might be thawing a little toward Mr. FBI."

"I wouldn't say that," Rae responded, making a point to turn away from him.

Kez stepped over to them. "You girls ready for some white sand and blue water?"

Rae snorted. "Like you'll leave the room to see it."

A wanton smile lifted the corners of Kez's mouth. "I'll at least see it out the window," she said.

V rolled her eyes, but Rae stopped her. "Don't act like you have any room to judge, Doc. Dave is going to be serving you several specialty *cock*tails while we're there."

V blushed and Kez laughed. Dave came up and put an arm around V's waist. "What are you girls laughing about?" he asked, making V turn even redder.

Rae laughed harder and pushed her sunglasses up into her hair. "Nothing for you to worry about, Dave."

Van came up to them, loaded down with baggage. "Any time she says not to worry about something, that's when you should worry," he said, dropping several bags onto the sidewalk.

Rae's laugh died and her lips flattened into a thin line. "Don't presume to know me anymore, McLeod." Turning on her heel, she strode through the automatic doors.

Van watched Regan walk away from him, her carry-on bouncing with the swivel of her hips. He ran a hand down his face and looked heavenward. Jackson clapped a hand to his shoulder, but it was Kez who spoke.

"Few men get a second chance presented on a silver platter, complete with first-class tickets to paradise," she said. Her eyes darkened as she continued, "Don't screw it up."

"I'm trying not to," he said, doing his best not to whine.

"Try harder," she said sharply and followed Regan into the airport.

Van felt Jackson's hand tighten on his shoulder. "My wife better be in our honeymoon suite tonight, Van. Not busy giving Rae a shoulder to cry on."

V laughed. "I think you mean, you hope she's not a shoulder for Rae to lean on while she stumbles back to her room." She fixed Van with an almost pitying look. At least, it would've been but for the gibe she launched next. "Although Rae's never had a problem finding a brawny arm to help guide her home after a night out."

Van's guts twisted at her innuendo.

"V," Dave said in a chastising tone.

She looked at him unrepentantly. "What? You know Rae, and you know I'm right." Her mouth twisted in a wry grin. "And you saw the bathing suits I packed for her. Rae won't be lacking for *any* attention once we get to the resort." V's eyes practically burned a hole through Van. "That, you can be sure of."

Once she, too, went inside the airport, the men stood around the mountain of baggage. Jackson's hand remained on Van's shoulder, and he slumped dejectedly. Dave and Jackson exchanged a quick look. A tremor of unease worked its way up Van's spine at their tense expressions. "What?" he asked.

"You've stirred up the hive," said Dave. Van didn't know the guy well but had the sense Dave rolled with the punches and let little worry him. There was something bigger at play here.

"What the hell does that mean?" Van asked. He dragged a nervous hand through his hair as he waited for the answer.

Jackson signaled a skycap and said, "What Dave means is that both his girlfriend and my wife want Rae to be happy. They've spent the past several years trying to get her to open up about why she never dates." A guy in blue pants and a matching vest walked up and gulped when he saw the amount of luggage. Jackson gave him an encouraging smile and a fifty-dollar bill. "Make sure it all gets inside, okay?"

Delighted, the man pocketed the money. "Yes sir!" he said and started organizing the various suitcases, duffels, and bags.

Jackson resumed their conversation. "So, after all this time of her dodging and refusing to answer questions, boom"—he clapped his hands together in emphasis—"here you drop out of the sky. The answer to those questions and, according to Kez, the source of many more. She thinks, and I'm sure V agrees, you're the reason Rae won't get serious with anyone."

Van's heart latched onto this bit of news. "Regan hasn't dated at all?" Dave and Jackson cringed. Van's optimism stymied. "What?"

"He's your buddy," said Dave to Jackson.

Jackson swore under his breath but answered Van's question. "No, Rae doesn't 'date.' She . . ." He paused, seemingly calculating his response and looking wholly uncomfortable with the topic.

"She what?" Van asked, all at once dying to know and hating to hear the answer. It wasn't like she'd been a wallflower when they met, and she'd made it perfectly clear she hadn't turned to a nunnery to seek solace from their breakup. He'd expected to hear that she'd dated some, but at the same time, the idea of her with someone else sat like a brick in his gut.

"She hooks up," Dave finished. "A lot."

Van's head jerked toward Dave. It wasn't that different from what Regan herself said the night before, but it didn't make it easier to hear. Reflexively, he took a step toward Dave, but Jackson held out an arm and stopped him. "Calm down, man," he said. "He doesn't mean it like that."

Dave held his hands out in a reassuring gesture, his face apologetic. "Not at all, man. I swear. I like Rae. She's one badass chick. But she's as big a player as any guy I've ever met. Love 'em and leave 'em is the style I've seen."

"I don't get the sense 'love' has been a factor for Rae in a long time," Jackson said.

Van's stomach revolted at that thought, chased by a crushing wave of guilt. He bore some responsibility, maybe even all of it, for her withdrawing further into herself. Regan had always been guarded about her emotions, but she'd let *him* all the way into her life. She'd loved him—he knew that. And look what that had gotten her. The shame was all-consuming, dragging him so far under he might drown in it. God, he'd screwed up so badly back then. Was it even possible for him to remedy the damage?

"So, anyway," Jackson went on, "the girls are deciding whether to help you get her back."

"And if they decide against it?" Van already knew the answer.

"Let's say they'll make sure this vacation is anything but pleasant for you," Jackson said.

Dave shuddered. "They're vicious, dude. I mean, I love V more than anything, but her and Kez together and happy are scary enough. The two of them pissed at you . . ." He shook his head. "It was nice knowing you."

*Fucking perfect,* Van thought. "What do I do?" he asked.

"You've got a week to figure that out," said Jackson. He gestured for Van to go in front of him. "Time's a wastin'."

# 14

At the bar in the first-class lounge, Rae felt that same cosmic shift in the air. The atmosphere in the room heated with an almost electric charge. It rippled over her skin and settled in her chest before sliding lower. How could he still have such an effect on her? Bracing herself against the flood of awareness caused by Van simply entering the room, Rae concentrated on ignoring both him and the stupid, giddy sensations coursing through her. The bartender, a delicious mix of dark skin and light eyes, smiled as he placed three champagne flutes in front of her.

"Here you go, beautiful," he said with a wink.

She smiled back at him. "Thank you,"—her eyes flicked to his nametag—"Henry."

Those pretty eyes crinkled at the corners. "Please let me know if I can get you *anything* else," he said.

The back of her neck tingled right before Van's forearms materialized on either side of her. "Let me help you with those," he said, his words tickling her ear. That stupidly familiar *zing!* spiked through her. It pulsed lower at the familiar scent of his cologne. A memory from the night before skittered across her consciousness. Her leaning into him on the swing last night, snuggling against him and kissing his throat. With a decisive shake of her head, she chased the thought away, but the longing lingered.

*Get it together, girl,* Rae thought. *Think unsexy thoughts. Long division, baboon butts, garbage disposals.* She took one glass, allowing Van to carry the others. After a small sip of the bubbly liquid, she faced him. "Thank you," she said, using her old trick of looking over his shoulder rather than directly at him. Locking eyes with him now might make her burst into flames or ravage him in the closest closet.

He shifted and let her lead the way to join the rest of their party. Rae could feel his stare on her back. Well, really her ass, so she did what came naturally—added an extra shimmy to her hips. No reason for her to be the only one hanging on by a thread here. Thank God her trainer was a fan of squats, she thought.

"Happy honeymoon!" Rae called out cheerfully when they reached the table. Van handed glasses to her friends, and the three of them clinked the crystal.

Dave looked at Van with a false pout. "What, none for us?" he asked with a laugh.

Van shrugged and looked at Rae. "I had my hands full."

From her place on Jackson's lap, Kez said, "Oh yeah, you do."

Rae glared at her friend, but Kez grinned and curled closer to her husband. She'd wrapped around him like kudzu, sinking into a newlywed love bubble. V wasn't much better, although rather than using Dave as a recliner, she perched daintily on his knee. That left two chairs, and Rae dropped into the closest one. Van settled into the chair across from her.

Ignoring him, she took a long drink of champagne and asked Kez, "What's the plan for the week? Other than sun, sand, and sex?"

"Do we need plans beyond that?" asked Jackson. He made Rae think of a pirate in disguise, his semi-preppy T-shirt and khaki shorts contrasting starkly with his full beard and tattoos. Roguish was a good word for him, she thought. He always looked like he had something up his sleeve.

Rae gave him a wicked grin. "I don't." Van's knee hit the underside of the table with a *thunk*, making her glass wobble. *Gotcha,* she thought, overcome with a need to see him squirm. He'd been so sure of himself this morning, with that shirtless schtick. If she were honest, it had worked just like he'd hoped. She'd been privately salivating over him all morning. Now was the time to take him down a few pegs. Remind him who was in charge. And also remind *herself* she was the one driving this crazy train. No matter how mixed up or confused he made her, nothing was completely out of her control. She could handle this.

"No," she said, twisting the stem of her glass, "I can't argue against a week of nothing but long days by the pool and longer nights with the guy you met at the pool." Van's hands wrapped so tightly around the arms of his chair, she could see the whites of his knuckles from across the table. This was like using a sawed-off shotgun to shoot fish in a barrel.

"Makes me think of our Bermuda trip," Rae said, noting Van's ears perk up like a golden retriever. She had his attention now.

V laughed. "Oh God, that was a fun weekend." She snuck a glance at Van and winked surreptitiously at Rae, letting her know she knew what Rae was up to. She tapped a blunt but still manicured nail to her chin. "What was the name of that guy?"

"Which one?" Rae asked. From the corner of her eye, she saw Van's mouth turn down, and if he didn't loosen his grip, he was going to snap the arms off his chair. She knew V could see it, too, as she kept going with the story.

"You know, the Scottish one." She scrunched her nose in thought then snapped her fingers. "Fergus! That was his name."

Kez got into the act. "Oh yeah, the dive instructor."

Van looked like he was going to burst a blood vessel. Not so cocky now, was he?

Jackson squeezed Kez's hip. "Dive instructor?" he asked, his baritone dipping to a low growl.

Kez stroked his arm. "Down boy," she said. "Fergus only had eyes for Rae. Probably because she was topless ninety percent of the time."

Rae hummed, continuing to side-eye Van. "He was a very *hands-on* instructor," she said and licked her bottom lip.

Van shoved back his chair and surged to his feet. "I—" he started but didn't finish, looking simultaneously pissed off and completely lost.

In pretend embarrassment, Rae put a hand to her chest and finally looked directly at him. "Oh, I'm sorry," she said. When the tension in his shoulders eased a little at her words, she delivered the kill strike. "I had forgotten you were even here." Rae knew the moment her words hit the target when the wounded bleakness flashed across Van's strong features.

Quickly, he shuttered his expression into a bland facade. "This was a mistake," he said and left the table.

"Something I said?" Rae called after him, unable to keep the evil glee from her voice.

Jackson shifted Kez off his lap and stood, rubbing a hand over his beard. His eyes held a touch of rebuke when he looked down at Rae, and a tiny sliver of guilt pricked at her heart. Maybe that last part went too far.

"I won't defend him, Rae," Jackson said. "But just consider hearing him out before spending the next few days raking him over the coals left behind from the inferno that ended what you two had."

Rae was at a loss for words when Jackson jogged off to catch Van. Kez took the seat he'd vacated and Rae's hand. Breaking the silence that enveloped the table, she said, "Just because I married him doesn't mean we agree on everything."

"Maybe I should . . ." Dave waved a hand toward Jackson and Van.

V popped off his lap. "Go ahead, babe," she encouraged.

Once he left, Rae released Kez's fingers and leaned back in her chair. She took a sip of champagne then asked, "Is it wrong to want him to hurt, maybe even bleed a little?"

Kez shook her head, red hair tumbling over her shoulders. "No, ma'am. If I were you, I'd want to crush him like a bug."

V nodded. "Same here," she said, but Rae could tell her heart wasn't in it. V was the most emotionally in tune of them. She considered the feelings of others to a much greater degree than either Kez or Rae.

"Why don't I think you mean that?" Rae asked.

"Well," V said, switching into psych mode, "from what you told us, it sounds like you bolted after finding out the truth."

"Can you blame me?" Rae asked, her defenses rising.

"No," V said slowly. "But I can worry about you. I know he's the reason you're spooked about relationships. We didn't know the pre-Van Rae, but something tells me she might have kept a guy around for more than the occasional booty call."

"Not that we are judging either pre- or post-Van Rae. Both chicks rock," Kez added.

"Sure," V agreed. "I'm not saying anything to the contrary. But I don't want to see you trapped in this headspace forever. Maybe talking to Van will free you up to a certain extent. Even if you don't give him another chance, it at least lets you move on from that time in your life knowing you've gotten the full story."

Their description of a pre- and post-Van version of herself wasn't too far off the mark. She'd dated other guys before Van, but nothing serious. It wasn't because she'd been diametrically opposed to having someone special in her life. She'd been busy, first with school then with work. Allocating a slice of her already-full plate to a guy hadn't ranked high in her list of priorities. Until Van. He had been the first one she'd believed worth the investment. The returns on *that* had been abysmal, so she'd pulled everything out of the emotional market, content to dabble solely in . . . short-term, high-yield assets. Which worked, so long as you didn't hold onto them for long and kept a varied portfolio. V was advocating for a reevaluation of her strategy and an accompanying shift to a more stable, less speculative approach.

Kez reached out once again and placed a hand over Rae's. "I have to agree with V on this one," she said. "You owe him nothing, but you owe it to yourself to take every chance for happiness. Whether it's with Van or someone else."

V put her hand on top of theirs. "But whatever you decide, we'll be here for you."

"Hold up, man!" Van heard Jackson call from behind him. He was almost to the exit. Part of him wanted to keep going without looking back, but he couldn't do that to Jackson. The guy was starting his honeymoon, for Christ's sake. So Van stopped and waited for him.

"My coming on this trip was a mistake," Van said when Jackson reached him.

"No, what you're doing right now is a mistake."

Van recoiled, still smarting from Regan's earlier cut. "You heard her, right? She's over there fantasizing about some kilt-wearing motherfucker right in front of me!"

Jackson snorted and rolled his eyes. "And here I thought you'd dated Rae." He jerked a thumb over his shoulder toward the table they'd just left. "The pretty brunette with green eyes sitting over there. You dated her, right?"

Van wasn't in the mood for games. "What are you trying to say, man?"

"That if you dated her, if you love her like you claim to, then you know she absolutely *lives* to get under people's skin."

Van shook off his anger and considered what Jackson was saying, trying not to pin too much hope on the idea that Regan's story had been fictional. He had no doubt the girls had gone to Bermuda or that they'd garnered a lot of male attention while there. Maybe, though, she'd embellished her dalliance with the Scotsman solely for Van's benefit.

"She's fucking with you, dude!" Jackson confirmed, earning a dirty look from an elderly couple entering the lounge. He ducked his head in apology then continued in a lower tone, "She's fucking with you, and you're letting her. I don't know her as well as you did once, but there is no force in the world that can make Rae do something or go somewhere she doesn't want to. If she didn't want to be here, she wouldn't be." He slapped Van on the back. "She might not admit it, but Rae wants to be here, Van. You just need to remind her why."

Renewed resolve formed deep within Van, fortifying him to withstand the war of words Regan had started. Jackson was right. While Regan did want him to hurt like he'd hurt her, she'd had the chance to tell him not to come. He'd offered as much the night before, and she'd refused it. Which, at the very least, meant she no longer hated the very sight of him. It would be a tough road this week, for sure. He didn't doubt for a second that she would push him to the brink, but once there, he'd get her to tumble over with him.

"There they are," Jackson said.

"Huh?" asked Van, confused.

"Your balls. You finally found them." Jackson's only reaction to Van's shove was a loud laugh. "C'mon, dumbass."

❧

An hour later, Van sat next to Regan in first class. To the casual observer, she appeared disinterested in him, but even after all this time, he could read her body language. He saw her reaction to him in her stilted posture and the tension surrounding her full lips. She wasn't the only one affected. Nerves dampened his palms like he was getting ready to knock on the door of his high school crush.

A flight attendant leaned into their row. "Can I get you anything?" she asked with a polite smile.

Regan tucked her sunglasses into her bag and pushed it under the seat before she answered. "I'd love a glass of champagne," she said.

"Certainly," the woman replied then looked at Van. "Anything for you, sir?"

He gave her his double-dimple smile. "Champagne sounds good, thanks."

Her eyes twinkled. "Are you two celebrating something?"

Regan answered for him. "We're here with our friends who got married yesterday. Sort of a group honeymoon."

"Oh, how nice! Where are the newlyweds?"

Van pointed behind them. "They're two rows behind us. They'll be the ones that can't keep their hands off each other." He lowered his voice to a whisper. "I'd keep a close watch on the first-class lavatory if I were you."

The attendant laughed. "Thanks for the tip," she said. "I'll be right back with your drinks."

Silence descended between Van and Regan. He needed to break it, but his mind was blank. After their stolen moment together on the porch, he knew she still wanted him. But she'd made it clear, even while hammered, that despite being physically drawn to him, old anger at his deception was alive and well in her heart. "Hate" had been her word of choice. He abhorred the thought of her spending the last few years despising him while all he'd done was long to fix the mess he'd made of their lives. Fate, or rather Kez and Jackson's generosity, had handed him that chance, and now here he was, tongue-tied and afraid to take it.

"Here you are," the flight attendant said as she reappeared with stemless plastic champagne flutes. He and Regan each took one from her.

"Thank you," Regan said, and Van nodded.

"My name is Mary. Let me know you need anything. I think it's such a sweet idea to take a couples' trip as a honeymoon," she chirped.

"Oh, we're not . . ." Regan said but was talking to Mary's back as she walked to the galley. "Together," she finished quietly.

She lifted her glass, but Van put a hand on her wrist, stopping her before she could take a sip. Her forearm twisted in his hand, and she frowned. "What are you doing, McLeod?"

He touched his glass to hers, the plastic making a weak tap. "Cheers," he said. "To new beginnings."

When their eyes met over the cheap glassware, he didn't think she would say anything. A shadow passed over her eyes so quickly he might've imagined it. Then she tapped her glass to his. "Cheers," she said.

Van watched her elegant throat move as she swallowed. Even in her casual outfit of white shorts and green tank, she had a regal air about her. She crossed her legs, and Van couldn't help but appreciate the expanse of slender thigh that appeared as her shorts rose with her shifting posture.

"Eyes up here, McLeod," Regan said, and he jerked his gaze away from her legs and met cool green eyes. They were lighter this morning, mossy instead of emerald, which he took as a good sign. In the past, they'd gone darker when she was angry. She curved her upper body, tucking her shoulder against the side of the plane. Her leg brushed against his, and his skin pulsed at the incidental touch.

"So," she said, looking into her drink instead of at him. "We'll be in each other's presence for the next week. I, for one, am not inclined to let what happened between the two of us wreck my week in paradise. You and I"—she flipped a finger back and forth between them—"need to coexist without either killing each other or making everyone around us miserable."

Other passengers walked by their seats as they boarded the plane, but Van blocked out the ambient noise and focused on Regan. "I agree with that."

Her eyes hardened with her next words. "But don't mistake some veneer of decorum for forgiveness. It doesn't mean I've forgotten what you did. It means I'm going to tolerate you so I don't ruin my best friend's honeymoon. Are we clear on that?"

He nodded, taking whatever morsel she tossed in his direction. "I would like to ask one thing of you though," he said.

She scoffed. "You've got balls, McLeod, I'll give you that." After a brief pause, she asked, "Well, what is it?"

Van smiled, his lips feeling tight around his teeth and his mouth dry from nerves. *No guts, no glory,* he thought then plunged ahead with his request. "It's really two things." An eye roll was her only response, so he kept going. "First, would it be too much to ask you to call me Van?"

Her smile was thin and brittle when she answered, "My calling you a wrong name never bothered you before."

Refusing to take the bait, he said, "Please, Regan."

In a huff, she said, "Fine, *Van.* What else?"

This was the big ask. He knew she'd want to refuse, but he had to try. Wiping his hands against the fabric of his shorts, he said, "I'd like for you to give me at least one actual shot to explain everything."

Van imagined her bones clacking into place when her whole body went rigid at his question. She didn't respond, just looked out the window, as though the right answer were out there suspended on a cloud. He held his breath, waiting for her to say something. If she said no, he wasn't sure what he would do. He could ambush her while they were down here, try to make her hear him out. But he knew that wouldn't work. Even if it could, that wasn't how he wanted to handle it. He needed her to *want* to hear his explanation. Otherwise, he could talk until he was blue in the face, and it wouldn't do any good. If he forced the issue, anything he said would fall on deaf ears. If she were willing to listen, it could lead to a different, maybe better result. One that involved having her in his arms and in his life again.

Regan set her drink on the tray in front of them and crossed her arms over her chest. When she looked at him, her expression was impassive, except for her eyes. There was a challenge in them, and he vowed to meet it, whatever it was. "Prove you deserve one," she said.

Confusion wrinkled his brow. "What?"

"You want a chance to 'explain,'" she said, hooking her fingers around the word. "You have to prove you deserve it."

Van battled against the feeling of hope that grew with every inch she gave. He couldn't afford to be too confident. They had miles to go before reaching solid ground with each other. "How do I do that?" he asked.

She lifted one shoulder in response, seemingly uninterested in how he would achieve the task she'd given. "That's for you to figure out. Those are the terms, McL—" Regan pulled her lips between her teeth for a second then said, "Van. Take it or leave it."

"I'll take it," he blurted out, eager for any chance at all. When a feline smile of satisfaction curled over her lips, Van knew he was well and truly fucked. And he couldn't care less.

15

*Rae* flipped her tray table down to accept her in-flight meal. A *full* pour of white wine accompanied her serving of grilled chicken with artichokes, more than making up for eating with miniature plastic utensils. Van had the short ribs and a Woodford Reserve, neat.

Once she'd thrown down her "prove it" condition, they'd settled into somewhat of a détente for the balance of the flight. They engaged in surface conversation about things of little substance. It was a polite facade that scraped over Rae's already raw nerves. Snapping and snarling at Van over their past was preferable to stilted discussions about weather in the Caymans or the inferior quality of airline blankets.

She considered asking him what he'd been up to the past five years, but pride made her hold her tongue. She didn't want Van to think she harbored any curiosity about him. But her steadfast refusal to admit any real interest in his life or entertain his brief attempt to delve into hers left them with a banal politeness that had her climbing the walls.

*Screw this,* she thought. It was time to make her own in-flight entertainment, using a tactic she liked to call "Go Fish." Letting her arm graze leisurely along Van's, she leaned across her seat and picked up his drink.

She saw the hairs rise on his forearm at the brush of hers and hid her grin. He'd been about to take a bite, but the tines of his fork stopped before touching his lips.

Rae tilted the glass toward him in question. "You don't mind if I steal a taste, do you?"

Van's eyes dropped to her mouth, and she wet her lips. His pupils dilated, the dark contrast with his raw amber irises resemblant of a solar eclipse. She toggled the glass back and forth. *Hook's in the water.* Wishing the plastic cup was a heavier crystal tumbler, she gave the decadent liquid a small swirl. The "tic-tic" against the plastic wasn't as satisfying as the tinkle of ice against crystal, but it would do.

Van cleared his throat, his fork hanging forgotten in midair. "No, go ahead."

Rae lifted the glass and, right before taking a swallow, darted her tongue out along the rim. *Wiggle the bait.* Over the lip of the cup, she watched him, taking in the tightness of his jaw and the heat in his eyes. "Don't want to smear my lipstick," she said, her voice low and sultry.

The bite of beef slipped from Van's fork and hit his plate with a soft *plop*. The fork followed suit, clattering on his tray as he set it down— too focused on her to continue eating. Tilting the cup back, she took a small drink. The bourbon hit her tongue with the expected sharp bite, tempered by a delicate hint of caramel before coasting down her throat, coating it with sweet, spicy heat. "Mmm," she closed her eyes in appreciation of the rich flavor.

She heard Van make a strangled noise and opened her eyes. "God, that's good," she said. "All you have to do is open up and let it glide over your tongue." She watched his chest expand as he inhaled slowly, eyes never leaving her mouth. *Fish on the line.*

Again, Rae leaned into his space to put the bourbon back. She flipped her hair over her shoulder and looked at him, eyes half-closed.

"Thanks for the taste, Van," she said. "Let me know if I can return the favor." *Here's the tricky part. Reel slowly, so you don't lose it.*

Lust at its most primitive glittered in his eyes, but he didn't move. "You'd give me a taste, Regan?" The question was a rasping whisper, as though forced from his lips.

She fanned her lashes at him. "Of course." *Almost in the boat. Easy does it.* Rae rested her chin in her hand, her elbow on the armrest between them. A tiny lean to the right had their arms touching ever so slightly, making her shiver a little at the contact. And reminding her not to get too cocky, or she'd lose the game she'd started.

Van's Adam's apple bobbed jerkily. Then he licked his lips and leaned toward her. "Regan?" he asked, breath warm on her cheek.

"Yes," she replied. Inches separated their faces, and his cologne wove its way into her nose, tickling her memory. *Focus, don't let it off the hook.*

He dropped his head infinitesimally closer to hers. "About that taste." His eyes were molten swirls of the darkest chocolate. She'd almost forgotten the way they shifted colors with his moods, dark to light and back again.

"Mm-hmm," she said, biting her lower lip. "Would you like one?"

His hand brushed hers. "I think you know I would."

She pulled back into her own seat. Plucking her wineglass from her tray, she handed it over to him. "Here you go," she said sweetly. "I mean, it's basic white wine, but you're welcome to a taste of it."

Van blinked slowly, the yearning in his eyes muddling to uncertainty. He looked from the offered glass of wine to her face, not yet comprehending what just happened. She grinned in triumph. *Hook, line, and sinker!* Van flopped on the bottom of the boat, gasping at his predicament, tricked by her shiny lures and ready to be fileted.

She thought he would at least be annoyed with her antics, maybe even pissed at her teasing him like that. Which made the smile spreading across his face unexpected. The booming laugh that followed was infectious, and she joined in.

Van took the proffered wineglass from her hand. "Well played, Regan, well played," he said. Then he sipped what was likely an eight-dollar bottle of wine. His lips pursed like he'd just sucked on a lemon, and he set the glass back on her tray. "I think I'll stick with my choice," he said.

"Can't blame you there," she replied.

The tension between them was broken. Rae was far from comfortable, but being near Van no longer made her feel like crawling out of her skin. It was a start.

Once they finished their meals and Mary cleared their plates, Rae pulled a small throw from her bag. She'd learned long ago to pack a light blanket, because the airlines often seemed determined to freeze you to death. Rummaging deeper in her bag, she found her sunglasses and slipped them on. Tucking her feet underneath her and a pillow against the side of the plane, she burrowed back into her seat, the throw draped over her. They still had an hour before landing, so she was going to try for a catnap.

From behind her sunglasses, Rae watched Van stand up and stretch. The man hadn't skipped the gym much, if at all. Rae's fingers twitched with the urge to trace the *V* shape peeking out from the waistband of his shorts. Van was still fine as hell. The memory of him in bed that morning replayed in her head—lines of muscle, ridges of abs. The way he'd stretched over her in the bathroom doorway, displaying himself for her unfettered perusal and his sexy smirk when she'd done just that. And now, she was en route to spend a week with him in nothing but board shorts, glistening with sweat and sunscreen. All of it made her mouth water and her skin heat, with certain other parts growing more interested by the minute.

"Regan?" Van asked. She shook her head, wrenched from her attempts to mentally map out the lines of his body. Judging by the look on his face, he'd said her name more than once.

"Sorry, what?" she asked, lifting her sunglasses.

He held out a package of Swedish Fish. The plastic crinkled as he shook it in her direction. "These used to be your favorite," he said. "That still the case?"

When they were together, he brought her some of the cherry-flavored gummies every Friday at lunch. Even if she'd been out of the office, upon her return, the bright-yellow package rested in the middle of her desk. Most of the time, there was a note. Sometimes it was a bouquet of flowers. Rae hadn't thought of that sweet gesture, or others like it, in a long time. Surprisingly, her heart didn't harden against the memory.

She took the candy from his outstretched hand with a tentative smile. "You remember that?"

He smiled ruefully. "I remember everything, Regan."

This would usually be her cue to make a snarky comment like, *"Except for your real name,"* but she didn't. Maybe her resistance was worn down by the replay of the morning, or the way he'd laughed at her little prank earlier, or maybe in that moment she was just tired of pushing against the door keeping him out. Whichever it was, she didn't unleash a scathing reproach or cutting remark. Instead, she let herself enjoy having a cute boy hand over her favorite candy.

Van watched Regan tear open the cellophane and pop a small red fish in her mouth. She hummed in enjoyment.

"Still good?" he asked.

Regan nodded and tilted the open end of the small bag toward him. "Want one?"

His fingers were a lot thicker than hers, so he eased the opening wider and picked up some of the candies. As he chewed, he watched her sample a few more, then put the bag in her purse.

"I'll save those for later," she said. With a look that would be called shy on anyone else, she said, "Thank you." It was a small two-word phrase, but the way his heart reacted to it, you'd think she'd agreed to marry him. He had a long way to go, but she was talking to him—not hurling insults his way and then stomping off. It wasn't much, but it was something, and he celebrated the minor victory.

Regan lowered her sunglasses over her eyes and curled back into her corner. Taking a chance, he flipped up the armrest that sat between them. "Hey, Regan?" he said, crossing his fingers that he wasn't pushing too hard, too fast with what he was about to do.

She looked over, or at least he thought she did, since her dark glasses hid her eyes. "Yeah?" she asked.

He tapped his thigh with one hand. "If you want to stretch out a bit, I wouldn't mind."

She didn't immediately respond, picking at the blanket covering her legs and nibbling her lower lip. Finally, she said, "Van, I don't—"

Van jumped in before she could finish. "I'm just making the offer, no ulterior motives." That was a complete lie. Her feet in his lap provided an innocent way for him to touch her. Although, judging by her hesitation, she wasn't fooled. She knew he wanted her. That was how she'd gotten him to fall for that little "taste" production she put on earlier.

They sat silently for a few seconds, and then her pink-painted toes peeked out from under the blanket. She slowly slid one foot, then the other across the seat and into his lap. He pulled the blanket down to cover her feet.

Under the blanket, Van eased off one of her flip-flops. When his fingers curled around a slender ankle, Regan jerked and tried to pull her foot from his grasp, but he held on. "Just relax, Regan," he said while he used his other hand to massage the instep of her foot. He felt her tense in resistance and pressed a little harder right at the ball of her foot. She gave a soft groan and let go, sinking farther into her seat.

"See, it's not so bad, right?" he asked, using both thumbs to rub against the arch of her foot.

"I've had worse," she said, with a begrudging smile.

He glared at her and tickled her foot, making her yelp and try again to pull away. They shared an easy smile, and he kicked himself for the millionth time for letting her slip away. No, that wasn't a fair characterization, because it implied she caused their split. That had been all on him.

The night she left, Van had heard her come in. At least, he thought he had. He'd called to her, but there was no answer. In their bedroom, he found his briefcase open on the bed with his badge tossed down on it. His vision pinpointed down to a five-inch circle around that badge. Never in his life had he experienced the innate dread that swallowed him that night. It devoured his heart in one gulp, its voracious fangs tearing the rest of him to shreds. He'd lost the most important person in his life because he'd been too scared to tell her the truth. Too scared she'd leave him. In the end, it happened anyway, and he was left with only his own cowardice for company.

The worst of it had been the look on her face when he confirmed what she'd found out. Disbelief, pain, and anger had all been there, but also a fierce longing when she asked who he was. It signaled how badly she wanted him to give a different answer than the one she expected. To say he was Ray Edwards, the easy-going guy she'd met at the little café. That he hadn't orchestrated their meeting to use her to get to her boss.

When he didn't deny what she'd discovered, all hope vanished from her face in a blink. And then, she was gone.

He couldn't track her down wearing nothing but a towel, so he'd rushed to change. In the three minutes it took him to get dressed, he lost her. They were days away from making an arrest, and he couldn't drop everything to find her. His only option was to finish the case. Of course, he'd alerted his superiors that she'd blown his cover. So they sent other agents into her office to make sure she didn't tip off her boss. It was a waste of resources. She never came back to the office. She snuck back into their condo at some point to get her stuff, except for her phone, then she simply vanished.

As soon as the Hasselhoff arrest happened, Van should've tried to find her. He'd justified his failure to do so by telling himself it wouldn't do any good. That there was nothing he could say to explain his lies, that would bring her back to him. His inaction when he'd had the chance had doomed their relationship, and it wouldn't be fair to try to find her and make her relive his betrayal. But that was a bullshit excuse, and he knew it. He could've found her, could've pled his case to her. And it wasn't *her* he was trying to spare from reliving it but himself. The truth was he couldn't face her or the possibility of her rejection.

What he did instead of going to her and begging her forgiveness was take leave from the bureau and spend some quality time with Jack Daniels, wallowing in the misery of his world without her in it.

When he finally emerged from his whiskey-sponsored sabbatical, he'd considered leaving the FBI. But if he did, what did he have left? Regan was gone, along with the life he'd wanted to build with her. Without her, it crumbled to dust around him and left Van standing in the ruins, unable to pick up the pieces and move on. If he'd left his job, too, he would've had nothing.

So he'd stayed and was now supervisory special agent, assigned to the Charleston office. He'd had overtures from private companies, eager to hire him away as an in-house security consultant. The pay was light-years above what he made as an SSA, but he'd sacrificed so much to get where he was now, including the love of his life. Leaving would mean all that had been for nothing.

But now, Regan was here. The feel of the delicate bones of her feet beneath his kneading hands reassured him that somehow, after all this time, life led her back to him. She was here, in the flesh. This wasn't one of the thousands of dreams he'd had starring her. He wouldn't wake up and feel her loss all over again. This was real, and he had the next seven days to convince her that whatever brought them together the first time around, whatever name he'd used while they were together, didn't matter.

But would it matter he was still with the Bureau? Would she be able to get past the havoc his job had wreaked on her life? Or would it always be a stumbling block between them?

Van shook off the doubts, pushing them out of his mind. What mattered was how they felt about each other. That wasn't fake or a lie. It had been so real and raw, his heart still ached with it. Regan had felt that too. He knew it, because he'd seen the pain that ravaged her when she ran out the door. He had to show her that the man she loved was him—not the fictional Ray Edwards but him. They were his eyes into which she'd looked when they made love, his arms she slept in, and his words when he'd said "I love you." She might've met Ray Edwards, but Donovan McLeod was the man with whom she'd shared her life. He just needed to prove that to her.

# 16

*Well* isn't this cozy?" Kez rested a hip against the side of Van's seat.

Rae tried to pull her feet from where they were resting in Van's lap, but his hands were like manacles around her ankles, keeping her in place. When he wouldn't let go without a fight, she ceased struggling. His warm palm caressed her calf in acknowledgment. The trailing of his fingers along her leg ignited every nerve ending, her body buzzing with awareness. And that was just him touching her leg! She was venturing into dangerous territory but couldn't muster up any legitimate desire to retreat.

Rae stretched and took off the sunglasses she'd been using as a sleep mask. "I didn't think you two would come up for air until we landed," she said to Kez.

"Nature called," she said. Inquisitive hazel eyes dropped to Van's blanket-covered lap. "Do I need to check under that blanket to confirm everything is PG?"

Van's thumb brushed over Rae's ankle, and she fought off a shudder. "Why don't you worry about what's going on under your own blanket?" she snapped.

The captain came over the intercom system. "Ladies and gentlemen, we're going to be making our final descent into Grand Cayman in about twenty minutes. Please return to your seats and keep your seatbelts fastened for the rest of the flight. Flight attendants will come around to gather any last articles you wish to dispose of prior to landing. Thank you."

Van grinned up at Kez. "Saved by the bell," he said.

She gave his shoulder a playful nudge and headed back to her seat.

Van let Rae reclaim her feet and her flip-flops. She folded the blanket she'd napped under, hyperaware of Van next to her. Gummy candy and foot rubs. He was pulling out all the stops. She only had herself to blame, though, throwing down the "prove it" challenge. It did seem like he'd been prepared to engage in a certain amount of wooing well before her challenge. Either that or he carried around packs of Swedish Fish.

After stowing her bag, she stole a glance at Van. Even in a plain blue T-shirt, he made her breath catch. Time added a few lines here and there, but his eyes were still warm and his smile easy. And based on the peek she'd taken earlier, his ass remained spectacular.

Maybe Van's reappearance in her life wasn't the apocalypse she'd originally believed. There were worse ways to spend a week than on a tropical island with a gorgeous man on a mission for forgiveness. The past twenty-four hours had knocked her off her game, but she could feel her mojo recharging and moving back in place. Van's reaction to her asking for a "taste" helped, as did the impromptu foot rub he'd given her. If Van wanted to spend a week catering to her every whim and satisfying all her needs, who was she to stop him? Even if she did give him a chance to explain, it wasn't like she *had* to forgive him. She could listen and send him on his way.

After all, Kez did something similar eight months earlier. She'd needed closure with her ex and ended up with not only that but also managed to come out on the other side engaged to Jackson. Why couldn't Rae do the same? Well, not the same exactly, because Van wanted a second chance, not closure. And she was looking for . . . Well, she wasn't sure, but she *didn't* want to get married, especially not to him. Only, she *had* at one time, but not really, because she'd loved Ray, not Van. Right? Rae rubbed her temples, trying to chase away the fuzziness in her brain from the mental gymnastics she'd just done.

Van rested a tentative hand on her shoulder. "You okay?" he asked. The press of his fingers was light as he probed the tense muscles under his hand.

She sighed. "Yeah, I'm fine. Just . . . thinking."

"About what?"

It was tempting to lean into the feel of his fingertips on her bare skin. When his large hand worked to loosen a wicked knot, she could barely keep from moaning. It was tempting to chuck all her anger and resentment out the window and spend a week reminding Van how good they'd been on the physical side. Reawakened mojo or not, she knew that was a mistake. Keeping her pesky feelings and emotions locked down outside of Van's presence was one thing. It was a whole other ball game with him right next to her. The whirlwind of conflicting thoughts spinning through her head proved that.

Dipping her shoulder, she reluctantly moved away. "I don't think I can put it into words," she said.

His hand dropped away, and he plucked at the hem of his shorts. Nervous Van was an unknown phenomenon to her. He'd always been so confident and in control, but then, she supposed he had to be.

A slight jerk as the plane touched down surprised her. Trapped in her own thoughts, she'd missed the last announcements from the crew. As the plane taxied toward the gate, passengers around them gathered their things, eager to deplane and ready to start their vacations.

Was she prepared to spend a week with Van? Just in the span of the flight down, she'd run through a gamut of emotions and reactions to him, some of the time wanting to hear him out, some wanting to make out with him, and a not-insignificant portion wanting to chuck him out the emergency exit door. All of which boiled down to the answer that no, she certainly wasn't ready for a week with him, but it didn't matter. Because, ready or not, their week together in paradise was about to begin.

Van flopped facedown onto the bed that took up almost an entire wall of his hotel room. Turning his head, he looked out the sliding glass door to the patio. A tropical vista of brilliant blue water stretched to the horizon, dotted with sailboats and yachts. But that wasn't the door that held his interest.

Rolling over, he stared at the nondescript white door on the opposite wall. There was nothing special about it—just an ordinary door with a deadbolt currently set in the locked position. It wasn't the door but the person on the other side that held him captive: Regan. By some small miracle, or more likely the well-intentioned meddling of Kez, he and Regan had adjoining rooms.

She hadn't resisted his touch on the plane. At least not completely. Her skin was like satin—smooth and soft over toned muscle. The memory went straight to his groin, making his pants tighten. It seemed that would be his constant state around her this week. If touching her calves was enough to get him hard, he might spontaneously combust when he saw her in a bikini.

He grabbed his phone from the nightstand and checked the time. They'd reached the hotel around two o'clock and agreed to meet in the lobby within an hour to grab drinks and apps at one of the hotel bars. He still had about half an hour before he needed to be downstairs, so he opened the sliding glass door and stepped onto the balcony, a warm, salty breeze carrying with it the strains of "Three Little Birds" from the pool area below him.

White sand sparkled in the sunlight. Rows of beach loungers in lines so straight they could've been made with a ruler covered the beach in front of him. Umbrellas sprouted here and there between the chairs like cultivated blue-capped mushrooms. Those who weren't afraid of getting a little island sun lounged around an infinity pool. Waiters hustled from the beach bar behind the pool to fetch drink or food orders for guests. Flowers bloomed everywhere in brilliant splashes of color. It was beautiful, but the plain white door called to him more than the idyllic paradise below.

Van crossed back over the threshold and to the connecting door. He raised a hand to knock but stopped before his knuckles hit the wood. Pressing a palm to the surface, he leaned his forehead against it. *What was he doing?* Regan told him to prove he deserved the chance he'd asked for, and rather than do that, he was lurking like a perv outside her door. It wasn't like he'd come up with some grand plan in the thirty minutes since they'd left the front desk. If he knocked, what would he say? He had to get it together, otherwise the week would end with him no closer to her than he was right now and with bigger barriers than drywall between them.

A knock sounded on the main door to his room, and he leapt backward. For a moment, he fantasized it was Regan. That she'd been having the same thoughts he had but also the courage to act on them. "Just a second," he said. Opening the door, Van was disappointed to find Jackson and Dave. He checked his phone, but it showed he had plenty of time before he was due downstairs.

Dave noticed and grinned. "We're here to stop you from climbing the walls." He looked beyond Van and his smile widened. "Or to stop you from opening door number two."

Van let them into his room. "I figured the two of you would be . . . busy," he said.

Jackson leaned against the bureau, hands in his pockets. "So did I," he said with a grumpy frown. "Turns out my wife had other plans. Plans that involve her, V, and Rae rummaging through various pieces of luggage in our suite."

Dave laughed, less put out about the turn of events than Jackson. "I told you it was a mistake to bring other people on your honeymoon."

Tugging at his beard, Jackson muttered, "I wanted to elope, but Kez reminded me that would've done nothing but break Nana's heart. Then she decided to have you all join us on the honeymoon." His gravelly voice took on a feminine quality as he mimicked his wife. "Just think, babe, you'll have them to golf with and the girls and I can hit the spa! It will be so much fun! Like spring break for adults!" He dragged a hand down his face. "We should've eloped."

Van retrieved his wallet off the dresser, making sure his room key was inside. Sliding it into his back pocket, he motioned to the door. "Well, I don't need you to go through my suitcase."

Jackson snorted out a laugh and pushed off from the chest. "I need a drink," he said.

"My thoughts exactly." Van led the way to the elevator. When the doors opened to the lobby, the casual extravagance of the place struck Van once again.

All the colors were light and beachy, naturally. Coral chandeliers hung from the ornate ceilings, and brightly colored rugs broke up the cool marble floors. A huge circular teak table occupied the center of the lobby under an intricately designed blown glass mobile. The floral arrangement in a massive vase centered on the table rose so high, the tips of the blooms almost brushed the lowest pane of the artwork. The front desk was pristine whitewashed wood, gleaming in the sunlight coming in through the wall of glass that was the front entrance.

Together, they moved toward the rear doors that led to the beach and the casual bar Van saw from his room. The doors whooshed open, thrusting them into the warm sunshine and salty air. Van slid on his sunglasses to combat the glare and followed Jackson down a stone pathway.

Rather than snag a table under an umbrella, they elected to go directly to the bar. Circulating fans moved above the smooth bar top as servers hurried back and forth with various frozen drinks served with huge chunks of fruit as a garnish. Depositing himself on a stool, Van signaled the bartender.

"Welcome to Bar Louie," the man said, sliding three thin coasters across the granite surface. "What can I get you gentlemen?" His voice had a soft, musical lilt to it, and his smile was brilliantly white against his dark skin.

Jackson gestured to the tray of fruity drinks behind them. "As good as those look, I'll stick with a beer."

Dave agreed. "Sounds good to me."

"Bucket of Land Shark, please," said Van.

"Coming right up," the bartender said.

Once they had their drinks, the three of them leaned back against the bar, surveying the stretch of Seven Mile Beach in front of them. Van said, "Not a bad way to spend a Sunday afternoon."

Jackson touched the neck of his bottle to Van's in agreement. "Not how I planned it, but I can work with this."

Dave laughed. "You've got all week to test the stability of every surface in your room, man. After today, the two of you can disappear until checkout."

"From your lips to God's ears," said Jackson wistfully.

Van joined in Dave's laughter and felt the tension he'd carried all day loosen and unwind. Between the first hit of alcohol flowing through his veins, the gorgeous view, and spending time with these guys, the anxiety drained from his system. He needed to get out of his own head. Spending every waking moment analyzing how he was going to "prove it" to Regan wasn't getting him anywhere. He needed to loosen up. Sheer will couldn't force the answers Van needed, and he'd just drive himself crazy and Regan farther away if he wasn't careful. The answer was out there, and it would come to him. He just had to take his time to figure it out, without wasting a second of the week. Easy, right?

# 17

*What* suit are you wearing?" asked V from one side of the expansive bedroom in Kez's honeymoon suite.

"I'm still looking for it," Kez answered, her head buried in one of the multitude of suitcases lining the wall opposite the wraparound balcony. Their conversation volleyed above Rae as she lounged in the middle of the giant bed between them.

"Why on earth are you sorting through clothes instead of screwing your husband's brains out in this fabulous bed?" she asked Kez.

Her redheaded friend held up an arm in victory. "Found it!" She held up a shredded piece of emerald-green fabric and gave it a jaunty twirl.

"Found what?" Rae asked.

"My swimsuit," Kez replied. She tossed the green scrap onto the bed next to Rae, who scooped it up. Unfurled, the fabric didn't increase in size, but Rae could discern somewhat of a front and back with stringy sides.

"Damn, girl," Rae admired. "Breaking out the big guns!"

"Oh, trust me, honey," said Kez, "that's one of the tamer ones."

"Oh, I love that," said V. She pulled a filmy cover-up from a different bag and tossed it to Kez. "Put this over it."

Rae nodded in agreement. "Yes, that will be perfect." She looked at V. "What did you pick?"

"The blue and black bikini," V answered.

"The one that almost caused a car wreck in South Beach?" Rae asked.

V giggled. "Yep, that's the one."

"Are you trying to give Dave a stroke?" Rae teased.

"Just trying to keep him interested," V replied.

"Sweetie, I've seen the way he looks at you. You could walk out in a burlap sack tied with baling twine, and he'd think you were the most beautiful woman in the world," Rae said.

V smiled widely "Thanks, girl." Her gaze turned sly. "Someone's been looking at you like that for the past twenty-four hours."

Kez dropped a knee onto the bed and chimed in, "Yeah, things looked *pretty cozy* on the plane ride."

"You two read too much into things," Rae denied. Her two friends exchanged a look that said they weren't buying her special brand of bullshit. Honestly, she was getting a little tired of trying to sell that one. She scrunched down into the fluffy pillows and sighed. "I told him I'd give him a chance to offer *some* explanation for what happened in Charleston." Excited and juvenile *ooohhhs* greeted her words, but she quieted them when she added, "But only if he proves he deserves one."

V settled next to her on the bed. "But you are going to let him try, right?"

Rae crossed her arms. "What do you mean?"

V elbowed her side. "You know exactly what I mean, Rae."

Rae rubbed her ribs. "Ouch, you pointy little witch! And no, I don't know what you mean."

From her other side, Kez said, "Girl, please—yes, you do." Rae opened her mouth, but Kez held up a palm. "Don't bother denying it," she said. "And I'm not saying there's anything wrong with making him grovel, or walk over hot coals, or whatever ninja warrior obstacle course you have in mind. At the end, though, once he's run that gauntlet, you need to hear him out. Like a wise woman once told me, it's better to stay and have the fight than spend your whole life running."

Rae shrank into herself when Kez parroted back the very advice she'd given to Kez not even a year ago. It had been good advice then, and it applied equally now. It was also a lot easier to give than receive.

Kez tossed her long hair over her shoulder and headed to change into her green seduction suit. "Plus," she called back to Rae, "I'm sure V and I could help you think of a few challenges for Van this week." With an evil cackle, she slipped into the bathroom.

V rested her head on Rae's shoulder; they twined their fingers together. "Kez is right, you know," she said, squeezing Rae's hand. "Torture him all you want, but if he earns it, give him the chance you promised."

"I'll think about it, okay?"

"The torture or the chance?"

"Trust me, I've thought about the torture for the past five years," Rae said with a wicked smile. "The chance is a recent development."

V laughed and rolled off the bed. "I need to go change." She eyed Rae with a naughty twinkle in her baby blues. "I'm guessing the torture starts with the white suit?"

Rae batted her lashes. "It's like you know me or something. Meet back here in twenty minutes?"

"Kez, twenty minutes work for you?" V yelled.

The bathroom door opened, and a redheaded vixen wrapped in thin strips of green material appeared. "Like a charm," Kez said.

Rae and V whistled and clapped as Kez pirouetted for them. She bowed and then clapped her hands together. "All right, ladies, get a move on! We've got shots to take and men to slay."

Back in her own room, Rae shed her tank and shorts and sorted through her suitcase until she found *the* suit. It was white—blindingly so. You could call it a one-piece, except to do so didn't do it justice. It consisted mainly of slits and cutouts, held together by little more than a hope and a prayer. The back was nonexistent and the reason she spent most mornings on the stair machine or treadmill. She'd found it in a boutique in Wilmington the summer before. Beaches in North Carolina weren't the best place to wear a suit made of thin white straps. The Caribbean, however, was a different story.

Carefully, she navigated the openings of the suit, only backtracking once or twice. Rae adjusted the single strap over her shoulder and tucked her breasts into the top, displaying the girls to perfection. She oiled her limbs with sunscreen and ran a brush through her long, dark hair. White wedges with cork bottoms accentuated her legs, and a wide brimmed straw hat completed her look. She had a crocheted sarong that would complement the suit.

Rae tied it at her waist and regarded her reflection. It was pretty and flowed delicately around her thighs and over her knees. She turned to see the back. Undoing the knot at her hip, she revealed the straps crisscrossing her backside. They pulled and stretched taut over her firm butt. She took a test strut, and the suit stayed in place as she walked. Van had always been an ass man. There was no way he'd keep his eyes off her in this suit. The sarong was staying in the room.

Dropping a few essentials into a big straw tote, she left her room and went back to Kez's suite. The door swung open at her knock. A low whistle sounded at her back when Kez got the full rear view. V came in from the balcony, wrapping a hair tie around the end of her braid. All the places that should bounce did so in her tiny bikini.

"This must be the infamous white suit," Kez said. "Let me be the first to say, holy shit, girl! That thing is hot as hell!"

"I'll say," V agreed. "No cover-up?" she asked as she looped her own around her hips and knotted it.

Rae shook her head, setting her bag on the table by the door. "No reason to cover this up." She gestured down her body and shimmied her hips, making her friends laugh.

Kez put her sunglasses in her beach tote and grabbed her key card. "Y'all ready?"

"What, no pre-drink?" Rae pointed at the fully stocked bar in the corner. "You're letting that go to waste?"

Kez put her bag in the same chair as Rae's. "She has a point, you know?" she said to V. "I know you don't like shots, but it *is* my honeymoon, so I'm hoping you'll make an exception."

V's pert nose wrinkled, but she agreed. "Fine, fine, but please make it something that won't burn my nostrils."

Rae gave her a side hug. "But, V, that's how you know it's good!"

"No, that's how you know it's going to turn your liver to ash. Not that you worry about such things. Yours probably resembles Swiss cheese by now." V playfully pushed Rae's side.

Rae laughed. "Thanks for the diagnosis, Doc. But that's better than the macramé I'd imagined."

Kez broke up their lighthearted squabble with pink frothy shots that smelled of strawberries. "Here you go, girls!"

"What's this?" V asked.

Kez's smile was devious. "I learned how to make them for this trip. It's called the G-Spot."

The three of them clinked glasses and took the shots. The pink concoction tasted fruity and delicious. Rae licked her lips. "Oh my, that's good."

"Well," said Kez, "that's the desired response from the G-Spot." She took their glasses then asked Rae, "What I want to know is whether

Van is going to get the opportunity to elicit that sort of reaction while we're here."

Van had no problem getting that and more out of Rae. Hot shivers erupted over her skin at the thought. His hands had wrung every ounce of pleasure from her on more than one occasion. That wasn't counting what he could do with his lips or any other part of his body. She fanned herself with her sun hat.

Kez noticed. "Something I said?" The implication in the question would've been obvious to a deaf man.

"Why don't you make us one more round before we head downstairs?" Rae asked Kez. "I think even V would like another."

V nodded. "Those were good. Much better than Rae's go-to tequila shots."

Rae bumped her hip against V's. "I'm letting you ease into it, darling. I'll have you taking tequila shots like a pro before the end of the week."

"We've known each other for years," V countered. "If I were going to shoot tequila like you two experts, don't you think it would've happened by now?"

Their laughter drowned out the noise of Kez shaking up another batch of her pink potion. With a flourish, she filled their glasses once more, and again, they held them aloft. "May these drinks not be our only encounter with the G-spot this week," toasted Rae.

"Cheers!" chorused Kez and V, and the three of them downed the second round. V gathered their glasses and put them in the sink next to the bar.

"Now"—she wiped her hands on a small towel—"let's get downstairs." She adjusted the strings holding the small squares of her top in place and set the slit in her sarong so that it allowed the smooth line of her leg to part it all the way to hip level as she walked. Kez and Rae hooted at her and she blushed, waving her hands to get them to knock it off.

"Dave is one lucky man," Kez said.

V gave Kez a swat on the butt. "I'd say your husband is just as lucky, if not more."

Kez pivoted to Rae, but Rae stopped her before she could say anything. "Don't, Kez. Don't think I didn't notice that you put Van and me in adjoining rooms. I know you were the one who made the seating arrangements on the plane too. Not that I expected you to sit with anyone other than your new husband, but you've been manipulating this trip from the start. Don't get your hopes up. I've told Van he can earn his shot. But I'm not promising anything beyond that. What he did to me—the utter and abject humiliation, not to mention him almost costing me my career—the impact of those things isn't something you can understand. I'm not wholly convinced *any* explanation can make up for it. So, please, don't compare whatever may or may not happen this week between me and Van to what the two of you have with men who have never betrayed you."

A frown pulled down the corners of Kez's mouth, "Rae, I . . ."

Rae slung a comforting arm around her friend. "I know you have only the best of intentions, and I appreciate it. All I'm saying is that it isn't a foregone conclusion this week will end with a happily ever after. Or even this famed 'closure' I've heard so much about."

Kez returned the hug and V joined in, turning the hug into a three-way huddle. "You can't tell us not to hope for you, Rae," V said.

"Yeah," said Kez. "That's what friends do."

Rae stepped out of the group hug. "I know, I know. And I love both of you for it." She held the two of them at arm's length. "No reason to hide all this sex appeal up here. Let's get down to that bar. I can't wait to see the look on your guys' faces when they see you."

She could tell Kez bit back what she wanted to say. Rae knew it had to do with Van's face when he saw her, but then she was looking forward to that herself.

When the doors opened and they exited the lobby, humidity rolled in to compete with the cold-pressed air of the hotel's interior. Kez made a face, and Rae knew she was worried about her hair. It tended to absorb moisture in the air and expand to ten times its original size. She playfully pulled on one of the red waves falling down her friend's back, and Kez shot a glare in her direction.

At the hostess stand for the beach bar, Kez looked around for their male companions. Her height, coupled with her heeled sandals, gave her a good vantage point from which to search. It was obvious when she spotted Jackson because a goofy grin split her face. Red cartoon hearts might as well have swirled around her.

The minute he saw her walking toward him, Jackson bolted from his seat. He drew her into his arms and practically bent her in two when he kissed her. Kez was breathless when he let her up, and Rae's friend—her powerful, no-nonsense, litigator friend—giggled like a schoolgirl and melted into him. If they weren't best friends, Rae was pretty sure she wouldn't have been able to swallow the bile she felt rising at their ooey-gooey display of affection.

Sidestepping the happy couple, she saw Van and felt a *ping!* of excitement all the way to her toes. He remained in the casual shorts and T-shirt he'd worn on the plane. His feet splayed wide in front of him, planted firmly on the ground. The arms of his shirt stretched as he lifted his beer to his lips and took a long drink. Those mocha-brown eyes inventoried her body from head to toe.

Carefully, she constructed the perfect seductive half-smile—lashes at half-mast, eyes inviting, and lips puckered but parted a tad with a slight curve to one corner. She added an extra swish to her walk as she closed in on him. On a whim, she gave him a little extra—a slow, 360-degree spin. Once she faced forward again, she didn't miss the stunned gape of his jaw. Confidence surged within her at his reaction.

Reaching his side, she laid a hand on the metal arm of his stool. With the other, she tilted the brim of her hat. "Something catch your eye, Van?"

Van's ears rang and his blood roared. Regan had come down for drinks in a glorified thong. Her suit was stark white, with one shoulder strap. Asymmetrical cutouts ran down the front of it, almost making her look bound by white ties. He wasn't prepared for the bolt of lust that shot through him at the thought. Her cleavage teased him from a wide horizontal slit in the top, while multiple narrow strips wound around her ribcage. The bands of white constricted across her slim waist and over the curve of her hips. The tiered openings in the fabric became larger, exposing bronzed skin almost from hipbone to hipbone. They continued dangerously lower, flashing hints of flesh with no tan lines. She wore no cover-up, just a large floppy hat and sandals. Van's heart felt like it was going to pound out of his chest. It probably would've, but for the fact all of his blood flow was currently pumping south.

He guzzled his beer, his mouth as dry as the Sahara. He couldn't look away from the straps of fabric that barely covered her hips and chest, nor could he erase the image of her ass. Not that he wanted to. Hell, he wished he could print and frame it.

Regan's hat shaded half of her face, but there was no hiding her gloating smirk as she waited for his response.

He didn't know whether to grab the largest towel he could find and wrap it around her or enjoy the display of all that glistening skin. The slight scent of coconut wafted up, and he wondered if she tasted as good as she smelled. Belatedly, Van recognized he was still sitting there staring mutely, which, if he read the laughter in Regan's eyes correctly, was the reaction she'd expected. Forcing his lips to move, he asked, "Can I get you a drink?"

She rounded the back of his stool, positioning herself to his left, her back to a group of men across the bar. Van glanced over, noting their leering appreciation of the view of her backside. His jaw clenched, and he fought the need to put an arm around her waist and let his hand grip the swell of her hip, staking his claim to the sensuous woman beside him. Since he couldn't be sure she wouldn't cut that hand off with the knife the bartender was using to slice limes, Van held back.

Regan picked up one of the laminated drink menus and reviewed the selection, glancing at his beer. "Not feeling very adventurous?" she asked him. Her eyes met his in challenge. "I guess things have changed over the past few years."

She rocked forward on her toes and leaned over the bar to place her order. As she chatted with the bartender, her hat dipped down to the middle of her back, and Van's eyes dipped to her ass. If her goal was to tease him to the brink of madness, she was well on her way. That suit, what little there was to it, molded to her body—her very toned and lithe body. The metal bar of the armrest bit into his palm as he tightened his grip on it, trying not to touch her. Regan made it clear he had a long way to go to earn the chance she'd promised. He would not screw up by giving into the baser urge, no matter how fierce, to get his hands on her.

On his right, he was vaguely aware of Dave guiding V to stand in front of him. "Wanna sit down?" Dave asked her.

She smiled up at him and flipped her braid over her shoulder. "No, there are fewer adjustments necessary with this ensemble if I stand." Her torso tipped backward. "But I might lean on you a bit."

Dave pulled her closer, widening his knees so the edge of her butt propped against the front of his seat. His hands remained on her hips as he said, "Lean away, beautiful."

Kez settled onto the stool on Van's left that Jackson had vacated, and the man himself stood behind it. Jackson wove a hand beneath all that red hair to lay a hand on her shoulder. Van envied his friends' ability to touch their women so easily with no fear of losing a finger. Jackson sipped his beer and said, "That's some suit, Rae."

Spinning around, she ran a hand down the front of it and grinned. "If you're nice to me, I might let your wife borrow it."

With a grave look across the bar, Jackson replied, "Not if you want her to leave our suite."

Regan followed his gaze and saw the five or six twenty-something guys seated on the opposite side of the bar. Once they saw her looking, they all puffed up, posturing like roosters. She snickered. "Honey, none of them would know what to do with a woman like your wife." She gave Jackson a sly look. "Especially not since she's been with a man like you."

Kez laughed while Jackson saluted Regan with his beer. "While you may be right, Rae," he said, "I'm not interested in anyone other than me seeing what she looks like trussed up in bits of nylon dental floss and patches of fabric."

Regan cocked an eyebrow at Kez's revealing suit. "She's not exactly wearing a muumuu."

The way Jackson looked at his wife, it was obvious he was more interested in what was under her suit. "No," Jackson admitted, "she's not." He tilted his beer at Regan. "But she's definitely *not* wearing that."

The bartender reappeared, carrying a tropical concoction. "Miss Rae," he said, "your Killer Bee."

"Thank you, Marcus," Regan cooed. She lifted the drink to her lips and took a sip. "Oh God," she groaned in appreciation, "that's so good!"

Marcus's delight at her praise stretched his smile. "I'm so glad it is to your liking." He took in the rest of their group. "Can I get anyone else a drink?"

V regarded Regan's cocktail with suspicion and said, "I'll have whatever you make that has half of the alcohol that hers does." Marcus's answering laughter was contagious.

"Actually, Marcus," Jackson said, "I think you have something special back there for the ladies."

Marcus looked puzzled for a brief second then beamed. "Ah, the honeymooners! Yes, yes, one moment!"

When he disappeared, Kez poked Jackson in the ribs. "What do you have up your sleeve, Mr. Jenkins?"

"Patience, Mrs. Jenkins," he said and kissed her lightly.

Regan pretended to vomit. "I need antacids or nausea medication if you keep this up all week. Dramamine for dry land." She pointed a finger at Jackson. "If you've taken my best friend and somehow brainwashed her into one of those women who talk about soul mates and eternal love, I'll never forgive you."

"Don't worry. We'll keep the lovesick romance behind closed doors as much as possible," Kez promised.

Marcus reappeared with a tray bearing a bottle of champagne and three flutes. V hopped up in excitement. "Veuve!" she exclaimed, clapping her hands.

Quickly, Dave wrapped protective arms around her chest and cautioned, "Baby, I don't think that suit was designed with jumping in mind." She flushed scarlet and righted her top behind the screen of Dave's arms.

The cork popped from the bottle, and Marcus filled three flutes with champagne. Kez looked at Jackson. "Don't you want a glass?"

He grabbed another beer from the bucket on the bar. "No thanks, Gorgeous. You ladies stick with your bubbles, and I'll stick with mine."

Van watched the three girls toast each other and then Jackson for his thoughtfulness. He leaned toward his friend and clinked the neck of his bottle to Jackson's. "Thanks for inviting me, man."

Jackson nodded. "Glad you could make it." He looked at the girls. "I hope you actually make something of it while you have the chance."

Van couldn't talk to Jackson with Regan a few feet away, but he wanted to tell him what she'd said on the plane. "She says I've got to prove I deserve a chance."

Jackson's eyebrows arched in question. "Is that right?"

Van nodded. "Yeah."

"How are you going to do that?" Jackson asked.

Keeping his eyes on Regan, Van shook his head, brow furrowed. "No idea."

Jackson passed him a fresh beer. "You're a smart guy. I'm sure you'll think of something. Hell, you made her fall in love with you once, right?"

"Yeah, but then I gave her a reason to hate me."

"Give her more reasons to love you," Jackson said, as if it were so simple.

"It's not that easy, man," Van protested.

Jackson put a hand on his shoulder. "Nothing worth it ever is. You know that."

Kez appeared and slid an arm around Jackson's waist. "This conversation looks way too serious," she scolded.

Jackson dropped a kiss to the top of her head. "I think it's time we get you something to eat, Gorgeous."

Kez sipped her champagne then stifled a hiccup. "Probably a good idea. Let's grab one of those tables."

"Van and I can do that," he replied. "Go corral Rae and the rest of the . . ." His voice trailed off as they watched Regan tuck the ice bucket and champagne in the crook of her arm, holding her flute in one hand and the Killer Bee in the other.

Van scrambled out of his chair. "You guys get the table. I'll get Regan." Not giving Kez a chance to argue, he was behind Regan in two strides. "Regan," he said to her back. The brim of her hat scraped against his chest when she turned around.

When she lifted her cocktail to her lips, a bead of condensation dripped off the side and dove into the slit in the top of her suit. It moved in a slow path down her chest, weaving its way over her skin. Van tracked the tiny droplet until it disappeared into her cleavage. The cold press of her drink to his chest gave him a start, and he found Regan staring at him.

"Huh?" he said dumbly.

Amusement flickered in her eyes, but she didn't smile. "Did you need something, Van?" she asked. "Or did you come to stare at my tits?"

Her question brought him out of his breast-induced stupor, and he wanted to slap himself. Leering at her would not win her over. Hastily, he cleared his throat and said, "I think Kez and Jackson want to get a table and order some food."

"Right," she said and toasted him with both glasses. "Well then, lead on, Macduff."

"Let me help you with that," he said and took the champagne bucket. Wanting to keep as many people as possible from staring at her ass, he extended his free arm. "After you." A derisive snort told him she knew what he was doing, but she didn't call him on it. Although he'd gotten his wish as she sauntered in front of him, he'd miscalculated how hard it would be to look anywhere but her ass. He watched as it flexed and plumped with each step she took. He was going to need a cold shower before they even reached the table.

Blessedly, Kez and Jackson chose a table close by. V and Dave were already seated and, after depositing the champagne on the table, Van pulled out Regan's chair for her. She looked down at the woven wire seat and frowned. Van looked at the chair but saw nothing wrong with it.

Kez chuckled. "Rethinking your decision to leave that cover-up in the room, huh?" At Kez's teasing, Van understood the problem. Given the mesh design of the seat, Regan would look like she'd been sitting on a waffle iron. In one swift move, he pulled off his shirt and laid it over the metal grating. Regan looked at him like he was nuts, but he shrugged and took the chair next to hers. She remained standing.

A waitress approached with menus and frowned at Van's bare chest. "I'm sorry, sir," she said, "but we require all men to be wearing shirts in the dining area."

"You're kidding, right?" Van asked. "She can dine in a thong, but I have to wear a shirt?"

The waitress was apologetic. "I am sorry, sir, but that's the rule."

Desperate to save face, he searched for another solution and locked onto the towel cart outside the rope fence around the patio. He slipped his shirt back on and said, "I'll be right back." Van cleared the low rope with barely a hop and speed walked to the towel cart. "Hey, man, can I get a towel for my . . . girlfriend to use while we eat? Her suit isn't really conducive to . . . sitting."

The young guy glanced over Van's shoulder at Regan and grinned. "Who needs it to be good for sitting?"

"Towel, please," Van said, shifting to block the kid's view. He trotted back to their table to deposit the fluffy blue beach towel onto Regan's chair.

A wry smile teased around the corners of her mouth before breaking free. "Who needs shining armor when you're armed with high thread count terry cloth?"

*18*

*Rae* avoided Kez's amused look by hiding behind the menu. Dodging the subtle press of Van's knee against hers under the table was not easy. She couldn't move without having the same problem to her right with Jackson. With over six feet of male times three, legroom was at a premium. The coarse hair on Van's leg teased her thigh, and she shivered.

Trying to think about anything else, she read over the menu. Her stomach grumbled with each item—everything sounded amazing.

"Rae," V called from across the table, "you'll eat oysters with me, right?"

She flipped her menu down and looked over at her friend. "Sure, sounds good. Kez, you want some?"

Kez nodded. "That sounds great." She looked over at Jackson. "Right, babe?" she asked with a laugh.

He shuddered. "It sounds disgusting." Jackson was notorious for his dislike of anything seafood related.

"Let me guess," Kez mocked. "A grilled chicken quesadilla, with just chicken and cheese?"

"It's like we're married or something," he responded.

Rae laughed at their banter then returned to the menu.

Van asked her, "You still eat your oysters with horseradish?"

She ignored the blip in her pulse at the fact he remembered how she liked her oysters. Lifting her eyes from the specials, she met his brown gaze. "I do."

He smiled. "I remember how much you liked the way they'd roast them at Shem's."

The blip increased, and her heart beat erratically. Shem's was a hole in the wall he'd introduced her to on Sullivan's Island. You could sit outside at scarred tables and watch boats sail out with the sunset. Its specialty was oysters: raw, steamed, roasted, or any other way you wanted. But the coup de grâce was their special recipe for horseradish. She remembered the sharp scent of the spicy sauce coupled with the briny taste of the oysters. Her mouth watered as she thought about a place she'd long since banished from her mind.

Van brought her there at least once a week to get her oyster fix. Some Saturday nights, they had a band on the waterfront. Band was a generous description, as it was usually one guy with a guitar, a microphone, and a stool. They pushed tables back to create a dance floor overlooking the water. She and Van often found a spot on the worn boards, wrapped in each other's arms and swaying to the music. She'd felt loved and safe with him then. Except, it hadn't been Van taking her there, but "Ray," the persona he'd carefully crafted to slither into her world. The happy memories caught on the twin shards of humiliation and anger jutting stubbornly within Rae's subconscious. The fragile happiness stirred by the memories didn't stand a chance against the jagged edges of those stalwart emotional peaks and was soon shredded beyond recognition.

"That was a long time ago, Van," she said, her voice quietly raw.

Luckily, he was the only one who noticed her shift in demeanor, and before he could comment on it, V summoned the waitress. "Everyone ready to order?" the server asked.

"Yes, I think so," V said. Once the server left with their orders, she asked, "What is our plan for the first night?"

Jackson said, "I didn't make any."

Kez put a hand on the inside of this thigh, just above his knee. "I did," she said. "But it's for two people, not six."

Dave pulled V closer to him. "That's funny, Kez, because it sounds like you and I have the same plans." V's cheeks pinked up, and she shook her head but didn't put any distance between them.

Dark mischief danced in Kez's hazel eyes as she looked at Rae and Van. "Looks like you're on your own. That won't be a problem, will it?"

Rae was sorely tempted to use the swizzle stick from her drink as a weapon. But it would be poor form to stab your best friend on her honeymoon. Especially when she'd brought you along with all expenses paid. Rae forced a smile. "No, that should be fine."

"Good, then it's settled," Kez said. "Tonight, we're left to our own devices, but tomorrow, there is a private cabana with our names on it."

There was no way Rae was going to pass up an opportunity to torture the boys over this development. She shot a devilish grin at Jackson. "That's great! Does it come with a lotion boy?"

His beer paused halfway to his lips. "Lotion boy?"

Rae nodded solemnly, while cackling internally. "Oh yes, all the high-end hotels have them now. It's a guy who makes sure you have all the sunscreen you need," she paused for effect, "and that it's applied properly in all those hard-to-reach places." Somehow, she kept a straight face.

Jackson's big hand choked the neck of his beer at the suggestion that another guy would get within ten yards of Kez with a bottle of lotion.

Not surprisingly, he summarily dismissed the idea. "Kez travels with her own personal lotion guy—me. We won't need his services."

Rae looked to V. "Guess he can spend more time on us."

Dave's easygoing grin faltered for the first time. "Yeah, I don't think that will be necessary. I'll take care of all of V's, uh, lotion needs."

Here was what she'd been waiting for. Rae didn't miss Van's frown when she said, "Sounds like I get some quality one-on-one time with the lotion boy. Things are looking up." She taunted him with a flutter of her lashes. "I mean, unless you're interested."

He sat up straighter in his chair. "Interested?"

She crossed her legs, dragging her foot up his calf. "Well, yeah. Are you interested in the proper application of sunscreen?"

A rough swallow moved his throat as he stared at her, eyes like the color of molten chocolate and every bit as heated. He leaned forward, resting his elbows on the table. "Oh yes, I'm very interested."

*Sucker!* Rae dropped her leg from his. "Great, then we'll let him start with you. I'd hate for that pretty skin to get burnt."

"Wait, what?" Van spluttered as the rest of the table collapsed with laughter.

In mock seriousness, Rae turned to him. "You just said you were interested. We'll let the lotion boy get you all greased up with SPF, then he can do me. Mine will probably take longer, more places to cover, you know? So, he'll start with you."

Van frowned so hard the skin around his mouth turned white. "I am not having some kid put lotion anywhere on me."

He was making this so easy, it was almost a shame to engage in it. But this wasn't horseshoes or hand grenades so *almost* didn't count. Rae shrugged. "Suit yourself. Looks like I get him all to myself then." She gave him an evil smile and sat back as the waitress delivered their oysters.

Van stood up. "I need some air," he said and walked off.

Four sets of eyes moved from Van's retreating form to Rae. She squirmed under their scrutiny. "What?" she asked, feigning innocence.

Jackson sipped his beer. "You going to do this all week?"

She grabbed an oyster, sprinkled it generously with the horseradish, and swallowed it whole. It wasn't Shem's, but it was still good. Dropping the shell into the discard bowl, she said, "Maybe. Is that a problem?"

"You tell me," he answered.

Rae slurped down another oyster and flicked the shell into the bowl. It hit with a *ping!* She kept her eyes on Jackson's passive face. "Why would it be?"

Despite her bravado, guilt over her petulance had already set in. She'd been the one insisting to Van they needed to get along, and less than a full day into the trip she'd goaded him into abandoning them.

Jackson's left shoulder rose upward in a lazy shrug. "Just seems like a waste of paradise to spend it dredging up the past."

"For some of us, the past is closer to the surface." Her defensiveness was as much to deflect her embarrassment over her behavior as it was a genuine response to Jackson.

Jackson set his beer next to his empty plate and steepled his fingers in front of him. "Rae, I'm not saying you shouldn't *be* angry. Van messed up big time, but he didn't do it to hurt you. He did what he did because it was his job."

Kez put a hand on Jackson's arm. "Babe, we don't need to be in the middle of this."

Jackson was undeterred. "Rae needs to hear this, because otherwise she's going to keep blaming Van for something he couldn't help."

Okay, hold on. Rae would coexist with Van this week, but that didn't include rehashing old wounds with the rest of their party. Especially when it sounded distinctly like Jackson was taking Van's side and trying to justify what he'd done.

"Couldn't help?" she asked incredulously. "What exactly couldn't he have helped, Jackson? Setting me up on that first meeting? Lying to me *every single day* about every aspect of his life, from his fake job to his fake friends? Parading around in front of all my friends as someone he wasn't? Letting me call him by his fake name every time we screwed? And, oh yeah, not telling me—the woman he now claims he was totally in love with—that I was working *for a drug dealer*. Which one of those couldn't he help?"

He shook his head. "I'm not talking about any of those things, Rae."

"Then what?"

Jackson's blue eyes were soft in the face of her anger, and his voice lacked any edge. "He couldn't help that the two of you fell in love, Rae, but you've blamed him for it ever since you walked out the door."

Rae scoffed. "Please. He played me for a fool, Jackson. He used and manipulated me to get what he wanted, with zero regard for how it would affect my life." The oysters she'd eaten soured in her gut and her face flamed as she admitted to being such a fool. Her eyes burned with tears she refused to shed, and she looked past Jackson to the glimmering sea behind him.

"Rae, you need to—" Jackson didn't finish, because Kez cut him off.

"The only person who *needs* to do something," she said in a firm voice, her small hand gripping his arm tightly, "is you, Jax. Drop. It. Let the two of them sort it out."

The newlyweds stared at each other for a long moment without speaking, then Jackson brought Kez's hand to his lips. He brushed a kiss across the tips of her fingers and smiled sheepishly. "Sorry, Gorgeous." Then to Rae, he said, "Sorry, Rae. I'll back off."

Her renewed shame at being played by Van was miniscule in comparison to what she felt at being the source of their rancor. It wasn't fair for her past with Van to interfere with what should be one of the best weeks of their lives. Time to act like an adult. She picked up her drink and laid her napkin on her plate. "It's okay, Jackson. I know you're standing up for your boy. It's what Kez or V would do for me."

"Where are you going?" asked Kez when Rae stood up.

Rae tipped her drink in the direction Van had stormed off. "I'm going to smooth things over with Mr. Sensitive."

"What about your food?" V asked.

Rae thought longingly of the grilled shrimp tacos she'd ordered. "Have them box it up for me."

Van regretted his decision to stomp away like a sulky child as soon as he'd done it. But pride kept him from going back to the table. He'd kowtowed to Regan the entire night before, let her take her swings and jabs at him, been the butt of her jokes and object of her disaffection. He pushed her too far by bringing up Shem's, and she'd retaliated as only she could. Van knew he could only expect more of the same, all of which he would readily admit he deserved. But, Christ, there was only so much he could shoulder in twenty-four hours. So he'd fled the laughter and derision she so easily tossed his way, cognizant the whole time that he'd go crawling back.

Once he descended the stone steps to the beachfront, he turned left. A thatch-roof bar with weathered clapboard walls that may have been red once but were now sun-faded to a dusky pink sat in a grove of trees. A long horizontal shutter was open above a thin tin ledge that served as the bar. Brightly colored plastic stools sat under the shelf, and a few scattered picnic tables ringed the perimeter of the place. It had a few patrons, but there were plenty of empty seats. Van snagged one and ordered a beer. He'd foolishly left his behind on the table.

When the bartender set his beer down, Van drained half of it in one swallow. A chalkboard menu advertised conch fritters and grouper bites, with a few other small plates. Not the lavish fare of the hotel, but his stomach rumbled in response to it. He ordered and twisted on his stool to watch the water. In a matter of hours, Regan had gotten under his skin and pushed all his buttons. He should've known better than to fall for her seductive act *twice* since leaving Charlotte. He was an idiot to think she'd offer anything to him. She enjoyed toying with him, largely, he knew, because she thought that's what he had done to her.

He asked for another beer when the paper boat containing his conch fritters arrived. The small, breaded morsels were piping hot, and he burned his tongue on his first crispy bite. Downing the rest of his first beer to soothe his scorched mouth, Van slouched in his seat. Today had started out so promising, yet here he was eating bar food alone.

"Is this bar restricted to lying jackasses, or can anyone sit down?" Disbelief horned in on his pity party when he saw Regan poised next to the empty stool beside him. He did his best to hide his excitement.

"I'm pretty sure no one would turn you away while you're wearing that," he said. She'd kicked off the heeled sandals and stood barefoot in the sand. Because she wore heels constantly, it was easy to forget how short she was. It had always amazed him when she came home from work, slipped off her shoes, and shrank four inches.

With a knowing grin, she perched one bare cheek on the plastic stool next to his, setting her now watered-down drink on the bar. She eyed the conch fritters, and he slid them toward her. "Help yourself," he said, "but be careful—they're hot."

She plucked a fritter from the waxy brown paper and blew on it then took a bite. "Mmm," she said, "these are pretty good."

Choosing his own from the small container, he popped it in his mouth and chewed. "Yeah, they are."

She snagged a napkin from the dispenser and delicately wiped her fingertips. Grabbing his fresh beer, she took a sip. "So, taken any more undercover assignments destined to ruin the lives of some unsuspecting ladies, or am I the only lucky one?"

He choked on his bite of fritter, coughing and wheezing. Regan whacked him on the back, maybe a tad harder than strictly necessary. But she hadn't let him choke to death either, so he'd take it as a win. Once he recovered, he took a sip of beer. "I haven't worked undercover in a long time, Regan."

"Well, you did blow it pretty badly the last time, right? I mean, sleeping with the mark had to have gotten you a little *X* in your fancy FBI file, even if you did bring down the bad guy."

"Regan, I—"

She waved a hand in the air and sighed. "Sorry, sorry. I told everyone I'd come down to make peace with you and yet, the first words out of my mouth stir everything back up. Let me start over. So, Van, you still with the FBI? How's that going?"

Her delivery of the last two lines was robotically cheery, and Van wiped his mouth to hide a smile at her effort to make small talk. She'd always hated it, he recalled, much preferring to cut straight to the core of the problem. She must *really* not want to bring up whatever topic brought her looking for him. But she was here, so he'd play along. Plus, her reaction might give him a chance to see whether his still being with the Bureau was going to be a problem for her.

"Pretty well," he said. "I got a promotion recently, so I head a small team now. I'm still in Charleston, but I get to travel a fair amount, which is nice. On the whole, yeah, it's going pretty well."

They talked generically about his work and hers for a bit, munching on the fritters and trading sips of his beer. Once the food was gone, Regan took her time balling up her napkin and putting it in the empty basket.

Spinning on her stool, she leveled those piercing green eyes at him. Their color was so unique; it was mesmerizing to look directly at them. He'd lost himself in them so many times while they were together. Drawn to her once again, he leaned her way with no conscious thought of doing it.

She put a hand on his chest. "I'm sorry for what I said."

He covered it with his own. "I'm the one who's sorry."

Regan pulled her hand away and eased back in her seat. "I'm not ready for the deeper 'I'm sorry' conversation yet, Van. I came looking for you because, like I said before, I won't let what happened between the two of us jeopardize Kez and Jackson's honeymoon. They don't need to spend this week taking sides in our war. They came here to enjoy paradise and were sweet enough to invite us along. I respect them too much to do anything to detract from this week. And"—she blew out a harsh breath—"that should include provoking you." She looked at him from beneath her lashes. "Even if you make it ridiculously easy."

He laughed. "So does this mean you're calling a ceasefire?"

Her deep chuckle sent sparks flying through him. "I guess you could say that."

Van recognized he had an opening and seized upon it. "Have dinner with me tonight," he asked—or sort of ordered.

Her lips quirked into a half-smile, but she pulled away from him. "What?"

He gestured back toward the hotel. "The four of them all have 'plans' tonight, but we don't. Have dinner with me, please?"

Regan poked at the empty container in front of her. "Didn't we just do that?"

Van put a tentative hand on her knee. "Regan, please." He felt her muscles quiver under his palm, tensing up for either fight or flight. She looked toward the surf and didn't answer. She also didn't move his hand from her leg, so he left it there, enjoying being able to touch her.

Without looking at him, she said, "I can't do that, Van." Disappointment speared him, until she said, "At least, not yet."

"I can handle 'not yet,'" he said, relief coursing through him. "It's a lot better than 'fuck off.'"

She laughed then—a real, genuine laugh that rolled out on the sea breeze. He joined in, and finally, she looked at him. The sadness behind the laughter made his heart ache, knowing he was the reason for it.

"I've missed laughing with you, Van," she said. "That's probably what was hardest the first few months after . . ."

*After she'd uncovered his lies*, he thought, as her voice faded.

Regan went on. "You could always make me laugh. No matter how crazy things were at the hotel, you made things lighter. Life with you was . . . brighter." She stood up, and his hand fell away from her knee. "Which made the aftermath that much darker."

He wanted to say something, anything, to erase the haunted tone of her voice, but words failed him.

The wind rippled the brim of her hat, and she reached up to secure it. She brushed a stray hair from her eyes. "Come back to the table, Van. I promise I won't bring up lotion boys, cabana boys, or any other type of boy."

He tossed a few bills onto the bar to cover his food and beers, then followed her to the hotel. When they reached Bar Louie, Jackson and Dave were paying the tab and Kez held two takeout boxes. "Good timing," she called out and handed a box to each of them.

"Y'all finished already?" Regan asked.

Jackson nodded. "Yeah, we thought we'd get a jump on those 'plans' we had for tonight." He looked at Kez like she was his own personal hot fudge sundae, the hunger in his eyes positively savage.

"Go get 'em, tiger," Regan encouraged and winked at V and Kez. "See you ladies in the morning."

"You're not coming with us?" V asked.

"To what? Watch the four of you fondle each other in the elevator? I think I'll pass," said Regan. "Plus, I need to tip Marcus."

"I'll walk her home, V," Van promised with a grin. After agreeing to meet for breakfast, the other couples walked into the hotel, leaving Van and Regan alone.

"You don't have to wait for me," she said.

"I don't mind," Van insisted. He followed her over to the bar where she placed a twenty-dollar bill in Marcus's hand.

"Mr. Jenkins already paid with a generous tip, Miss Rae." Marcus tried to give the money back.

Regan pressed it back into his palm. "Marcus, we'll be here all week, which means you and I are going to become close friends. Close friends don't fight about money."

Reluctantly, he tucked the bill into his server's apron. "Thank you, Miss Rae."

"See you tomorrow, Marcus," she promised with a jaunty wave. Their exchange reminded Van of the way Regan had treated the employees at the Carson. She'd always had a kind word and a sweet smile for every bellman, maid, or janitor. She knew them by name and treated them as equals. It was one of the things he'd loved most about her. Despite being in the top tier of management, she never acted as though her position made her better than anyone else. Based on her conversation with Marcus, that hadn't changed.

They strolled through the lobby to the elevators. As they waited in air-conditioned comfort, Van asked, "Are you sure you won't join me for dinner?"

Regan fiddled with the lid of her to-go box. "Van, I—" The elevator opened, and a rush of people exited around them. Once the crush of bodies passed, they stepped into the elevator.

"You what?" he asked after hitting the button for their floor.

She stared straight ahead. "I can't."

"Can't or won't?" he pressed her.

"Does it matter?" she asked.

"Of course it matters!" he said, the cardboard container squeaking in his hands as he shook it.

The door dinged on their floor, and she hurried in front of him, but he wasn't willing to let her escape so easily. He caught up to her at her door and asked again, "Can't or won't, Regan?"

She fished out her room key. Slapping it to the electronic lock, she said, "I can't, Van." The door closed behind her with a soft click.

He remained briefly at her door, the lingering scent of her tempting him to knock and beg her to reconsider. Reason won out, and he trudged to his room. A small smile crept onto his face as he thought more about her answer. A door shutting in their face might dishearten most men, but not him. Because she said she "can't" have dinner with him, not that she "won't." There was, he knew, a vast difference between the two. "Won't" meant that she was refusing to go to dinner with him, that she didn't *want* to have dinner with him. "Can't" implied a whole other meaning. "Can't" meant you wanted to, but something kept you from it. Something like resurgent old feelings you didn't want to admit. Van could deal with "can't" because it gave him the freedom to show Regan she could.

*19*

*Rae* heard Van's door close and slumped against her own. There was no way she could've had dinner with Van tonight. Spending the past twenty-four hours with him stirred up too many feelings, not all grounded in hate, and that scared the shit out of her. She needed to keep her distance until a good night's sleep gave her more perspective. Then maybe she could hear him out.

Rae pushed herself off the door and walked deeper into the room. She avoided looking at the door to Van's adjoining room. No sound came from inside, but she knew he was just on the other side of the wall. She put the container of food into the small refrigerator hidden in the armoire. The clock on the nightstand read 5:30. She tossed her floppy hat on top of her suitcase and kicked off her shoes. In the bathroom, she started the shower and peeled off her suit.

As the water pummeled her back, she planned her evening. After her shower, she'd put on something comfy, order room service (cold shrimp tacos sounded less than appetizing), and call it a night. Normally, she wouldn't have wasted a perfectly lovely evening in a swanky hotel by staying in, but she needed to recharge after the last few days. A solo dinner overlooking the ocean would be heavenly.

Once she'd scrubbed away all the sand, sunblock, and the remains of the day, she wrapped herself in the luxurious hotel robe and piled her hair on top of her head in a messy bun. Rooting around through her clothes, she found a soft pair of sleep shorts and a matching tank. Ditching the robe for the shorts and tank, she combed out her hair and dialed room service.

Waiting on her food, she flipped through a magazine extolling the virtues of Stingray City. Her stomach growled, and her mind wandered back down memory lane.

*The tangy smell of sautéed shrimp hit her nostrils when she opened the door. Eric Church crooned on the condo's sound system, and the parted drapes showcased the city below.* Someone was in the mood for seduction, *Rae thought. She dropped her keys and purse on the small table next to the door. Kicking off her heels, she followed her nose into the kitchen. Leaning against the doorframe, she took a second to admire her man in his element.*

*Dressed in faded jeans and a well-worn T-shirt, he stood barefoot at the stove. Over the sizzle of the succulent shrimp, she heard him humming along with the music. With a flick of his wrist, he flipped the shrimp into a separate pan that held linguini, cherry tomatoes, and small pearls of mozzarella. He drizzled a little more olive oil into the pan then added a sprinkle of fresh garlic. The pan hissed at the addition of the oil, and he expertly swirled the contents to blend the ingredients.*

*Rae clapped her hands. "Bravo, Emeril," she said as she crossed the wide-planked floor.*

*One hand still on the skillet handle, Ray glanced over his shoulder. His handsome face broke into a smile. "Hey there, beautiful. You're home early. I'd planned to have everything ready when you walked in."*

She pushed onto her toes to give him a kiss. "Benson had some meeting tonight, so he sent me home early." The pan in his hand tilted slightly. "Careful there, Chef," she cautioned. "You're about to send dinner spilling onto the floor."

"What would I do without you, baby?" He righted the pan and set it on a back burner. With both hands now free, he gathered her in his arms and kissed her. It wasn't a quick peck but a dedicated exploration of her mouth. Her fingers curled into the fabric of his shirt and her knees went weak. When he pulled back, she blinked owlishly.

"What was that for?" she asked then hurried to add, "Not that I'm complaining!"

He kissed the tip of her nose. "What? I can't kiss my girl hello when she comes home from work?"

"Well, yeah, but that was more like I was home from war," she teased. "You just saw me this morning."

His eyes turned serious, and he caressed her cheek. "I want to do that every time I see you, Regan. Even if you're only gone for fifteen minutes."

Her heart almost tripped out of her chest and her insides went gooey at the sweet sentiment. "Well"—she wrapped her arms around his neck—"who am I to stop you?"

They'd been so good together, so right. Except now, she saw all of it through the lens of his deceit. Every time he'd taken an interest in her work, it was because he was trying to wheedle out details related to her boss. Each work function he'd come to hadn't been to support her but to scope out Hasselhoff's business. Even if she could move past it and accept that was a necessary evil of his real job, what about the more mundane aspects of their lives? Like, when she'd asked him about *his* day at work—had he told her about his real day, or was even that a lie? Or when he'd say he was going for a run, was he meeting someone that he couldn't tell her about? How much of all of it had been lies?

But over the years, the few times she'd allowed herself to wonder about him, a part of her had always believed that everything couldn't have been fake. The way he touched her, or the warmth in his eyes from across a crowded room. Those things . . . they felt so real and genuine that even in the flaming shitstorm that rained down on her after the Hasselhoff arrest, she'd been hard-pressed to believe that had been a lie too. At least, until the weeks turned to months and she didn't hear from him. Not a single word. If anything between them had been real, surely he would've reached out to her then. Yeah, she'd left and done her best to disappear, but c'mon . . . the guy was *FBI*, for God's sake. If he wanted to find her, he could have. And he didn't. And that was what hurt the most. Because it meant he hadn't really cared at all.

A knock interrupted her musings, and when she answered the door, the delicious scents arising from under the covered dishes on the cart wheeled into her room made her mouth water. She asked the waiter to set it up on the balcony and, after tipping him, Rae sat down to her feast. Everything looked so good on the menu, so she'd gone a little crazy. There were plates of mango carpaccio, sea bass, duck fat fries, and grilled veggies. And, of course, a half carafe of wine. It was way more food than she could eat, but she couldn't help herself. She wanted to try it all!

Spreading a napkin in her lap, she dug into the mango carpaccio first. The sweetness of the mango blended with the tart tomato and creamy avocado in an explosion of flavor on her tongue. She couldn't hold back a moan of pleasure at the taste.

"Regan?" Van called.

Spinning in her seat, Rae looked around frantically but didn't see him. "Van? What are you doing?"

"The same thing you are," he answered, flapping a napkin over his railing. "Looks like we'll be having dinner together after all."

This was not the laid-back culinary experience she had planned for tonight. At least a wall separated their balconies. A tiny wall that offered little protection, but she'd take it. "So it would seem," she said. "I hope you enjoy your meal."

"It certainly sounds like you are," he said, and she heard the playful tone in his voice. Rae pictured the half-grin that would go with it and the creases of amusement by his eyes.

She made a noncommittal response and returned to her food. She could hear the scrape of his chair when Van sat down. Based on that, he was sitting directly behind her. Determined to have the tranquil night she wanted, she took a deep breath and an even deeper drink of wine. The sea bass was as yummy as the carpaccio, and the duck fat fries were salty, delicious heaven. The veggies tasted as good as grilled vegetables could. She had just scooped the last of the fries into her mouth when he spoke again.

"I should've told you, Regan." When she said nothing, he kept going. "The first time I said I loved you, I should've told you who I really was. Hell, I should've told you before that. As soon as we got serious, I should have told you the truth. For the longest time, I justified it by saying I couldn't, that I had to keep you in the dark for my job until the case was over. But that's not true."

Rae picked up her wineglass, pulling her feet into her chair and hugging her knees. She wanted him to shut up but was also dying for him to say more. To explain why he hadn't been honest with her. Why he'd built their life together on a lie. And why, when it all came crashing down, he'd so easily let her go.

Van kept talking. "It wasn't true, because I know I could have trusted you with the truth. You wouldn't have betrayed me to your boss. Instead, I betrayed you. What's crazy is that I'd decided to tell you. That's why that stupid file you found was in my briefcase. I was going to tell you everything, but you found it first, and I never got the chance."

Tears threatened, but she willed them back as she hung on his words. For so long, she told herself that whatever his explanation was, it wouldn't matter. That she didn't care why he'd done what he had. The simple act of it was enough to tarnish everything she thought they had. But as his words spilled over the concrete barrier, she knew that wasn't true. It *did* matter, and she *did* care. Rae had a painful, consuming desperation for this man to tell her everything hadn't been one big lie. She voiced none of that but willed Van to keep going. He did.

"You must know, Regan, that I wasn't lying about who I was. Well, not really. I lied about my name and my job, but not about the man I was." He paused, then huffed. "God, that sounds so stupid and trite."

She heard his chair grate against the concrete again and assumed he'd stood up. Moments later, she heard the pad of his footfalls as he paced, still talking.

"It started as a way to get inside the Carson, but what grew between us, what we shared was real, Regan. What I felt for you was real. When I talked about our future together, I meant it. *You* were who I wanted to spend my life with. You still are. My life, Regan, not Ray Edwards's life. I want you in *my* life forever. It was me who took you to Shem's and danced with you to cheesy eighties love songs. It was me telling you I love you all those times. Each time we made love, it was me making you cry out. Every single thing between us was real, Regan. None of it was a lie."

Her hand trembled as she brought her glass to her lips and drank. Could she believe him? Why, after five years, would he lie to her? It couldn't be to get her in the sack. He could find someone else downstairs at the bar with a lot less effort. What was his angle? Did he even have one? Was all of it true or just another ploy? But if so, for what? Question after question tumbled through her mind.

"I love you, Regan," Van said so faintly she almost didn't hear him. "I've never stopped loving you."

Rae set down her wine and stood up. She stepped back inside her hotel room and slid the glass door shut. Pushing down all her doubts, questions, and residual anger, she went to the door separating their rooms. She flipped the deadbolt and opened the door on her side of the wall. Raising a hand, she rapped loudly on the remaining closed door and waited.

Not even thirty seconds after her knock, the door flew open, and Van stood in front of her. His hair was damp, and like her, he'd changed clothes. He wore black lounge pants and a charcoal-gray T-shirt. Stubble dotted his jaw, and his hand clutched the doorknob as he stared at her.

"Regan, I—"

She put a hand to his mouth to silence him. "I don't want to hear any more tonight, Van. Not about the past or the future. Let's just enjoy the present." Sliding her hand from his mouth to the back of his neck, she arched up on her tiptoes and brought his mouth to hers. She felt his sharp intake of breath at the contact and the briefest moment of reluctance on his part. When she continued pressing her lips to his, a greedy moan rumbled through him, and he released the door handle to swing her into his arms. Instinctively, her legs wound around his waist and his hands cupped her ass.

When his lips parted beneath hers, Rae slanted her head and tangled her tongue with his, eager for more. He groaned deep in his throat and stepped backward into his room. Quickly, he crossed over to the bed, kissing her the whole way. Deep, insistent kisses that left her breathless. He sank down onto the mattress, keeping her in his lap. Finally, they broke apart, each panting for air. Van touched his forehead to hers, his hands stroking up her back.

Again, he tried to speak, and once more, she silenced him. "You've talked enough for one night, Van. There are other things I want you to do with that mouth."

She ripped his shirt over his head and sat back, marveling at his body on display in front of her. Rae took her time studying him, trailing her fingers over the taut lines of muscle. He was the same but different. Briefly, she wondered if he'd think the same about her.

Van hissed in a breath at her touch. It came out in a moan as her lips followed the path of her fingers, licking and sucking lightly on his torso.

"Regan," he said, his tone almost reverent while she worked her way down his body, stopping with a nip to his side right above his waistband. Impatiently, she dipped her hand beneath his pants, but he stopped her with a hand on her wrist. Fire blazed in her eyes as she looked up at him.

"I need to see you, baby. I need to see all of you," he said, voice hoarse and eyes desperate.

Nimbly, she whipped her shirt over her head and cast it aside. When he reached for her, she slid forward on his lap. Her breasts grazed his hard chest as his hands splayed across her shoulder blades. Lifting her lips to his ear, she sucked the lobe into her mouth and bit down. His answering groan told her he still enjoyed the sting of her teeth capturing his flesh. She soothed the bite with a subtle flick of her tongue, purring into his ear. "Seen enough yet, Van?"

He gripped her upper arms and, before she could process what he was doing, had her flipped onto her back with her head resting against the pillows. Desire pooled in his luxuriant brown eyes as he held himself above her. His large hand cupped her breast and gave the nipple a quick tweak. A moan ripped from her throat when he repeated the maneuver on her other breast.

"Van," she panted, reaching for him.

He lowered his face to her chest, nuzzling the silky skin as he said, "I'll never get enough of you, Regan. Twenty-four hours a day, seven days a week wouldn't be enough."

She ground her hips against his knee between her thighs, seeking more contact.

He eased his leg backward, and she growled. She felt more than heard his quiet laughter at her anger. "Patience, Regan. It's been five years since I had you in my bed. I'm going to savor this moment, not rush it." His hungry lips traveled up between her breasts and across her collarbone. Van dropped soft kisses against her throat, and she tilted her head to allow him better access.

The need rushing through her veins overpowered her subconscious shouting, *Slow down! It's too soon!* As he continued kissing up her neck and licked the curve of her ear, rational thought gave way to primal urges, and she wrapped her legs around his still-clothed hips. She clung to his shoulders as the bridge of his nose traced the line of her jaw. Then they were eye to eye. He stared down at her, and she could see equal portions of lust and wonder in his expression. Gently, he stroked a finger over her cheek and crooked it under her chin. That tender touch severed the last link of her self-control and in a beseeching tone, she said, "Please, Van, please."

The sound of his name—his *real* name—on her lips in that moment hit him in the chest. It cracked open, and a torrent of pent-up longing poured out, surging all around him. He had pictured Regan Murphy in his bed countless times since she left him. Some of those images needed NC-17 warnings, but none held a candle to the real thing. Hearing her use his name in such a desperate plea did more than simply stoke the flames of passion. It rekindled the devotion he'd long carried for the woman lying beneath him. She could have asked him to do anything then, and he would have. Anything but walk away from her.

With his fingertip, he outlined her face, sketching over her delicately arched cheekbones and elegant nose then down to her kiss-swollen lips. It was as though he were committing her face to memory, using as many senses as he could. His worship was short-lived, because adoration wasn't what Regan was looking for, and she told him that with a sharp bite to his finger as it rubbed over her lips.

"Ouch," he said, tapping the tip of her nose.

She was unrepentant and dragged her heel up the back of his leg. "I'm half-naked and fully turned on, Van. It's not my face you need to focus on right now."

His laughter pressed his chest tighter against hers, making her nipples harden. Teasingly, he shifted his weight back and forth on his elbows, letting his coarse hair scrape over her sensitive skin. Her breathy gasp and wide eyes told him she enjoyed it. Lazily, he slid down her body, not breaking their skin-to-skin contact until he reached the waistband of her cotton shorts. He plucked at it with his teeth, and she wriggled her hips encouragingly. Lifting his eyes from the cloth, he dragged them up her body and met hers. From his vantage point between her thighs, there was a small ring of green around her heavy, darkened pupils.

Her hand drifted up to cup her own breast, lightly teasing a nipple with the tips of her fingers. She watched him watching her. "I didn't know this was a spectator sport. Am I going to do all the work?" Her other hand drifted down her taut stomach and a finger dipped under her shorts. As hot as it would be to watch her get herself off, he'd earned that privilege tonight. There was no way in hell he was giving it up. He grabbed her wrist, pulling her hand back and placing it above her navel.

"Not so fast," he said. "I told you I'm not rushing this."

Her hips flexed upward and bumped his chin. "If you move any slower, I'm going to have to check for a pulse," she retorted, saucy as ever.

His fingers slid under her loose pajamas, and he palmed her ass in his hands. She hummed in pleasure as he dug his thumbs into her inner thighs while his long fingers gripped her cheeks. In a single move, he flipped his hands over, grabbed the legs of her shorts and yanked off the skimpy bottoms, leaving her in nothing but a pair of sheer black panties. He tossed the tiny boxers over his shoulder, not caring where they landed. Leaning back onto his haunches, he ran his hands up the inside of her thighs, luxuriating in the velvety texture of her skin.

She writhed at his touch, her hips pressing into the bed and fingers plucking at her nipples while she stared up at him. A sensuous smile curved those gorgeous lips, and she nodded her head toward his pants. "Seems like you're a little behind, McLeod." This time, the use of his last name was playful instead of resentful. While he continued caressing her thighs, she hooked a leg around his waist and delved a foot beneath his waistband, trying to push his pants off his hips.

He laughed when her eyes rounded upon discovering he wore nothing beneath the lightweight sleep pants. Her toes brushed across bare flesh, and she grinned. "You naughty boy." She pushed harder against the fabric at his waist in her attempt to get him naked, so he did the gentlemanly thing and slid back off the bed. Her foot trailed against his abs as he stood up. Keeping his eyes on hers, he hooked his fingers under the drawstring and shoved. When the pants dropped down his hips, he felt the heat of her eyes rake over him from head to toe, with one noticeable pause at his groin. As she licked her lips, he kicked his pants away and knelt on the bed, placing his hands on either side of her ribcage.

He looked at her panties. "Now who's behind?"

Regan pulled her bottom lip between her teeth and lifted a hand to her throat. Slowly, she slid two fingers down her chest, between her breasts. Van watched her nipples tighten further as she circled them. Her fingers slipped lower, over her flat stomach. His eyes followed, and when she reached the scrap of lace, he looked back at her face. He felt her hips lift then tilt and the slide of her legs against him as she slipped out of her underwear. With one hand, she brought her panties into his line of vision, draping them across his knuckles.

Putting all his weight on his other arm, he picked up the scrap of lace and put it on the nightstand. "I'll hold onto those," he said.

Her nose scrunched when she laughed. "A souvenir?"

It was then that he broke eye contact and took in the sight of her naked body. Its lush curves called out for his touch. His mouth watered at the thought of tasting her. He crawled toward her until they were once again chest to chest. Their breath intermingled as he dipped his head and kissed her. His tongue probed between her lips and they parted, allowing it to slide over hers. He cupped her face in his hands, supporting his weight on his elbows so as not to crush her. Using his grip on her jaw, he angled her head and deepened the kiss, capturing and swallowing her moans. Her hands strayed over the expanse of his back, and he felt the hot sting of her nails when he nipped at her bottom lip.

"Van," she sighed, as he trailed fervent kisses down her neck and across her shoulder. With her hands at the back of his head, she tried to direct his path, but he resisted, content in taking his time to explore the body he'd once known better than his own. Van feathered kisses down her arm and into the crook of her elbow. His mouth continued its downward journey, earning a full body shiver from her when he sucked gently on the underside of her wrist.

After placing a kiss in her palm, he started at her belly button and kissed his way back up her body. When he reached her breasts, he took both of them in his large hands, relishing the weight of them in his palms as Regan arched into his touch. He rolled her nipples between two fingers, and she cried out in bliss. This time, when she tugged at his hair, Van let her guide him down to one breast and pulled a stiff peak between his lips. He licked and sucked as she clenched her hands around the base of his skull, pinning him to her. His name fell from her lips like a chant. He lifted his head, and she whimpered at the loss of his mouth, only to groan when he lavished the same attention on her other breast. With a last tug, he released her breast and drew a line down her stomach with his tongue, swirling around her belly button before diving lower.

He gripped the inside of her thighs and guided her legs apart. Regan's sharp inhale ended in a reverberating purr of encouragement. Van flattened his palms on the crease between her hip and thigh, pushing her legs wider. The sensual spectacle before him awakened a primal need to claim, his hips rutting forward instinctually against the mattress. The tangy scent of her arousal had him panting to taste her, to lap at her spicy slickness until she was as crazed as he was. When he glanced up her body, she stared down at him between her legs. Sizzling hunger arced toward him from the green depths of her eyes. With her golden skin flushed tawny and her hair spread over the pillow, her fingers still teasing at her breasts, she looked like a pagan goddess, and he was ready to worship her. He kissed the underside of her thigh. She made an unintelligible sound and clasped her hands around the curve of her breasts, shoulders pulling back and arching her spine.

"Please," she moaned, "please, Van. I need you."

A subtle shift of his mouth and he was there. He used his lips, his tongue, and his fingers to tease, tantalize, and finally give her the release she wanted. She thrashed against him, lost in her own pleasure. Van worked her until the last tremble of her thighs ceased and she lay pliant and spent under his mouth. As she came down from her orgasm-induced high, he fumbled in the nightstand for the condoms he'd bought at the airport on a hopeful whim. She watched him roll it on with hooded eyes and then reached for him, guiding him to her center.

That first slow push made his eyes roll back at the tight, throbbing heat of her. Even through the latex, he could feel her body welcome him, stretching and rippling to draw him deeper. Again, the need to claim her ripped through him, urgent and feral. He thrust harder, loving the feel of her under him and relishing the passionate collision of their bodies. Van clamped his hands on her waist as he steadied himself against the rising tide of need.

Regan undulated against him, her hands now at his shoulders, grasping and clutching. The sharp bite of her nails spurred him faster as together they found their rhythm. Skin against skin, sweat mingling and breaths whispering. Anytime they'd come together had been amazing, but this was something else entirely. It was as close to a divine experience as he'd ever had. The feel of her, the sounds she made, the way her body meshed so perfectly with his, it was almost too much. And then, when he felt her stiffen and her core begin to contract and roll with her orgasm, it was the final crescendo of sensation that triggered his own release, and he buried his face in her neck as he came.

Coming back into himself, Van raised his head to kiss her neck, and she sighed contentedly. Both of them were still breathing hard, and a light sheen of sweat coated their bodies. Van rolled out of bed and dealt quickly with the condom. Upon his return, Regan hadn't moved from the center of the bed. Her dark hair was a tousled mass, and her eyes were half-lidded and sleepy. Her lips parted in a languid smile, and she beckoned him to her. Once more, he was a mere mortal, summoned by the goddess who ruled him.

When he got back in bed, she rolled toward him, laying her head on his shoulder and resting a hand on his stomach. He cradled her next to him, idly drawing abstract shapes on her naked hip. Kissing her temple, he said, "Regan, I—"

Her fingertips at his lips stopped him. "I don't want a postmortem discussion, Van. Whenever we talk, things tend to get . . . messy. Let's not ruin this with words. Let's just enjoy it." Those long, sooty lashes swept upward as she looked at him, keeping her fingers against his mouth.

Not wanting to do anything that would make her leave his arms, he nodded once, kissed her fingers, and resumed stroking her hip. Satisfied, she nestled against him. He felt her relax and her breathing even out as she fell asleep on his chest. Doing his best not to disturb her, he used his foot to maneuver the blanket folded across the end of the bed to within his reach. He draped it over them. The exhilaration thrumming through his veins succumbed to exhaustion. Regan shifted in her sleep, and her leg twined with his. Sleep claimed him with a smile still on his face.

Later, they came together twice more. Once with her on top and then again in a position he couldn't explain but thoroughly enjoyed. He'd loved this woman for years, and now, against all odds, she was back in his life. He wasn't letting her go again.

20

The smell of coffee roused Rae from the best sleep she'd had in months. Coming awake slowly, she cracked one eye open and took a deeper whiff. Was that bacon mingling with the heavenly aroma of freshly brewed caffeine? The possibility was enough to get her to open her other eye. On the nightstand next to her—no, wait—next to *Van's* bed was a steaming cup of coffee. Its pale-mocha color looked suspiciously similar to the way she made it at home.

"Splash of milk and a spoon of sugar, right?" The question came from behind her, and she looked over her shoulder. Van stood there, the low-slung pajama pants hanging at his hips. His naked torso woke up much more of her body than coffee ever could.

Last night had been . . . Hell, it had been spectacular. He'd played her body like a finely tuned instrument, getting notes out of her she hadn't hit since, well, ever. It seemed Van had perfected certain skills and learned a few new ones while they were apart. Regret, rather than jealousy, settled within her, because she hadn't been celibate for the last few years either. Too bad she'd missed out on his honing those techniques on her. An indulgent shiver skated down her spine at the thought of practice making things even more perfect.

"Regan?" Van pulled her from her dirty daydream. "That's still how you take your coffee, right?"

Plumping the pillows behind her, she pushed herself up and curled her hand around the mug. One sip told her he'd gotten it right, and she was pleased he remembered. She nodded to answer his question and took another swallow. "Did I smell bacon?"

He grinned and pointed to the table by the glass doors. Two plates, still with the covers on, sat next to glasses of orange juice. "I ordered breakfast." His grin dimmed for a second and doubt clouded his eyes. "I hope I got something you like. I mean, I went with what I remembered, so I think it should be fine. But if you want something else—"

"Van," she interrupted his adorably nervous rambling. "I'm sure it's fine." Setting her coffee next to the bed, she threw the sheets back and stood up. She'd slept naked and still was. After a long stretch, she glanced at him, enjoying the voracious way he looked at her. She worked damn hard on her body, and knew it showed in the lines of her limbs and trim frame. But as much as she appreciated Van looking at her like she was his breakfast, eating naked wasn't something she wanted to try. At least, not with bacon and eggs. Strawberries, chocolate sauce, and whipped cream? That was a different story.

Her tank and shorts lay crumpled at the foot of the bed. "Mind tossing me my clothes?"

Van's mouth snapped closed, and he gave his head a subtle shake that made her laugh. He smiled back and said, "Do I have a choice?"

An impatient waggle of her fingers was her answer, and he reluctantly retrieved the pajamas and handed them to her. Before she could put them on, he skimmed a hand down her side, and her skin tingled in anticipation. He bent down slightly, and she put her arms around his neck. Van looped his hands together at her lower back, pulling her into him. "If it were my choice, you'd spend the rest of the week like this."

A smile played on her lips. "You mean starving and with morning breath?"

His fingers curled tighter over her hips. "I mean naked and pressed up against me," he countered.

A flutter raced through her abdomen at the idea of spending all week holed up with Van, only sending out for food and more condoms. "That sounds tempting," she said, her nails scratching lightly down his chest. His body responded to her touch with a riot of goosebumps and a shuddering breath as her fingers dipped lower to trace the line of the *V* at his hips. Pausing, she smiled up at him, "But then, so does bacon." With one last stroke of his abs, she stepped away and shimmied into her tank top. As it flowed down to her waist, she pulled on her shorts.

His choked laughter made her smile. It struck her how not awkward this morning after was. There was no uncomfortable silence nor any clumsy exchanges between them. Their interactions were light and familiar, as though they'd never been apart. But those five years had happened, as had the prior year of deception.

Van's confession, for lack of a better word, played through her mind. He'd said a lot of pretty words, but why had he waited so long to say them? A lot of what he said was what she wanted to hear, but there was one glaring omission. If he'd loved her all this time, if his life had been miserable without her, surely he had the resources at his disposal to end his exile from her.

And even if she could finally come to terms with the big lie—was the reason behind it enough to make her forgive the ripple effect it had on her? Yes, Van lied, because it was his job to lie. He'd lied because her boss, unbeknownst to her, was a very, very bad guy. One whom the FBI tasked Van with apprehending.

That was all well and good, but that wasn't the end of the inquiry. If she were as important to him as he claimed she was, he should've done more to shield her from what happened. Instead, she'd had to shoulder all that alone. Because not only had he eliminated her job, he'd cost Rae her friends as well. Not that they were the cream of the crop, but still. Because of him, she was alone and adrift in a sea of uncertainty and fear. And he'd left her there for weeks, months, and eventually, years. One night of mind-blowing sex didn't change that fact, nor could it erase the black stain of it from their history. Would their past always hover in the background, casting long shadows over any possibility of a future? The unsettling thought made her steps falter.

"You okay?" Van asked as he caught her elbow.

She shook him off, although not as violently as she would have yesterday. "I'm fine," she said and sank down into a chair. Van's dark eyes looked troubled, but he didn't push. Beneath the dome cover, Rae discovered a breakfast of scrambled eggs, bacon, roasted fingerling potatoes with fresh fruit. A basket of multiple kinds of toast sat in the middle of the table, with jars of jellies and jams encircling it. Her stomach grumbled, so at least one organ in her body wasn't conflicted. Unfurling her napkin from the silverware, she dug in with gusto.

Van sat next to her and ate with equally ravenous speed. "Guess we worked up quite the appetite, huh?" he asked.

Washing down a bite of egg with a bit of juice, Rae laughed, "I think so." They ate in companionable silence for a while. Scraping up the last of her eggs with a piece of sourdough bread, Rae popped it into her mouth. She patted her belly and sighed as she swallowed the last bite. "I'm stuffed." She waved off Van's offer of more coffee and leaned back in her chair, closing her eyes contentedly. They popped back open as Van's fingers grazed down her arm.

"Last night was unbelievable," he said.

"Yeah," she agreed, "you were pretty incredible. Makes me think you haven't been a monk these last few years, sitting in self-imposed exile and doing nothing but thinking of me."

"I always thought of you, Regan." His eyes were serious. "Always."

"I'm sure a lot of ladies would be heartbroken hearing that," she said, trying to keep the conversation light.

Van wasn't having it though. He took her hand in his and slid forward in his chair. "Regan, you're all I've thought about since you left. I meant what I said last night. I've never stopped loving you."

She pulled against his hold, but he held fast. "Van, I'm not ready for all that. I mean, it's a lot to take in. I haven't seen or heard from you in five years, then you randomly pop up at my best friend's wedding, and two days later we're having breakfast together the night after you fucked my brains out. Throw in a declaration of undying love, and it's making my head spin." *Plus, I'm wondering if I can really believe in this again.* That little tidbit she kept to herself.

His thumb rubbed over her knuckles. "I'm sorry, Regan." His gaze moved to the breathtaking view beyond the balcony then refocused on her. "Actually, that's not true. I'm not sorry, because everything I said last night was the real, unvarnished truth. I made the mistake of lying to you before. I'll never do that again."

Suddenly, the room was too hot, and he was too close. She wrested her hand from his and stood up so quickly her chair tipped backward and clattered to the floor. Her pulse was thready, and her mind raced with conflicting thoughts. What he said sounded so good, so right. Did how long it had taken him to say it truly matter? Would she even have listened to him back then if he'd tried? Wasn't the point that he was here now, admitting he'd been wrong and groveling for her forgiveness? But after such a long period of silence and being forced to wonder if he'd ever cared at all, it scared her to believe it so quickly. Rae clutched her shaky hands together and turned her back on him, looking out to the calm turquoise waters below. She heard him right the overturned chair, but he didn't approach her, nor did he speak. Instead, he waited for her to regain her composure.

Wrapping protective arms around herself, she said, "Van, you talk like we're getting back together. Like this is the start of something." When she stopped to gather her thoughts, he remained silent. Resolutely, she turned from the floor-to-ceiling glass and looked at him. "Last night was amazing. Being with you like that was wonderful. But a singularly remarkable night doesn't erase a year of deception that decimated my life, nor does it make up for the fact that you never cared enough until now to try and explain."

Hurt flashed in Van's eyes, but she kept going. "Plus, there's the fact that you let me continue to work for a freaking drug dealer! I can't fault you for doing your job, Van. You had to do what you had to do. I'm sure the more time that goes by, the better perspective I'll have on that. But I still can't reconcile the fact that even after everything we shared, all the times I let you into my most private spaces and intimate thoughts, you let me think you were someone else. That whole time, I didn't even know your real name."

Tears formed behind her eyes, but she breathed through them, willing them to dry up. Van reached for her, but she backed away. "How can I trust anything you say to me?"

"Regan, there won't be any lies this time," he pledged, his arms still outstretched. "And back then, if you'd been in danger, I would've gotten you out. I wouldn't let anything happen to you. Ever."

*But you did,* she thought. *So much happened, and you didn't stop it or help me. I had to do it all on my own, without you.* Still, she heard the sincerity in his promise, and even with her unspoken misgivings, she allowed him to gather her in his arms. She heard his heartbeat beneath her ear as she laid her cheek against his chest. "I want to believe you, Van."

"I'm not asking you to put your blind faith in me, Regan," he said. "I just want the chance you promised me. Let me prove myself to you—please."

She drew in an unsteady breath and let her arms wind around his waist, focusing on the slow thud of his heart in her ear. His request wasn't any different from what she wanted, was it? One way or the other, she needed to know whether he was the man she'd fallen for. That she'd been romanced by a man caught between a rock and a hard place, not hoodwinked by a conman. If that were true, if she hadn't been as big a fool as she'd believed all these years . . . Rae felt the bands around her heart weaken and crack, the muscle beneath stirring with a fervor it had lacked since she'd left Van. This time, she was the one who tightened her arms around him, keeping him close.

He crooked a finger under her chin and lifted her eyes to his. "Is that a yes?" he asked.

Rae didn't trust her voice, so she nodded.

Relief flooded Van's face, and he smiled. "You won't regret it, Regan. I promise," he said then dipped his head to kiss her. It wasn't the steamy, sensual exploration of her mouth from the night before. This was tender, a heartfelt vow that he'd hurt her for the last time.

He broke the kiss and brushed a finger across her cheek. "I'm glad we got that settled," he said. "Now, about that morning breath . . ."

Pushing away from him, she slapped his stomach with a sharp *thwack*. Laughing, he pulled her back and kissed her again. Before he could get carried away, Rae wiggled free. She skipped to the connecting door. "I guess we don't need to keep these locked anymore."

"There won't be any more barriers between us, Regan." His words, and the heady promise they contained, broke the last of the bands around her heart. She only hoped it wouldn't be the next thing to shatter.

Ignoring Van's pleas to "conserve water" by showering together, Rae returned to her room to get ready for the day. The light on the phone blinked red, signaling a message. Her lips curved at the sound of Kez's hesitant drawl in her ear.

"Hey, Rae, just, um, calling to check in. We missed you at breakfast this morning. Van wasn't there either." There was a pause. "Anyway, we're heading to the cabana. It's number fifteen, but I'm sure you'll see us. Okay? Bye."

After a quick check of her cell to make sure no crises at work had arisen overnight, she brushed her teeth and took a brief shower. She was toweling off when she heard the door from Van's room open. "Regan?"

"In here," she called back to Van, tucking the towel between her breasts. He rapped lightly on the doorframe, and she turned. He was almost edible in bright-blue board shorts and black shirt. The outfit itself wasn't tantalizing but knowing what it covered had her lady bits in overdrive. "Hey," she said, dragging her eyes away from his chest to his face.

His lips twitched with amusement at her drooling over him. "Hey, yourself." He lasered in on the swell of her breasts. "Nice towel." The hair on the back of her neck stood on end when he prowled toward her. Reflexively, she retreated a step, her back bumping the counter. In seconds, he was in front of her, pinning her against the marble top. One hand cupped her jaw, while the other tugged at her towel.

"What are you doing?" she asked, perfunctorily batting his fingers away.

"This," he said, taking her mouth in a demanding kiss while undoing the knot. The towel pooled onto the counter then slid to the floor when he pulled her against him. She felt his smile against her lips. Before she could speak, he hoisted her onto the bathroom counter. She flinched a little when her ass hit the cold surface. Van moved between her legs, placing his hands on the tops of her thighs but never breaking the kiss. His tongue delved deep into her mouth, tasting all of her as she clung to his shoulders. Her legs wove around his, urging him closer as he plundered her mouth. His hands moved up her thighs, and she moaned, scooting her ass to the edge of the counter. God, she wanted him!

She fumbled with the laces of his suit, finally tugging it open. Running her hands around to the back of it, she pushed it over his hips. Before it could join her towel on the floor, Van grabbed it. He pulled his lips from hers, and she blinked in disappointed surprise, relieved when two of his fingers slid into the side pocket and pulled out a condom. Then he released his grip, and the shorts fell to the floor. Rae took the condom from him and tore open the foil, wasting no time in rolling it down his length. Van groaned at her touch and rocked forward in her hand.

"Eager, are we?" she taunted him.

He grabbed her ass and pulled her to the edge of the counter. "Eager doesn't cover it, Regan," he said as he slid into her. Her legs locked around his hips as he surged forward. Her hands sought purchase on the smooth ledge, knocking her toiletries into the sink and onto the floor in a series of crashes and clangs. Tipping her head back, she arched her body into each of his thrusts. "Eyes on me, sweetheart," he grunted. Obeying his command, she lifted her head up to look at him. "You feel so good, baby," he murmured, watching her face with hazy eyes.

Releasing her grip on the counter, she brought her hands to his jaw, guiding him to her for a kiss. They swapped frenzied breaths as he plunged into her over and over. "Oh God, Van!" she cried, feeling the curling tendrils of an orgasm building within her.

He tightened his grip on her hips and doubled his already frantic pace. "Just let go, baby, I've got you. Let go."

She did, and for a second, she felt like she was levitating as pleasure exploded through her entire body. She cried out in garbled gibberish as she felt him join her, his forehead falling to her shoulder as he rode out his own climax. Rae kissed his cheek as his gulping breaths drifted hotly across her breasts. His thighs trembled with exertion, and he leaned heavily on the counter. "Guess you got your cardio in for the day," she said.

He huffed out a laugh. "I noticed you let me do all the work."

Tracing a finger down his sharp jawline, she gave him a sly grin. "You're the one that asked for a chance to prove yourself. I'm giving you what you wanted."

A loud knock sounded from the door of her room, and she jerked upright. "Rae?" called V. Another knock sounded. "Rae, are you in there?" Kez called through the door.

Van looked at her with a playful glint in his eyes. He angled his head toward the door and opened his mouth, but Rae quickly covered it with her hand. "Don't even think about it!" she chastised in a quiet voice. He grinned beneath her palm and kissed it. She twisted her hand, centering it on his face, and shoved. Off-balance, Van had no choice but to stagger backward, which allowed her to hop off the counter. Fixing him with a warning glare, she whispered, "Do not open your mouth and under no circumstances are you to come out of this bathroom. Nod if you understand."

Still grinning, Van nodded obediently. Rae hurried past him, stark naked. Rifling through her bag, she found a short robe and slipped her arms through its silky sleeves. Jerking the tie into a knot, she crossed to the door and cracked it open. "Good Lord," she said, "are you two trying to wake up the whole hotel?" She propped one hand on the doorframe and the other on the knob. Given Kez's height, her efforts to block their view were probably futile, but she had to try.

V looked at her phone. "It's after eleven, Rae. I don't think anyone but you is still in bed."

Kez craned her neck to see over Rae's head, but she pulled the door tighter, eliminating the line of sight into the room. It was an overcorrection, and Rae cursed her stupidity when a knowing gleam came into her friend's hazel eyes. "Just exactly what, or should I say who, has got you staying in bed until eleven, Ms. Murphy?"

Rae was grateful for her olive complexion, because without it, a telltale flush would've spread over her cheeks. When she didn't answer, Kez reared back to look at the next door down. "Maybe we should go check on Van. V, what do you think?"

Panic gripped Rae. "No!" she said quickly, without thinking. *Crap!* Van had her way off her game today. Kez's eyes glimmered brighter, and Rae knew she'd stepped right into the trap. *Shit!* "I mean," she backpedaled, "I heard him moving around in there, so I know he's awake."

"Mm-hmm," said Kez. "Right."

"Look," Rae said, struggling to keep her voice even and calm, "I got a late start today. Give me fifteen minutes, and I'll meet you in the cabana. You said it was number fifteen, right?"

With one last knowing grin, Kez let her off the hook. "Okay, that's fine, but a word of advice?"

Rae arched a slim brow at her. "Yeah?"

Kez thumped a finger against Rae's neck. "Slap some concealer over that love bite."

Rae slapped a hand to her neck. "What!"

Triumphant, Kez formed a gun with her hand and shot off an imaginary round at Rae. "Gotcha! Tell Van we said hurry." As they headed back down the hall, V dissolved into giggles, and even after shoving the door closed, Rae could still hear Kez's gleeful peals of laughter.

Van poked his head out of the bathroom. "Is it safe for me to come out?"

Rae signaled for him to come forward, raking a hand through her hair in frustration at being so easily discovered. "It was a waste of time to have you hide. They knew you were here the whole time."

His eyes widened. "Really? How?"

"Never underestimate a woman's powers of deduction. Especially if said woman graduated from either law or medical school. Outsmarting the two of them is impossible."

Van laughed and pulled her in for a brief kiss before he spun her toward her suitcase. "Then I guess you need to get dressed for the beach." He settled onto her still-made bed with his hands tucked behind his head.

She crossed her arms. "And what do you think you're doing?"

He grinned. "Enjoying the view."

Seizing the opportunity, Rae decided to toy with him a bit. "Oh, really?" she asked, untying her robe and letting it fall open. Watching him closely, she let it slide off her body. "How's this for a view?"

With an animalistic noise, he lunged toward her, but she stopped him with a palm on the center of his chest. "Ah, ah, ah," she chided. "You said I needed to get ready for the beach. So you just lie back and wait, okay?" At her push, he tumbled backward onto the bed, and she pranced around the foot of it to get to her suitcase. Bending over a little more than strictly necessary, she searched for her black bikini. While it wasn't on par with the white suit from yesterday, she knew it would keep Van's attention.

Plucking the suit from her luggage, she stood and hazarded a glance back at Van. His jaw was set, and his eyes were hot coals of lust. His hands fisted the comforter, physically restraining himself from lunging at her once more. The long muscles in his forearms stood out in ropy cords. He ran his tongue along his bottom lip. "Find what you were looking for?" His voice was deep, the timbre of it sending electric jolts over her skin.

She let the bikini dangle in front of her. "Sure did."

He looked at the miniature swaths of fabric she held out, eyes narrowed. "Where's the rest of it?" Her answering grin was sinful, and he swallowed hard. "There is more to it, right?" She didn't miss the hopeful tone in his voice, which made her laugh.

Turning her back, Rae slid the bottoms up over her legs. After, centering the ties at her hips, she adjusted the rouching to gather the fabric over the curve of her ass. It was a Brazilian cut, high on the hip and minimal coverage in back. The top was a single piece bisected by a keyhole over her cleavage. Once she'd hiked the girls up into their perky and upright positions, she turned to Van and struck a ta-da pose. "What do you think?"

"I think you're the sexiest woman I've ever seen in my fucking life," he said, rising from the bed. His hungry approach made Rae feel like a rabbit cornered by a wolf. Her heart fluttered in her chest and her muscles twitched as he stalked closer.

She watched, transfixed, as he traced his thick finger down her bare cleavage and dipped inside her top to stroke the underside of her breast. Her breath hitched as his lips followed the path of his finger. When he placed an open mouth kiss on the center of her cleavage, she shuddered and leaned into him. Her skin tingled at the rough scrape of his stubble as his kisses climbed higher. When his teeth pinched the tender flesh of her neck, she whimpered. His lips were at her ear when he whispered, "You're wearing a cover-up today."

⁂

A thick rope barrier strung between wide wooden posts separated the veranda and cabanas from the powdery white sand of the beach. The cabanas themselves had white canvas roofs and three slatted sides, with their wide-open entrance facing the ocean. Filmy white curtains were available for privacy but stood open at cabana fifteen.

As he and Regan rounded the curve, Van spotted their group lounging on catty-cornered couches facing the ocean. Kez waved when she saw them. Regan waved back and looked at Van from beneath her wide-brimmed hat. She was wearing the cover-up, although the name was misleading. It was a sheer caftan that billowed around her in the breeze. When the wind blew, it plastered to her body, displaying the curves underneath.

She'd asked him not to say anything about last night or what happened on the sink less than an hour before. He knew the surreptitious look she'd given him was to confirm he would stand by his agreement to keep quiet. Given the chance, he would've yelled from the top rail of the balcony to everyone within earshot that she was his again. Only he wasn't sure she was. He'd asked for another chance, and she'd agreed, but what did that mean? They weren't together if she wouldn't tell her friends. And if they weren't together, what were they?

"Hey there, you two," Kez greeted them. "We missed y'all at breakfast this morning."

Regan tossed her bag onto the low table in the center of the half-circle of seating. Her hat landed on top of it, and she ran her fingers through her dark hair to fluff it up. "Sorry about that," she said but didn't elaborate.

A waiter appeared from behind the palm fronds. "May I get you something?"

With a sparkling smile, Regan asked for something with mango. Van picked up a beer from the bucket on the table. "I'm good," he said.

"Very good, sir." To Jackson, the waiter asked, "Will you be lunching in the cabana this afternoon?"

"Yeah, I don't think we have any plans to leave here until you kick us out," Jackson said.

The young server had a musical laugh that made their group smile. "We would never do such a thing," he assured Jackson. "I'll bring out some lunch menus with another round of drinks." With a slight bow, he left them.

Regan peeled off her caftan and stuffed it into her bag before she took a seat on the empty couch across from Kez and Jackson. Van sat next to her, not as close as he wanted, but made up for it by stretching his arm along the back of the cushion. His thumb grazed her hair, and she didn't pull away. If having four people stare at them like a science experiment bothered Regan, she didn't give any outward indication of it. She was as serene and calm as the surface of the Caribbean.

Removing her sunglasses, she looked between Kez and V. "So did you ladies have a good night last night?"

V was the first to answer. "Oh yes!" she exclaimed then blushed a little. "We ate at the Italian place here. It was so good."

Van watched V curl into Dave, her feline smile showing the Italian place hadn't been the only good part of their evening.

"What about you, Kez?" Regan asked.

Kez exchanged a heated look with Jackson. "We had dinner in, and it was . . . delicious."

"I'll bet," snickered Regan.

"Well, your night must've been interesting if it made a sun worshipper like you sleep in until almost noon," Kez countered. "Care to tell us about it?"

Regan yawned and said, "Had dinner in my PJs on the balcony overlooking the water. Very mellow."

"And?" Kez pressed her for more information and Van held his breath, waiting to see what she'd say.

"And what, Kez?" Regan asked evenly.

"Sounds like a good night all around," Jackson intervened before Kez could continue her cross-examination. "I hope we can all have dinner together tonight."

"Works for me," Regan said then looked out at the line of lounge chairs one step down from their cabana. "Do those go with this setup?"

Jackson nodded. "Yeah, we get the four right in front of us."

"Nice," she responded then looked to V and Kez. "How about it, ladies? Care to join me for a little sun?"

There was some secret girl code transmitted among the three women. V and Kez bobbed their heads and rose from their seats. Regan did, too, then turned to Van. Smiling sweetly, which automatically made him nervous, she asked, "Van, will you put some sunblock on my shoulders? I meant to earlier, but I got . . . distracted."

The source of that distraction rocketed through his brain. Given her wish to keep things between them under wraps for right now, her request for him to act as her lotion boy took him by surprise. Wordlessly, he accepted the sunblock from her and watched as she twisted her hair into a makeshift knot. Then she turned her back to him and knelt between his knees, her hands on the tops of his thighs. With her head bent slightly forward, she looked like a sacrificial offering. He took in the graceful slope of her shoulders and the way her ribcage tapered down to her slim waist, right above the dimples on her lower back.

When she called his name, he stopped ogling her backside, shaking the bottle and squirting the coconut-scented cream into his palms. Using broad strokes, he massaged the lotion over her shoulders and down her back. She leaned into his touch, and he heard her quiet hum of pleasure. If she kept this up, he would be hard as a rock. Smoothing the last of the lotion onto her skin, he capped the bottle and mentally ran through how to take apart, clean, and reassemble his service weapon to distract himself from the feel of her skin beneath his fingers.

Rising from her crouched position before him, she took the bottle back and dropped it into her bag. She tapped a finger to his cheek and said, "Thanks, Van. You could have a real future as a cabana boy." With a quick tousle of his hair, she joined her friends at the front of the cabana. He stared after her as she sashayed down to a chaise, fluffed out a huge beach towel, and offered her body to the bright Caymanian sunshine.

Jackson's laughter pulled his attention from Regan's glistening midsection. "What's so funny?" he asked.

After a swig of his beer, Jackson answered, "I never thought I'd see the day when a girl totally had your number, man." He tipped the bottle toward Van. "It looks good on you though. You're a lot less gloomy."

Van took a pull of his own beer. "You're one to talk, loverboy. If you were wrapped any tighter around Kez's finger, it would fall off from blood loss."

Jackson lifted a shoulder in a careless shrug. "I cannot, nor would I even want to, dispute that." His beer tilted sideways to include Dave. "And I'm pretty sure this guy is in the same boat."

Dave's ever-present state of chill was clear from the way he lifted his palms in a gesture of cheerful acceptance. "What can I say?" he asked. "That girl freaking owns me."

The petite blonde in question poked her head over the back of her lounge chair and smiled at Dave. The besotted look on his face confirmed it—he was a goner.

Van reclined into his seat, stretching his long legs in front of him. "Well, now that we've each established ourselves as totally and completely whipped, what's next for our little therapy group?"

Jackson mimicked his easy posture. "I certainly hope you're not about to encourage us to sit in a circle and share our feelings."

Van scoffed at the idea of chanting kumbaya or some other drivel with these guys while they got in touch with their inner children. He scanned the beach in front of them, his eyes landing on a volleyball net stretched across the sand. "How about a little friendly competition?"

Jackson's eyes lit with the challenge. "Competition? Absolutely, but I'm not so sure about the friendly part."

Van couldn't help but razz Jackson as he stood. "Don't worry, old timer. I'll take it easy on you."

Stretching to his full height, Jackson had a couple inches on Van. "We'll see about that shit, McLeod," he replied. Looking at Dave, he asked, "You up for it, man?"

Dave polished off his beer and set the empty bottle on the table. He slapped both Van and Jackson on the back. "Well, somebody's got to show you two how it's done, right?"

The beach volleyball court was diagonal from their cabana, directly to the right of the girls' chaises. Jackson tugged his shirt over his head and tossed it to Kez as they passed. "Hang onto that for me, will you, babe?"

In an exaggerated motion, Kez slid her sunglasses down her nose and let loose a loud wolf whistle at her husband. He obliged her with a brief flex of his biceps, and she fanned herself through a pretend swoon against her chair. Dave was more subtle, tucking his shirt through the slats of V's chair and placing a light kiss to her temple.

Van risked squatting down beside Regan. She looked at him over the top of her oversized sunglasses. "Did you need something?" she asked. Without responding, he reached back and pulled off his shirt with one hand. Her vivid green eyes tracked over his bare chest and down the planes of his stomach. He didn't miss the slight flare to her nostrils or the way her throat bobbed with a deep swallow.

Holding out his shirt, he asked, "Mind tucking this into your bag?"

With a vague nod, she took it from him, letting her fingers glide over his palm.

God, did he want to kiss her, but he also didn't want to push her. He was treading in uncharted waters, but she had instigated the lotion application, so he figured giving her his T-shirt to hold was a safe bet. "Thanks," he said and started to rise, but she reached for his arm.

Her touch was feather light, and she looked as surprised as he was that she'd done it. As they both looked down at her fingers on his arm, Van spoke her name in question. "Regan?"

Her thumb rubbed the underside of his wrist, and she said, "Shirtless is a good look for you." When she tugged lightly, he swayed in his crouched stance. He gripped the opposite arm of her chair to steady himself, which put his face level with hers. She put a hand to his cheek. Her abs tightened to raise her upper body toward him while she brought his lips down to hers. The kiss was light and quick, but it carried so much weight because she'd kissed him in front of her friends. *She'd kissed him,* not the other way around.

Pulling back, she smiled at him, "A *very* good look indeed." Adjusting her sunglasses, she laid back. "Now, go do whatever manly thing it is that required the three of you to take off your shirts. You're blocking my sun."

# 21

As Van trotted down the beach, Rae knew without checking that Kez and V were staring at her. Their curiosity was like a living thing, clutching her lounge chair and salivating for details. And, okay, her decision to plant a smooch on Van in front of God and everyone else probably wasn't the best plan, but she couldn't help herself. In the past few hours, *not* touching or kissing him had somehow become impossible. If he were within three feet of her, hell, if they were in the same room, she *wanted* her hands on him. She craved physical contact with him like a junkie needing a fix.

Kez cleared her throat, and Rae rolled her head toward her friend. Sure enough, both Kez and V were sitting up in their loungers, expectant looks on their faces. "What?" Rae asked.

Kez waggled a finger at her. "Don't you 'what' me, young lady! I don't know what happened in the past twelve hours, but you better come clean right now." V moved from her chair on the other side of Kez and plopped down on the foot of Rae's chair. They had her surrounded.

Rae gazed down the beach. The guys had drafted another man into their game and were warming up two-on-two. She jerked her chin in the direction of the game. "View's much better that way." Neither of her friends spared a glance down the beach. Rae knew they would not budge without her spilling at least a few salacious details. She threw up her hands in surrender. "Fine, what do you want to know?" The sooner they finished their interrogation, the sooner she could sip frosty drinks and watch Van run around shirtless. Talk about motivation.

Kez flipped onto her side, propping her head in her hand as she readied her questions. "I want to know *everything*, but I'll settle for what happened after we left yesterday afternoon."

"That's the same thing as 'everything,' isn't it?" Rae quibbled.

"Potato, po-*tah*-to," Kez responded.

"C'mon, Rae," V pleaded, nudging Rae with her foot. "You always wheedle the details from us. Turnabout is fair play."

"And may I point out," Kez added, "that normally we don't even have to ask what happened without you volunteering every little, or sometimes large, detail. If you're holding back, there's more to this than a casual island fling."

*Crap,* Rae thought. Her caginess only heightened her friends' interest in her night with Van. She should've been ladling out the sexual innuendos and draping herself across his lap. That would have been her standard approach—not this newly guarded attitude about her sexual conquests. Trying to dodge Kez's question, Rae said, "Let's not get carried away. Just because you're floating through life on a heart-shaped cloud doesn't mean the rest of us are ready to hop on too." She shot a pointed look at V. "At least not *all* of us."

V shoved Rae's foot. "Quit stalling," she warned. "I deal with teenagers going through puberty, the true masters of diversion and misdirection. Your paltry tactics won't work. Something happened with you and Van last night."

The appearance of their server saved Rae from having to answer just yet. "Ladies, here you go." Frozen drinks in a soft shade of yellow with a spike of red in the center rested on a tray. A chunk of mango and a slice of strawberry garnished each one.

"These look divine," said Kez. "What are they?"

He smiled. "The drink of the day—A Kiss on the Lips."

Kez wiggled her eyebrows at V and Rae. "How perfect."

With a slight bow, he retreated into the cabana to deposit the second bucket of beer and the promised lunch menus. They each took a drink off the tray and sampled the fruity concoctions.

After appreciative murmurs over the tangy sweetness, Kez resumed her questions. "No more dodging, Rae," she demanded. "Spill."

Rae's reluctance to talk about Van wasn't exactly genuine. While she had certain doubts still swirling in her head, she was excited and cautiously optimistic, which made her want to spill her guts to her girlfriends. These women had the insights she needed to make sure she wasn't being overly cavalier, so she obeyed Kez's command. She told them everything from Van's confession on the balcony to their sweaty tumble across the sheets for most of the evening. The time on the counter had both Kez and V fanning themselves with approval. It was easy to tell them about the sex. Sex was the most basic part of the equation. The emotional landscape, however, was harder to navigate, much less explain.

"How can I trust someone who consciously deceived me for over a year?" she asked. "For more than three hundred sixty-five days, he lied straight to my face about every aspect of his life."

"But were the lies directly about you?" V asked.

"What do you mean?"

"What I think she means," clarified Kez, "is that were his lies about you or his feelings for you?"

Rae considered their joint question, experiencing the same expansive sensation in her chest from earlier, as though a knot were being untied and she could take a full breath. "The way he tells it, no, they weren't," Rae answered.

"Do you believe him?" Kez inquired, toying with a long strand of red hair that had fallen from her topknot.

"I believed his name was Ray Edwards, so I don't know if what I believe is the best test," Rae said wryly.

V shook her head. "No, I don't think so, Rae. That's the *only* test that you should use. What you believe is paramount in this situation." She repeated Kez's question. "Do you believe him?"

*Did she?* Rae wasn't sure. She wanted to. There was no question about that. Even if she did, where did that leave them? Van obviously thought it offered them a chance to start over . . . together. The notion that he had been grieving the loss of her since she'd run out the door turned everything on its ear and left her reeling. In her mind, he'd gone on after she left without a hitch in his life—content to bask in the glory of his big bust and move on to bigger and better things. Without a backward glance at her or the life they'd built. But if she were wrong and he wasn't the heartless bastard she'd painted him to be but a man trapped in the ultimate catch-22, then she'd wasted years of her life being angry and distrustful of any promise of forever. And, if she were honest, *she* was the one who'd run, not Van. He might not have followed, but if she'd talked to him back then, she could've saved them both years of misery and loneliness.

Her role in the demise of their relationship was too much to consider on this beautiful beach. Heavy thoughts had no place in paradise, so she banished them to the innermost reaches of her brain—at least for the next week. She didn't want to spend the time she had left psychoanalyzing what was happening with Van. It was too much, and she didn't want reality intruding right then. Any major decisions about the future could wait until they were back home. Screw being responsible while she was on vacation. Days and nights of naked, sexy time with Van were much more appealing.

She lowered her glasses and *sort of* answered her friends. "I believe he looks ridiculously hot when he is sweaty, shirtless, and covered in sand. For now, that's good enough."

V's head whipped around so quickly, Rae worried she'd get whiplash. Kez sat up for a better look. Dissatisfied with her vantage point, she wedged herself between V and Rae on Rae's chaise.

"Oh my," said Kez in a breathy voice as she watched the remake of the volleyball scene from *Top Gun* currently taking place about fifty yards away.

It was a sight to behold. The four men were not playing a friendly game. It was a no-holds-barred match full of spikes, dives, and spraying sand. Van dove to dig out a particularly well-placed slam by Jackson and skidded across the powdery surface. When he pushed up from the ground, grains of white sand stuck to his tanned torso. Rae got out of her chair, headed to the beach without even thinking. V and Kez were hot on her heels.

Like a trio of teenage girls watching varsity football practice, they stood in a gaggle on the surf side of the "court." Water lapped at their ankles while they watched the ball sail back and forth over the net. Sand churned underneath Van's feet as he chased a deep shot from Dave. It landed just outside the lines, giving Van and his teammate the serve. He tossed the ball in the air a few times, catching it easily. Long, tanned fingers curved up the sides of the ball with each toss.

Thoughts of what those fingers did the night before made Rae a little woozy. When Van finally pitched the ball high enough to serve, his arm arced through the air, every muscle straining with his long reach.

On the downswing, defined obliques torqued as he whipped his hand against the ball. The broad expanse of his back flexed as he waited for the return, resting lightly on the balls of his feet. His fluid movements played out in a slow-motion masculine ballet, only instead of pirouettes and pliés, there were blocks, sets, and spikes. She didn't know the score or who was winning, nor did she care. They could play to a hundred and it wouldn't matter, so long as she didn't have to give up her front-row seat. A quick glance at her friends' mesmerized expressions confirmed they were also willing to watch the glistening display of shirtless machismo all damn day.

Van called out, "Match point!" and then sent the ball streaking over the net. Only Jackson's miraculous bump set back to Dave saved an ace. The battle wore on as each team came up with save after save until finally Van sent the ball spinning out of Dave's reach but barely within bounds. He sank to his knees in the soft sand, chest heaving from the exertion of the last volley. His nameless teammate extended his hand, and Van clasped it, levering himself from the ground. They did the standard handshake/bro hug thing then slapped hands with Dave and Jackson.

Part of Rae wanted to run and congratulate him with a kiss, but she pumped the brakes on that idea. While she planned to let loose and enjoy herself for the rest of the week, that didn't mean she should hype up Van's expectations and play the part of the doting girlfriend. She needed to make sure all signals she sent to him were clear and not open to misinterpretation. It didn't help that her mind was a muddled mess over what she wanted to happen between them. When the transmitter itself was scrambled, how could she keep the signals from getting mixed?

Van solved the immediate problem by walking down to meet her at the water's edge. Jackson and Dave wasted no time in lifting Kez and V into their arms for consolation hugs and kisses over their loss. As though he sensed her turmoil, Van stopped next to her. Sweat ran in rivulets down his chest, forging damp paths through the sand coating his skin.

"Jackson really made you work for it, huh?" she asked.

He chuckled in agreement and brushed a hand down his body, trying to dislodge some of the tiny grains. It didn't work.

"Well," Rae said, "look at it this way. They charge big bucks for that type of exfoliation at the spa here, so you've saved yourself hundreds of dollars."

Van rolled his eyes. "Just what I was hoping for."

Playfully, she shoved his arm. "Cheer up, McLeod. You won! I'll buy you a celebratory drink once you get cleaned up."

His dark eyes moved to the clear blue water then back to her face. His eyebrow waggle would've made Magnum, P.I. proud, and it telegraphed exactly what he was thinking. Her eyes widened, and she backed away, hands outstretched to ward him off.

"No, Van," she said, with a quick shake of her spread fingers, "don't even think about it."

"Think about what?" he asked innocently, right as he charged forward.

If he'd allowed himself time to consider what he was doing, Van never would have tackled Regan into the ocean. He would have worried about pissing her off, or that it was too much of a display, or any number of other things. But he didn't think or consider. He just grabbed her and plunged them both into the crystal waters of the Caribbean. He heard her screech as she went under and felt her flail against him in the gentle surf. When they surfaced, water droplets hung from her lashes, and she was spewing ocean water along with several colorful curse words.

Shoving her hair back, she jabbed a finger at him. "Oh, you're gonna get it now."

Laughing, he shook his head, spattering her with saltwater, which only made her that much more determined to drown him. She launched herself at him, and he stumbled back into a wave. Pressing her advantage, Regan latched onto his shoulders like a koala and dunked him. Opening his eyes underwater, Van saw her hips directly in front of him and hooked an arm around them, hoisting her out of the water when he stood. With a piercing shriek, her fists pummeled his back as he held her on his shoulder. A firm swat to her ass made her redouble her efforts to punch him in the kidneys. Lucky for him, his torso was long, and her arms weren't. She landed a few more jabs to his ribs before he relented and let her slide down the front of his body.

Regan stood on the tops of his feet with her hands gripping his forearms. He smoothed the wet hair off her face and said, "You're so tiny."

"Goliath thought the same thing about David," she retorted and slapped his stomach.

He *tsked*. "Your first instinct shouldn't always be to maim or kill, Regan."

"It's served me well this far," she argued but let him draw her in until their bodies were flush against each other. Her hands glided up his arms, and he let his palms rest right above her ass. They swayed with the tides as the water washed around them.

Van lowered his head until their lips were inches apart. "What are your instincts telling you now?"

She nibbled on her lower lip and stared at him. "That I'm in big trouble."

Over Regan's shoulder, Van saw a flash of silver in the water. He knew from experience Regan liked only one type of sea creature: cooked and on a plate. If that flash was what he suspected, she would freak out.

Trying to keep her attention on him, he slid his hands down over the swell of her ass and lifted her up. Her heels hooked behind his back, and she curled her fingers around his biceps, smilingly oblivious to the barracuda cutting through the water a few feet away.

"In a hurry, cowboy?" she joked.

"It's easier to do the things I want to do to you on dry land," he answered, keeping one eye on the 'cuda. Giving it and its mouthful of huge teeth a wide berth, Van made his way back to shore.

Regan wriggled against him, a move he would've welcomed if he weren't trying to navigate his way out of the ocean without either running into the fish or letting her see it. "I can walk, you know," she protested when he tightened his grip.

"I can't help it if I want to take every available opportunity to touch you." The line was tacky as hell, so her answering eye roll was not unexpected.

"Jesus, McLeod, no wonder you're still single, with lines like that."

The barracuda swam farther out to sea and disappeared. He set her down in the shallows but took her hand in his. It hadn't been a lie when he said he wanted any chance he had to touch her. Cheesy? Sure, but not a lie. She didn't pull her hand away though.

"Holy shit, Rae!" Kez called as she scampered toward them. "Did you see that—" Van gave a slight shake of his head, and her question died on her lips. As one of Regan's best friends, Kez had to know about Regan's fear of sea life.

But it was too late. Regan tugged her hand away. "Did I see what, Kez?"

Kez fumbled briefly, but she recovered. "A parasail," she lied.

Regan turned back to the water and searched the sky. "Where?"

Before Kez could answer, Dave appeared with V trailing behind him. "Man, did you see that giant barracuda? It was right next to you!"

All the color drained from Regan's cheeks, and she reached back to Van. He steadied her with a hand at her waist. "What did you say?" she croaked out.

Dave's brow wrinkled in confusion. "Uh, there was a barracuda swimming next to you out there. How did you not see it? We could see it from the beach!" To Van, he said, "You *had* to have seen it. You were looking right at it!"

Kez and V exchanged a worried look, and V tugged on Dave's forearm. "What?" he asked, genuinely confused. "What'd I say?"

"I'll explain later," V said as she pulled him toward the cabana. Kez mouthed "Sorry" to Van and followed them.

Regan faced Van. "Did you see it?"

This could go one of two ways. If she wanted an out, she'd twist this into some farfetched example of why she couldn't trust him. Or she'd be grateful he'd kept his cool and carried her out of harm's way. Her poker face gave him no inkling of which direction she was leaning. Van bit the bullet and nodded, admitting he'd seen it.

"Death was swimming two feet from me, and you didn't tell me?" Her voice rose a whole octave at the end of her question.

Honesty was the best policy here, he thought. "I didn't want you to freak out."

Two spots of color returned to her cheeks and her palm came up to his chest. "That's why you picked me up?"

Another nod.

"And that's why you left the water?"

Yet one more bob of the head. He waited anxiously to see how she would react to his explanation.

His heart sank as she said, "You hiding things from me isn't new." Well, that sealed it. She'd elected to blow this out of proportion as an excuse to back away. *Fuck!*

Except she didn't drop her hand from his chest. It slid to his shoulder then higher. Her other hand took the parallel route. Oh-kay, this was not what he was expecting to happen.

The press of her fingertips to the back of his neck brought him closer. Tentatively, he put his hands on her hips. She stepped into him, rising upward as he bent down. He really hoped she wasn't gearing up for a swift knee to the family jewels. His abs tensed at the thought. But her feet stayed planted firmly on the ground, and a smile blossomed on her face.

"Doing it to protect me, however, is a nice, unexpected twist," she said right before kissing him. The kiss was sweet, almost demure. Well, except for the small bite to his lower lip when she pulled away. She batted her lashes at him, clutching at imaginary pearls. "My hero," she purred in an over-the-top breathy voice.

He knew she was messing with him. She was the heroine of her own story. Regan didn't need, or want, a savior or hero. She was perfectly capable of fighting her own battles, even against pointy-toothed sea beasts. Knowing all that didn't keep his chest from puffing out a bit at her acknowledgment, even in jest, of his role as rescuer. Van sketched a deep bow to her. "At your service, milady."

With a snort, she bumped his shoulder with a hip. Off-balance, he tumbled backward and landed on his ass with a loud splash. Laughing, Regan skipped out of the water and headed back toward their cabana. Over her shoulder, she called, "Get a move on, Aquaman. I at least owe you a drink for your tidal pool heroics."

Jackson jogged over and stood in the surf, dipping out a few handfuls of crystal clear water to rinse off. With a lopsided grin, he offered a hand to haul Van to his feet. The two of them fell into step toward the shaded sanctuary and cold beers.

"Seems like you're making progress," Jackson commented casually. He was never one to pry into another man's business. He was a good sounding board if you were willing, but he wouldn't force the issue. Hence the blasé reference to how things had obviously shifted between Van and Regan.

Van rubbed his neck and lifted one hand in a "Who knows?" gesture. "I think so, man," he said. "But with her, it's going to be day to day." He stopped and let loose a rueful laugh. "No, scratch that, more like hour to hour. I don't blame her for being gun-shy after what happened, but it's also hard to keep banging my head against a wall."

"I get that," Jackson replied. "But remember, it's been less than seventy-two hours since you waltzed back into her life completely out of the blue. Don't expect her to skip blithely off into the sunset with you yet."

"I know, I know!" Van said, frustration creeping into his voice. "Last night was . . . Well, you can guess what it was. But this morning, she agreed to give this thing between us a chance but also says not to say anything to any of you. Then she does the thing with the sunscreen and kisses me." As they wove between two chairs, Van waved a hand toward the water. "Back there, on an inhale, she brings Charleston back up, but on her exhale, she's flirting with me. I don't know what she wants!"

Jackson checked to make sure they remained out of earshot of the others before he spoke. "Van, for a smart guy, you can be a real dumbass sometimes."

Van stopped short. "Huh?"

Jackson halted his long strides and faced Van. "You fucked up five years ago, Van. Big time. You lied to this girl the whole time you were together, right?"

Jackson's blunt delivery momentarily stunned Van, but he recovered enough to argue. "Well, yeah, but it was because—"

Jackson's large palm shot up to stop him. "I know *why*, but it doesn't change the fact that you did. If the shoe were on the other foot, how would you feel? If Rae had been the one undercover back then and was *still* an FBI agent now? Would you trust your own feelings about her? Wouldn't you at least have some concern that the past might repeat itself? That if called upon to lie again for her job, she'd do it? You burned her, man. You burned her badly. If she's waffling or uncertain about what she wants or how she feels, that's part of the territory. If you love her, then you'll gladly slog through it with her."

Jackson started walking again, and Van hurried to catch up.

"Trust isn't something that's freely given by any of these ladies," Jackson reminded him. "You had it and threw it away. You know Rae, probably better than I do. She won't just hand you a do-over. She'll make you fucking grovel." Jackson glanced over to see Regan chatting with the waiter as she wrung water from her hair. He looked back at Van. "You've got one choice, Van."

"Oh yeah? What's that?" Van asked, his stomach twisting nervously.

"Get your head out of your ass and accept whatever punishment she metes out." With a grin, he added, "I mean, it can't last forever . . . right?"

"McLeod!" Regan yelled, brandishing two shot glasses filled with a violent-pink liquid. "I've got a G-Spot with your name on it."

Laughter burst from Jackson's lips. "Oh man," he wheezed, "you are so fucked. But what a way to go!"

## 22

*Rae!* V scolded, glancing around at the neighboring cabanas. "Do you really think it's appropriate to shout 'G-spot' across the beach?"

"Normally," Rae answered, "it's the G-spot that makes me shout things, so I think it's okay."

"Good Lord." V sighed and shook her head in resignation. "We can't take you anywhere."

"She's worse if you feed her after midnight," Kez said.

Rae tuned out the rest of their comments as Van and Jackson walked up. Several female heads swiveled their way, taking notice of the duo. Rae couldn't blame them. Separately, they were hot. Together, they were a ten-alarm blaze that could engulf the hotel. Jackson's larger build, slightly shaggy hair, and thick beard made him more rugged than Van's sharper-featured, more clean-cut look, but neither would get kicked out of bed for eating crackers.

Jackson bumped her shoulder as he came into the shade. "No G-Spot for me?"

Rae inclined her head toward Kez. "Sure, she's right over there. Although, if you can't find it on your own, I really can't help you."

Kez came to his defense. "Trust me, Rae, Jax is *well*-acquainted with its location."

"Thank you, Mrs. Jenkins," he said, lifting her onto his lap.

She kissed him. "You're welcome, Mr. Jenkins."

Rae gagged. "Please, you're going to make me vomit, and I don't want to revisit that mango concoction from earlier." She passed one of the pink shots to Van. "Bottoms up, hero." Clinking her glass to his, she took it in one swallow. It really was delicious. She'd convinced the staff to whip up an entire batch of the stuff, which was currently chilling in a metal pitcher tucked into an ice bucket.

"Want another?" she asked Van.

His grin was dirty. "Have you ever known me to shy away from the G-Spot?"

Her own lady parts sparked to life, as did certain parts of last night. She could answer that question with an emphatic *no*. "Not to my knowledge," she answered, pouring another round of shots.

She passed them out to their group and then raised hers in a toast. "To Kez and Jackson, may all the ups and downs of your marriage be under the sheets!" Everyone laughed and downed their shots, and she quickly refilled their glasses.

"What else should we toast?"

"To women," Van offered.

Rae quirked a brow. "To women?"

He nodded, lifted his glass and said, "To women. Let us cherish them, support them, and respect them. And," he looked directly at Rae, "if we get the chance to love them, let us do it unconditionally."

"To women!" called out Jackson and Dave.

Rae got her arm to move and direct the shot to her lips. She tilted the glass and swallowed automatically. The man had a way with words. He wielded that skill to manipulate his way into her life the first time. Now he was relying on it to convince her to let him back in. Rae was willing to allow him back into her bed, or bathroom counter, but she needed to keep him a safe distance from her heart—for now.

"Well, well, well, what do we have here?" The strutting newcomer was the most flamboyantly gay man Rae had ever seen. He couldn't have been over five feet six, and his itty-bitty teal shorts bordered on indecent. His white shirt fit closely to his slim physique—a physique she got a good glimpse of since he'd unbuttoned the shirt almost to his navel. Dark-mahogany skin glowed against the fabric, almost as brightly as his pristine white sneakers. His shaved head gleamed, and his eyebrows were better shaped than hers. A sparkling gold nametag read "Robbie."

Jackson's lips twitched, and he asked, "Is there something we can help you with?"

Robbie took his time looking Jackson over. "I'm sure there are many, *many* things with which you could assist me." Dark eyes scanned over Dave and Van, inventorying them as well. "And then your lovely companions could finish wherever you left off."

A snort of laughter escaped Kez's lips at his theatrics. He fanned his hands out dismissively. "But, my lovelies, I am not here to see what you can do for me." He cast another long look at Jackson. "As temptingly scrumptious as that sounds." He clapped his hands together in a staccato fashion. "No, no, no. I am here to find out if there is anything Robbie can do for you." He rolled the *r* at the start of his name for so long it took on several additional syllables.

Van cleared his throat and asked hesitantly, "Do for us?"

Robbie sidled closer to Van and purred, "Yes, darling. I'm the director of recreation, so I wanted to make sure you beautiful people were taking advantage of all our . . . opportunities." His inflection made the innocuous word sound positively pornographic.

It was Rae's turn to laugh when Van blushed at Robbie's proximity and insinuation. She asked, "Why don't you give us the rundown?"

Robbie's narrow hips swished as he made his way to the couch and sat, crossing his legs and linking his fingers at his knee. "Well, we have all the watersports—parasailing, banana boats—and of course, snorkeling and scuba diving."

"We swam with a barracuda this morning," Rae said. "I think I'll pass on any more water sports for the time being."

Robbie's laugh was a dainty little tinkle of sound. "We have plenty of things to keep you occupied on land too. There's karaoke night and of course the talent show."

Rae's ears perked up. "Talent show? Tell me more."

He leaned forward, sending the smell of coconut and vanilla wafting toward her. "Well, it's more for the ladies."

Rae mimicked his posture. "Do tell."

"It's an all-male show," he said, "made up solely of guest volunteers competing in a few contests to be crowned the winner. It's held every Monday in the amphitheater."

"So there's one tonight?" Rae asked.

Robbie nodded enthusiastically, almost bouncing in his seat. "Yes." His excitement waned, and he sulked theatrically, looking down at his buffed nails. "But we are a few contestants shy of having a full slate."

Rae, Kez, and V shared a sly grin. Jackson shifted in his seat, while Dave and Van looked increasingly nervous.

"Exactly how many more contestants did you need?" Kez asked. Jackson shot her a censoring look, which she studiously ignored.

Robbie perked up. "If we had three more volunteers, it would be fabulous." His elfin hands shot out into a jazzy arc to demonstrate just how *fabulous*.

"Well," said V, "you're in luck, Robbie." Dave tensed beside her, his eyes pleading.

Kez nodded while putting a preemptive hand over Jackson's mouth. "Yep, you came to the right place." Jackson mumbled incoherently behind her palm, shaking his head.

Robbie bounded from his seat, clapping his hands in an ecstatic frenzy, eyes alight with excitement. "Really?"

Locking eyes with Van, Rae confirmed it with a wide smile. "Absolutely. We've got three able-bodied volunteers right here who'd love to participate." Was there a better penance for Van than to have him humiliate himself in front of hundreds of strangers? If there were, it didn't immediately spring to mind. While it wasn't even close to the same level of embarrassment he'd caused her in Charleston, Rae thought it was a good start.

"Now wait a—" Van tried to say, but Robbie's jubilant squeal cut him off.

"What time do they need to report for duty?" Kez asked, keeping her hand clamped against Jackson's lips. His blue eyes held more resignation than anger though.

Robbie popped up onto his toes, then down, then back up—a human Tigger, giddy with enthusiasm. "The show starts at nine. Make sure they are there by eight-thirty."

Rae hugged Robbie. "They'll be there with bells on."

Once Robbie skipped away, Kez lowered her hand from Jackson's mouth. It was an unsmiling line behind his beard. "What. The. Hell. Did. You. Do?" he clipped out.

Unphased, Kez kissed him, pressing her lips to his until he kissed her back, albeit begrudgingly. "Relax. It'll be fun!"

"For whom exactly?" he asked, but he no longer looked as grim.

Kez circled her arm to include V and Rae. "For us, dummy!" The girls laughed, but Dave and Van were less than pleased.

"What's the matter, McLeod?" Rae razzed him. "Have a little performance anxiety? I hear that happens as men get older."

He pointed his index finger at her. "You'll pay for this, Regan Murphy."

She shrugged off his threat. "You know where to find me, McLeod."

❧

Dave adjusted his fedora. "This is not cool, man."

Van glowered at him while tugging at the hem of his plaid skirt. "What do you have to complain about? You're Michael Jackson pre-molestation accusations." He gestured to the white shirt tied below his pecs and the scrap of plaid fabric that barely covered his ass. "I'm a frigging pop princess!" His protests made the ratty blond wig shift around on his head.

Jackson adjusted his own wig and said, "You're more Captain Caveman than Britney in that getup. Nice legs, by the way. Leg press or free squats?"

Van moved his glare from Dave to Jackson. "You're one to talk. Who are you supposed to be anyway?"

Jackson looked down at his own costume—a flowing dress with a ruffled hem accentuated by a brown wig. "Celine Dion, I think."

"You look more like a cross-dressing extra on *Little House on the Prairie*," Van grumbled.

Robbie twirled into the back room where they were sequestered. He carried a tray with a fifth of tequila and three shot glasses. "For my starlets," he chirped. Setting it on a small table, he poured three generous shots and said, "Bottoms up!"

When they finished the first three, Robbie quickly splashed a second round into their glasses. As they took the next shot, he said, "You three are my closers, so the ladies will be primed and ready when you walk out. We'll start with you, Michael." He tapped the brim of Dave's fedora. "Then we'll move to Celine," he said, looking at Jackson. "And the true finale"—he danced in a circle around Van—"will be you, Britney!"

Van grabbed the tequila and poured himself a third shot. It was room temperature and tasted cheap, but he could feel the alcohol taking effect. He'd need all the help he could get to endure this humiliation. When Jackson told him to take whatever punishment Regan doled out, dressing up as Britney Spears in front of hundreds of people hadn't been within his realm of expectation. The reflection staring at him from the mirror on the back of the door looked ridiculous. He'd be lucky if he didn't give the folks a show they hadn't signed up for, as short as this skirt was. He gave his boxer briefs a self-conscious tug, wishing they were more boxer than brief.

Jackson passed him another shot, and Van gladly sucked it down. Robbie shepherded them out of the room but not before Van grabbed the tequila. From the side of the stage, they watched men of various ages "perform" as everything from Mick Jagger to Donna Summer. Some really got into it with high kicks and hip thrusts. Others shuffled side to side *almost* to the rhythm of the music.

After escorting an overweight Justin Bieber off the stage, Robbie signaled to Dave and mouthed, "You're next."

Dressed in black pants and a matching vest with no shirt, Dave looked extremely uncomfortable. Jackson nudged his shoulder. "Relax, man, you've emceed countless of these things at the bar back home."

Dave gulped. "Yeah, but I wasn't the one *doing* the twerking."

The first few strains of "Billie Jean" played over the speakers, and Robbie said, "Ladies and gentlemen, please welcome a man with all the right moves—Michael Jackson!" Cheers and whistles sounded through the crowd as Dave made his way to center stage. Van and Jackson watched as he gave a valiant effort at a leg kick and toe pop. Nowhere close to the King of Pop's skills, but the crowd was generous with their applause. Dave danced across the stage as best he could, getting through the entire song and ending with a decent moonwalk back into the wings.

Sweat shone on his chest, and he was breathing hard. He made a *gimme* gesture with his hand, and Van passed him the tequila. Dave drank straight from the bottle, lowering it with a wheezing sound. "God, am I glad that's over!"

Robbie was announcing Jackson as Celine Dion before either of them could congratulate Dave on surviving his turn in the spotlight. Personally, Van thought Jackson had drawn the easiest card. His outfit was outlandish, but his ass wasn't hanging out and all he had to do was sway to that song from *Titanic* and he'd be through.

He had to admit it, though, Jackson got into it. So into it that with one sweeping arm move during a high note, he ripped the back of the gown he was wearing. That brought more cheers than anything else, especially when Robbie "helped" him by pulling it off. Jackson finished the song wearing nothing but a pair of athletic shorts. Based on the audience's response, including Kez's excited clapping from her front-row seat, that was the best part of his performance.

Perspiration beaded on Van's forehead as Jackson's song wound down. He was next. The tequila had helped the onslaught of stage fright so far, so more should make things even easier. Taking it from Dave, he too drank right from the bottle.

"Well, well, well," Robbie crooned into the mic while he fanned himself. "I've never seen that side of Celine!" Van heard the laughter and took another slug. The fifth was less than half-full. Robbie went on with his shtick. "The only person I know who could follow that is the gorgeous lady we slated for our grand finale! The one and only—Miss Britney Spears!"

Jackson gave him a fist bump as he came off stage right when "Baby One More Time" started. When Van emerged from behind the curtain, the crowd erupted into raucous applause and female shouts of approval. Temporarily blinded by the spotlight, he couldn't tell who was yelling or how many people were there. Fueled by tequila and catcalls, he moved to the music. Van had a good sense of rhythm, so dancing wasn't hard for him. As the song continued to play, he got more comfortable, egged on by women cheering and the tequila humming through his bloodstream. He gyrated his hips and stroked a hand down his abs, stopping right before it got beyond PG-13.

"Take it off!" Regan called. Van pivoted in the direction of her voice. She wasn't hard to spot, seated in the middle of the front row between Kez and V. One hand cupped around her mouth as she cheered, the other held her cell phone to record his one time in drag for posterity.

If she wanted a show, then that's what she'd get. Keeping his eyes on her, he crawled on all fours to the edge of the stage and ground his hips into the floor in time with the music. For emphasis, he pounded one hand to the beat with each thrust of his pelvis. Regan bit her bottom lip and bobbled her cell phone as she watched him simulate sex on stage. He grinned, knowing what she was thinking. Hell, if he didn't stop thinking the same thing, his miniature skirt was going to become a miniature tent.

The song ended, and he sat back on his heels, careful to keep a hand at his crotch, just in case. The crowd went wild. Regan jumped up with V and Kez, all three of them yelling and clapping. Rising to his feet, he blew kisses to his adoring fans and jogged off the stage, holding his skirt down and plotting his revenge the entire way.

# 23

The way the three of them jumped up and down screaming, you'd think it was 1999 and they had front row seats to NSYNC. Van's performance left Rae weak in the knees, and if she were totally honest, her panties a little damp. The man could flat-out *rock* a schoolgirl skirt. The wig, not so much. When he disappeared behind the curtain, she dropped back into her seat.

Next to her, Kez sighed deeply. "Good Lord, girl. That was hot!"

V giggled. "I feel bad I didn't have any ones!"

A tap on her shoulder made Rae turn to see a well-dressed older woman behind them. "Excuse me?" she said.

"Yes, ma'am?" Rae said reflexively.

The woman aimed her finger at where Van had walked off the stage. "Is he yours?"

Rae felt her face heat. "Um, I'm sorry? Is who my what?"

"That young man who mated with the floorboards—is he yours?"

Unsure of how to respond, Rae stuttered, "Well, um, I—"

"If he is," said the woman with a bawdy wink, "you are one lucky girl." Then she smoothed her blouse and directed her eyes back to the stage.

Rae's mouth hung open, and she looked from Kez to V, both equally stunned. Kez's lips started to curl, and so did Rae's. A titter of laughter burst from V, and that sent them into a laughing fit. Their chuckles devolved into snorts, and all three struggled to get themselves under control. Rae dabbed a tear from under her eye and sucked in a deep breath. They reined in their hysteria when Robbie reappeared on stage.

"As usual, Miss Britney Shut. It. Down!" he exclaimed with a saucy snap of his fingers. "Whew!" He wiped a hand over his gleaming head. "Is it hot in here? Fear not friends, that little musical delight is a tiny sample of what we have prepared for you tonight!"

Kez leaned over and whispered to Rae. "There's more?"

Robbie continued his spiel. "We've got feats of strength coupled with challenges of mental agility." He waved a hand in front of him. "There will be magic, there will be death-defying stunts! So sit back, relax, and enjoy the rest of the show!"

"This ought to be good," V said under her breath.

And it was. The feat of strength was a push-up contest with a twist. Each time the chest hit the ground, you had to take a shot. The mental agility portion of the show was Robbie getting the contestants to recite the alphabet backward while chugging a beer. Death-defying stunts? Baseball bats rested at even intervals on the stage. Each man had to place his forehead on the top of a bat and spin in a circle for twenty seconds then run in a straight line to get a beer, which, you guessed it, he then had to chug.

By the time they'd reached the magic segment, Jackson, Van, and Dave were all less than steady on their feet. Rae had lost count of how much alcohol they'd consumed in the hour they'd been on stage. In the push-up contest alone, Jackson had downed multiple shots, with Van and Dave close behind him. She considered it a minor miracle they were still standing, albeit listing slightly with goofy, drunk grins on their faces.

"Holy crap, are they hammered!" Kez said.

When Dave blew her a sloppy kiss, V laughed and pretended to catch it. "You can say that again."

Van pointed at Rae then leaned over to Jackson, who whacked him on the back. Van was either too drunk, Jackson too strong, or a combination of both, because it sent Van stumbling forward and he almost plowed into Robbie.

"Well, hello, sailor," Robbie said into the mic.

Van smiled drunkenly down at him. "Hiya, Robbie." Rae was impressed he didn't slur . . . much.

Robbie looped an arm around Van's waist, and Van tucked the smaller man under his shoulder. "A girl could get used to this," Robbie said coquettishly. The audience hooted as Robbie led Van back to his place in the lineup.

"Now, ladies and gentlemen, as sad as it is, we have come to the closing segment of our show." A chorus of boos came from the crowd, and Robbie signaled for them to quiet down. "I promise you, we saved the absolute best for last. Please join me in welcoming a very special guest to the stage—Madame Fruita DeLoome!"

A smattering of applause broke out as a rotund black woman came onto the stage. Sequins strung through her ruby-red caftan made it waft around her in glittery ripples when she walked. A matching turban sat atop her head, and she gave the crowd a regal wave.

"Madame DeLoome has a unique talent," Robbie informed them. "She is not only psychic. By looking at a man, she can tell with absolute certainty one thing about him." He paused for dramatic effect, then said, "Boxers, briefs, or nothing at all."

It dawned on the three women all at once. "Fruit of the Loom!" they cried out in unison.

"Oh my God," said V. "She's an underwear psychic!"

"This must be why they've been funneling them liquor all night," said Kez. "No way a sober man gets on stage to discuss his underwear preference in front of strangers." She pointed a finger at Rae. "You, my dear, are the exception to every rule, so don't even waste your breath saying you'd be fine doing that. We *all* know that's true."

Rae sniggered behind her palm as she watched Madame DeLoome weave her way down the line of contestants, sizing each one of them up and asking a bare minimum of questions before revealing her prediction as to their preference of unmentionables.

When it was Jackson's turn, Madame DeLoome craned her neck so far back, Rae worried she would tip over. "My, my," she crooned, sizing him up. "Aren't you a big boy?" Jackson's only response was a lopsided grin.

Kez let loose a shrill whistle of appreciation, and DeLoome laughed. "Sounds like someone agrees with me." With a last caress of Jackson's arm, she announced, "There's really no question here, ladies and gentlemen—but especially the ladies—that this scrumptious male specimen could only wear boxer briefs."

Jackson's cheeks flushed, and she threw back her head and whooped with delight, tapping him lightly on his ruddy cheeks. "That pretty pink color you're turning says I was right on the money, honey! Care to confirm?"

Kez used her hands as a megaphone and called out, "I can!"

Jackson blushed even deeper, and the underwear expert grinned broadly.

DeLoome spread her arms wide, her sleeves flowing out like wings. "There you have it, folks!" Everyone applauded, with Kez clapping the loudest.

Dave was up next, and he slumped slightly to the side, but Jackson pulled him back to stand straight. One flick of her eyes up and down his body and DeLoome was ready with her prediction. "This man wears briefs!"

Dave leaned down into the mic. "Why don't you ask the blonde in the front row?"

V paled and hid her face behind her hands, but Madame DeLoome refused to let her off the hook. Facing the auditorium, she put a hand up to shade her eyes from the spotlight and focused on V. "You mean that cute little number shriveling in her seat?"

V groaned and peeked out from behind her fingers while Kez and Rae laughed at her embarrassment.

"What about it, honey?" asked DeLoome. "What type of drawers is your man wearing? I'm picturing navy blue and tight in all the right places. Am I close?"

"Sooner you give her an answer, the sooner you're off the hook," advised Rae.

With an audible gulp, V sat up in her seat and said, "The only thing you missed was the color. Tonight's are black, not blue."

DeLoome's shoulders shook as she shivered in response. "Mm-hmm, now that's a visual I can work with. Thank you, baby!" She gave Dave a quick swat on the ass, and he jumped.

DeLoome moved to the last man in the contest—Van. Rae's palms got damp watching DeLoome circle him, cocking her head this way and that way as she eyeballed his hips. Coming back around to face him, she stopped, putting her elbow in her opposite hand and tapping a finger to her lips in thought. "This one," she mused, "is a puzzle. I'm having a difficult time conjuring a vision."

Van leered at Rae but kept quiet while the psychic revolved around him in a weird orbit. Suddenly, she stood stock-still in front of him and snapped her fingers. "I've got it," she cried. "I know why there was such a weak signal! Because there's nothing for me to pick up on." She cocked a finger at him. "Shame on you, young man," she scolded playfully. "Going commando in front of all these people!" Women in the crowd shrieked so wildly at that declaration, Rae feared for her eardrums. Madame DeLoome reveled in the crowd's fervor and said, "You gonna tell me I'm wrong, boy?"

Wordlessly, Van turned his back to the audience and wiggled his ass. The crowd roared in approval. *No way is he about to do what I think he's about to do*, Rae thought. Van unbuttoned his pants, thrilling his audience. He didn't drop trou in front of the whole resort, but he lowered the waistband enough to let everyone see the top of his ass shine whitely beneath the tanned skin of his back. He looked over his shoulder and, with an exaggerated wink, tugged his pants back into place. Several women booed, which made him laugh.

From beneath the voluminous folds of her gown, DeLoome retrieved a fan and snapped it open. She fluttered it furiously over her ample bosom. "Whoo, Lord!"

Laughter echoed through the auditorium, and Robbie reappeared on stage. He asked for another round of applause for all the guys and Madame DeLoome, which the crowd enthusiastically provided while the men filed out behind the curtain.

Kez looked at Rae and laughed, giving her a side hug.

"What's so funny?" Rae asked.

Still laughing, Kez replied, "I couldn't imagine a more perfect man for you than one who will drop his pants on stage to prove he's going commando."

<br>

Concentrating on setting one foot in front of the other, Van shuffled unsteadily along behind Dave and Jackson, back into the room they'd occupied before hitting the stage. The walls seemed to tilt inward, and he blinked slowly, trying to get them to straighten back out. It didn't help, just made the walls shift back and forth. Jackson leaned against the far wall while Dave slid gingerly into a chair by the door. Van propped himself on the ledge below a small mirror, no longer confident in his ability to remain standing.

Robbie sprang into the room, bubbling over with glee. "My three stars!" His happiness was effervescent as he flitted around the room, giving each of them little pats on the arm. "You were wonderful, just wonderful! And the way your lady friends chimed in—oh, I couldn't have asked for a better night!"

Noticing the empty tequila bottle on the ledge beside Van, he said, "Oh, we can't have you darlings going around without a drink. Let me go grab—"

"No!" shouted Jackson from his position against the wall. He shook his head and winced, gripping his temples with one hand. "No more tequila," he said in a softer voice while he tried in vain to hold onto the wall behind him. If Van hadn't also been clutching the ledge he was perched on, he would've laughed at Jackson's big hands scrabbling against the smooth surface, desperately searching for a handhold to help him stay upright.

"Well," said Robbie, fingering his scarf. "I could certainly get you something else."

"No," Dave said. "No more booze." He held his head as still as a statue and seemed to strain to see Robbie's slight figure. "I don't know which of the three of you is the real Robbie, but whichever one it is— no more booze."

Van wanted to nod, but he worried that the ceiling and floor might join in the sway of the walls if he did. "Please," he said, "could we have some water?"

Robbie laughed and fluttered his fingers. "Okay, okay. No celebratory drinks. There are a few bottles of water in that fridge below you." He pointed to Van, who slowly bent over to look under his countertop seat. Sure enough, there was a mini fridge. Kneeling, he opened it and pulled out three waters. He clumsily rolled bottles to Dave and Jackson, then took a deep gulp from his own.

"Where can we meet the girls?" Jackson asked Robbie.

"I told them to pick you up at the door where you came earlier. I'll lead you back to it. This place is a maze."

Dutifully, the three of them followed Robbie back through the warren of passageways in the amphitheater's backstage. At last, they emerged into a main hallway of the resort. Standing in a straight line across from them were Regan, Kez, and V.

"Why do I feel like a groupie right now?" Kez asked as she kissed her husband.

"Enjoy the show, babe?" Jackson asked her.

She eyed Van. "Oh, it was some show."

Van tried to bow, but he tipped forward with the movement. Regan caught his arm then put hers around his waist. "Easy there, Casanova."

He draped an arm over her shoulders and flashed a boozy grin. "Thanks, baby." Pulling her tighter against his side, he kissed the top of her head. "Mmm," he mumbled into her hair, "you smell nice."

"You smell like a distillery," she said but kept her arm around him. To the others, she said, "I don't think he is in any condition to do anything more than pass out."

Van nuzzled her ear. Or at least he tried, but in his inebriated state, he missed and got a face full of brown hair. Choking on the inhaled strands, he coughed and wobbled on his feet. "You trying to take advantage of me, Regan?"

Her side-eye could've cut through steel. "Oh yes, McLeod, I've been biding my time, waiting to have my way with you after your drunken public strip tease." She fought to keep him upright as his big body leaned against her. "Let's get you back to your room."

He shot a wink over to Dave and Jackson. "She wants me." He tried to mouth the words to them, but a sharp elbow to his ribs let him know he'd said the words out loud.

Jackson and Dave laughed, then Jackson asked, "You need help herding him up there?"

Kez slapped his chest lightly. "As if you can offer any help! You can barely stand up." Her hazel eyes darkened under her lowered brow when Jackson teetered backward. She grabbed his arm and yanked him forward. The sudden movement put him even more off-balance, and he tripped over his own feet. With arms flailing, he crashed into Kez, and her heels clattered as she fought to support his weight. Jackson threw out a hand and braced himself against the wall, clamping the other at Kez's waist to keep her from falling. Their drunken tango ended with her sandwiched between his broad chest and the wall.

"Seems like I've still got some pretty good moves," he said proudly.

Kez's shove was purely for show. "Get off me, you big oaf." Her smile took the edge off her words, and Jackson kissed her. She didn't let it linger though. Ducking out from under his arm, she said, "C'mon, ladies, let's put these guys to bed."

Their progress was slow as they wound their way back over to the main building. Van was drunk, but that wasn't the reason he draped his arm across Regan's shoulders. The black one-piece pantsuit thing she had on was strapless and exposed the satiny curve of her shoulders. His fingers rubbed gently along her bare skin, feeling firm muscle under soft flesh. Goosebumps popped up beneath his touch. The other two couples walked ahead of them on the cobblestone path, so he angled his head down and dropped a small kiss on her cheek. Regan's fingers tightened their grip at his waist, and she leaned into him. Her heels put her at the perfect height to notch right under his arm.

Around them, tree frogs sang from their posts in the palm fronds. Water gurgled by the stone walkways in decorative concrete and steel lanes on its way to the fountain at the rear lobby entrance. Discreet outdoor lights illuminated the pathways but still allowed the stars to be seen in the sky above. It was like walking through a rainforest in moonlight. Van chuckled inwardly at his overly romantic thoughts. He had to be drunk if he was waxing poetic like that. A glance at Regan's profile made him wonder if his buzz was from the tequila or from being with her.

"You certainly put on a performance tonight," she said.

Van's fingers fanned out, covering her shoulder. "Too much?"

Her laugh floated away on the evening breeze. "I don't even know how to answer that question. I'll say this though. The lady behind me was a big fan. Who knew the over-sixty set was into male burlesque?"

Fueled by old feelings and tequila, he said, "I only saw one woman tonight."

She stiffened against him. "Van, now is not the best time to have some sort of in-depth conversation."

He hurried to reassure her. "That's not what I'm trying to do. I just want you to know how I feel."

Regan shifted her shoulders, and his arm dropped from around her. She kept walking next to him as she spoke, "Van, that's just it. How you feel about me *is* part of that larger conversation." She stopped and swept an arm out, taking in their surroundings. "Let's enjoy paradise while we can. Reality will infringe soon enough, so let's not ruin anything before we have to."

It pained him to hear that talking about a future with him could ruin things. Even drunk, he knew what would happen if he forced the conversation before she was ready. That was a surefire way to send her running in the other direction. If all she offered were their next few days on the island, then he'd have to use those days to make her see that life with him could be everything she wanted.

He hastened forward to take her hands in his. Unfortunately, he was looking at her, not the path, and didn't see the uneven brick before his toe snagged the edge. He pitched forward, arms flailing wildly. His reflexes, dulled by the alcohol flowing through his veins, didn't kick in. Pain bloomed at his lip when his face hit stone.

"Van!" Regan cried when he face-planted at her feet. Her shout made the others in their group turn and rush back to them. Regan knelt next to him as he pushed himself up on his hands and knees. "Oh my God, are you all right?!" she asked, reaching out to touch his face.

He felt a warm, wet trickle run down his chin and rubbed a hand under his lip. His fingers came away bloody. Running his tongue behind his teeth confirmed they were all still in place. He'd escaped any major injury, except to his pride.

"Damn, man," Dave said. "Are you okay?" He helped Van stand up. V produced a tissue from her clutch and handed it to him. Van dabbed at his split lip, and V shook her head, sending her curls bouncing.

"You need constant pressure on that to make it stop bleeding," V instructed. With an apologetic grin, she added, "Especially with all the booze you have in your system right now. You're going to bleed like a stuck pig." She put her hand on top of his and pressed the makeshift gauze firmly against his lip.

"Thanks, V," he mumbled from behind the cloth. Humiliation at his clumsiness heated his cheeks. A light touch on his arm brought his eyes to Regan. Her own were dark with concern.

"Are you okay?" she asked, gripping his forearm tightly. "Do we need to go to the hospital?"

He grimaced at the suggestion. "No, other than my dignity, I'm fine. Just a scrape." The five of them didn't look convinced. "Really, guys, I'm fine. I promise."

When V and Kez hesitated, Jackson went into action, shooing them away. "Let the man have a little space to regain his self-respect." He grinned over at Van. "I mean, damn, dude, I've never seen anyone actually *throw* themselves at a woman." His grin moved to Regan, and he winked. "He must have it bad." With a hand at the small of her back, Jackson guided Kez toward the hotel.

Dave tugged a reluctant V away. "Doc, your patient's in excellent hands." V let Dave lead her to follow behind Kez and Jackson but not before she gave Van a stern warning to keep pressure on it and follow up with an ice pack.

Once they were alone, Regan's fingertips dusted over Van's cheek. "Are you sure you're okay?"

Her concern buoyed his spirits. "If I'd known all I had to do to get you to care about my well-being was skim my face along concrete, I'd have fallen down the steps at Jackson's two days ago."

She flicked his earlobe with her middle finger. "Smart-ass."

Van took her hand and interlaced their fingers. "I'm fine, I promise."

With one last long look at him, she turned toward the hotel. "Then let's get you upstairs and get some ice on that."

When they reached his room, Regan transformed into a little drill sergeant. She ordered him to take off his shoes and get in bed but resisted any effort on his part to get her to join him. "I've got to get some ice for your face," she said and pointed a warning finger at him. "Stay."

He held up both hands in surrender and settled against the pillows. With a swish of fabric, she grabbed the ice bucket and sailed out of the room. Upon her return, she put a generous amount of ice into a washcloth and held it out to him. "Follow Doc V's orders, please."

"Regan, really, I'm—"

She pushed the washcloth to his lips with an irritated sigh, effectively silencing his protests. "Don't be an idiot, Van. Male pride needs to take a back seat to common sense at this point. If V says ice it, then you ice it." She sat on the edge of the bed next to him, keeping a hand on the ice bundle.

He covered her hand with his, shifting the icepack a bit so he could talk. "Thanks, Regan." His eyes roved over her outfit. "That's a pretty fancy nurse's uniform."

She rolled her eyes and stood up, slipping her hand from under his. "I'm going to go next door and change clothes."

Uncertainty gripped him. Van wanted to ask, no, *beg* her to stay the night with him, but he also didn't want to risk pushing her too hard. He asked, "Are you going to bed?"

Laughter flashed in her eyes, and she leaned down, tracing a finger along his jawline. "I don't know. Are *we* going to bed?"

He started to smile, but pain from the split in the center changed it to a weak lift of the corners of his mouth. "I thought you'd never ask," he said.

With a chuckle, she tweaked his nose. "I'll be right back, McLeod."

When the door between their rooms shut behind her, he closed his eyes. He must have drifted off to sleep, because the next time he opened them, it was fully dark in his room. His lip throbbed, but that dull ache was an afterthought at the discovery of the compact form snuggled next to him under the covers. With a start, he realized he was completely naked and could feel every inch of Regan's slender body against his. Her breathing was deep and even as she slept with her back to his front, their bodies curved together. His hand rested on her stomach. She wasn't naked, but whatever she was wearing was thin and filmy to the touch. Her legs were bare and intertwined with his, her shapely backside nestled into his groin.

His body stirred to life at the feel of her next to him. Slowly, he lifted his hand from her stomach and slipped it underneath the hem of her top. The loose fabric gave him easy access, and he smoothed his hand up her ribs until he reached her breast. He cupped his palm around its curve, skating the tips of his fingers across her nipple. Even in her sleep, she arched into his touch. Emboldened by her body's innate reaction, he kneaded the soft flesh. His efforts elicited a breathy moan from her, and she twitched her hips back against him.

Feeling her awaken, his hand stilled. Her voice was low and husky with sleep. "No one told you to stop doing that." Her fingers ghosted down his arm and soon her hand was on top of his, encouraging him to continue. Van kissed her neck and nipped at her earlobe. Her hand left his and traveled back to curl around the base of his skull, pulling him tighter against her. His hand moved lower while she writhed against him, encouraging his caress.

Hooking a finger in the waistband of the tiny shorts she had on, he dragged them down her hips. She shifted slightly to let him pull them off. A quick wriggle and she divested herself of them completely, leaving them somewhere under the covers. He dragged his hand up the back of her leg and she opened herself to him, draping one leg over the top of his. Accepting the physical invitation, his hand moved to the inside of her thigh, then higher. As his fingers brushed her sensitized flesh, she opened her legs wider. A few delicate strokes had her calling his name and chasing his touch. When he took his hand away, she groaned, but shivered in excitement when he reached for a condom from the bedside drawer.

He made quick work of the foil packet and hastily rolled on the thin layer of protection. Van ached to have her bare, but he had to earn the right to ask that of her again. He had her back in his arms, in his bed and, hopefully, in his life. That was enough, and he was thankful for all of it as he sank into her from behind. He groaned at the feeling, hesitating to even move, but Regan held no such qualms. Her hips bucked back against him, and she gave a frustrated whimper. Van gave her a sharp smack on her ass, and she cried out but didn't stop moving her hips.

"If you think spanking is going to do anything but turn me on," she said on a ragged breath, "you must've forgotten a lot about our time together."

Van gripped her hips, holding her still. "I forgot nothing about being with you, Regan." He punctuated the statement with a hard thrust and an accompanying bite to her shoulder. "Not. One. Single. Thing." The sound of his hips slapping against her ass spaced each word, and she moaned her approval.

"Oh God, Van! Yes, please!" she begged.

Soon, both their words dissolved into primal grunts and guttural sounds as they lost themselves in the pleasure of each other. Their sweat-slicked bodies moved in a roiling embrace, hands grasping, teeth nipping, and hips undulating in feverish pursuit of pleasure. It was a hard, almost voracious coupling as they clung to one another, seeking more contact than was physically possible. They drove each other to the brink, both trying to stave off release, until they had no choice but to succumb to their bodies' visceral demands. Van's shouts echoed Regan's cries as they tumbled over the sharp edge into bliss.

As their breathing slowed and their bodies cooled, Van held Regan against him. His hand rested below her breast, and he could feel the rapid strike of her heart against her ribs. He placed tiny kisses along her shoulder and up her neck. Reaching her ear, he whispered, "I love you."

She said nothing but laid her hand on top of his and squeezed.

# 24

Using the filigreed mirror above the chest of drawers in her room, Rae tucked a wayward strand of hair back into place. She slid one, then the other, of two thin silver hoops into her earlobes. The lightweight jewelry swayed as she tilted her head from side to side. Her hair was pinned up off her neck in an understated style that was island chic. The dress she wore was a deep lapis blue with a flowing skirt that stopped above her knees. Its halter neckline showcased her cleavage, and the vivid color set off the rich tan she'd developed over the past week.

It was their last night in the Caymans, and Jackson had arranged a private dinner for the six of them at the Grand Old House. One last hurrah to put the perfect seal on what had been, despite her initial misgivings, a wonderful week. In the mirror, she watched her lips form a subtle smile as she remembered the past few days.

She'd woken up in Van's arms the morning after he'd literally, if not intentionally, kissed the ground at her feet. The sensation of being cocooned under the covers with him was as familiar as it was unsettling. When things between them had gotten serious the first time, they would spend every night together wrapped around each other like moss on a live oak. Since she'd left him in Charleston, Rae had never allowed that with another man. Even if, by some fluke, they finagled a way to stay in her bed all night, there was no cuddling, spooning, or any other nonsense. Her side of the bed was sacrosanct, and any man who crossed into it would limp back over to neutral territory.

But Van. Van was something else entirely. When she returned and found him passed out fully clothed, there hadn't been a moment's pause in her decision to undress him. The boxer briefs tucked into his pants' pocket gave her a good laugh. When she slid under the covers next to him, he rolled over and pulled her against him. The two of them fit together seamlessly, his long frame curving around her petite one. His hand lay on her stomach just underneath her breast, and his breath tickled the shell of her ear as he slept. In a blink, they were back in bed together like nothing had ever happened, two long-lost puzzle pieces interlocked once again.

Rae no longer had any desire to run from him. In its place was an acute craving to draw his arms tighter around her and burrow farther into the warmth of his body. He had been her safe space when she was truly starting out. Her PR career had been in its fledgling stages when they met. The job with Hasselhoff had been her big break, and some days, the enormity of responsibility thrust upon her shoulders at the tender age of twenty-five weighed heavily on her confidence. Those days were the ones that had made her fall hardest for Van. Because when a glitch or issue at work threatened to drag her into a spiral of self-doubt, Van was there to assure her she could handle anything life threw at her. Seeing herself through his eyes then helped her become the woman she wanted to be—someone who deserved the success she received because it wasn't given but earned.

As he snored softly behind her that night, all of that ran through her head. She no longer saw Van through lenses tainted by past duplicity but as a shining example of how a man should treat the woman in his life. He had supported her from success to failure and all the gradations between. When they were together, there was never a time he wasn't there for her.

Her cynical view before was that he had to be the perfect boyfriend or it would've blown his cover. Peeling back the hurt and anger let her see that everything he'd done for her—from his leaving Swedish Fish on her desk every week, or taking her out for oysters, and especially falling asleep with her cradled against him—wasn't part of an assignment. He could've nailed her boss without doing any of those things. No, he had done none of that to get close to Hasselhoff. He'd done all of it to get close to her—because he loved her.

As the scales fell away from her eyes, the Pandora's box of feelings burst open, freeing a tumultuous riot of emotions that crashed over Rae in a long overdue catharsis. Reveling in finally having the freedom to *feel* everything she'd suppressed for so long, she allowed her tears to fall freely, thankful that the tequila-fueled evening turned Van's naturally deep sleep into more of a coma. Rae cried—not only to mourn the wasted years she'd spent away from Van—but also to help flush any remnants of the anger or resentment she harbored toward him. Both took up too much space in her heart, and neither had a place in her life any longer.

Later in the night, when she felt Van's feather-light caress on her skin, she'd freely given into her need for him. Their union was as electric as ever as their bodies fused together. His touch made her catch fire from the inside, burning white-hot as she lost herself to the familiar sensation of his body against her and within her. When she surfaced from the hedonistic abyss, she felt his lips moving against her shoulder and up her neck.

His whispered "I love you" was so faint, she almost didn't hear it. The earlier revelation she'd had was still too fresh and raw to allow her to respond, but she didn't want his declaration to go unanswered. Rae did the only thing she could. She gave his hand a soft squeeze. Her touch was as an acknowledgment not just that she'd heard the words but that she welcomed them.

When he found her still nestled against him the next morning, they'd taken a more leisurely approach than the night before. He'd taken his time with her body, stoking a fire that built slowly but was a raging inferno by the time it was all over. That morning, she'd accepted his offer to "wash her back," and they'd showered together. Together was all they had been the past several days. Whether it was lounging in the cabana, trying out the infinity pool, or holding hands under the table at dinner, they'd been inseparable. Jackson joked that it was hard to tell who among them were the honeymooners.

Van hadn't pressured her about what would happen when they returned from vacation. His actions made it clear he wanted to be in her life. But honoring her request, he'd made no demands and asked no questions, and for that, she was grateful. It let her adjust to the new, or rather, renewed feelings that grew each day she was around him. She tried to show him how she felt, rather than saying it out loud. Because while she had let go of the majority of the hurt, Rae still wanted to know why he hadn't come for her. If fate hadn't shoved them together at the wedding, would they have spent the rest of their lives apart? She'd come a long way toward forgiveness, but she couldn't shake the need to know what had held him back. At the same time, she knew if she voiced the question, there was a very real possibility the bubble of happiness they had created could burst. Theirs was a rekindled passion while simultaneously fledgling, which made it uniquely fragile. Rae found herself wanting to protect it at all costs, but still the need to know *why* simmered within her.

Van's sharp rap on the adjoining door brought her back to the present. "Coming," she called, slipping into a pair of silver sandals. Her jaw dropped when she opened the door and laid eyes on Van. She'd grown accustomed to seeing him in either board shorts and a T-shirt or nothing at all, either option equally enticing. Their group had mostly skipped fancy dinners and outings, electing instead to keep things casual. But tonight, she wasn't the only one who'd put a little more effort into her appearance.

Decked out in a pair of tailored white trousers topped by a crisp, indigo-blue blazer and white dress shirt, Van was dreamily dapper. A seersucker pocket square and simple loafers worn with no socks completed the look. His hair was still wet from the shower, and he'd left a scant bit of stubble on his face. Nothing close to the full beard Jackson sported, but enough scruff to look a little wicked. The man was sex on a stick.

When she didn't say anything or move aside, Van tapped a finger to the bottom of her chin. "If you're not careful, you're going to catch flies."

She smacked his hand away, and he made a show of adjusting the starched cuffs of his shirt, so they were just visible beneath the sleeves of his jacket.

"You look"—Rae ran her hands up the edge of his lapel and pulled him into the room—"like we shouldn't bother with dinner."

His hands found her hips. "Don't tempt me, Regan. The way you look in that dress is going to have me hard all night as it is. If you're sitting across from me with sex eyes, I'll end up dragging you into the bathroom for a quickie." Humor lit his warm brown eyes, "And I'm pretty sure Jackson would kill me if I got us kicked out tonight."

"I guess we should head downstairs and get around other people before I change my mind, lock the door, and strip you out of your snazzy suit."

His fingers dug into her hips, and while his eyes were still warm, it was desire not humor emanating from their brown depths. "Regan." Her name was a gravelly caress, said like a warning.

She slid her arms around his neck, stepping into the warmth of his body. His hands slid lower, pulling her flush against him and enveloping her in the intoxicatingly male scent of him. Angling her chin, she offered her lips to him, eyes sliding closed in anticipation.

A knock sounded against the door of her room, and her eyes flew open. "Just in the nick of time," she breathed. Van snorted in irritation and released his grip, letting her answer the door.

Kez, Jackson, Dave, and V all waited on the other side. "I thought we were meeting in the lobby?" Rae asked, her body still singing from Van's embrace.

Jackson harrumphed his disapproval. "Kez didn't want to take any chances on the two of you getting tangled in the sheets and not making it for our final night dinner. I told her there was nothing wrong with that idea and that it actually sounded like a good plan."

Kez elbowed him. "Please, you're as excited about dinner tonight as I am. Save your caveman act for someone who might actually buy it." Turning to Rae, she said, "Let's go, you two. The bed will still be here when we get back."

With an evil twinkle in her eye, Rae asked, "Who says we were even planning on using the bed?"

A lighthearted mood enveloped the six of them as they made their way to the lobby. Laughter, smiles, and subtle touches between her and Van had replaced their stilted interactions. As they walked, he kept a hand at her waist, centered over her spine. The weight of Van's hand on her back, together with the slight stroke of his thumb, wasn't there to help guide her across the lobby. It served a dual purpose—foremost as a gentle reminder of his presence, as if she really needed one, but also as a signal to others, no matter how understated, that she was his.

They emerged from the hotel, and a liveried driver opened the door to an early 1960s Lincoln Continental limousine. Kez grabbed Jackson's arm at the sight of the suicide doors. "You didn't!"

He grinned. "I did."

"What's the deal?" Van asked Rae.

"Kez, for some inexplicable reason, is fascinated with 1960s Continentals. I think it has to do with the doors. Who knows? But I'm guessing Jackson went the extra mile to arrange our ride tonight. If I didn't like them both so much, I would find the lengths to which he goes to make her happy positively revolting."

Van let out a deep chuckle but took her arm, turning her to look at him while everyone else was getting in the car. "Is it so horrible to have your happiness be that important to someone else?"

Rae put her hand in his. "So long as I get the benefits of it? No, I guess not." It was an artful dodge of the underlying meaning of his question, but he let it slide. "Come on," she said, tugging him along to the car. As they slid across buttery white leather seats, she spied a few bottles of champagne chilling in buckets atop a retro console. When Jackson popped the top on the first bottle, she nudged Van and said, "Yeah, turns out I'm perfectly okay being along for the ride on the love bus, so long as it includes free champagne."

The long car rolled slowly down the street. Through the tinted glass, they spotted luxurious oceanfront mansions and meticulously hedged yards. The drive was short, and soon they pulled into a parking lot in front of a white clapboard building with a shiny tin roof. The front porch had a lattice railing, and ceiling fans stirred the humid air. Mammoth palm trees flanked the entrance and lined the front of the building. When they entered the restaurant, the dark hardwood floors gleamed against the white of the painted wood-paneled walls. A crystal chandelier hung in the center of the large room, and a mahogany bar stretched to the right.

Across from them was a large triple-arched doorway, framed in the same dark wood from the bar. Rae saw another larger chandelier through the archway. Amply spaced tables draped in white linen allowed diners their privacy. Heavy floral curtains hung from dark rods over massive windows.

When they checked in with the hostess, a shorter man in a white dinner jacket joined her. Jackson's height dwarfed him, the difference in their stature almost comical. He took Jackson's hand, pumping it enthusiastically in greeting. "Welcome, Mr. Jenkins."

"Thanks, Pierre," Jackson said. "This is my wife, Kez. Our friends Rae, Van, Dave, and V." He gestured to each of them.

The diminutive man dipped his head slightly. "A pleasure to meet you all. Please, if you would, follow me this way."

He led them from the dining room to a wide covered porch with dark paneling on the ceiling above. The porch opened onto an ocean-front veranda that spanned the entire length of the restaurant. Beyond the railing, crystal-blue waves crashed against weathered rocks. There was a panoramic view of the ocean and the sunset. Rae looked around for a table for six, but Pierre didn't slow down. Passing a lattice divider, they stepped off the patio and onto a concrete path. Rae heard Kez gasp and peered around her friend to see what had left her speechless. Her hand went to her chest. "Oh, wow!"

Lanterns on the edges of the walkway cast flickering lights over sprinkled rose petals leading to an elevated dais. A gazebo perched on the edge of the rock outcropping, framed by large timbers. Gauzy white curtains draped each side, and twinkle lights encircled the top of the open cabana. On the side facing them, the curtains had been tied back to reveal a table set for six with pressed linens, crystal, and fine china. A candelabra sat in the center of the table, its candles sputtering in the ocean air. There was romance, and then there was something like this.

Pierre asked Jackson, "This is all to your liking, yes?"

Jackson clasped the man's hand. "Pierre, you have truly outdone anything I could've asked for or described. This is perfect."

Pierre's cherubic cheeks crinkled when he smiled. He bowed in thanks. "I am so glad it meets with your approval. Please, take your seats. Arianna will be right over to get your drinks." With another bow, he scuttled back down the path.

Each man pulled out a chair for his date, and once everyone was seated, all six of them turned to look at the sunset.

Kez leaned over and kissed Jackson's cheek. "I can't believe you set all this up."

With his thumb and forefinger, he took her chin in a gentle grip, placing a kiss on her lips. "I wish I could take credit for it, but it was all Pierre. All I did was call and make the reservation." Jackson stroked his knuckles against her cheek. "But I'm glad you like it."

The only other time Van could remember being this full was when he'd accepted one of Jackson's invitations to join him for Thanksgiving dinner at his nana's house. The woman had prepared enough food for an army, and they'd all done their best to eat themselves into a food coma. Tonight was a close second to that feeling. Everything on the menu looked delicious, so they'd gone overboard with their orders. From the mango and crab salad, lobster risotto, seafood curry, sea bass, and of course, filet with baked potato for Jackson, there hadn't been a single dish that wasn't extraordinary. As for the desserts, his favorite had been a tie between the red velvet lava cake and the passionfruit cheesecake.

The sun had set long ago in a spectacular display of purple and red shot through with vibrant streaks of orange. Stars twinkled over the sea, and the crash of the waves had dulled to a soft, pulsing *whoosh*. Stuffed and sated, they sipped after-dinner drinks in a companionable silence. Jackson and Kez had retreated to the railing closest to the ocean so he could indulge in a cigar with his bourbon. Dave and V lounged across the table from Van and Regan, V leaning her head on Dave's shoulder. Van toyed with a few tendrils of Regan's hair loosened by the ocean breeze. Under the table, her hand rested above his knee and her fingers drifted in a lazy half-circle against the inside of his thigh.

Dave patted his trim waist and sighed. "Man, this was unbelievable." He shifted in his seat. "Except you guys might have to roll me out of here."

"Get in line, Blondie," Regan said. "If anyone is getting carried out of here, it's me."

Strains of music wafted over from the main veranda. Van rocked backward in his seat to get a better view. A band warmed up in the far corner. Nothing elaborate, just a few guys with guitars and a microphone. Tables had been cleared away, freeing up a space that could serve as a dance floor. A sense of nostalgia came over him as he remembered the summer evenings he'd spent with Regan at Shem's. There were no cicadas singing here, and the crash of the Caribbean wasn't the gentle lapping of a Carolina inlet, but the urge to hold her in his arms was every bit as strong.

He rose from the table and extended his hand to her. "Ms. Murphy, may I have the pleasure of a dance?"

She looked over her shoulder toward the musicians then up at him. His hand hung suspended before her as he waited for her answer. Her fingers sat in a *V* around the stem of her martini glass, and she gently sloshed the clear liquid around the crystal. With a flourish, she picked it up and tossed it back in a single swallow. "What the hell," she said and put her hand in his. He led her to the veranda, the scrape of chairs signaling his friends had followed suit.

They made their way onto the floor, joining the few couples already moving to the music. This time, when he urged her closer, there was no resistance. She came willingly into his arms. His hands curved around her waist, and he felt her laugh.

"Last time we did this, I was in cutoffs and a Panthers T-shirt."

"We danced at the wedding," he reminded her.

"No, you shanghaied me at the wedding, and I didn't have a choice if I didn't want to make a huge scene. This"—she scratched her nails along the nape of his neck—"is something completely different."

Her admission was equivalent to a profession of undying love from any other woman. She might not have said the words, but her yielding to his embrace told him all he needed. Regan Murphy was not a woman prone to letting a man lead her anywhere, be it on the dance floor or anywhere else. Her surrender to the moment and his touch meant she was warming to the idea of seeing where things between them could go.

"You even smell sexy," she said.

Van chuckled. "Thanks, sweetheart." He dropped his voice to a low rumble. "As I recall from this morning, so do you." He felt her shiver and knew she was remembering waking up to find his head between her legs. Ducking his head so his lips were right at her ear, he said, "But you taste even better."

Regan lifted her head. "Could we just take a taxi back to the hotel?" Desire made her exotic eyes glow.

Van replied, "I'm ready if you are." Regan was spinning out of his arms and back toward the exit before he had even finished his sentence. She tugged on his hand, encouraging him to match her quickened pace.

Jackson's booming laugh followed them. "Guess we'll see you guys in the morning," he called to Van's back. Van threw up a hand but didn't turn back. He was too focused on the swish of Regan's delectable hips in that sexy-as-hell dress.

When they spilled out the front door of the restaurant, Regan dashed to the taxi stand. Cars were lined up, waiting patiently to ferry patrons from the stylish restaurant to their next destination. Opening the door to the first one in line, she slid into the back seat, and Van joined her. Regan allowed him to give the address to the driver but then grabbed his lapels and pulled him down for a kiss.

Her lips parted under his, and her tongue stole into his mouth. It was velvety soft and slid against his as she moved onto his lap. Her skirt slid up her thighs, and she ground against him in eager abandon. Lost in the sensation of her mouth on his and her hips rolling against him, he groaned and clamped a hand on the back of her neck. He kissed her deeply, savoring the small sounds she made in the back of her throat as he took control. His other hand slid up her thigh and was on its way under her skirt when the driver clearing his throat brought Van back to reality.

When he pulled back, his breathing was labored. Regan's eyes were hazy, and her lips swollen to a plump ripeness from his kisses. "Why'd you stop?" she asked. Leaning forward, she tried to kiss him again, but he gripped her neck gently to stop her, his thumb trailing over her jaw.

"We've got an audience," he said as he jerked his chin toward the driver.

With a sinful smile, she drew her fingertips over his hand resting on the top of her thigh. "So?" she said, a rising challenge in her eyes. Her fingers tightened around his wrist, and she pulled his hand higher.

"Regan," he said darkly but didn't stop her. Her skin was smooth under his fingers as she brought his hand under her skirt, climbing higher until it reached her hip. His fingers spread out, expecting satin, silk, or lace but feeling nothing but skin. He groped higher but still felt only supple skin. By this time, he was cupping her ass cheek in his palm.

"You're not wearing any panties," he said in an accusatory whisper.

"You've got only yourself to blame, Donovan," she teased. "Ever since you pulled that little stunt on stage, I've been biding my time. Tonight seemed like the perfect opportunity to show you weren't the only one willing to go commando."

All the blood in his body rushed to his crotch at the realization that the only thing separating them was the fabric of his dress pants. She grinned and rocked against his erection.

Her eyes sparkled fiendishly with lust. "Think you can get me off before we get to the hotel? I'd owe you one then."

If his dick got any harder, it would snap in two. "That depends, baby," he said and massaged her ass, enjoying watching her eyes grow heavy and darken with pleasure.

"On what?" she asked, teasing a finger beneath his shirt collar.

"On whether you think you can keep quiet so we don't get thrown out of this cab."

Regan leaned forward and bit his earlobe. "I'll be good, I promise," she whispered into his ear, and Van thought he might actually explode.

He glanced over her shoulder at the cabbie, who was keeping his eyes pinned on the road in front of him. Van knew the guy knew what was going on but was doing his best to ignore it. He had one helluva tip coming his way if he stuck to that plan. Moving Regan off his lap and back onto the bench seat made her frown until he slid his hand up her thigh and back under her skirt. She let her knees fall open, giving him more access. The heat from her core called to him, beckoning him closer.

Van draped his other arm around her, tilting her head back to rest in the crook of his shoulder. He kissed her right as his thumb brushed against her clit. Regan moaned, and he felt the vibration of it against his lips. Her fingers gripped his shirt tightly as he explored her mouth with his tongue. He pushed one finger inside her. Her back arched, and she tilted her hips up, moving in time with the rhythm of his strokes.

Lifting his lips from hers, Van looked down. She'd hiked her skirt up far enough to let him see her ride his finger. She bit her lip, and he knew she was struggling not to cry out.

"Do you like that, baby?" he said hoarsely in her ear.

"Mm-hmm," she said in the sexiest little groan-whisper he'd ever heard.

"What about this?" he asked as he rubbed her clit with this thumb, continuing to thrust his finger in and out of her. A sharp inhale and a jerk of her hips against his hand told him the answer even before she nodded her head.

He kissed her neck right below her ear and sucked gently on her flesh, sliding one more finger inside her then curling them both to caress her inner walls while his thumb increased its pace. Her breathing turned to quick pants, and he smiled against her skin, kissing along her jawline. The jerks and spasms of her body became frantic as he worked his fingers against her. He knew the instant she was about to come, because her whole body stiffened and the most intimate part of her wound snugly around his thrusting fingers. Van tightened his arm around her shoulders and his lips crashed into hers, smothering the sounds of her orgasm as she came apart in the cab's back seat. His tongue swept into her mouth and mimicked the rhythm of his fingers inside her. He didn't break the kiss until he felt the last shuddering pulse of her body and she went limp against him.

Withdrawing his hand, he plucked his pocket square from his jacket and used it to help her clean up. He'd just smoothed her skirt back down when they pulled up in front of the hotel. Her eyelids fluttered open, and she looked up at him, her full lips slightly pursed and eyes unfocused. Van smiled and kissed the tip of her nose. "Looks like the answer to your question was yes, beautiful."

25

Rae didn't miss the sizable tip Van gave their driver before getting out of the car and coming around to open her door. She gladly accepted his hand and exited the back seat on unsteady legs. His arm slid around her waist, keeping her close. The woodsy, spiced scent of his cologne teased her nostrils, and she drew in a deep breath.

Van's laugh ruffled her hair. "Did you just smell me?"

She pinched his side. "Don't ruin the moment, McLeod."

"Apologies, milady," he said as he steered her through the lobby to the elevator. As they rode up to their floor, she smiled at their reflection in the brass doors. "You look happy," Van said with a grin of his own.

She pushed onto her tiptoes to kiss his jaw. "That's because I am, Van."

He squeezed her hip. "I'm glad, Regan. So am I."

The doors parted when they reached their floor, and Van followed her to the door of her room. She carded them in, and when the door clicked shut behind them, Van wasted no time in pinning her against the wall and kissing her senseless. His mouth slanted over hers in a dominating fashion, and she welcomed the attack. Her lips parted, and his tongue slipped inside.

Van moaned as he kissed her, and his hands moved to her hair. He pulled out the pins and let it cascade down her shoulders in luxuriant chocolate waves. His fingers pushed into it, and he angled her head, his kiss becoming even more demanding. She clutched at his shoulders, clinging to him as he took her mouth, greedy and desperate. When he finally raised his lips from hers, they were both gasping for air, eyes wild with need.

He stepped closer, pressing his body against hers from chest to knees. She felt his cock, hard and insistent against her stomach. "I want you, Regan," Van said with his lips only inches from hers. He shook his head and his eyes burned into hers. "No, it's more than want. I *need* you, baby."

Rae cupped his jaw in her hand. "Let me get out of this dress, and I'll see what I can do to help you with that."

Van turned his head and kissed her palm. "Don't take too long," he said.

With a laugh, she slipped out from between him and the wall and walked toward her suitcase. "You can't rush perfection, McLeod. It'll take as long as it takes." Shooting him a sultry look over her shoulder, she added, "But I can promise it'll be worth the wait."

He reached her in two strides, wrapping his arms around her from behind and pulling her back against him. His lips trailed down her neck and over her bare shoulder. "I've been waiting on you for the past five years, Regan. But even if it had been forty, it would've been worth it to have you back in my life."

Rae's throat went dry, and she felt tears prick at the backs of her eyes. It wasn't from the romance of his words, although that was surely how he'd intended them. It was from the sharp slash of pain caused by his making their time apart sound like some sort of forced exile, as though he'd had no choice in the matter and was just awaiting her return. As though he hadn't had the power to end their separation, to find her and have her back in his life long before now. Instead, he'd been content to do nothing and let her spend the last five years questioning whether anything they'd had was real, berating herself for being a sucker, and rebuilding her life all on her own. Rae couldn't delay the question any longer—she had to ask, or it would strangle her. "Why?" she asked, her voice scratchy with emotion.

Oblivious to her sudden shift in mood, he kissed his way back up her neck, nuzzling the skin behind her ear. "Why what, baby?"

Taking a deep breath, she stepped out of his embrace and turned to face him. The question had jumped out without a plan, but now it was dangling between them like a suspension bridge. She hadn't had the guts to cross it all week, too scared of what would be on the other side. But now she had to know the answer. "I asked why," she said.

Van's brows drew down in confusion over the sudden shift in the mood. "Why what?"

"Why did you wait? Why not try to find me once the case was over? You knew what your investigation would to do my career, to my entire life. You had to know I would be"—she searched for words, needing him to know the true depth of pain she'd endured—"devastated, humiliated, heartbroken, and, most important, alone. But you did *nothing*. You wrapped up your case and went on with your life while mine was in ruins, and you didn't even try to reach out to me. And what I want to know is *why*."

Van stepped toward her, hands outstretched. "Baby, you know why. It was my job, I had to—"

Rae stepped back, shaking her head. "I'm not asking about why you had to be Ray Edwards. I'm asking why Donovan McLeod never tried to contact me. If he was the one in love with me, if he was the one

I spent a year of my life with, and if he was the one I'd given my heart to, then why would he put me through the agony of the last five years, when all he had to do was click a few buttons to find me?"

"I—" Van paused, his uncertainty palpable in the air. He glanced away then dragged a hand over his face. When he looked back at her, his eyes were dark with sadness. "It's not that simple."

Rae's heart wrenched. "It's not a complicated question, Van."

"You ran out on me!"

She shook her head. "I ran out on Ray Edwards, but Donovan McLeod made the decision not to follow me. And I deserve to understand why. You're asking me to trust you, to believe in what we have. But the truth is that you didn't, Van. When it came down to it, you didn't think what we had was strong enough to weather the storm you caused."

"Regan, that's not true," he protested.

She smiled weakly. "Isn't it? Because if you had, if you'd honestly thought our relationship could've survived, you would've come to me then. It wouldn't have taken an act of the cosmos throwing us together for you to have a second chance. That chance was there for the taking— you just passed on it. You passed on us, Van. And that was after we'd been together for a year! It's been a week, Van. If a year isn't long enough to convince you we had something worth saving, why should this last week change anything?"

"Nothing's changed between now and then, except maybe the fact that I'm more in love with you than ever," Van said, coming closer and touching her shoulder. The warm press of his hand made her want to forget this conversation, lean into his touch, and stay in paradise forever, but she knew she couldn't. The door had been opened now, and she had to walk through it, regardless of what waited on the other side.

He went on, "Don't you think I wanted to find you? For weeks, I couldn't function, because all I thought about was you. Where you were, whether you were all right . . . thoughts of you consumed me, Regan! How can you even question that?"

"How can I not, Van? You had every resource at your disposal to find out the answers to both those questions, and you didn't use any of them!" Rae twisted away from his touch. "I deserve to know why!"

She crossed her arms and waited. And waited. Van looked everywhere but at her, as though the answer was somewhere painted on the wall behind her or bobbing on the ocean in the distance. When he finally met her gaze, the raw grief in his eyes lanced right through her heart. It took all she had not to go to him and offer some comfort, but she held her ground. He owed her an explanation, no matter how hard it might be for him to give it or for her to hear it.

His throat constricted with a jagged swallow, as though the very words were strangling him. He took one step toward her then stopped. She could see in the set of his shoulders that he wanted to reach for her, but he didn't. With a dejected sigh, he said, "Finding you would have meant facing what I'd done to you. I would've had to look you in the eye and admit I was the person who'd destroyed everything you'd worked for. That I'd used you and lied to you, even if in the end it led to so much more between us. I'd have to stand before you and confess all my wrongs with no guarantee that you'd do anything more than slam the door in my face when I was through. It would be like losing you all over again, and I just couldn't . . ." He raked a hand through his hair, his face haggard and pained. "I couldn't bear it, so I took the coward's way out."

His words echoed in Rae's head, swirling and colliding with one another. Her question had been answered, but the answer was almost worse than not knowing. Because the truth was he'd loved her . . . just not enough to risk his own further heartbreak. The weight of that truth pressed down on her chest so hard it was difficult to breathe, much less speak.

Somehow, she found her voice, albeit shaky, and said, "Whether to forgive you was my choice to make, Van, and you took it from me. Which is the most selfish part of this whole thing, because you didn't do that for a job. You did it to protect yourself at my expense. And I don't know if that's something I can forgive."

"Don't do this," Van said, coming closer and touching her arm. The fear in his eyes almost broke her. "Please, Regan. Don't shut me out. I'm here now, doing what I should've done then. It's all out there now. There are no more secrets between us. We can finally move forward. Together."

"Again," she said, her voice stronger now and threaded with the conviction of a woman wronged, "*you* don't get to make that choice for me, Van." She shrugged off his hand. "At least not this time."

As he packed, the cold light of dawn crept in around the edges of the floor-length curtains in Van's room. A glance at the clock showed it was just after six. After he'd left Regan's room last night, he hadn't slept much, if at all. Every time he closed his eyes, he remembered her face when he'd told her why he hadn't looked for her once she left. The pain that had ravaged her features and dulled her eyes was almost too much to bear. Worse was the knowledge that once again, he'd been the one to put it there.

She'd asked him to give her some time to sort through how she felt. He wasn't sure whether she wanted hours, days, or weeks, but he would give her whatever she needed. Which made the decision to book an earlier flight an easy one to make. There was no way he could sit next to her at breakfast, in the taxi to the airport, or on the excruciating flight home without begging for yet one more chance. Pleading for her forgiveness once more. Knowing that, he'd booked the first flight out that morning, determined this time to put her needs ahead of his own.

Grabbing his phone, he shot a quick text to Jackson: *Sorry for the early text, but something came up with work and I have to head back early. Thanks again for everything, man. Enjoy your last day in paradise.*

## Four Weeks Later

"I'm sorry, sir, but Ms. Walsh isn't available," Kez's receptionist said, her smile kind but firm.

Van glanced at the nameplate on her desk. "Marjorie—may I call you Marjorie?" He upped the twinkle factor in his smile, hitting her with all the charm he could muster.

The pink tint to her cheeks gave him hope. She fingered the reading glasses hanging on a gold chain around her neck. "Well," she said with a coquettish smile, "I think that would be all right."

"I only need a few minutes of her time," he coaxed, making sure his smile didn't appear forced. "Fifteen minutes max." He touched an assortment of fingers to his forehead in what he hoped was the Boy Scout salute. "You've got my word, Marjorie."

Marjorie's resolve was weakening. "Maybe I could—"

Kez's office door opened. "Marjorie, can you get me the Goodman file, please?" Her eyes were on the legal pad in her hand instead of the reception area.

"Well, I—" her receptionist started to answer, but Van jumped in.

"Kez," he said, and her eyes shot to him in an instant.

"Van? What are you doing here?" The pad in her hand bowed a little as her fingers tightened, and for a moment, he worried she might throw it at him. He had to act quickly.

"I'm here to confess and confirm that I am a gigantic coward and do not deserve to be in Regan's life but am willing to beg, borrow, wheedle, plead, and prostrate myself in any way necessary for you to help me try to get her back."

She regarded him like a scientist might examine a particularly noxious disease under a microscope—eyes narrowed, nose wrinkled slightly, with nostrils twitching and lip curled.

"I can start the begging portion now, if that helps," Van offered.

Her assistant had been watching this exchange with avid interest, wide-eyed and nibbling on the corner of her reading glasses. His life had been reduced to the comic entertainment of a stranger, but the ding to his dignity was worth it if he could get Kez to help him.

Kez blew out a breath then said, "Marjorie?"

The glasses fell from Marjorie's lips. "Yes?"

"Hold my calls," Kez instructed. To Van, she said, "Well, get in here. I don't have all day to listen to your sniveling, so we might as well get on with it."

Relief flooded through him as he followed Kez into her office. For the first time in weeks, he had hope. It was a small, weak glimmer in a cavernous black hole, but it was there.

Kez sat behind her desk and indicated he should take one of the visitor chairs on the other side.

"I really appreciate—"

"Stop." Kez held up a hand, and Van obediently closed his mouth. Steepling her fingers in front of her, she watched him—those gold eyes, flinty and unyielding. He fought not to squirm in his seat. "Do you recall, Van, what I told you before we left for the Caymans?"

"Well . . . of course, but—"

"It was a yes or no question, Van. Please only respond to the question asked."

Apparently, he'd missed the part where she'd sworn him in as a witness. "Yes," he said.

"And what was that?"

Van swallowed, heat rising up his neck. "I believe you said, 'Don't screw it up.'"

"Very good, but there was a follow-up piece of advice, correct?"

He gritted his teeth, reminding himself that he needed Kez to make this work, and if letting her hone her cross-examination skills on him was what it took to get her on board, then he would do that and more. "Try harder," he said.

"And yet . . ." She spread her hands wide. "Here we are." Kez sat forward in her chair, resting her elbows on her desk blotter. "Just so we're clear, I don't buy that work excuse you gave Jackson to bail early. *Something* happened between you and Rae that last night. She's been tight-lipped, as usual, but I'm not an idiot. I saw things unfolding between the two of you and then it all unraveled. What I don't understand is how, after I handed you the golden ticket to redemption—an entire week on a tropical island with her—you still managed to do something to screw it up." She slapped her desk then threw up her hands in frustration. "What is wrong with you, man? What part of *try harder* did you fail to comprehend?"

"That's why I'm here now," Van said, crossing an ankle over his knee. It kept him from bouncing his foot, a sure tell of how nervous he was. He didn't need to give Kez any more ammunition.

Kez arched one eyebrow, her glare turning calculating. "So, what, your plan is to just throw yourself on my mercy and beg for help? I'll give it to you, Van—you've got a lot of balls to walk in here and think that's all it will take for me to offer up my best friend to you. Just who do you think you are, anyway? Rae could have her pick of—"

"I left the FBI, Kez," Van said, quietly interrupting her rant.

Her mouth dropped open, eyes rounding in surprise. "Say what now?"

He cleared his throat and ran his hands down his slacks. "I said I left the FBI."

"But you . . . but it's . . . but . . . why?" Flustered, she sank back into her chair hard enough for it to squeak.

Van's smile was small but determined. And then he told her his plan.

## 26

*You'd* have thought the asphalt parking lot outside her office held the key to all life's mysteries with the amount of time Rae had spent staring out her window over the last few weeks. It didn't, of course, because then she would've known definitively what she wanted to do about Van. And . . . she didn't. At least, she didn't think she did.

"Ugh!" Rae tossed down her pen and shoved out of her desk chair so hard it spun in a wild circle. It was eerily familiar to what Rae felt she'd been doing since the morning she got Van's text in the Caymans.

Van: *I'm not leaving you, Regan. I'm just giving you what you asked for. That's all I plan to do from here on out.*

It had pinged into her phone around eight-thirty the morning of their last day on the island, not waking her up since she'd never really gone to sleep after asking Van to leave so she could think. Which is all she'd being doing since then. It sucked. Big time. She was used to thinking about other people's problems and how to strategically untangle the matted and snarled messes they'd made of their lives. But now . . . now she had to think about what to do with her own life and would have much preferred to hand it over to someone else. To dump the giant, smelly pile of crap that was her love life into their lap and say, "Fix this, please. Give me the answer I've been searching for the past few weeks and cannot find."

He'd texted her a little over the past few weeks. Nothing too serious or pushy. Just a few "hope you're doing well," or "saw this and thought of you" with a picture. One such picture had been of a sunhat embroidered with "Silently Judging You," which made her snort laugh. She appreciated him letting her know he was there but not pressing her for any sort of answer.

Her desk phone bleated, and Rae pounced on it, grateful for the distraction. Hopefully someone had some huge mess that needed her full attention immediately. God, she hoped it was a sexting scandal, one that included leaked nudes. That would be the perfect thing to take her mind off her own life. And she'd be helping the person, so it wasn't a wholly selfish prayer.

"Yes?" She sounded eager and breathless, even to her own ears, so she made a mental note to dial it down from an eleven to a more manageable five.

Her assistant paused then said, "I have Ms. Walsh, er, Mrs. Jenkins on the line for you."

Rae swallowed a disappointed sigh. Kez had been sniffing around her for weeks, as had V. Both of them knew something happened on their trip and were dying to know what. While their intentions were pure—she knew they only wanted to know so they could be there for her—Rae wasn't ready to talk about it. How could she tell them how she was feeling when she wasn't completely sure herself?

"Put her through, please."

"Rae?" Kez's voice sounded excited.

Rae braced herself, sinking back into her chair. "Afternoon, Mrs. Jenkins. How can I help you?"

"Actually, I'm in a position to help you this time."

"Really? How so?" Out of habit, Rae grabbed the small notepad next to her phone, ready to jot down details if necessary.

"Well, I have a new client who could use your unique services."

*Please let it be nudes or a secret love child,* Rae thought. "Tell me more," she said.

"Before I get into the details, I should warn you he needs someone immediately. As in today. If that's not doable, I'll need to let him know to see if he's willing to wait for you. I'd of course tell him you're totally worth it, but it's his decision."

"Actually, that's perfect for me," Rae said, pumping a thankful fist in the air. She clicked over to her calendar just to confirm. "I have an opening at three this afternoon. Is that soon enough?"

"That should be fine," Kez said.

"Then lay it on me," Rae instructed, pen in hand.

"I'll let him give you the nitty-gritty details, but the gist of it is that he's moving to Charlotte to start a new business. He'll be dealing with high-end, wealthy clients, so he needs to make sure what he described as a 'delicate personal issue' doesn't impact his transition up here."

"Delicate personal issue, huh?" Rae's interest was piqued. It didn't sound like the ultimate scandal she was looking for to occupy her brain, but *delicate* could include a wide array of things.

"That's what he said," Kez replied. "Since I'm handling the corporate end of things, I don't need those details. But I was only too happy to steer him over to my best friend who just so happens to be the best in the business."

"You flatter me," Rae said. "Please, continue."

Laughing, Kez said, "I'll let him know the time. Thanks for doing this, Rae."

"No problem. But don't you think I need his name? That seems like an important detail."

"Right! God, sorry. It's been a morning. His name is Eduardo Ramon."

Rae paused in writing. "You're joking, right?"

"I've got a check here with his name on it, so no, I'm not."

Rae scribbled the name on her notepad. "Okay, I'll see Mr. Ramon at three."

At two forty-five, Rae checked to make sure everything was set up in the smaller of their four conference rooms. Its white wainscotting and cool gray walls were at once soothing and elegant. She'd chosen the smallest room because it evoked a sense of discretion. Like the room itself cocooned the client from whatever crisis had erupted, protecting them from prying eyes. Satisfied everything was as it should be, she circled back to her office to grab her tablet and trusty notepad. Sometimes folks were a little skittish about handheld electronic devices, since a lot of the reason they were coming to see her in the first place stemmed from an unfortunate experience involving one. Hence, the notepad just in case.

Her assistant poked her head in. "Your three o'clock is a little early."

"No problem. Go ahead and take him back to the conference room, and I'll be right there."

"You got it, boss."

Rae pulled a pocket mirror from her desk drawer and checked her reflection. PR was all about image, and no one would hire a rep who had lipstick on her teeth or a poppy seed trapped in her gumline. Confirming no smudges or stray hairs were present, she smoothed down her skirt and left her office.

The door to the conference room was closed, so she gave a quick rap to announce herself then opened the door. "Good afternoon, I'm Regan Murphy. It's a pleasure to—"

"Hey, Regan," said Van, rising from his seat at the table.

Rae stopped so short she almost came out of her heels. Clutching the tablet and pad to her chest, she blinked rapidly. Like he was a mirage she could dispel from her line of vision. But he didn't disappear. Instead, he stood there looking way too good in a suit. "Van? What are you doing here?"

Sweat dampened his brow as he watched the shock of seeing him play across Regan's face. He hoped he hadn't overplayed his hand or bungled things further by coming here. But this wasn't a text conversation, nor was it a voicemail to be left. This was a face-to-face kind of thing, because he needed to see her. Needed to know she was hearing him, absorbing what he said.

"I have an appointment," he said, resting his palms on the top of the table so he couldn't fidget. It was a bit of an aggressive pose, so he backed up a bit and shoved his hands in his pockets. Then he remembered the body language class about how that made it look like you were hiding something, so he pulled them out again. So much for not fidgeting.

Regan came farther into the room and set down her things. "*You're* my three o'clock?" Her lips twitched a little and she muttered, "Guess this is payback for Jackson showing up on her doorstep."

"What?"

She shook her head. "Nothing, never mind. What are you doing here, Van? And the answer is not that you have an appointment. That's what got you into this room, not what brought you to my office in the first place."

"I need some help with a little romantic issue from my past and I think you're the woman to assist me."

One brow rose, along with the corner of her mouth. "Is that so?"

He gestured to the seat in front of her. "Can we sit?"

Regan hesitated briefly then lowered herself into the chair. Van took his seat opposite her, breathing a sigh of relief that she hadn't thrown him out on his ass.

"So," she said, her hands resting lightly on the table, "tell me more about your PR problem, Van."

*Here goes nothing*, he thought. "Well, you see, I made a big mistake a few years ago and didn't take the right steps to remedy it. Which put me in a bit of a predicament with someone very important to me. It made them question the depth of my feelings for them, even if whether the way I felt about them was real. Whether I truly believed in what we had together. If I were the person they believed me to be, deep down, or just some cowardly asshole too afraid to face the consequences of his own actions like a human being with fully developed emotions."

Regan huffed out a small laugh. "Sounds like you have sort of an image problem."

"You could say that," Van said, encouraged by her smile. "But the good news is I think I've figured out the best way to address it."

"Oh?" She cocked her head to the side, her smile widening. "Then why do you need me?"

"You're an integral part of my plan, Regan. Without you, it doesn't work. At all."

"I see. Tell me more."

Van leaned forward. "The first and most key feature of the plan is that I've already cut out a large part of my life that started the problem in the first place."

"You have?" Her brows dipped and she frowned.

He nodded. "Yep, I've left my past employer."

Regan sat up straight in her chair, her lips forming an *O* of surprise. "You did what?"

"I'm no longer employed by the Federal Bureau of Investigation."

"But . . . why?" She looked flabbergasted by the news. He hoped it was in a good way and not in a why-in-the-hell-did-you-do-that way.

Van smiled and lifted one shoulder. "It was an impediment to what I wanted in life."

"Which is?" Regan leaned forward, mirroring his posture, eyes bright and sharp. She was fully invested in his explanation, but he cautioned himself against rushing things. This had to be paced properly, no jumping to the big finish.

"I had a life with someone. A great life. Actually, it was beyond great. It was everything I ever wanted." He paused to let that sink in, then went on, "There was one glaring exception. Because of my job, I had to lie. To everyone, but worst of all to the person who mattered most. I had to put up walls and hold in secrets from the one person I loved more than anything in the world. I can't blame the job for everything though. My own selfishness and immaturity played a major role too. But it all started with my job. I knew if I stayed with the FBI, the specter of what happened would always be lurking in the background as a reminder of my mistakes. So I left."

"Just like that?"

"Just like that."

"What are you going to do now?"

"I've taken a job in private security consulting. Better hours, better pay, fewer slimeballs."

That got him a laugh. Regan tapped her pen against her notepad, nibbling on her bottom lip. "In Charleston?"

Van shook his head slowly, trying not to read too much into her question. "No, that's the best part. They want me to open and run a new branch office—right here in Charlotte."

Regan's whole body jerked at that news, and Van hurried to reassure her, dropping any pretense that this conversation wasn't about them. "Please don't think my moving here is trying to pressure you. I know you said you needed time, and I'm going to give you that. I promise. But I want you to know that *you* are the most important factor in every decision I make. There was no way I would turn down a job that brought me closer to you, Regan. I made the mistake of letting you walk away before without fighting for what I wanted. Without owning my own part in what happened to us and giving you the chance to decide if you could forgive me for it. Without showing you that you are the single most important person in my life and that without you in it, my world exists in shades of gray and levels of average. I'm not making that same mistake again. I needed to tell you that in person, not over the phone. But I don't want it to feel like pressure. You asked for time, and I want you to take as much as you need. When you're ready, I'll be here."

She had to give it to him, Van certainly knew how to make an impassioned plea. And look damn good doing it. The suit alone was enough to make any woman consider his argument. Which she was, obviously. It wasn't every day a guy who looked like Van set up a fake meeting just to pour his heart out to you and accept blame for everything except the Kennedy assassination. He'd done exactly what she'd wanted him to do five years ago. Did the timing of his confession matter? Wasn't the point *what* he said, rather than *when* he said it?

Regan pushed her tablet to the side and rested her elbows on the table. "I've spent the better part of the last decade being pissed at you, Van. And I gotta tell you, it's freaking exhausting."

"I know and I'm sor—"

She shook her head, and Van stopped talking. "I'm not looking for another apology. Anything that follows what you just said is going to fall woefully short, I'm afraid. I couldn't have drafted a better *mea culpa* myself. And I'm the best there is."

Van grinned. "I don't doubt it for a second."

"You shouldn't. The Eduardo Ramon thing was a nice touch, by the way. Ray Edwards's Latin cousin, perhaps?" Regan smirked and got up from the table. Van looked panicked until she walked toward him and not the door.

Standing in front of him, she said, "What I'm trying to say is that the entire time I was mad, the undercurrent powering that anger was how badly it hurt to feel  not just used and abandoned but so alone. Loneliness that ran bone-deep because the man I loved tossed me aside and moved on. But the thing I never let myself consider, even for a moment"—she held out a hand to Van, and he wrapped his warmly around hers—"is that you might have felt the same way when I left you. Well, not the used part; that's *all* on you, buddy."

Van laughed and tugged lightly on her hand. She came willingly and settled into his lap, glad the door to the conference room was opaque. "I did, you know," Van said, stroking her palm.

She cupped his jaw, brushing a thumb over his cheek. "Yeah?"

"Soul-crushingly lonely, Regan."

"Would you think less of me if a not-so-tiny part of me were glad?"

His laughter rumbled against her shoulder, and he shook his head. "I'd expect nothing less."

Regan shifted a little on Van's lap so their gazes were level. His arm wound around her waist, and his hand curved over her hip. "I'm tired of being pissed, Van."

"Yeah?" His hand moved to her ribcage, the light press of his fingers urging her closer.

She nodded, dipping her head until only a breath separated them. "I think it's about time I tried something a little different."

"What did you have in mind?" His words ghosted over her lips in a whisper.

"I was thinking," Regan paused, her lips quirking into a hint of a smile. "I was thinking something more along the lines of a happily ever after. I've never had one of those before." She cocked her head to the side, eyes bright with humor. "Man, I don't think I've ever said that to a guy before."

Van pinched her side, grinning from ear to ear. He mimicked the tilt of her head. "Regan Murphy, are you asking me to be your first?"

Her smile grew to match his, until they were smiling at each other like complete lovesick fools. Regan closed the last millimeter of distance between them, brushing her lips to his. Before he could deepen the kiss, she pulled back. "Even better, McLeod, I'm asking you to be my last."

# Epilogue



*Six Months Later*

**How** in the ever-loving hell did I let you talk me into helping with Thanksgiving?" Rae bemoaned as she tried to wrestle a four-hundred-pound turkey into a roasting pan.

Kez poked her head out of the pantry. Flour streaked across her forehead, and wisps of red hair stuck out in every direction from her once-immaculate braid. "A better question is, how in the hell did you not talk me *out of* hosting Thanksgiving?"

Rae gave up on the bird, and it flopped sideways into the pan. She looked at Kez. "Fine, we're both morons. Does that make you feel any better?"

Kez blew her hair out of her eyes and swiped at the flour on her face. "Not particularly, no."

"Can't we call Nana and tap out?" Rae pleaded, clasping her hands under her chin and expertly batting her eyelashes.

Kez rolled her eyes. "Have you met Jackson Jenkins—the most competitive man to ever walk the earth? 'Tapping out' isn't in his vocabulary. He told Nana we'd host this year, so that's what we're going to do."

"Can't you call a caterer?" Rae asked.

"Trust me," Kez said, frustration clear in her tone. "I tried. They're all booked." She threw an arm across Rae's shoulders, enveloping them both in a cloud of flour. "It's you and me, sister."

"The blind leading the blind," Rae grumbled and dusted off the white fingerprints Kez left on her shoulder. It was the evening before Thanksgiving, and Kez had called in a panic about getting everything ready for dinner tomorrow. Why she'd called Rae, who was the most culinarily deficient of anyone they knew, was a mystery. But Rae'd agreed to help. Facing the ass end of a turkey, she regretted that decision in a big way.

"Well, alcohol helps everything else. Maybe it will help in this situation. Why don't you pop out to Jackson's man cave and snag us a bottle of bourbon?" Kez asked as she regarded the lopsided turkey. "I'll figure out how to wrangle this thing into submission, what a giblet is, and how to get it out of this bird."

Not wanting any part of that, Rae scrambled out of the kitchen and headed to the smokehouse. She really liked the little one-room building with its leather furniture and hint of cigar smoke in the air. It was a very masculine setting, perfect for Jackson.

Pushing open the door, the glow of dozens of candles lining the room surprised her. A second look revealed scattered rose petals on the floor and a bottle of champagne chilling in a corner. Well, shit. It looked like she'd stumbled into Jackson's seduction scene. Before she could retreat, she heard Van call her name. With a startled yelp, she looked around.

Candlelight flickered as he stepped out of the shadows next to the champagne. Dressed in one of his custom suits, he looked sexy as hell. The dark jacket draped just right across his shoulders and tapered in at his trim waist. The Windsor knot in his deep-crimson tie centered perfectly at his throat.

"What are you doing here?" she asked in bewilderment. He'd had to work late tonight, or so he'd said.

"Something I've wanted to do for a long time," he said and moved toward her.

Rae smirked and said, "I'm pretty sure we've already done it in here, but if you're offering a quickie, I'm totally into that." She glanced over her shoulder toward the house. "Kez is in there talking about giblets and pulling stuff out of a turkey's ass. I'm so not into . . ." She trailed off when she turned back to find Van on one knee holding up a ring box.

Her ears began to ring, and her palms went clammy. "Um, what are you doing?" she asked, pushing the question out from her tight, suddenly dry throat.

Van laughed and said, "Well, I'm trying to propose to my girl-friend if she'll ever stop talking about quickies and stuff coming out of a turkey's ass."

Rae swallowed hard past the burgeoning lump in her throat. "You're proposing?"

Van nodded. "I am."

"To me?" she asked. He laughed, making his eyes crinkle a little at the corners and showcasing both dimples. God, he had a magnificent smile.

"Yes, baby, to you," Van confirmed, giving the velvet box a little waggle. Light glinted off the stone.

"But I'm here to help with the giblets," Rae said, still lagging mentally. He was there, on bended knee, holding out a ring, and she couldn't comprehend this was happening.

"No, Regan," Van said patiently. "That's just something Kez came up with to get you over here."

"So we're not cooking Thanksgiving dinner?" Rae's brain felt like it was moving two steps behind normal speed, and she stared at the giant rock nestled in the box in Van's hand.

"Oh good God, no," Kez said from behind her. Rae whipped around to see her friend standing in the doorway.

Kez cast an apologetic glance at Van. "Sorry, I couldn't help myself. I had to see it in person!" Her hair was now suspiciously immaculate and her face free of any flour.

To Rae she said, "Nana's older, not senile. There's no way she'd trust us with making Thanksgiving dinner. She flew in two days ago and has been hiding out at V's." Kez pointed at Van, who was still down on one knee with the most beautiful diamond solitaire extended in front of him. "But you've got more pressing questions to answer right now."

Rae blinked down at Van, who was trying gamely not to laugh. "Marry me, baby," he said.

Rather than answer, Rae launched herself into his arms, sending them both tumbling to the floor in a flurry of rose petals. She peppered kisses all over his face, making him laugh out loud. "So is that a yes?" he asked.

"Yes!" she said, tears of happiness welling in her eyes as he slipped the ring on her finger. It glowed in the romantic light of the candles, and she heard Kez sniffle.

"I'm guessing she said yes," said Jackson as he came up behind Kez and wrapped his arms around her.

From his position on the floor underneath Rae, Van called back, "She said yes!"

"Congrats, man," Jackson said. He led Kez away from the door. "We'll give you guys some privacy." Right before he closed it, Jackson said, "Oh, and Rae?"

She looked up at him. "Yeah?"

"Please don't leave your panties behind this time."